The Good Book of Oxford

By
Hilary Andrews
And
Bernard Andrews

Chapter one

'Mr Nichols?' asked the police officer.

'Yes, what the hell's going on?! What's happened?'

'It appears someone's broken into your flat, sir, and made a right mess in the process. They've really turned it upside down.'
The officer gestured as if Mike's gaze needed guiding, to the wreckage indicated by the officer's words.
Another policeman stumbled out of the lavatory covering his mouth with his hand. 'Oh, my goodness, you do *not* want to see what they've done in there!' Mike remained just outside the doorway of his pokey, Streatham flat, surveying the damage at a safe distance from the policeman. He wasn't quite sure what thought to deal with first: The combination of the presence of the police, the car keys in his hand and the obvious smell of alcohol on his breath? He stuffed the car keys into his pocket, trying to veil the action with a faux-shocked shake of the head. The fact that his flat had been broken into? Strangely the TV was still there; his laptop was in the satchel slung over his shoulder; the door would need fixing but other than that it was just slightly more messy than usual. Mike looked awkwardly at the ground before clumsily constructing an expression of horror for the benefit of the still-heaving policeman.

A foul-mouthed exclamation woke Mike from his concerns. It came from the rancid, fatless face of Jackie from next door who had slithered up beside him. Mike spotted her blackened fingernails creep onto his shoulder. He just about managed to smother the shiver of disgust.
'Yeah, what a pain!' Mike turned to her. He was pleased that his turning also forced her to remove her spindly, drug-ridden digits from his person.

'Oh, I'm so sorry Mike! They've really done you over. They've trashed the place!' I've reached a real low, thought Mike. Even Smackie Jackie, the junkie is shocked by how I live.

'Come 'ere love.' Jackie held out her twig-like arms, offering Mike a hug. Mike reluctantly leant forward to accept. Her skin had the texture of an unwashed potato and she smelt like the juice at the bottom of his fridge that he guiltily remembered was marinating the salad he'd bought in a rare moment of optimism last week.

'Ah thanks, Jackie,' said Mike, holding his breath and trying not to be disgusted by her thinness.

He wasn't really bothered by the break in. He just wanted everyone out. He wanted his space back. He wanted some time to enjoy the valuable excuse for a bit of self-pitying. He wanted the cheap bottle of hock the trespassers had rather tastefully allowed to remain sitting on the sideboard.

Chapter two

Seventeen-year-old Andrew Tremayne awoke with a gasp. He felt a sudden sense of relief upon realising he´d been dreaming. It had been a terrible dream of his parents being killed in a car crash. He groped around in the fug of his brain, searching for something solid, some firm ground that could orientate his thoughts. But as the fug dissipated, nothing familiar made itself known. The walls of the room were covered in some faded flowery wallpaper. – Oh this is my Gran's! He shuffled himself upright, accompanied by the unfamiliar squeak of some aged bedsprings. –Oh no! His breaths shortened. –My Mum! There was no firm ground, nothing familiar, just a dizzying sinkhole of the despair. He remained sitting in his bed, his shoulders locked at an awkward angle, unable to move except for a strange unconscious flicking between the little finger and thumb of his right hand

Andrew heard footsteps walking quietly down the passage outside the door. His grandmother was probably bringing him a cup of tea and after hearing his crying, had moved away. He suddenly felt ashamed. His Grandma was equally upset. She had lost her daughter. He opened the door.
'Grandma, Grandma,' he called, 'it's all right. I just had a nightmare'.

Margaret Nichols turned round and smiled at Andrew.

'I know. I heard you calling out in the night. I thought you might like a cup of tea.'

Andrew smiled,

'Yes, I would. Let me take it from you. Tea's great.'

'I'm just going to meet Michael from the station. You remember he's coming today?'

'It will be good to see him but I thought he was driving.'

'His car broke down. It's a very old one, you know.'

Andrew laughed,

'I do know. It broke down the last time I went in it.'

Andrew went back into the bedroom, sat on the edge of the bed with his elbows on his thighs, and drank his tea. He stared at the floor between his feet. It was now over a month since his parents had been killed. During that time, he had been living with his grandmother. He should have been at school doing his A-levels. He had refused to go back to school. What was the point? He couldn't read, study or do anything much. His relatives had said that it would do him good to see his friends. Some friends had come round to visit him but it had been unbearably awkward. He felt guilty thinking it, but his friends had seemed so shallow in that moment, so devoid of any real substance, they were incapable of behaving in any scenario not already fully rehearsed and peer-reviewed. Andrew's anger grew as he struggled to understand why he was the one who felt embarrassed after trying to put them at ease by telling jokes. He could almost see his comments hanging there, like conspicuously ignored social-media posts.

Andrew sighed and then shrugged in defiance. His Grandma was great. She didn't criticise him or tell him to 'get a grip' or to 'snap out of it', but he could tell she was trying to think of things he could do. He thought about Uncle Mike. He liked him but he was considered a bit of a joke in the family.

Michael Nichols was an apparently failing schoolteacher in a failing school. He drank too much, always looked in need of a shave, wore scruffy clothes and was altogether without ambition. Andrew could hear his mother, Mary, talking about him – 'he was very clever at school you know and everybody liked him. He was wonderful on the cello. He could have been a musician'.

Andrew got dressed slowly. He tried to stretch out everything he did so that it filled up the time between meals and bedtime.

'Andrew, Andrew, we're here' called his grandmother.

Andrew went into the kitchen, where his grandmother stood next to his Uncle Mike.
'Hello Uncle Mike, sorry to hear about the MG'

Mike nodded to Andrew,

'Yes, I suppose she's nearing the end but I keep trying to keep her going a bit longer.' Andrew laughed. He was pleased to see Mike and glad that Mike didn't give him big, masculine hugs like some of his relatives. He knew that they were being kind and showing that they cared but somehow it was easier if they didn't appear to care at all. Andrew hadn't seen Mike since the funeral and then Mike had said nothing to him. He remembered Mike's face, ashen, grey, staring ahead like a zombie.
'So, Uncle Mike, what brings you to Lathbury?'

'I do come and visit my poor, old mum occasionally'.

Margaret laughed,

'Oh, he comes for the food, I know'

Mike pulled a studied expression of offence,

'Mum, Mum what a thing to say but you do make a good pie. Doesn't she Andy?' Andrew nodded, playing along with the scene for the benefit of his grandmother, aware that he had not been suitably appreciative of her cooking in recent weeks.

Margaret went over to the cooker,

'Well, how about a late breakfast?'

'Yes, brunch they call it, Mum,' said Mike.

The three of them sat companionably around the kitchen table while Margaret dished up, eggs, bacon, sausages and beans. Mike tucked in hungrily and to his own surprise and that of his grandmother, Andrew also consumed a fair amount. Mike then kept them all amused by a tales of misbehaviour at his school, told in a manner that betrayed his anarchist sympathies.

In the afternoon Andrew and Mike went out for a walk. They walked up to the top of Sifford Hill where there was a good view. Andrew was out of breath.

'Sorry, Uncle Mike, I'll have to stop for a bit. I've been a bit lazy recently.'

They sat on a log and Mike pointed out various landmarks. After a while Mike said,

'How about coming back with me to Streatham for a few days?'

Andrew was taken aback. He had only ever been to Mike's fetid flat once and had a vague recollection of being concerned about contracting some form of incurable disease.

Mike went on,

'I know it's not the Ritz but I would appreciate the company and you could give me an insight into the world of the "you". It's difficult to empathise with them when you are thirty-four.'

'Thirty-four! I thought you were a lot older than that. But as you say thirty-four is knocking on a bit,'

'Oi!' grinned Mike, 'no need for that!'.

'Oh, I didn't mean to insult you. It's just that my mother was forty-four and you being her brother . . .'
'Well, I was the baby of the family.'

'Oh, I thought you were the eldest?'

Before Andrew realised it Mike had pushed him off the log and he was struggling to stop himself rolling down the hill. Mike shouted after him,
'Are you coming to Streatham then? To keep a poor old crusty company?' Andrew extricated himself from some nettles.
'Ok, then – give it a go,' he said.

Andrew was quiet as he and Mike made their way back to his grandmother's house. He was dreading telling her that he was going to stay with Mike. He didn't want to offend her. He wondered if he should change his mind. After all he didn't really want to contract rabies or vole's disease or whatever from Mike's grubby Streatham shack.
When they got in the house, his grandma smiled,

'Well, that's put some colour in your cheeks!'

'Mum,' said Mike, 'Andy's going to come to Streatham with me for a bit.'

Andrew was shocked that Mike had announced it so suddenly, so abruptly.

'Well, I don't know I...' he trailed off. Margaret was beaming at him,

'That's wonderful,' she said, 'a change of scenery will do you good. Come on, go and have a wash and I will get some supper. We can pack up later. I suppose you need to be back at school on Monday, Mike, so you will have to go tomorrow.'

Later that evening, Mike and Andrew sat in Margaret's sitting-room watching an old war film. Margaret had gone to bed.

'I thought she'd be upset!' said Andrew petulantly, 'she sounded as though she was glad to get rid of me.'

'She probably is,' said Mike, helping himself to some left-over apple crumble, 'I mean you have hardly been a laugh a minute and she does have friends. She probably hasn't been to have coffee with any of the thousand Eileens she knows or been to the Bridge club for ages.'

Andrew was about to protest but he felt his eyes well up. Instead, he threw a cushion at Mike and after about ten minutes, Margaret came down in her dressing-gown to protest at the noise and at the dilapidation of her best cushions. The following morning, Andrew was pleased to find that his grandmother had done most of his packing. He was rather surprised that she had packed so much stuff.

'I'm only going for a short time Grandma. I'll be back here shortly.'

'I know dear but you may decide to stay a bit longer. I shall miss you and if you want to come back sooner than you intended that's fine by me.' After breakfast, Margaret took them both to the station.

Mike groaned when he saw that the next train was a slow stopping train but

Andrew
didn't mind. He wasn't looking forward to their arrival at Streatham so he was glad for it to take longer. Mike found some seats with a table in front so they could sit opposite each other and both sit by the window.

'I'm afraid I am going to be rather unsociable as I've got to read something for school tomorrow,' said Mike.

Andrew was pleased. He was happy to just look out of the window. It was a sunny, spring day and the Berkshire countryside looked rich and beautiful. The hedgerows were white with hawthorn and the fields were dotted with buttercups and dandelions.

The train stopped at Reading, Maidenhead and Slough. Andrew watched the people getting on and off the train. He wondered about them. A group of girls were laughing, possibly more loudly than was necessary – their fits interspersed with almost imperceptibly short, scrutinising glances of one another. A quieter girl stood on the periphery of the group, her shoulders about her ears. Her eyes were darting from one face to the next, as if she were permanently chasing the social flow. Andrew's gaze followed one old lady scurrying down the platform clutching her hand-bag unreasonably close to her chest. She looked sad and scared. He wondered if she had lost someone, perhaps her husband or maybe her daughter, or maybe both like his grandma. Andrew felt his thumb flicking his little finger on his right hand. He turned back inside the carriage and looked at his roughly shaven uncle reading a crumpled collection of papers. Mike acknowledged the attention with a brusque flick of his unkempt brow. –I hope this isn't real, Andrew thought. I hope this life isn't a turd rolled in glitter. The phrase made him smile. The train neared London. It rushed through Hanwell station. He remembered his

Grandma telling him the story of how Queen Victoria had said that if she were not

Queen of England she would have liked to have been the wife of the vicar of Hanwell. It certainly looked pretty with the viaduct behind and the church spire rising through the trees. The train finally pulled into Paddington and Mike found them a bus to Streatham. Andrew fell asleep on the bus. He was awoken by Mike shaking him,

'Come on. Wake up. We've got work to do'

Andrew wondered vaguely what 'work' he was supposed to do. Surely Uncle Mike didn't want him to resume his school work. That didn't seem characteristic of Uncle Mike who despite being a teacher, didn't seem to value education or at least work. His curiosity was aroused further when after arriving at the Streatham flat, Mike said,

'You go and unpack. I'll order a pizza for our lunch and afterwards there's something I want to discuss. Andrew's heart sank once again. Perhaps Mike was going to play the part of the authoritarian uncle and tell him to, 'pull his socks up'. Still, he reflected as he pulled his pyjamas out of his suitcase, his room wasn't bad, relatively tidy with a view over the railway.

<u>Chapter Three</u>

Mike put down his knife and fork and sipped his glass of beer.

'Do you drink beer? I mean I don't want to lead you into bad ways.'

'Dad quite often gave me a glass of beer.'

This wasn't strictly true especially the 'often' but Mike happily filled up his glass.

'Now to business,' he said.

Andrew could see that Mike was as unwilling to begin this 'business' as Andrew was to hear it. 'This might upset you,' he said. Mike looked out of the grimy window, the sun showing up all the dirt. His face was unusually solemn. 'Your parents were the nicest, kindest people I ever encountered. I owe it to them' 'Owe what?' asked Andrew, puzzled.
Mike turned round suddenly then said very quickly,

'The truth; there's something someone isn't telling us about how, or why your parents died.'
Andrew went cold inside. He was shocked, bewildered and yet. . .?' 'Yes', he murmured, 'they were the best, but what... what do you think happened?'
His voice trailed off. He didn't want to cry in front of Mike but he realised he was shaking. Mike looked at him. He showed concern in his eyes.
'Let's go in the other room and sit on comfortable chairs'

Andrew nearly laughed, despite his trembling, as he sank into a 'comfortable' chair and a sharp spring scratched his thigh.

'Why are you saying this? Everyone, including the police think it was a straightforward car crash. Something drove them off the road and they crashed into a tree. The car went up in flames and . . . and they were both killed outright.' 'Look Andrew, I don't know what happened, I just don't believe that the story that the police are giving us is right. It doesn't fit. I'm not saying it definitely isn't the truth, but at the moment, there are way too many unanswered questions. For starters, what drove them off the road?'

'I thought it was wet and slippery or . . . or Dad fell asleep at the wheel or they were avoiding someone who drove on.'

'It was three o'clock in the afternoon and they had only left Ebbchester three quarters of an hour before.'

Andrew screwed up his face as if in pain. 'Well, it must have been one of the other reasons.' Mike pulled his chair closer.

'Andy, I know it's painful but it's got to be faced. The police found no trace of another car and the road was wet but not unusually slippery. Do you know what they really think?'

'No, no, no I don't'

'They think your dad was drunk!'

'No, Uncle Mike, don't say that! He couldn't have been drunk. He would never drink and drive, never, never!'

'I know. That's what I think.' Andrew stared ahead.

'Does Grandma know what you think?'

'No, she thinks as you did that it was just a tragic accident. I have spoken to your father's brother; Simon and he thinks like I do.'

Andrew brightened. Uncle Simon was a solicitor and was a much more dynamic figure than Mike.

'Is he going to do anything about it?'

'No, your Auntie Melanie was too shocked. Simon said she wouldn't hear of it.'

'Even if it cleared Dad's name?'

'No, she said that it made no difference and it wouldn't bring them back.'

Andrew frowned,

'Well, I think it makes a lot of difference. It does to me anyway.'

Mike smiled,

'Good lad! You will help me then?'

'Uncle Mike, I will do whatever I can but is there anything we can do?' 'Well, I have already been to the police and told them what I have told you but they think I am some kind of nutcase and they have no intentions of looking any further.'
Andrew sighed,

'It would be difficult to do anything without the police.'

Mike leaned forward,

'Yes, they have everything at their disposal – scientific stuff, DNA and so on.

That's why I think you should have a go at them.'

'But why would they take any notice of me? They would just think of me as a child even though I am seventeen.'
'Because you are the nearest relative. You have the most right to demand some action. When you, the son, says his father never, ever would drink and drive it means more than the word of a brother-in-law.' Andrew stared ahead. He felt himself shaking.
'I suppose I would have to go to the police station in Birford. Would you come with me?'

'I think you would be better on your own. If I was there, they would just think that your daft uncle had put you up to it. I could of course go with you to Birford and wait outside but I have to work Monday to Friday and you could go immediately.'

'What! Tomorrow!'

Mike laughed,

'If you like. If you think you're up to it. I know you are a bit fragile at the moment and you might want to wait until you feel a bit stronger.'

'No, I'm OK but you would need to advise me what to say.'

'I could but it might come better just out of your head so you are not using my words.'

'But, what about the fare to Birford? I have no money.'

'I can support you for the moment.'

'You can't do that. You're not rich'

Mike laughed,

'No, I'm not but actually you will eventually have quite a lot of money. Have the solicitors spoken to you?'

Andrew put his head in his hands and this time the tears began to flow uncontrollably.

'I didn't want to know,' he sobbed, 'I don't want to be rich because my parents are dead. Grandma just said not to think about it for the moment and she would look after things.'

Mike waited for a bit until Andrew had calmed down.

'Andy,' he said gently 'no-one would think that you wanted your parents' money and, in any case, there is some complication about it but whatever there is, it's yours.'

Andrew wiped his face with his sleeve.

To my husband,
children and grandchildren

'I'm sorry, Uncle Mike. You must think I am a pathetic drip. I don't know what came over me.'

'Andy, you have just undergone a terrible tragedy in your life. I am finding it hard to cope with, so, I can't imagine how it is for you.'

'But, but. . . I want to do this thing. I want to find out what really happened in that car crash and. . . .and if I need to use my parents' money to do it, I will' 'At the moment, it's OK. I do have some savings and if things begin to get expensive, we can sort it out later. Let's not think about money for the moment.

We'll do whatever it takes.'

Mike leaned over and replenished their beer glasses. He lifted his.

'Whatever it takes,' he said.

Andrew smiled and lifted his glass of beer,

'Whatever it takes.'

Chapter four

'My name is Andrew Tremayne. I have an appointment to see Chief Inspector

Wilkinson.'

Andrew tried to sound as grown-up as he could and was grateful that there was a desk between him and the young Police Constable so that she could not see his quivering knees.

Police Constable Claire Walters looked at the young man in front of her with curiosity. He was tall, fair-haired, thin and very pale. He looked a nice lad but very nervous. She wondered why he had an appointment with old 'Wilkie'. She picked up the telephone and pressed the Chief Inspector's number,

'A Mr Tremayne to see you Sir.'

'Show him up' was the quick response.

Claire opened a door,

'Straight upstairs, third door on the left'.

Andrew knocked timidly on the door, hoping that it was the right one. He wished he could be bolder, more confident and adult. He was afraid he might break down when talking about his parents' death in front of an aggressive policeman. That would never do. He must steel himself.

'Come in,' said a voice. Andrew was glad the voice didn't shout, 'Come' which seemed to be the fashion amongst the 'men about town' these days.

The room that Andrew entered was a pleasant, comfortable room with arm chairs and potted plants.

Inspector Wilkinson, a large, athletic-looking man with unruly, fair, curly hair, rose from his seat behind an imposing, large, oak desk and held out his hand. Andrew put his hand out aware that it was weak and clammy.

'Mr Tremayne?' Andrew nodded.

'Do sit down'.

The inspector indicated a large armchair covered in dark blue leather and seated himself in a similar one opposite.

'I'm so pleased you could come, Mr Tremayne, but first of all you must be parched after your long journey. I'm sure you would like a coffee.' He didn't wait for a reply but leaned over and pressed a button on his desk,

'Two coffees please, Angela and don't forget the biscuits.'

Andrew didn't have the courage to say that he had just consumed three cups of coffee at the station buffet as he had arrived too early.

'I must say, Mr Tremayne, I think it is very brave of you to make this journey after such a terrible tragedy in your life.' The inspector leaned over and said in a quiet voice, 'I really am so sorry about what happened to your parents.' He put his hand on Andrew's arm, 'not many of us can survive intact after such an experience. I had a similar tragedy myself years ago. It takes a lot of time and some courage to come to terms with it.'

Andrew looked up at the inspector's face. He looked to be near to tears. Andrew looked away. Why was it that kindness produced this weakening effect on him? At all costs he wouldn't cry. Fortunately, Angela arrived with the coffee. Andrew looked at the comfortable-looking, slightly over-weight middle-aged woman and liked her. Inspector Wilkinson pulled over a coffee table and Angela put the tray down. She smiled at Andrew, 'I hope you like Hobnobs. We have run out of chocolate biscuits.'

Andrew smiled back,

'I do like Hobnobs. They are one of my favourites.'

Angela withdrew. The Inspector poured out the coffee and then looked up. 'I know you have come to find out the details of the accident which killed your parents.'

'I am grateful to you for seeing me' said Andrew, 'and I apologise for taking up your time.'

'Not at all, not at all,' said the Inspector, 'it's natural that the nearest relative should want to know all the details. I can see that you are a plucky young man and so I won't spare you the horrors. I will show you a photograph of the accident. This gives you the knowledge of what happened.' He took a picture of a burnt-out car next to a scorched, sycamore tree and handed it to Andrew. It was horrific. The car was completely burnt and he could just about make out two bodies in the front seats. Andrew felt sick and could feel his face becoming ashen.

He gripped the arms of his chair in an attempt to remain calm.

'Yes, it's shocking isn't it' said the inspector sympathetically.

Andrew was determined to achieve the purpose of his visit.

'What were your conclusions as to the cause of the crash?' He deliberately avoided the use of the word, 'accident'.

The Inspector screwed up his face as though it was difficult to answer the question. 'It's hard to say but probably a wet road and another car racing past. There again your father could have had some kind of seizure. We couldn't do any tests on the bodies as they were too badly burnt.'

'My father had very good health,' said Andrew.

'Yes, we know that but it could happen to anyone'

'My father would never drink and drive.'

The Inspector laughed,

'No, of course not. There's never been any question of that.'

'What about foul play? They could have been murdered.'

The Inspector laughed again,

'You've been watching too much television, young man. No there has never been any sign of foul play'.
'Why not? How do you know?'

Andrew could see that at this point the Inspector's bonhomie began to crumble

'I think you can leave these things to the police, Andrew. They know what they are doing.'
'But I know my parents and my father was always a very safe, careful driver.' 'Nobody is disputing that, Andrew. I can assure you that if there was any sign whatsoever, however small, of foul play, my men would have spotted it. I think we deserve your trust, don't you?'

Andrew did not answer the question which he thought was rather silly. He noticed the new condescension with the change from 'Mr Tremayne' to 'Andrew' He couldn't think of a way to continue the conversation. Then the Inspector laughed,
'I hope you haven't been influenced by your relative, Mr Nicholas, is it?' 'Nichols' said Andrew.

The Inspector laughed again in a derisory way, then seeing the expression on Andrew's face, changed tack.

'I think he was so upset by the accident that he didn't make sense, quite understandable but I think I'd better get on with catching criminals.' He laughed at his joke and stood up. Andrew understood that the interview was at an end.

'Thank you for your time,' he said, 'and good luck with the criminals'.

The Inspector walked with him to the top of the stairs.

'It was good to meet you, Andrew. I hope I managed to put your mind at rest.'

Andrew stared out of the window of the train. He was puzzled. Inspector Wilkinson had treated him kindly. He was obviously a well-respected, competent police-man, but why was he so adamant that there had been no foul play? Was it because they had too much work on and didn't have time to pursue it? The photograph of the wrecked car with the two bodies kept floating into his mind. He was rather surprised that he had been shown it. Perhaps it was to show him that they were treating him as an adult. It certainly showed that the bodies were practically unidentifiable. He knew that his Uncle Simon had identified them as far as he could and they had used dental records and various bits and pieces. He shut his eyes. He didn't want to think about it anymore. He would have a sleep and discuss it later with Uncle Mike but sleep didn't come easily. There was something wrong somewhere. He couldn't identify it but he was sure that was the case.

Chapter five

Andrew heard the door bang.

'Hi, Andy, sorry I'm so late. We had a wretched, parents' evening. It went on and on and I had some terrible stroppy parents. They either think you are unkind to their lovely children or they want a return to corporal punishment. They'd be happy if I beat them black and blue if it would get them a few Cs at GCSE. Good heavens! What are you doing?'
Andrew looked embarrassed,

'I hope you don't mind. I am quite good at spaghetti Bolognese so I thought I would give it a go. I don't mean to interfere.'
'No! no! not at all. Wonderful! I love spaghetti Bolognese. I'd have invited you before if I'd known you were a 'Jamie Oliver'.
Andrew laughed,

'Not quite. It should be ready in about twenty minutes. I haven't put the pasta on yet.'
'Great!' Mike sat down at the kitchen table. 'How did it go with the police?'

Andrew turned down the heat on the Bolognese sauce and joined him at the table.
'Not very well I'm afraid – I mean I didn't get anywhere on the murder suggestion.

Inspector Wilkinson seemed a very nice man . . .'

'Hmmp . . .You mean a smarmy git. He dyes his hair. Did you notice?'

'No, I didn't, but surely that's irrelevant. He did seem to be sympathetic.'

'Yeah – seems I know not seems.'

'What?'

'Hamlet.'

'Oh, well as I was saying. He did understand. He said he had suffered a similar tragedy some years ago.'
'I expect his cat died.'

Andrew put his head in his hands and shook.

'Andy, are you OK? I'm sorry if I sounded flippant!'

Andrew looked up. He was creased up with laughter.

'I gather you didn't like the handsome Inspector?'

'No, not my type. Now tell me word for word what happened.'

After Andrew had related the whole conversation, they both sat in silence for some minutes. Mike spoke first,
'I'm surprised that he showed you that photograph. He didn't show it to me. Perhaps he thought you would be so shocked you wouldn't continue the conversation or that somehow it was the clincher to prove his point.'
'But why should he want to do either of those things. He should be looking for the truth?'
'Exactly, there's something wrong there. It looks as though someone is getting at him.'
'Or he may have a lot of work on and didn't want to waste time on it.'

Mike thought for a bit,

'I don't think it's that,' he said, 'He has a reputation as a good policeman. They are used to worrying away at things until they get the right answer. And another thing – this is a high-profile case. Your parents were quite well-known, English, middleclass intellectuals. He couldn't really afford to get it wrong. There are a lot of people out to get the police at the moment, rightly so in my opinion.'

Andrew smiled,

'We mustn't let our personal prejudices get in the way but I think you are right. There is something wrong. Do you think he is being black-mailed?'

'Could be and in any case, I am not prejudiced. My opinions are based entirely on experience.'

Andrew thought back to three years ago when Mike lost his driving licence for six months but said nothing.

Andrew stood up and put the spaghetti in the saucepan.

'The point is – what do we do now?'

Mike sighed,

'I suppose there must be another policeman that would have investigated the accident.'

Andrew stirred the spaghetti. He nodded,

'I'm sure there is. He or she is probably wondering why they didn't continue with it but it would be difficult to get past Wilkinson.'

'You're right there. He probably runs his force with a rod of iron. We'll have to think of something different.'

Andrew put down his wooden spoon,

'What we are really interested in is – why did they do it? Who wanted to kill my mum and dad? I mean we're not so interested in the police angle – locking them up and so on'

Mike grunted,

'I am. I want them hung, drawn and quartered, apart from the fact that I don't believe in Capital Punishment, but it's true we need to think about why someone would want them dead'

'Let's have our dinner and then we could make a list of reasons why people commit murder.'

'Good idea! You know Andy, you are a very organised sort of guy – clear thinker perhaps you might become a lawyer.'

'Like Uncle Simon – no thank you.'

'He's a good bloke. What's wrong with him?'

'I don't know I suppose he's OK. Have you got a cheese grater?'

'No but I've got plenty of cheese. I practically live on cheese sandwiches.'

'Well, I will just have to cut it in small chunks.'

'You will make some lucky girl a great husband.'

'Stop talking about me. What about you? Have you any girlfriends? Or don't you like girls?'

Mike put his head on one side as though he were considering the question.

'Yes, on the whole I do like them.'

'Haven't you thought about getting married?' said Andrew as he dished out the spaghetti.

'Yes, I have given it some thought – think about it most of the time actually but I haven't had much luck. I mean you need a girlfriend first.'

'Haven't you had any girlfriends?'

Mike thought as he munched away at the spaghetti,

'Yes, I've had a few. There was Rosie. She was fun but I don't think my mum would have taken to her.'

'Why not? Grandma likes most people'

'I don't think she's very keen on tattoos and Rosie had a stud in her nose and in various other places actually. Anyway, Rosie moved on. Chloe was nice. I was quite keen on her. I thought it might work.'
'What happened?'

'I brought her back here one evening and . . .'

'Oh, I see'

'No, you don't and don't interrupt. I really gave the place a good clean and organised a nice candle-lit supper'
'She didn't like pizzas?'

'There's no need to be superior just because you have culinary skills. In fact, I had a really slap-up meal organised, one of those meals for two from Marks and Spencer's.'
'Yes, I've seen those advertised - two meals with two courses for ten pounds.

Wasn't it any good?'

'Yes, it was great and I got an extra bottle of wine – fizzy. She liked that Prosecco stuff, can't say I do myself.'
'And?'

'I never really saw her again. I don't think she liked my life-style.'

'What gave you that idea?'

'Just a few comments she made – why didn't I throw out newspapers? and why didn't I invest in a bookcase instead of piling up books on the floor? and didn't I mind cracked plates? You know, that sort of thing. I mean it's no good if she wanted a different lifestyle.'
'I didn't know this was a style.'

'Of course, it is. I mean I don't value things that don't matter like matching plates or milk jugs.'

'I just thought it was laziness,' said Andrew throwing more cheese over the Bolognese.

'There you go again. I think you would suit the law, mixing with all those poshos.

Have we got any pudding?'

Chapter six

'So, we won't think about your parents at all. We will just think about why murders happen. Have you got a pen and paper?'

'Yes', replied Andrew. 'I have an old exercise book'

'OK, then, sex is a common one, jealousy, love turning to hate – crimes of passion.'

'Money' said Andrew 'people wanting money, stealing from the rich, not wanting to lose it, inheritance,'

'Then there is power,' said Mike, 'control, people wanting to organise other peoples' lives, megalomania.'

'Fear, being afraid of someone, what they could do to them, beat them up or destroy their good name.'

'Yes', said Mike 'and going on from there you have possibilities of someone losing their job.'

'Or their wife or husband,' put in Andrew.

'And talking of reputations, it isn't just a well-respected person being accused of being a paedophile, it could be someone's reputation as an academic or a great artist or musician.'

'Pride' said Andrew.

Mike laughed,

'I think we have gone through most of the seven deadly sins – Lust, Pride, Envy, Greed. What else is there?

'Sloth?' suggested Andrew.

'Nobody's going to kill somebody for Sloth.'

'Well, say you had a certain lifestyle which involved a great deal of Sloth – you might . ..'

'Shut up,' said Mike.

'Well let's go through the list,' began Andrew, 'Sex – that's out.'

'Why?'

Andrew looked exasperated,

'Because, my parents were a happily married, middle-aged couple. They were not interested in that sort of thing.' 'You'd be surprised!'
'Mike! They loved each other.'

'Well, how about this – There was some chap, a real geek, you know the sort I mean. He had never had the courage to go out with girls and then he began to work with your mother. She was very kind to him, smiling at him and encouraging him – that sort of thing and he mistakenly thought she was giving him the 'come hither'. He approaches her and she has to let him down with a bump. Now some of these quiet chaps can go out of their minds about a thing like that.'
'We-ell,' said Andrew, 'but my Mum! I mean she was in her forties. I can't imagine some young chap going for her.'
'Andy, forty-four is quite young and your mum looked younger. It's difficult for me to assess her attractions. Being her sister, you don't look at her in that way but she was always regarded as being a bit of a looker and she was slim and lively and all that. The 'young chap' could be as old as her or have some kind of 'mother complex'.
'I suppose it is a possibility – worth looking into. Then there is money. Have you any ideas about that?'
Mike looked thoughtful,

'I never got the impression that they were rich people and you would inherit what they had, but there is some dispute about the will. We could look into that.'
Andrew screwed up his face in distaste,

'I don't really want to talk about money in connection with my parents.'

'I know that, Andy but we have to look into everything if we are to find the killer. I could make a few discreet inquiries. Simon would know.'

'Don't say I asked you to do it.'

'No, I think I could find a way.'

'OK then,' said Andrew, 'but be careful. The next motive for murder is power.'

'That's an interesting one for two intellectual academics.'

'How about, if they had uncovered something that destroyed someone's life's work?'

'That's a good one, or it could destroy their reputation.'

'My parents would always be kind. They wouldn't want to hurt anyone.' 'No, they wouldn't but they might feel they had to. Say someone was defrauding someone else or lying about something. There could be some powerful rich, bully who was hurting everyone. Sometimes people are afraid to speak up. It's like that in schools. Most people are a load of wimps. Your parents would be the kind to speak out.'

'You could be right there, Mike. That's something we could look into.'

'I think you've forgotten something'

'What?'

'What's happened to the 'Uncle Mike' I deserve a bit of respect.'

'Shut up Mike and let's get on with it.'

Mike pulled a face but continued

'I think we have covered most of the relevant motives and they all lead back to their work.'

'Well, they do have other friends – did have,' muttered Andrew.

'Let's start with their work. They are both attached to Ebbchester University and have been for some time – right?'

'Yes, they have been there most of their working lives. Dad did some research at Oxford for about three years and then returned to Ebbchester. Mum had some time off when I was born and then had a few months resting as she kept having miscarriages and she thought that might help but in the end she had to have a hysterectomy and that was the end of that. Poor Mum, she would have loved a big family and she somehow felt it was her fault that I was the only child.'

'Yes that was rotten luck.'

Andrew ignored the implication.

'So, we have always lived in Ebbchester. So, I suppose whatever work colleagues or friends they had will be there.'

'Didn't they go to America for a while?'

'Oh, just for three months. That was something to do with work'

'So, Frank was a Physicist and Mary did History and then turned to Archaeology.' 'Yes, she got very enthusiastic about that, but it wasn't just digging, it was old manuscripts and that sort of thing as well. Dad was quite involved too. He seemed to get quite excited about it.'

'They both published stuff, didn't they?'

'Yes, usually with the Ebbchester University press.'

'And they went on the radio and television.'

'Yes at first I would watch them but more recently I couldn't be bothered. They would be wheeled out for some topic that was in the news.'

Mike scratched his head,

'Didn't Mary go on the television to talk about that treasure that somebody dug up in East Anglia?'

'Yes – "here we have Doctor Mary Nichols to tell us what it's all about" – that sort of thing'.

'So,' said Mike, 'there were lots of people who knew them or knew of them. Did any of them come to the funeral?'

Andrew shook his head,

'Mike, I didn't notice anyone. Afterwards, when people came back to the hotel, I just skulked in a corner and as soon as I could, I went back to Grandma's and hid in my bedroom. I behaved really badly. I didn't think anyone for coming.'

'You didn't behave badly, Andy. I was just as bad. I didn't speak to anyone. Mum would probably know. She organised everything, spoke to the vicar, booked the hotel for the food. She was great really.'

'Yes she was. Uncle Simon and Auntie Melanie were good too.'

'Andy, I'll give Mum a ring and see what she remembers. She was going round, pouring drinks and talking to everyone.'

'What reason will you give? I don't want to upset her.'

'Oh, I'll think of something.'

Mike pulled out his mobile phone and dialled his mother.

Andrew felt uneasy. Sometimes Mike was so blunt. He dreaded listening to the phone call.

'Hello Mum. It's me, Mike. This is just to let you know that Andy's settling down fine. I'd have asked him before if I'd known he was such a dab hand at the old cordon bleu. How are you?' (silence)

'That's great! I didn't realise you were such a champion Bridge player. You will have to teach me sometime' (silence)

'Mum, I was just chatting to Andy and we both felt a bit bad about not talking to anyone at the funeral' (silence)

'I know they wouldn't mind but it would be nice to get in contact with them and I think Andy would be interested in the work his parents were doing. You know how it is when your parents talk about their work you pretend to be interested and just let it pass over you and then later wish you had taken more interest.' (silence)

'Hang on, I'll get a pen.' (silence while Mike scribbled down names)

'Thanks Mum, that's great.'

Mike came over and sat down clutching his piece of paper.

'Mum remembers speaking to about six work mates. There were two professors who seemed to know Mary and Frank quite well but probably came to the funeral to represent the two departments'

'Have you got their names?'

'Yes Professor Simpson from Archaeology and Professor Patel from Physics. There was a married couple who socialised with them but Mum didn't get their names.'

'Oh, I think I remember them – the Martins, Stuart and Heather, a nice couple. They would come round for meals sometimes but I don't think they worked with them recently. Heather worked with Dad some time ago I think, but they stayed friends.'

Mike continued,

'There was what Mum called "a young girl" – probably a sixty-year-old. Mum said she was terribly upset. She could hardly speak and kept saying, "They were so lovely and so clever." She was called Lucy Hammond – well she thinks it was "Hammond"'

'And the other person?'

'I think he was the one Mum liked the best – Hayden Lewis.'

'Why did Grandma like him?'

'I think he must have talked to her quite a bit. Old people like it when younger people make time for them. He probably said what wonderful people Frank and
Mary were.'

'Well, they were.'

'Yes of course but Mum likes to hear it. It helps. Do you find it helpful?'

Andrew thought for a minute,

'No, I don't think I do. I suppose I expect people to say nice things about them and if they don't, I assume it. I don't think I need to hear it. On the other hand, if someone criticised them I would be hurt or angry. I was incensed when I thought my father had been accused of drunk driving. By the way Wilkinson said there was never any question of drunk driving.'
'That's not what he said to me.'

'What exactly did he say?'

'Oh, something like – the chances are he lost control of the car because he was intoxicated – could have been drugs but probably drink.'
'Did you hit him?'

'Nearly, I couldn't believe what I was hearing.'

Mike looked at the scribbled list in front of him,

'Our next job is to get in touch with these people – friends and work mates.'

'Yes,' said Andrew, 'we need addresses and phone numbers.'

'I think,' said Mike thoughtfully, 'that we need to meet them face to face. In that way we can see their reactions to our questions and not just hear it.'

'Mike, I should be grateful if you would come with me. You are more confident than I am. I didn't do too well with Wilkinson.'

'I think you did do well. I don't think he would have said anything different whatever you said. But I will come with you. It's easier with two.'

'Thanks Mike. I should be grateful. I know that limits us to weekends.'

'Not necessarily, it's getting towards the end of term and I don't have the sixth form or Year 11 anymore. It doesn't take that long to get to Ebbchester. We could easily do it in an evening. I suggest that you set to work on the internet, looking up University departments and finding addresses and telephone numbers. We need to get on with it as the University term has practically finished and they will soon be sunning themselves in the south of France.'

'Or Fiji'

'I don't think they are rich enough for Fiji and they need to be near something of historical interest or a major University.'

Andrew yawned,

'I'm tired. I've not been used to actually doing anything for ages.'

Mike looked concerned,

'Are you OK, Andy? I mean we don't have to do everything so soon.'

'I'm fine. It's good to be getting on with something and I feel strongly about getting to the bottom of things. What old Wilkinson didn't realise was that his attitude, far from discouraging me from investigating has had the opposite effect.

I'm convinced he's hiding something.'

Mike laughed,

'A cover-up! That's the 'in' word. You get to bed, Andy. I'll do the washing up and you can start on the internet tomorrow'
Do you need a password on your computer?'

Mike blushed,

'It's Chloe. She was the love of my life when I bought the laptop. I couldn't be bothered changing it.'
Andrew laughed,

'Lucky you didn't go in for tattoos!'

Chapter seven

Lucy Hammond sat in Ebbchester University library and stared out of the window. The windows were large and took over the whole of one side of the library. Lucy didn't like this new library much. She preferred the old one with its medieval wooden beams and lovely oak panelling.

She looked down into the park which was alongside the new library. A little boy was racing down the pathway on his scooter and his mother was trying to keep up with him while wheeling a buggy and clutching the hand of a toddler who had obviously refused to go in her buggy. Lucy wondered what it was like to have children. It looked fun but then it was obviously hard work. Still there was no point in thinking about it. She hadn't had a serious boyfriend since she was an undergraduate.
Lucy wondered if the academic life was really for her.

She had been so delighted to be accepted for a PhD. And then to work with Dr. Mary Nichols! It was like a dream come true, but now . . .?' The tears welled up in her eyes until she could see the boy on the scooter no more. What had really happened? How could Frank Tremayne have been pushed off the road and have smashed his car against a tree, killing himself and Mary? Lucy knew she was wretched not just because her career had been ruined but because she had loved Frank and Mary Tremayne. They had been like a family to her. Lucy's mother had died of cancer when Lucy was fifteen years old. Her father, Peter, had married again when Lucy first went to university. Lucy liked her father's new wife, Nancy, and was pleased that he had a nice person to keep him company but as soon as she returned home for the holidays, she realised that things had changed. It was inevitable that they would. Their comfortable old sitting room with the shabby leather chairs had gone. The floor was a beautiful polished wood and the chairs and sofa were white. Instead of the velvet curtains, there were modern, colourful blinds.

'I hope you like it, Lucy,' Nancy had said.

'It's beautiful,' Lucy gasped and she did think it was, but nevertheless she ran up to her bedroom and wept.

Lucy shook herself. This was no good. She was acting as though her whole world had fallen apart. She would get a new job, maybe teaching or journalism? In the meantime, she would get some fresh air. It was a lovely day. She would go for a walk by the river. Lucy picked up her books and shoved them in her bag. She noticed that a light was flashing on her mobile phone. She would look at that after she had left the library.

After wandering down to the lakeside, Lucy sat on a bench and took out her mobile phone. There had been a call from an 'unknown' number. She pressed the number and put the phone to her ear. After a few rings a nervous voice answered,

'Hello,'

'This is Lucy Hammond. You rang.'

'Oh, thank you for ringing back. My name is Andrew Tremayne. I understand that you worked with my parents'.
 Lucy's voice came back eagerly,

'You are their son? Yes, yes I did work with them, particularly with Mary.' 'We wondered if we could come over to Ebbchester and meet you. There are a few things we would like to ask you.'
'Yes of course. I should be delighted to meet you. Who are 'we' by the way?'

'Sorry, the other person is my uncle, Michael Nichols. He is my mother's brother.

We should have spoken to you at the funeral but we were very distracted.' 'Of course, you were. When do you want to meet? Could it be in the evening or do we need to wait until the weekend?'
'The evening is fine. We could get to you before seven. When are you free?'

Lucy hesitated,
'I'm free tomorrow, Wednesday, and then on Friday. I'm afraid Thursday is out. Is

Wednesday too soon?'

'No that's fine. Please suggest a place and we will meet you there.'

'Well, you won't have had time to eat. I wish I could invite you for a meal but I'm afraid my flat is very pokey. I used to eat sometimes with your mother at the
Maison Bleu in Salisbury Street. Would that be OK? I could give you directions.

'No that's fine. We'll find it – seven o'clock then?'

Lucy sat back on the bench and shut her eyes, Mary's son and Mary's brother! Oh, how badly did she want to meet them! Lucy felt impatient for the rest of the day. After a quick snack in the evening, she decided to visit the Martins, Heather and Stuart. She didn't know them very well and they were considerably older than her but she knew they were very close to the Tremaynes. They lived in Oldbridge which was a twenty-mile drive from Ebbchester. As she drove along she wondered why she wanted to see them. Was it just the comfort of someone else who had lost a precious friend? She felt that somehow it was more than that – some kind of unfinished business. What had really happened on that dreary wet day in March? It had never made sense. She decided that she would not say anything of that sort to the Martins. She drew up outside the Martins' house. She was surprised to see that it was quite grand. She had never been to their house before but she had imagined it to be like the Tremayne's house, an Edwardian Terrace which had seen better days. This house was probably less than twenty years old and was detached with an imposing driveway leading up to the front door. Lucy parked the car by the roadside and walked up the drive through a pretty garden full of daffodils and flowering cherry trees. She was glad she had telephoned to say she was coming. 'Lucy, how lovely to see you!' Heather opened the door before Lucy had time to ring the bell and came running down the drive to embrace her.
'I saw you at the funeral, Lucy, but I think we were all so shocked, it was difficult to speak. You know Stuart has had disturbed nights ever since. Come in, come in.
Have you eaten?'

Lucy replied that she had and they entered the spacious hallway. The floor was covered with beautiful Italian tiles. Heather saw Lucy looking at them.

'Aren't they lovely? We went over to Carrara especially to get them.' Heather took Lucy into the sitting room. Stuart stood up to welcome her. Lucy had to stop herself from gasping. Stuart looked terrible. He had obviously lost a lot of weight and his face looked ashen. Lucy wondered if he was suffering from some serious illness. He managed to smile at Lucy and was his usual, pleasant, courteous self.

'Hello Stuart, I just thought I would let you know that Andrew Tremayne and

Michael Nichols are coming to visit me tomorrow. I'm meeting them for dinner.'

'We know Andrew, of course,' said Heather but not Michael'

'Oh, he's Mary's brother.'

Stuart looked slightly taken aback,

'I thought he was some kind of waster, on drugs or something.'

'Stuart!' exclaimed Heather, 'he's Mary's brother. She was very fond of him.'

Stuart smiled at her,

'That doesn't necessarily make him a paragon of virtue.' He turned to Lucy,

'What do they want? Why are they coming?'

This time it was Lucy's turn to be taken aback.

'I think they were just looking up friends of the Tremaynes'

Heather turned to Stuart,

'It's quite natural, dear. They want to keep their memories alive. Now Lucy, what will you have to drink? Do sit down and we'll renew our happy memories together.'

After a few minutes, Lucy was seated in a comfortable armchair and conscious of driving home had accepted a small glass of white wine. Heather had placed a tray of 'nibbles' on the glass coffee table and Lucy who was quite hungry had to restrain herself from eating the lot.

Lucy had met the Martins a few times but didn't realise how well they knew the Tremaynes.

'I met Frank when he was an undergraduate,' said Heather, 'I'm a few years older than him and I was already doing research into String theory. He was very anxious to join me and fortunately he got a first in Physics. He was very bright and in no time at all had surpassed me.'

'That's not quite true, Heather,' laughed Stuart, 'You had time off to marry me and to have three children.'

'Oh,' said Lucy, 'I didn't know your children'

'We got married young,' said Stuart and our children were born in the space of five years'

'That sounds fun' said Lucy.

'It was' said Heather 'but our youngest child contracted meningitis and died at two years old'

'Oh Heather' said Lucy, putting her hands to her face in horror, 'How terrible!' 'It was,' said Heather, 'particularly, as you know, I am Australian and Stuart's family were in Scotland. Frank and Mary were engaged then and they were so kind to us.'

'Our other children have survived,' said Frank.

'What do they do?' asked Lucy.

'Mark qualified as a doctor and works with *Médecins sans frontiers* in Africa and Sophie is a teacher. She got married two years ago and we hope to be grandparents in a few months' said Heather.

'Oh, I'm delighted for you both. You must be so excited' said Lucy.

'We are,' said Heather. Everything seemed to be so wonderful and then we lost our dearest friends. They seemed very happy too. Didn't they Stuart?'

'Ye-es,' said Stuart, 'in a way but they did seem to be acting rather strangely'

'You mean about money and that sort of thing?' put in Heather.

'What do you mean?' asked Lucy.

'Oh, nothing much,' said Stuart quickly, 'they just wanted to give away their money.'

'They were very generous,' said Heather.

They spent the next half-hour happily reminiscing about their mutual friends, the Tremaynes. Lucy was pleased that she had gone to visit them as she felt that it had been helpful to all three of them to talk about the life and tragic death of two people they all cared so much about. She left their house with promises to return and for them to let her know when the baby arrived.

Chapter eight

Mike and Andrew set off for Ebbchester as soon as Mike came home from work. The journey took them longer than expected as it was rush hour and the traffic was bad. They arrived at *The Maison Bleu* at about 7.15.

'Not too bad, just fifteen minutes late' said Mike, 'have you got your list of questions?'

'I have,' said Andrew, 'but we don't want her to think we've invited her to an interrogation'

Mike shrugged his shoulders and they went in. They spotted Lucy immediately. She was sitting at a corner table with a bottle of white wine. Andrew had met her before but only fleetingly. Mike was amazed at how young she looked. Lucy looked up and smiled. She was of average height with long fair hair tied back.

'I am so happy to meet you both,' she said. 'I – I suppose I am pleased to meet with people who were close to Mary. We saw such a lot of each other this last two years' – she added rather lamely.

They sat down and Mike picked up the drink's menu.

'I see you are drinking white. I'm a red man myself. How about if we order another bottle of each?'

Andrew seized the menu.

'How about if we order a large bottle of fizzy water?'

Mike sighed,

'It's time you passed your driving test. When we get back I'll teach you.'

Lucy laughed,

'Well, you can both share my Sauvignon Blanc. There's only half a bottle left so it won't make you drunk.'

They ordered their meals and Mike entertained them with some school anecdotes. Andrew felt slightly irritated as he felt that Mike was trying to impress Lucy with his rather exaggerated stories. They were half-way through the main course before Andrew was able to tentatively ask, 'What about you Lucy? Tell us about your work?

'Well, as you know I worked with your mother. I suppose I should say, "worked for your mother" but it never seemed like that. I have been studying for a Ph.D. in Medieval History and Mary was my supervisor. I was absolutely thrilled when she took me on as her assistant. We didn't think that was possible at first but we were sponsored by a rich, local business man, Hayden Lewis. You may have noticed him. He came to the funeral, a lovely man?'
Mike frowned,

'Did he have designs on my sister?' Andrew choked on his fizzy water.
'Mike!' he said.

'What? That's one of our questions isn't it?'

Lucy looked puzzled and Andrew was covered with embarrassment. After he had finished coughing he said,
'Well, I suppose we ought to tell you the purpose of our visit.'

'We believe Frank and Mary were murdered,' said Mike bluntly.

Andrew sighed. He wished Mike had a bit more sophistication. He expected Lucy to cry out in horror. She did gasp and then remained thoughtful'
'I did wonder, myself,' she said, 'tell me why you think so.'

'Well – it was the circumstances of the crash,' said Andrew tentatively. 'It was the middle of the afternoon in good light. It had been raining but there was no evidence of skid marks or of another driver pushing them off the road.
They just drove straight into a wall,' explained Mike.

Lucy screwed up her face in perplexity.

'Yes, I heard something to that effect. It always seemed strange to me. What do the police think caused it?'
'Drunken driving,' said Mike fiercely.

'No!' gasped Lucy, 'Frank would never drive after a drink. Even I know that.' She paused thoughtfully, 'was there evidence of alcohol?'
'No,' replied Andrew, 'the bodies were too mashed up for that'

Lucy flinched then turned to Andrew,

'Could your father have had a heart attack or something like that?'

'Well, my mother was in the car as well. She's a good driver, herself and would surely have grabbed the steering wheel.'
'Perhaps she had nodded off to sleep.'
Mike banged the table with his fist,

'No, they were only twenty miles from where they set off?'
Andrew was rather embarrassed by Mike's vehemence.
'It doesn't seem very likely,' he said rather lamely.

Lucy reached for another glass of wine and stared at the rose in a small glass in the middle of the table. Andrew's heart sank.
'She's going to disagree with us,' he thought.

Lucy looked up.

'Have you any ideas about who or why anyone would want to kill them?' 'Not really,' said Andrew mournfully.
'But' said Mike forcefully, 'we have made a list of why murders happen. That's why I asked you about the lovely Lewis'
Lucy laughed,

'The lovely Lewis is probably a happily married man and I never saw any sign that he was infatuated with Mary – still you never know!'

Mike took out a grubby piece of A4 paper and made a big tick beside the paragraph he had entitled 'Sex'.
'Mike, I honestly don't think that was the case.'

'Possibility though,' said Mike chewing the end of his pen.

'May I see your list?' asked Lucy hesitantly.

Andrew quickly produced a clean, type-written list from his pocket.
Lucy perused it carefully.

'I see what you mean,' she said, 'there are reasons why the nicest of people like Mary and Frank might seem to pose a threat to somebody, particularly in the academic field.'
'That's why we came to you' said Mike.

'Ye-es, I will have to think about this. There is a lot of jealousy in academic circles; you know people who have done painstaking work over twenty years and are hardly recognised – just the odd footnote. I know one professor, lovely, old man who recently published the results of thirty years work. It was mentioned in *The Times* but the reviewer said it was, "the most boring thing he had ever read". The Guardian was even worse; they said, "Professor Hetherington should retire to his garden or play bowls." Wasn't that unkind?' 'What was his work about?' asked Andrew.
'Something to do with the reproductive habits of a South American beetle.' 'Probably was boring,' sighed Mike. Lucy looked hurt.
'He was very well thought of in academic circles, reputed to have a brilliant mind.'

Mike frowned,

'And Mary and Frank had loads of accolades and even appeared on the telly. Was this old boy really miffed about his reviews?'

'Oh no! Nothing like that, he's lovely. He just laughed about it, making jokes about how 'Beatles' –with an 'a' were more popular than his beetles.'
Mike sniffed,

'Not that funny'

Andrew was embarrassed,

'Mike! He's an old man. You can't expect people in their seventies to have a good sense of humour,'
'Why not? My grandfather used to have me in stitches when I was a child.' 'Doing what?' asked Andrew rather curtly.
It was Mike's turn to look embarrassed.

'Well, wearing funny hats and that sort of thing.'

Andrew and Lucy laughed and after growling a bit Mike joined in.

The waiter then arrived with their meals, a salmon salad for Lucy, lasagne for Andrew and steak and chips for Mike. They all tucked in hungrily.
Despite having the biggest dinner, Mike finished first.

'Lucy,' he said, waving his last chip in the air, 'Have you any ideas? Are there people we could talk to?'
Lucy looked down at her plate, toying with a piece of lettuce.

'I don't know. It could be something to do with the research they were working on.'
'What was that?' asked Andrew, 'I know they were learning Welsh but I didn't take much interest.'
Lucy looked up in surprise,

'Were they? That's interesting. I didn't know that.'

Andrew laughed,

'Yes, they had all these grammar books and C.Ds. They kept testing each other.

Dad was really irritated as Mum had a much better memory for the vocabulary.'

Lucy stared into the distance,

'So, they were working on it,' she murmured.

'Working on what?' said Mike with some impatience.

Lucy looked round the restaurant and looked uneasy.

'Can't you tell us, Lucy?' asked Andrew gently.

'Of course, she can,' snapped Mike, 'this is life and death.' Lucy stood up.
'I think we ought to go somewhere more private' she said, getting her things together.
Mike looked impatient and Andrew looked longingly at the remains of his lasagne.

Lucy smiled and quickly wrapped it in her paper serviette.

'We can heat it up in my room' she said.

'Oh! So that's where we're going' Mike said rather belligerently.

Despite his obvious irritation Mike went down to the cash desk and paid for the three meals. Lucy protested but Mike snarled, 'We asked you to come.'

Chapter nine

Lucy rode her bicycle to her small flat in Ebbchester. Mike followed slowly in the car. Andrew was quiet. He was annoyed with Mike as he thought Mike had been unduly aggressive towards Lucy. Mike didn't appear to notice.

'I don't understand what's with this cloak and dagger stuff. Do you?'

'No but I'm sure Lucy wouldn't exaggerate things.'

Mike grunted,

'I don't know. Perhaps she likes a bit of drama.'

'I'm sure Lucy's not like that.'

Mike let out a raucous cackle,

'You're quite smitten aren't you? Mind you she's quite a looker.'
Andrew went puce-coloured with embarrassment and anger.
'Do you have to be so crude?'

Mike laughed,

'Oh, I could be a lot cruder.' He looked sideways at Andrew.

'Sorry Andy, I'm just teasing. I'll try and behave myself.

They drew up outside a tall Edwardian three story house. Lucy locked her bicycle in a small cupboard in the front garden.
You can park anywhere at this time,' she said, 'It's terrible during the day. Come on up. I'm afraid I'm right at the top.'
Andrew and Mark followed Lucy up two flights of stairs and she unlocked a narrow door at the top. They entered a small, light room with a big window overlooking Ebbchester.
'This is great' said Mike enthusiastically.

'Tea or coffee?' asked Lucy.

'Coffee for me but none of your posh stuff, I just like instant,' said Mike.

All three had instant coffee and Lucy produced some Hobnobs which reminded Andrew of his visit to Inspector Wilkinson. He told Lucy the story as they drank their coffee.

They sat round a small card table which Lucy had covered with a colourful little tablecloth given to Lucy by a friend who had visited Peru.

Lucy put her mug down firmly in the centre of the table.

'Well, I expect you're waiting to find out why I brought you here. I'd better start from about a year ago. As you know I have worked for Mary Tremayne for about two years. She is. . . was my supervisor. My first degree was in Medieval History. I became particularly interested in the early Middle Ages – what people call "the dark ages" but in my opinion they weren't "dark" at all but full of enlightenment and interest but I won't go into that. I did quite well with my degree . . .' 'Got a first I suppose,' muttered Mike.

Lucy ignored him and continued.

'I wanted to do research into that period of History and I particularly loved old manuscripts.'

'How can you – love – old manuscripts?' sneered Mike.

Lucy laughed,

'Oh, I do and when you can actually see and touch something that was written that long ago – well – it's thrilling. My professor introduced me to Doctor Nichols and she suggested that I should work on *L'Estoire des Engleis* by Geffrei Gaimar. This was written in a period somewhat later than I had hoped but Dr Nichols thought I was admirably suited to it.' 'Why' asked Andrew.

'Because it was written in old French and I am bi-lingual. My mother was French.' 'Ah, that explains it,' said Mike. Lucy looked puzzled.

'Explains what?'

'The 'je ne sais quoi', the Latin temperament, the mysterious, Gallic allure, the . .

. '

'Shut up Mike,' said Andrew. Lucy didn't appear to be at all embarrassed. 'I haven't got a Latin temperament. I'm quite prosaic and very English – stiff upper lip and all that, but I do speak French.' 'Go on,' said Andrew.

Well I started on the 'Gaimar'. Mary was with me every step of the way and we both became very interested in it. It's about the History of the English but includes a great deal about the British. Mary had been working on Geoffrey of Monmouth's, *History of the Kings of Britain*. Gaimar's book was written at the same time but they didn't appear to collaborate. The interesting part was that among others, Gaimar claimed as his source, *The Good Book of Oxford*. Geoffrey talks about 'a very ancient book'. Both of these books were given by an Archdeacon Walter so there is some speculation that they were the same book.

'And are they?' asked Mike.

'We don't know as the book has been lost – but . . .' Lucy stopped.

'But what?' Mike interrupted.

'I'm not sure, but both Mary and Frank took a great interest in *The Good Book* and in the beginning Mary kept saying things like, 'Wouldn't it be wonderful if we could find *The Good Book of Oxford*?' 'You say "in the beginning". Did they go off the idea?' asked Andrew.

Lucy screwed up her face in perplexity,

'I don't think so, far from it in fact but they suddenly didn't talk about it any more.

They became quite secretive.'

'Did you ask them about it?' inquired Andrew.

'Yes, of course. At first, frequently, then less, as they obviously didn't want to talk about it. I was a bit hurt at first but they were always so kind to me that I knew they must have a reason but . . .'
'But again' laughed Mike.
'This is difficult,' said Lucy 'and I must apologise to you both before I start' 'Go on,' said Mike.

'Well' began Lucy hesitantly, 'it was the weekend and the Tremaynes were away. I went into college to catch up on some work. I wanted some paper clips and as I had run out I went into Mary's room to see if she had any. The room was locked but the doors are old and my key turned the lock. I didn't think Mary would mind.
She was always very easy-going.

I mooched around looking for paper clips. I went over to her desk to look in the drawers there and then I saw it.'
'Saw what?' Andrew was puzzled.

'A folder entitled *The Good Book of Oxford*. This is the bit I'm ashamed of. My curiosity got the better of me. I opened it and began to look through it.' 'Was it actually there, the ancient manuscript?' Andrew was enthralled. 'No, it was a collection of notes. Some of it appeared to be translations and there was a photocopy of a small piece of an old manuscript but I couldn't make it out.
It was too damaged and I think it was in Welsh – or ancient British.'

'Did you get much information from the notes?' asked Mike curiously.

'Some of the translations were about the ancient History of the Britons, the kind of thing I had been working on in Gaimar. I was puzzled and slightly miffed that they hadn't included me on this and then I came to a whole section which was of a religious nature, morality and a description of the personality of Christ. It was fascinating. I am not a biblical scholar but I am familiar with most of the New Testament and these writings were a totally original view of Christ and his teachings.'
'In what way?' asked Mike.

'He seemed to come across almost as a revolutionary, a kind of Communist but not as we would think of a Communist but someone so compassionate and merciful, so forgiving and loving. I can't describe it but it was beautiful. I would have loved to copy the whole thing but of course I couldn't.'
'Why not?' asked Mike, 'I would have done.'

'That's because you've no conscience at all' said Andrew. Lucy interrupted quickly to stop the sparring.
'And then there was the money.'

'Mike looked up,

'You mean there was a stash of notes in the drawer.'

Lucy laughed,

'No, but there was a whole section on the use of money and wealth. You know in the Middle Ages, usury - taking interest on a loan was banned by the Church. Well this was much more extreme than that. The writer really despised wealth. He regarded the rich as we would regard criminals.'
'The camel and the eye of the needle,' said Mike.

'Yes, he took that quotation very literally.'

'Did you find anything else?' asked Andrew. Lucy looked guilty.

'Yes I did. I know I shouldn't have read it but I did. There was a letter from a professor in the University of Cardiff. Mary had obviously asked him to translate some stuff and he was saying that he would send it in a couple of weeks but there was a strange sentence at the end. I can't remember it exactly but he said something like – I can't stress enough the importance of keeping this secret. I do not do this work at the University but in a remote place. There is danger for all of us here.'

'Dramatic stuff' said Mike, 'do you think he was a nut-case?'

Lucy smiled,

'I can't imagine Mary and Frank having much to do with him if he was. They were so sane.'

'If he spoke about danger, it could have some connection with their deaths,' said Andrew thoughtfully.

'Yes, that's why I told you. I didn't want to. I was ashamed about snooping among your mother's things.'

'Good thing you did,' said Mike, 'this does make a difference. Did you see anything else?'

'No I don't think so. Well, there was one thing. There was a scrap of paper and on it was written in Mary's writing,

"Read *The Good Book of Oxford* and die?" that's all with a question mark after it. There were other bits and pieces, jottings – that sort of thing but nothing that stuck in my mind.'

The three of them sat for some minutes, thinking about what Lucy had said.

After a while Andrew said,

'Lucy, did my parents seem nervous? Do you think they were aware of any danger?'

'No, they seemed quite normal. My guess is they would have thought the Professor was exaggerating the danger. What about you Andrew? Did you see any difference in them?' Andrew shook his head slowly,
'No, but there was one day when they both were very angry about something.

That was unusual. I mean, Dad sometimes got into a stew about something but

Mum was usually very calm. She was always an optimist.' 'Do you remember when that was, Andy?' asked Mike.
'I should think about a couple of months before the accident – before they were killed. I know it was Ash Wednesday and Mum went to church with Grandma. Dad didn't go, said he was too "wound up". Does that ring any bells with you Lucy?' 'No because I was away before Easter and I wouldn't have seen them then.' 'But,' said Mike, 'it does look as though the danger and possibly their murder had something to do with *The good book*.'
Andrew turned to Lucy,

'Do you think it was dangerous because the book was very valuable or because of its content?'
Lucy shrugged her shoulders,
'I don't know. All I know is that for some time they were almost obsessive about finding it and included me in their investigations. We were all excited about the prospect of finding it. We told lots of people about it. Then all of a sudden the subject was dropped.'
'What did they say if you mentioned it?'

'Well it was Mary usually that I would speak to. She was as enthusiastic as ever about my work on Gaimar but if I said something like – wouldn't it be wonderful if we discovered the Good Book of Oxford? – she would say something like – yes wouldn't it?'
Mike looked at his watch,

'It's getting late and Lucy and I have to work tomorrow. I think we have to tread carefully with this. It would seem to be crazy to think that discussion of an old book would be dangerous. As I see it, there's two things we can do. We can look through all the writings and notes that Mary and Frank left and see what we can find. Lucy could you get into Mary's room again and lift that folder?'

'No, Mary's room has been cleared and there is someone else in there now. But I can inquire about her stuff. I can say it's relevant to my research which it is in a way.'

Mike turned to Andrew,

'Could you look through the house and any places where you think your parents could have left things. If it was that sensitive they could have hidden it.' 'Yes, I will,' said Andrew. He hadn't been back to the house since the death of his parents but now felt he could do it. 'What was the other thing we could do?'

'Get in touch with the old boy, the professor.'

Lucy said,

'If I found the letter, his address would be on it but failing that I can look up all the Welsh Universities and find some experts on the Welsh language.'

'Yes that would be good and I can do that as well. We have all the prospectuses at school for the children's applications for University'

'And I could look on the internet,' suggested Andrew.

'Good lad,' said Mike 'but what we mustn't do is tell anyone what we are doing. It sounds crazy but we have to be careful.' He turned to Lucy, 'Lucy, Mary was my sister and Frank my very good friend as well as being my brother-in-law. They are Andy's parents. You do not need to be involved. I don't want to be over dramatic but it could be dangerous.'

Lucy looked hurt,

'Of course I want to be involved. They were my very good friends and my life is not the same without them. I am actually very, very pleased to do something and
I hope you will include me in everything you do.'

'Of course we will Lucy,' said Andrew gently, 'we couldn't do it without you'.

Chapter ten

Andrew tossed and turned in his bed in Mike's Streatham flat. He had been relieved to find that he had a key to his family home in Ebbchester. He was glad that he didn't need to involve anyone else in finding it. He opened his eyes and looked at the key on his bedside table. It was on a key ring bearing the badge of Birford Football team that he carried around with him. He felt as though the gold of the Yale key was lighting up and flashing at him. He was obviously going crazy. Andrew got up and wandered into Mike's tiny kitchen. Andrew had tried to tidy it up a bit since he had been staying there but it was still a mess. He made himself a cup of tea and sat staring at the darkness of the London sky. He wondered vaguely why the night sky in London was never really black or even dark blue, just a muddy pink.

He knew he was nervous about going to the house in Ebbchester. He supposed it was because of all the memories it held. They had moved there when he was about three years old so he didn't remember living anywhere else. He knew he needed to go, not just because of their investigations but because he had to come to terms with what had happened. He finished the tea. He would get the train the following day and go.

Andrew stared up at number 23, Birford Road. It was a tall, red-brick, terraced house. He felt as though he was looking at it with fresh eyes. It had always been just 'home'. He looked furtively around. He laughed at himself. He wasn't breaking and entering. He had a key. This was his home.

Andrew turned the key and went in. The door pushed past a mound of letters. It was quite natural that there would be circulars from people who didn't know his parents weren't there. He turned into the first room on his right, the family sitting room. He stared in horror. Someone had been in and 'turned the place over'.

There were books strewn over the floor and the three-piece suite had even been slashed. Andrew felt like running straight out again. He listened. Was anyone there now?

Had squatters been in? The house was quiet. Andrew went cautiously through every room and discovered that whoever it was had done the same in each room. Even in the kitchen, plates and dishes had been thrown onto the floor. Andrew trembled. Had his kind, good-natured parents produced such hatred in someone?

He went upstairs; more of the same, cupboards emptied and mattresses slashed. He sat on the bed in his own room and gazed around him. His grandmother had brought most of his clothes to her house so there wasn't much in the wardrobe or the chest of drawers but the drawers had been taken out and turned upside down. His mattress had also been slashed.

He sat still for a while in order to contain his anger and then to control his tears. He looked around and then it dawned on him that the attackers were looking for something. They hadn't taken televisions or jewellery or things of value. He knew they had taken lap-tops because he hadn't seen those around. No, they were looking for something. He smiled to himself; well they obviously hadn't found it! Andrew felt calmer. He would go through each room himself and see if there was anything to find. He wondered when this intrusion had happened and whether someone would be back. He went downstairs and looked at the letters. He noticed that some had been carried into the kitchen and some had been ripped open in the hallway. He noted that the ones in the kitchen finished on March 22nd. That was a couple of weeks after his parents' death. He looked at the torn open ones in the hallway. The last one was from a week ago! He shivered. They must be coming back on a regular basis. He picked up the letters of the last week. He didn't think they would be much use but he put them in his pocket. Then he took them out again. He picked out the obvious circulars and advertisements for pizzas and put them back on the floor. He would go round the house but would leave it largely as he had found it so that no one would know he had been there.

Andrew went carefully round the ground floor trying to leave everything as he found it. He went upstairs. He was tempted to take a photograph of his parents' wedding that was in their bedroom. He realised that he had never really looked at it before. There they were smiling into the camera; his mother looking radiantly happy and his father looking rather embarrassed and perhaps a little proud of the pretty girl by his side. Andrew put it back where it had been knocked onto the floor. He prepared to return downstairs when he heard a key turning in the lock. He froze at the top of the stairs and then forced himself to move back into his parents' bedroom.

He heard two men come into the hall.

'Not much post' said one.

'Well I don't think there will be now,' said the other, 'most people will know by now that they've snuffed it and there's no point in writing to them'
'Yes but the boss wants everything, bank statements, car insurance, pay slips. He seems to think he can learn something from them. I wish we could find what he really wants. We could get good money for that'
'You're not thinking straight, Ken,' said the other, 'the boss is paying us good money as it is. He's a dangerous man. We can't make demands.'
His friend sighed,

'I suppose you're right. I don't think there's anything else here. Let's go.' 'We're supposed to make a thorough search each time'. Andrew's stomach contracted. It occurred to him that he could walk down the stairs and ask the two men what they were doing in his house but apart from being afraid he thought it might be unwise to let anyone know that they were suspicious. He was relieved to hear the front door slam. He sat on the bed for a while, trembling and waiting to make sure the two men had left the area. He finally decided that it was safe and was half way down the steps when he realised someone was at the door. He gripped the banister and stared at the door. Someone was pushing a letter through the letter box.

Andrew sat down on the stairs and remained mesmerised for some minutes. He finally stood up and still shaking made his way to the front door and picked up the letter. It had been sent some months ago and had had many destinations before arriving at number 22 Birford Rd. The last destination was 28 Birford Rd and it had obviously taken the occupants about ten days before they had got round to delivering it to number 22. Andrew put it in his pocket. He went out of the house by the back door and then went quietly down an alleyway which led to Bath Road. He looked furtively along the road and then set out on a brisk walk towards the station.

Chapter Eleven

'So you see Mike, I decided not to confront them as I thought it would be best not to let them know we were on to them'.
'And they could have knocked you on the head . . . or worse.'

'Well yes, there was that consideration, and then a letter was pushed through the door that had been posted ages ago then lost in the post.'
Mike looked interested,

'Have you got it?'

Andrew fished in his pocket.

'Yes, here it is. It was posted in France. It got lost because there was no country or post code on it. It was sent to an 'Ebbchester' in America.
Mike picked up the rather crumpled letter.

'The person who sent it must have been an idiot' he said, 'anyway let's have a look at it'. He tore open the envelope. 'Oh no!' he said, 'it's in French'.
Andrew laughed,

'Seeing it was sent from France, that did seem likely.'

They both poured over the letter. They knew a little French but the writing was shaky and difficult to read. The only thing they could decipher was written twice, on the top of the letter and on the back of the envelope. The letter was sent from a monastery in Brittany.
They felt quite excited

'We'll have to contact Lucy', said Mike, 'with her French connections, she should be able to translate it.'
Andrew was thoughtful,

'Mike, do you think they found the original manuscript in this monastery?'

'That could be the case. Let's phone Lucy,'

At that moment the telephone rang and Mike went to answer it. It was Lucy. Mike waved excitedly to Andrew and turned up the sound so that Andrew could hear. 'it's great to talk to you Mike, I have some news – not very good I'm afraid.' 'What's that?' asked Mike.

'Well, I contacted Cardiff University and asked someone about the Welsh department and in particular the professor and I was told that he died of a heart attack a couple of months ago.'

'Oh no,' said Mike, 'poor old chap. Was he the one who sent the letter?' 'Yes, I'm pretty sure it was. I knew it was a professor but had forgotten the name and when he said Professor Gwyn-Jones, I recognised the name. Also the letter was signed, Emlyn, and that came to me while I was on the phone so I said "Would that be Emlyn Gwyn-Jones and he said it would. He then asked me if he could put me through to the Welsh department and I said "yes". Now from here onwards I'm not sure if I did the right thing.'

'Don't worry Lucy I'm sure it will be OK,' Mike replied – a little sharply to Andrew's ears.

'Well' continued Lucy, 'I was put through to a senior lecturer, a Doctor David Thomas. He was very friendly and asked me what I wanted. I told him I had been anxious to contact Professor Gwyn-Jones and I was very sorry to hear of his death. He asked if there was anything he could do to help me and I said, "I'm not sure". He then asked whether I wanted to contact the professor about "Mrs Nichols' manuscript" I didn't know what to answer and I hesitated so he would have guessed that he was right so I just mumbled, "Yes". His next words were rather strange. He said,

"Exactly what do you want to know?" I muttered on about doing research with Doctor Nichols and how we worked together. In this case that was not strictly true but I couldn't say that I was investigating her murder. He then said in a rather fierce voice,

"Miss Hammond I suggest you come to Cardiff to discuss this. In fact I think it is imperative that you do so at your earliest convenience."

I put on a jolly, friendly tone and said that I would love to meet him and to visit Cardiff. I muttered on about going to a rugby match at the millennium stadium and said I would let him know when I was coming. He gave me his mobile number and said he had mine as I had phoned him on it.'

'Phew' gasped Mike, 'things are hotting up. We have something to tell you as well but I don't want to talk on the phone. Can we come and see you on Saturday?' 'Yes, of course. I'm free all day – well there are things I should do but I'm not in the mood for doing them.'

'Great! We'll see you on Saturday morning. We'll get there as soon as we can.' Mike put the phone down.

'Did you get that?'

'Yes, I did. That lecturer sounded a bit strange?'

'He sounded worried. What is it about that manuscript which gives people the jitters?'

Do you think it's because it's valuable and they want to get their hands on it?'

Andrew sighed,

'That would seem to be the most obvious thing but somehow I think it's what's in the manuscript that is important.'

'But Andy, it must be hundreds of years old. It's not as though it can hurt anyone. It can't reveal any dodgy dealings or even that the Queen's not the rightful heir to the throne. How could anyone be afraid of it?'

'I suppose it could contain some wonderful poetry and be valuable on that score', said Andrew thoughtfully.

'But nobody's going to murder someone over some poetry!'

Andrew laughed. He knew that despite Mike's aspirations to be a Philistine, he had a great appreciation of poetry and the written word generally.

'Lucy read a little bit of a translation. She thought it was very beautiful.' 'I suppose somebody might kill to get hold of a genuine Rembrandt,' suggested Mike.

'We might have some clues when Lucy translates our French letter. Did I give it to you?'

'No! You idiot! Don't say you've lost it.'

They spent the next half hour going through the flat but to no avail.

'You idiot' shouted Mike again.

'Well, if the flat was a bit tidier it would be easier to look.'

'So it's my fault that you've lost it.'

'I didn't say that.'

'Well let's think. Nobody has had the opportunity to steal it as we were looking at it less than an hour ago.'

'We were looking at it when Lucy phoned. You went to answer it.'

'So it should be still on the table. Look under the table.'

'I have done.'

'Look again'

Andrew bent down and went through all the books and newspapers that had their home under the table. As he stood up he caught his trouser pocket on the edge of a chair. It ripped.

'Oh No!' he exclaimed, 'that's your fault – oh Mike! Here it is. It was in my pocket.'

Mike took the opportunity to beat his nephew with a rolled up newspaper and Andrew was able to detach a similar weapon from underneath the table. After some time, dusty and exhausted, Andrew suggested that they find a safe place for the letter.

'Yes' agreed Mike, 'my flat's been gone over once already' 'What! When? You never told me,' said Andrew.

'Oh just before you came. Nothing was stolen but I didn't associate it with this business. I wonder whether they thought Mary gave me something to look after.' 'Unlikely I should think' said Andrew looking round the flat, 'but then they wouldn't know that,' Mike ignored the implication.

'My break in and the one at your house suggests they haven't found it.'

'Which is good. I think I will keep the letter in my pocket and under my pillow at night.'

'Yes it will be a great relief when Lucy's done the translation.

Chapter twelve

0Saturday morning in Streatham was dreary. The sky was overcast and the rain came down in a continuous drizzle.

Mike and Andrew hurried to Mike's old car, clutching pieces of toast as they didn't want to waste time having breakfast.
'You've got the letter' snapped Mike.

'Yes, it's in my pocket.'

'I hope it's not wet'

Andrew didn't answer but gazed dismally at the rain. Fortunately as they approached Ebbchester, it eased off. They got lost on the way to Lucy's flat and eventually got there at eleven o'clock.
'Sorry we're late Lucy,' said Mike, 'I couldn't get Andy out of bed.'

Lucy smiled,

'I was just about to make some brunch. Would you like some?'
'Excellent' said Mike.
Ten minutes later, they sat comfortably on the floor of Lucy's little flat enjoying bacon, egg and sausages. Andrew had told her about his expedition to his old home and the letter from Brittany.
'I can't wait to look at it,' said Lucy 'I'll just wash my hands'

Lucy sat with the letter on her knee and a pen and paper on a small table at her elbow.
After some minutes she said,

'This is really interesting. I'll read out my translation. I might get it wrong as it's hard to read and his writing is the old-fashioned French style.
'Dear Madame Tremayne,

It was wonderful to meet you and your husband in Brittany. I hope you managed to find a Welsh translator for the documents. What a pity so much of it is lost! I am writing because I have found a Latin translation of some of the 'Good Book'. I know that you will value this as I do. I do not want to send it in the post but as you said you would be returning with the Welsh document we could exchange at the same time but we must be very careful. These are difficult times particularly where money and power are concerned. Everybody is vulnerable! We must remember poor Hugo de St Sulpice. He was an unacknowledged martyr for our cause. I do not want you to be the same. I am an old man but you are a beautiful young couple with a lovely son. We must protect him.

I know you want to publish but we must wait until the time is right and with God's help it will soon be so.

I wish you every blessing in your glorious work. You are always in my prayers.

Jean-Phillipe Tessier O.S.B.'

'What's OSB?' asked Andrew.

'Order of Saint Benedict' answered Mike, 'he's a Benedictine monk.' Lucy looked round. There were tears in her eyes. 'Isn't that beautiful?'

Andrew also felt quite choked up. Mike sniggered,

'A bit over the top especially that bit about 'a lovely son'!'

'That's how my mother would have described me.'

Lucy laughed,

'I expect your mother would describe you like that, Mike!'

'Ugh! I hope not. But this is of some significance. What on earth is in *The Good*

Book that makes it so dangerous?'

'Something about money and power' said Lucy.

'But how can such an old book be of relevance now?' asked Andrew

'I read some of it, just a page,' said Lucy 'and it was very beautiful. It was like drinking clear, cool water in the desert. It's the only way I can describe it.' 'But what did it say?' persisted Andrew.

'I think it was a kind of interpretation of the gospels. I suppose even non-religious people have a vague idea of the wording of the gospels – the camel and the eye of the needle and that sort of thing, but the page I read didn't speak so much about the love of money and the root of all evil, it was more about the positive side, more like the beatitudes.'

'Are you a religious person, Lucy?' asked Mike.

Lucy hesitated,

'My mother was French and technically a Catholic. It was part of her background, her nationality. We hardly ever went to church except at Christmas or Easter but I was sent to a convent school' 'What was that like?' asked Andrew curiously.

'Oh it was great. There weren't many of the nuns there when I went but it was a good school and the sisters were lovely. What about your religious background?' 'Well my mother is Church of England and goes to church regularly,' said Mike, 'we were sent to Sunday school as young children but my mother didn't seem to expect us to go to church.'

'My background is similar,' said Andrew, 'Grandma goes to church but my Mum and Dad didn't. We would go with Grandma at Christmas but religion didn't seem to impinge on their lives much, except that . . . well they were good, kind people and I suppose you would describe them as Christian.'

'Loads of people are good and kind but they might be from any religion or none at all,' put in Mike.

'I know but I'd say my parents would have regarded themselves as, 'Christian' .

This Jean-Phillippe feared for my parents. He didn't want them to become "martyrs", but I suppose they did,' said Andrew.

'And who was Hugo de St Sulpice?' asked Mike, 'do you know, Lucy?'

'No I've never heard of him but we could look him up.'

'So,' said Mike, 'we've got two things to do, visit Cardiff and visit Brittany.' 'And in the meantime we could look up Hugo. I could do that. I've got a bit more time on my hands,' volunteered Andrew.

'And when do we go to Cardiff?' said Lucy, 'I can juggle my time so I could go any time. What about you Mike?'

'Well I have a 'day in lieu' coming up which I could take on a Tuesday or Thursday as Years 11-13 have now stopped having lessons.'

'How do you come to have a day "in lieu",' asked Andrew curiously.

'If you must know I stood in for the sports master for three Saturdays on the trot for football matches'

'I will contact Cardiff and try to go the earliest Tuesday or Thursday. Is that OK?' asked Lucy. The others agreed.

Immediately after they returned to Streatham, Andrew began looking up 'Hugo de Saint-Sulpice'. At first he had no luck. There were many towns and villages in France named after Saint Sulpice and many Hugos.

After some hours Andrew found a footnote in a description of a French monastery, containing the name, 'Hugo de Saint-Sulpice. There was no more information. Andrew found it very frustrating. He called Mike over to look.
Mike looked interested,

'That document has been translated into English and so it might be in the British Library,'
Andrew looked through the library catalogue and eventually found it.

'But you have to have a ticket to go there,' he moaned

'I've got one' said Mike, 'I'll go on Monday after school. I'll nip out early. I should get there in time.'
'How do you come to have a British Library ticket?' asked Andrew.

'Oh I do a bit of research now and again.'

Andrew was left with little to do over the weekend. He attempted to tidy the flat and cooked meals. Although he still missed his parents, he became very absorbed in his new task of both clearing his father's name and finding out the cause of their death. Every now and again he would still be shocked at the realisation of their death. He also found himself thinking more and more about Lucy. When he went to bed at night he would fantasise about how he would rescue her from burning buildings or a vicious attacker. He knew he was being silly and Lucy was unlikely to take much notice of a 'mere boy' but he did want her to think well of him and well – one could always dream? He decided he would try to read round the research that Lucy and his parents had been doing. He began by reading Geoffrey of Monmouth's *History of Britain.* He found it hard going at first but after a while became quite absorbed in it.
He was reading it when Mike returned from school on the following Monday.

'What's this then?' complained Mike, 'No dinner today?'

Andrew looked up,

'It's in the oven. You're late.'

'I went to the British library.'

Andrew was excited,

'Did you find anything?'

'Not a lot but Hugo was murdered. They think he was killed by some Italian financiers.'
'Did it say why?'

'Well as far as I could make out it was because he had been influenced by *an ancient book* and was condemning the financiers as being greedy and saying that their money was "tainted" '
'*The ancient book* is probably the same one that Geoffrey of Monmouth referred to and probably *The Good Book of Oxford*.'
'Yes, the thing seems to revolve around money and wealth generally' mused

Mike,

'The problem is, where do your parents fit in? I mean they weren't rich people - well no more than most of us.'

'Hugo was killed because he attacked the financiers; could my parents have been about to do the same?'
'Now there's a thought. Do you remember we put money and power on our list for possible murders? You know, Andy, I know you don't want to, but I think it's time to visit your Uncle Simon.'
'You mean about the will?'

'Yes.'

Andrew stared in front of him,

'No, I don't want to but you are probably right. There is something here that we don't understand. You said originally Uncle Simon agreed with you about the murder?'

'Yes, I think he still does but your Auntie Melanie was adamant he should forget about it.'

Andrew went to the oven and brought out the lasagne and for the next twenty minutes they tucked in with gusto. Andrew realised with a little guilt that his appetite had returned in force. He comforted himself with the thought that he needed his strength for the job in hand.

'Any news from Lucy?' asked Mike as he downed a glass of beer.

'Yes, sorry I forgot to tell you.' Andrew downed his own glass of beer, 'she says – is Thursday OK?'

'Great! That's fine with me.'

Andrew hesitated,

'I think I will go and see Uncle Simon. I've got to sort it out eventually. I'll phone him tomorrow.'

'Good lad! I think it would be better if you went on your own. I mean I'm not really related to him and although he did agree with me about the murder, I don't think he has a lot of time for me.'

Andrew laughed. He knew full well what Simon's views of Mike were.

'Why do you say that?'

'Oh he once told me that I lacked ambition and if I wanted to get a 'decent' girl, I needed to get a better job, more status, more money.'

'Did he actually say that?'

'Not in so many words but he did use the word 'decent'. I mean my idea of a 'decent' girl would be one who didn't care about money and especially not about status.'

'I can see him saying that but he is a good man and he's honest. My Dad reckoned he was a very good lawyer and he did care about us all'

'You're right. Take no notice of my prejudices and go and see him as if you just wanted to sort out your affairs. It might be better if you didn't mention murder.'

'Hello, is that Uncle Simon?'

'Andrew! How lovely to hear from you. How are you? Have you gone back to school?'

'No, not yet. I'll leave it until September now and repeat the year. I need to get good grades for University.'

'Yes of course. Have you thought about where to apply? I know Ebbchester is good but you might want to try somewhere further afield, maybe Oxbridge?' 'Oh I haven't thought about that yet. Uncle Simon, I was wondering if I could come and see you. I need to sort out my affairs, money and that sort of thing.' There was a short silence denoting Simon's hesitation.

'Yes, we need to do that but are you feeling up to it? I mean you didn't want to talk about money a short time ago.'

'Oh, I'm feeling a lot better now.'

'I'm glad to hear it but it's still early days. You might not feel like making major decisions.'

'Well, I'll know when I find out what they are.'

'Of course, it's your right. When do you want to come?'

'As soon as possible, Monday?'

'No, er . . .I'm a bit tied up Monday. How about Tuesday? How will you come?'

'I'll get the train.'

'Let me know what time it gets in and I will meet you at the station.'

'Oh, there's no need.'

'Yes there is. It's the least I can do. Tuesday then?'

Simon rang off and Andrew sat down. He felt quite weak. He didn't know why and felt rather ashamed of himself for being so childish.

Despite his hesitations, Tuesday found Andrew on the train to Cheltenham. He wished he could have walked to visit his uncle but Simon hadn't told him where to go so he had no option but to accept the lift gratefully.
'Delighted to see you, Andrew. You're looking well. I thought we'd be better going straight to the office as this is really official business. How's your grandmother,
Mrs Nichols?'

Andrew had scarcely time to reply before he was whisked off to Simon

Tremayne's office. Andrew had been to Simon's house frequently in the past. As a young child Andrew had enjoyed going there, as Simon's children, Fiona and Peter made a great fuss of their little cousin. Now they had both left home, Fiona had been to medical school and was now a consultant gynaecologist. She had married another doctor the year before and was now expecting her first baby. Peter was a barrister and lived in London.
'How's Fiona, Uncle Simon? Is she keeping well?'

'Oh she's fine but these gynaecologists know too much about what's going on.

She can see all the pitfalls!'

'And Peter?'

'Oh he's fine. He's specialising in Human rights. I thought he would do commercial law.'

'Human rights! That's great. He will be good at that.'

'I suppose so, well here we are.'

Andrew had never been to Simon's office. It was a discreet but imposing building in the main high street of Cheltenham, just a stone's throw from his house. They went up some steps then turned into an attractive room overlooking a neat garden. Simon indicated a comfortable armchair for Andrew and then went to get some coffee. He came back with a plateful of cakes and biscuits.

'I've put it on. It takes a while to percolate so we might as well get started.' Simon brought out a thick folder from his filing cabinet.

'As you probably know I have always been the solicitor for your parents but I wasn't expecting to have this job to do for them.' Simon's voice almost broke and Andrew was aware that this was almost as big a burden for Simon as it was for him. Frank had been his little brother and the two boys had had a loving, close relationship.

'Your parents bought their house jointly some years ago. They had not finished paying off the mortgage but in the event of their death, it is paid for, so you inherit that and its contents without encumbrances. They had some savings – a few thousand pounds in ISAs.'

'Did they make a will?'

'Oh yes, sorry I thought you knew. I advised them to make a will years ago. They left everything to each other and if both of them were deceased it all comes to you.' Andrew gave a rather sour laugh,

'So I'm a rich man.'

Simon sighed and looked out of the window. He fiddled with his tie, then turned to Andrew,

'Yes, but this is where it gets complicated. I'll just go and get the coffee and then we can talk about it.'

Simon stood up and went into the small kitchen adjacent to his office. Andrew was puzzled. He couldn't imagine what the complication might be. He wondered if his parents had huge debts or something. It seemed unlikely. They were eminently sensible and certainly weren't spendthrifts.

'Well here we are,' said Simon cheerfully putting the coffee down in front of

Andrew, 'Sugar?'

'Yes please,' replied Andrew helping himself to two spoonfuls.

'The complication is – your parents were given two million pounds shortly before they died.'

'Why? Who gave it to them?' asked Andrew

'It was given to them by Sir Gareth Morgan-Lewis because of their research into the kings of Britain. You have heard of Sir Gareth?'

'Yes of course, everyone has. He's a very rich man who gives a great deal to charity. Why was he interested particularly in their research?'

'Well he sees himself as a Welsh man.'

'I thought he was Canadian.'

'He is but likes his Welsh ancestry. His son, Hayden took an interest in Ebbchester and got to know your parents.'

'Oh, he was at the funeral. I didn't know he was Sir Gareth's son.'

'He just calls himself Hayden Lewis so it's not obvious.'

'What's the problem? I suppose the money will go back to Sir Gareth or go to the

University?'

'It's not as simple as that. The money was given to your parents, not to help them with their research but given to them personally as a kind of reward. Your parents refused it.'
Andrew laughed,

'Good for them!'

Simon smiled,

'I can see you are their son. The difficulty is Sir Gareth is a powerful man and the money was placed directly into their account to make refusal impossible and Sir Gareth made it known that he had made the gift. He was planning a big ceremony to advertise the fact.'
'I didn't hear about it?'

'No, most people didn't. I would not have known but Frank and Mary came to me with the problem. They had no intention of accepting the money and Sir Gareth had no intention of allowing them to refuse it. They decided in the end as it was already in their account, to get rid of it by giving it to charity.'
'So did they do that?'

'Yes and no. They intended to send it to an African village where they worked for a year, the first year they were married. They contacted the village and it was all arranged but then there was the accident.' 'Well why can't it still go through?'
'Because Sir Gareth wants you to have it.'

'But why? He doesn't know me.'

'I think he was furious about your parents' attitude.'

'But he's renowned for giving money to Charity.'

'Ah but that's when he gives it. He had told some high up people about the gift. Your parents were often on the television and were very well-liked. The public would have been pleased to see them rewarded. He was baffled at their refusal. To be fair they didn't give him a reason. When I asked them, they said it was better I didn't know but if Sir Gareth didn't leave them alone, everyone would know.'

'I expect they found out how he got the money in the first place.'

Simon laughed,

'What a cynical young man you are. But that's the problem. You have to make the decision.'

'There's no decision to make. It must go to the African village.'

'You could do a lot with two million pounds!'

'It wouldn't be good for my character.'

Simon sighed,

'You are a sensible, good boy but Sir Gareth is a very powerful man and I don't think he will leave it alone.'

'Can't we just send the money to Africa before he knows anything about it?' 'He has put out some legal prevention. His son came to see me a couple of weeks ago. He was very charming, very upset about the Tremaynes' deaths and anxious to be as helpful as possible. He went on and on about how you would need the money now you are an orphan with no-one to care for you, how it would help you in your career, you would be able to travel, meet 'nice' people and eventually set up home with your beautiful wife and talented children.'
'Did he really say that?'

'Well in slightly different words.'

Andrew laughed then coloured slightly. He was remembering Simon's past advice to Mike. He blew his nose vigorously to hide his embarrassment. Simon put out his hand and grasped Andrew by the arm.

'I know it's all very upsetting but in a way he's right, you know.'

'He's not. I do have people to care for me, there's Grandma and you and Auntie

Melanie and Uncle Mike and — well all my aunts and uncles and cousins' 'Of course you have, Andrew, and you know we will all care about you and help you in whatever ways we can but it's not the same as your parents. Is it?'

At this Andrew did become choked up. He nodded to his uncle, unable to speak. 'So I think you need some time to think it over. Discuss it with your grandma and your friends. I think they might advise you to keep the money.'

Andrew opened his mouth to speak but Simon interrupted him,

'Don't say anything now but think about it. I think Hayden Lewis wants to talk to you. He was very concerned and very charming. He said that although he didn't want that particular money to go to Africa, his father had given large amounts of money towards famine relief and the care of Aids victims. That is true of course. He said he would 'see what they could do' for that particular African village. I think he is a good man'

Andrew leaned forward and looked at his uncle.

'Uncle Simon, you know my parents wanted that money to go to an African village and that's where it will go. I don't need one minute to think about it.' Simon smiled rather sadly. He looked at his watch.

'Ten past twelve, I don't know about you but I could do with some lunch. There's a rather nice little place round the corner. Come on, let's forget about money for a while'

Andrew looked at the menu in front of him and tried not to look at the prices.

Simon saw his discomfiture and said,

'I'm having the sea bass. It makes a nice light lunch. How about you having the same. It makes things easier.'
Andrew nodded and smiled gratefully.

The food was very good and Simon even gave him a glass of white wine 'Chablis, a good vintage'. Simon chattered away talking about his childhood with Frank and all the scrapes they got into together. He was very amusing and Andrew laughed heartily at the reminiscences. They passed an enjoyable hour together. 'Well, we'd better get you to the station. I'll call a taxi. I don't want to be defrocked for drunk driving!'

Chapter Thirteen

'So you see Mike, I haven't any option but to send the money to the African village.'

'I can see that but aren't you tempted at all to take the money? I mean you could have a million and still give the rest away.'

'Of course it's a temptation in one sense. Most of us would like to be rich and have no money worries but would you take it if you were me?' Mike screwed his face up.

'Probably not but then I'm me and you're you.'

'What's that supposed to mean?'

'Well as you know I'm a committed Socialist and I eschew the wealthy lifestyle. I don't even like mixing with the rich or powerful. I aim to be a man of the people. Whereas you – well you've probably got different ideas or you may have when you are older.' Andrew laughed,

'Mike, I have exactly the same background as you. If I thought about it – lower middle class, I suppose. Our relatives were respectable teachers and craftsmen.' 'I try to forget about that. Another thing – you said that Sir Gareth wanted a big ceremony to present the money. Imagine the horror of that!'

'Yes that would be pretty ghastly but I don't suppose he would do that with me.' 'I shouldn't be too sure. It's not usually a case of secret donations for these so-called rich philanthropists.'

'That's a bit unfair. He does do a lot of good and I'm sure many rich people give money without anyone knowing.'

'Exactly!'

'Still there's no point in talking about it. The money is going to Africa and that's that.'

'Why do you think your Uncle Simon wanted you to take the money?'

'Oh I think he just wanted to make sure I was provided for in the future.'

'One burden less for him.'

'No, that's not the case at all. He is a generous and kind man and would provide for me completely if he needed to. I know that.'
'I expect you're right but there's another point. You know when I mentioned your parents' death not being an accident, he did agree with me. He might be afraid of what might happen to you.'
'You mean that Sir Gareth might have had something to do with my parents' deaths?'
'Could be.'

Andrew sighed and shook his head,

'I can't see that. You wouldn't murder someone because they wouldn't accept your money and in any case Sir Gareth is a well-respected man and his son, Hayden Lewis was a good friend of my parents. He was at their funeral.'
'But we don't know how he made his money. We don't know about all his shady dealings of the past.'
Andrew continued to look sceptical.

'I suppose we could look him up,' he said.

'I intend to,' replied Mike.

Mike managed to get the following Thursday off school and the day dawned bright and clear for the trip to Wales. Mike's car seemed to be going well and they picked up Lucy from Ebbchester with no hitches. Mike decided to put the roof down which proved to be rather windy over the Severn Bridge but they were all in good spirits. Andrew felt as though they were going on holiday and forgot to feel guilty about the feeling of happiness which swept over him. As they approached Cardiff, they began to become more serious in discussing how they were to approach Doctor David Thomas. Lucy said that they had no alternative but to be pleasant and matter-of-fact.

'But we need information' said Mike, 'I mean that's what we've come for.'

'But we mustn't make him suspicious,' argued Lucy, 'and we don't want to give anything away.'

'No' agreed Andrew, 'we'll just play it by ear. I will say that I want to have anything that belonged to my mother and Lucy can say she needs stuff for her research.'

'Yes,' said Mike, 'that sounds reasonable enough.'

Cardiff University was well signposted and they found it easily enough but had some difficulty parking the car. They argued about how much to put in the 'pay and display' machine, then found they hadn't enough coins between them. Lucy wanted to use her credit card but Mike declared darkly that she 'might never get it back'. Andrew went off to get some change and came back with a packet of 'kitcats'.

'Don't you know,' exclaimed Mike, 'that Kit-cat was taken over by Nestle?' Andrew looked blank.

'Very immoral record.'

'Come on!' exclaimed Lucy, 'we'll be late. I said eleven o'clock and it's twenty –to now.'

After finding the Welsh department and climbing two flights of stairs, they arrived at Doctor Thomas's office out of breath at exactly eleven o'clock. Dr Thomas was waiting for them. To Andrew's surprise he was quite a young man. Mike noticed his expensive suit and Lucy noticed his well-cut hair, his handsome tanned face and his highly polished shoes. He came to meet them and shook hands with them all. He seemed very interested to meet them especially Andrew, the son of 'such a distinguished couple'.

Doctor Thomas provided them with coffee, biscuits and comfortable arm chairs.

He leaned back, crossed his legs and put his finger-tips together over his chest.

'Now what can I do for such charming young people?'

Andrew looked warily at the expression on Mike's face and was grateful when

Lucy began,

'I had been working with Doctor Nichols for some time. She was doing research on Geoffrey of Monmouth's History of the Kings of Britain and I was working on *L'Estoire des Engleis* by Geffrei Gaimar. Our subjects over-lapped to some extent and so we saw a great deal of each other and worked together. I know some of the documents were in old Welsh and Mary asked for help from your department. I understand Professor Emlyn Gwyn-Jones was particularly helpful with translations. Because of the connection with my own research, it is important to me to retrieve any documents she sent here for translation.'

Doctor Thomas smiled sadly,

'That might be difficult, my dear. You see it was only Professor Gwyn-Jones that had access to these papers and he was an old man, very disorganised. At a guess,

I should say at the early stages of Alzheimer's.'

'But he must have had books and files in the college.'

'He did. My secretary went through them very carefully and there wasn't anything that might be helpful to you. I looked again before you came. Was there anything in particular that you were looking for?'
'Just the Welsh documents, I suppose,' said Lucy.

'Could the Professor have taken the documents home?' asked Andrew. 'A good question, young man' said Thomas, 'we asked his sister, who cleared out the house. She gave us what she had but there was nothing that might be of interest to you.'
'Did the Professor have a secretary?' asked Mike.

Doctor Thomas burst out laughing. After some seconds, he wiped his eyes and said, still laughing,
'Well, he had Edith. How much of a secretary she was to him, I don't know.' 'What do you mean?' asked Lucy.
Doctor Thomas leaned forward,

'Edith is an eccentric. She is completely batty.' He laughed again, 'in fact there was some gossip about their relationship – years ago- you understand.' He laughed again, 'I don't think the old boy would have had it in him in recent years and in any case – Edith!' He screwed up his face in disgust, 'probably nothing in it. I'm not one to listen to departmental gossip myself. Well, I'd best be getting on. I'm sorry if you have had a wasted journey. Have a look round Cardiff while you're here, a lovely city.' With that he showed them to the door and they began their descent down the stairs.
'Well, that was a waste of time,' sighed Andrew.

'I'm not so sure,' said Mike mysteriously, 'let's find the department office' 'I saw a sign to it on the ground floor' said Lucy. When they arrived at the office, Mike said,

'I'll go in by myself. It might be better that way'

Ten minutes later Mike came out of the office, looking very pleased with himself.

'Come on,' he said, 'we don't want to bump into Dracula.'

As they returned to the car, Mike explained that he had got Professor GwynJones's home address from the office and also the address and telephone number of Miss Edith O'Leary.
'She doesn't sound very Welsh,' mused Lucy.

'Oh, she is' replied Mike, 'her mother was Megan Evans, the famous Welsh poet' 'She can't be that famous. I've never heard of her,' grumbled Andrew.
'Do you read a lot of poetry in Welsh, then' said Mike sarcastically.

'I'm surprised they gave you her address,' said Lucy, 'is it in the prospectus?' 'No, but I have my ways' said Mike mysteriously.
'And what ways would they be?' asked Andrew, pushing Mike into a puddle. 'You idiot ' shouted Mike, 'these are new jeans. What do you think Miss O'Leary will think of me with mud up to my knees?'
Lucy and Andrew burst out laughing at Mike's unaccustomed concern about his appearance.
'You still haven't explained what your clever ways are' grumbled Andrew.

'I suppose I was slightly economical with the truth'

'Go on'

'Well I said I was her nephew and had been out of the country for a while and had lost her address book and wanted to take her a surprise birthday present.'
'That's not "slightly economical with the truth"'

'Isn't it?'

'No it's a big fat lie.'

'Anyway,' said Mike cheerfully, 'shall we go and see the lovely Edith first?' The others agreed and they set off.

Edith's address took them right out into the countryside. The weather took a turn for the worst and staring through the wind-screen wipers, they began to worry that the sat-nav wasn't working. They were directed down a muddy track which was filled with potholes.

'You have reached your destination'.

They peered out of the rain-smeared window.

'I can't see a thing' said Mike.

'Look' said Lucy, 'there's something behind those bushes'.

They got out of the car and walked down a muddy footpath to the door of what looked like a tumble-down cottage.

'Surely no-one can live here,' said Andrew. Mike tugged at a rope connected with a huge school-type bell. It rang loudly. They waited for a couple of minutes.

Suddenly a high, well-modulated voice came through the door,

'O'Leary residence. Please state your purpose.'

They looked at the battered door, mesmerised. Lucy spoke,

'Miss O'Leary. We were friends of Professor Gwyn-Jones. Could we come in and speak to you for a few minutes?'

The door opened. An apparition stood before them. Edith had a large amount of bright green hair surmounted by a red, floppy hat. She wore a long striped skirt and was draped in numerous colourful scarves. She looked very old but was upright, tall and thin. She smiled at them, her large, wide mouth stretching the width of her face. She clapped her hands,

'How wonderful to see friends of our erudite professor! It's just what I've been praying for. Come in come in. What do you want to drink? I have nettle, elderberry, dandelion and rhubarb.'
Lucy and Andrew settled for rhubarb but the more adventurous Mike went for nettle. They walked through a cluttered hallway into an equally cluttered sitting room.
Edith went off to the kitchen.

They looked around.

'She's got some terrific paintings,' said Lucy.

'Is the nettle, tea or wine do you think?' asked Mike.

The others shrugged their shoulders. Andrew stared at the well-stocked bookshelves. Many of the books were in Welsh but there were books about every subject imaginable, Religion, Philosophy, History, Science, Literature from various countries and heaped up piles on Mathematics and Astronomy.
Edith came in and plonked a tray down on a pile of books. The drinks were obviously her home-made wine.
'Now tell me how you know Professor Gwyn-Jones – a lovely, lovely, good man.

You do know he was murdered don't you.'

Lucy and Andrew looked shocked but Mike said,

'We were wondering about that. We had our suspicions.'

Despite the fact that Lucy and Andrew were somewhat aghast at Mike's statement, it seemed to have the effect of easing the conversation. All of a sudden they were together as co-conspirators and Lucy told her the whole story. Edith had met the Tremaynes and so was delighted to meet all three of them. She immediately announced that from the beginning she had no doubts that, 'That wonderful, brave couple was cruelly and wickedly murdered'.

Mike asked her on what grounds she believed that. Her answers, though more colourfully expressed, were much the same as theirs.

Andrew, who as yet hadn't spoken, leaned forward,

'Miss O'Leary, why did you describe my parents as "brave"?'

Edith looked slightly puzzled,

'Because of *The Good Book*.'

'*The Good Book of Oxford*?' queried Mike.

'Of course.'

Lucy looked excited,

'Miss O'Leary, have you actually read *The Good Book*?

'Before we go any further unless you want to be called Miss Hammond and so on, my name is Edith, only to my friends, you understand but I think we are going to be great friends.' With that she stood up, slapped Mike on the back, kissed Lucy on the cheek and gave Andrew a crushing bear-hug. 'Well I've read some of it, the bits we had from the monastery. Emlyn – God rest his soul- and I had a wonderful time translating it from the Welsh. Have you not read it?'

'I read that very short extract but that's all and the others haven't read any of it' Edith sighed and stared down at her long, gnarled fingers.

'Well, that is sad, very sad and what we had of it has been stolen, probably destroyed. It is a glorious book, probably the most inspiring book I have ever read apart from the Bible itself.'

'But why is it dangerous?' persisted Andrew.

Edith sighed again and shut her eyes,

'The gospels were dangerous, revolutionary, powerful. The good Lord was murdered because of his words. The rich and powerful fear those who might criticise them or suggest that perhaps it's not a good thing to be so rich and powerful. That lovely, black man, Martin Luther King was murdered because of his wonderful words. They say the pen is mightier than the sword and so it is but many a noble wielder of the pen has perished by the sword.'

'What was it actually about?' asked Andrew gently.

'Money, mammon, love of money – the root of much evil. Like the Church in the Middle Ages, it condemned usury but the *Good Book* was written in such a way that it spoke to us, people of the twenty-first century. It is particularly appropriate for our times when money, banks, the stock exchange etc. etc. seem to run our lives and the nations of the world.'

'Have you got any of it, Edith?' asked Mike.

'No, Mike I haven't. Emlyn and I worked on it at his home and after he was murdered, the house was ransacked. Everything connected with *The Good Book* was taken, the original manuscript, our translations, our notes, the two computers we were working on.'

'Doctor Thomas said that his sister cleared out the house,' said Lucy, 'Didn't she find anything?'

Edith smiled,

'Megan is a lovely person and would have collected Emlyn's files carefully but by the time she got there, they were all gone.'

Mike suddenly leaned forward and took Edith's hand.

'Edith,' he said gently, 'we should be most grateful if you would recount for us what actually happened, how the professor died, the order of events and why you think he was murdered.'

Edith stood up and went to the mantelpiece and picked up a battered old exercise book. She waved it at them.

'My diary,' she said, 'I try to write down as much ᵃ
memory is poor. Now where are we?' She flicked
of pages. She looked up at Mike then went to a drawᵤ.
brought him a pencil and paper. 'Make notes' she said, 'It might
be useful.

Emlyn and I worked on *The Good Book* for about two months, most of February and Marchl. It may seem strange to you but we didn't find out about the death of Mary and Frank until after the funeral. We don't watch much television. Emlyn's hearing wasn't too good and so he didn't listen to the radio. He was working at home on the manuscript and so didn't go into the University much. Lectures were finishing by then. I was away for a while, looking after a cousin in Ireland. When I got back, my parish priest phoned me up. He too had been away. He mentioned 'the terrible tragedy'. I didn't know what he was talking about. I immediately went round to see Emlyn who knew nothing about it. Nobody from the University had let him know! We were distraught as you can imagine. We read all the reports in the papers and found it difficult to believe that this was an accident. We even went to Ebbchester and spoke to the History Professor. He agreed that the circumstances were suspicious but dismissed murder as unlikely. I think he was troubled by it all. We voiced our opinions in Cardiff as well but most people treated us as fools and David Thomas was very unpleasant and I'm sure it was he that put it about that Emlyn was demented.

yn was very upset and his health did suffer at the time. We
didn't know what to do about the translations but I felt that we
should continue as the work was worth doing and for the sake of
Mary and Frank. Emlyn agreed and so we went on with the work.
I was rather surprised one morning when I turned up at Emlyn's
house to find his sister, Megan there. She said that she had
heard that Emlyn was ill and so had come to look after him. I
assumed that he must have mentioned his illness to her. I didn't
mind. Megan is so nice and a great cook. We had wonderful
meals for the few days that we were all there. Then one morning
. . .' Edith looked at her 'diary', 'Megan phoned up in great
distress to tell me that Emlyn had taken a turn for the worse and
the doctor said that he was dying. I rushed round but by the time
I arrived he was dead.'
Edith sniffed and wiped her eyes. The event was too recent and
her feelings too raw for her to talk about it. Andrew was surprised
when it was Lucy who persisted, asking gently,
'What did he die of Edith? What made you think he was
murdered?' Edith wiped her eyes again.

'The doctor was still there when I arrived and had already signed the death certificate. He said it was heart failure. I was shocked but not altogether surprised – if you understand me - at the time, because Emlyn had had a bit of trouble with his heart and about a year ago was fitted with a pace-maker. He had never mentioned having any trouble with his heart since. The doctor recommended a funeral director who arrived within a few minutes and then the Minister, a Mr Williams came from the local chapel. I am Catholic myself but Megan and Emlyn's family had always been Welsh Methodists. We all said some prayers together for Emlyn's soul and then the funeral director and Mr Williams sorted out the funeral arrangements. It seemed Emlyn had expressed a wish to be cremated. Megan wasn't very happy with that but as it appeared to have been his wish she agreed and the funeral was to be the following week. The funeral director arranged for the body to be taken to the funeral parlour. By that time it was afternoon and we hadn't eaten so Megan made some sandwiches and a cup of tea. We sat in Emlyn's sitting room in a kind of bemused fashion. Megan talked about their childhood, their parents, an older brother who had been killed in the war and a sister who had a family in Patagonia. She then talked about Emlyn's death. She said that Doctor Grant had been 'wonderful' staying with them until the end. I was surprised as although I had never met Emlyn's doctor, Emlyn often mentioned him. Aberfair is a small town where everyone knows each other and Emlyn played bridge with Doctor Yestyn Evans. I remembered him boasting that he was "fitter than Yestyn" who was overweight. I said that I thought Emlyn's doctor was Doctor Evans.

Megan agreed that he was and that they were good friends but said that Doctor

Evans was away. I didn't think any more about it until the funeral. I met Yestyn Evans then. He had just arrived back from a visit to his sister in Swansea the night before and was very shocked. After the service in the chapel, we had a wake in a local pub. Megan then went back to the house and I stayed chatting to Yestyn. I was curious because he seemed very angry. I assumed this was the way his sorrow had affected him but after a few drinks he said,

"I can't believe it. Emlyn was as fit as a fiddle". I mentioned his grief at the death of our friends. He just brushed that aside saying that he knew all about that but Emlyn was determined to continue with the translations. He then said, "Who is this Doctor Grant?" I said that I had assumed he was a locum. He said that he was only away for ten days and that Doctor Elizabeth Meredith would have covered his surgery and calls. He said that after such an unexpected death they should have had a post-mortem.

"It's too late now. They've burnt the body and that's another thing. Why didn't he go in the family grave?" I said that I thought that was his request. He just said "rubbish!" and had another glass of whiskey. I felt uneasy but decided it was time to leave. I went home for an hour or two then decided to go and keep Megan company for a while.

It was evening when I arrived. Megan opened the door and I could see she was very shocked and had been crying. This didn't surprise me as she had lost her brother but when I entered the sitting room, I too was shocked.'

At this point Edith stopped. Her grief and anger overcame her. The others waited in silence. After a few minutes she continued.

'They had taken down pictures from the walls, emptied the bookcases and left books strewn around the room. I went into the study. The computer and lap-top were gone and the filing cabinet completely emptied. Once again pictures were taken down and books strewn around. I went back into the sitting room where Megan was sobbing. She told me that the two men were there when she came back from the funeral. They told her that they were from the university and that it was important that they should retrieve "sensitive material". I immediately telephoned the University. It was difficult to get hold of anybody but the people I did speak to said they didn't know anything about it. I then telephoned the police. They were very good. They came round quite quickly, took particulars, looked for finger-prints and said they would be in touch. I then spent the rest of the day trying to comfort Megan. We drank a great deal of tea and I helped her clear up. Some of the stuff they had taken had belonged to her family, pictures and photographs. They had even been through the bedrooms and looked through all
Emlyn's clothes!'

Mike leaned over and took Edith's hand,

'Edith, that is really shocking. Did the police find out anything? Was anything retrieved?'
Edith clutched Mike with both hands.

'No that was the strangest thing. I stayed overnight with Megan. She was distraught and afraid. The following day we had a phone call from one of the young police officers. He said that they were working on the case and that although the thieves wore gloves, they thought they had a match from a fingerprint in the bathroom. He told Megan that he felt confident they would sort it out. Megan told him that she was planning on returning home but would return to Emlyn's house after she had sorted things out with the relatives in Australia.

She gave the policeman both our mobile numbers and also my address.' 'Did they sort it out?' asked Andrew.

'No, not at all, both Megan and I had phone calls from an Inspector Bains who told us that the young sergeant had made a mistake about the finger-prints and they had no leads at all.'

'So that was it' said Mike

'No, not quite, a week later I had a visitor. It was the young sergeant. He was dressed in mufti, wearing sun-glasses and one of those fleeces with the hood up. I recognised him when he took off the glasses. He told me that he was very sorry but there was nothing else he could do. He said that he would get into trouble if his superiors knew he was visiting me but he didn't want us to think 'all the police were corrupt'. He also said, "Ken Watson is a name that might be worth remembering." He made me promise that I would tell nobody about his visit but I don't think he meant people like you, otherwise there would have been no point in mentioning Ken Weston.'

Mike looked excited,

'So the implication is that some of the high up police have been corrupted. That's just what I thought, that Wilkinson for a start.'

Lucy laughed,

'I don't think you liked chief Inspector Wilkinson did you, Mike? We do have to be careful here though, as the sergeant said, 'not all police are corrupt.'

'And most of the police officers, particularly the younger ones are just doing what they are told' put in Andrew.

'Policewomen as well,' mused Lucy, 'Edith, what was the name of the Sergeant?' 'He wouldn't tell me,' said Edith, 'I probably could find out but I didn't want to betray his confidence. He was a brave and honest man.'

'He wasn't in that much danger' said Mike, 'with his hoody over his face.'

Lucy and Andrew turned on him angrily, 'He could lose his job!' said Lucy.

'Or be murdered himself,' shouted Andrew.

'OK, OK,' laughed Mike putting his hands up in resignation, 'I accept that he was a brave and honest man.'

'I should think so' muttered Andrew. He turned to the others, 'but where do we go from here?'

'This Ken Weston,' said Lucy, 'would there be much point in trying to find him?'

Mike shook his head,

'I don't think there would. He's probably just a petty crook and we haven't got ways of making him talk.'

'But we've got to do something' sighed Lucy.

'Father John,' said Edith abruptly.

The others looked at her in astonishment.

'Father John,' said Edith 'is my parish priest. *The Good Book of Oxford* is a very religious book. Mary and Frank were discussing the religious implications of the book and I suggested they talk to Father John Flynn. He's quite a scholar. They became good friends. I think they went to see him a few times.'

Andrew looked rather hurt,

'I'd never heard of him.'

'Andrew,' said Lucy gently, 'I think they were trying to protect all of us. We were all kept in the dark.'

'Edith,' said Mike rather sharply, changing the subject, 'Do you think it would be useful to go and see this John Flynn?'

'Yes, I do,' replied Edith, 'Father John probably knows more about them than I do.'

'We could go now,' said Mike. The others agreed and Edith wrote down the address and instructions and then phoned Father John to check whether he was in.

'Mary, that's the lady who cleans for him, said that he is out on sick communions but will be back in about ten minutes so if you go now you should catch him.' Edith practically pushed them out of the cottage door, kissing all three affectionately.

Chapter Fourteen

'Turn right at Dewi Lane' said Lucy, trying to read Edith's spidery writing, 'Oh! you've passed it.'

'You need to tell me before we get to the turn-offs,' said Mike testily, 'not after it' 'Sorry Mike' said Lucy meekly as Mike reversed at great speed.

'And I can see you and Andy grinning at each other like Cheshire cats. I'd like to see either of you driving with such useless navigators.'

They turned right down the little lane which wound up a hill and soon they had a magnificent view over the Welsh coastline.

'Mike! Mike! Be careful there's a huge drop on this side of the road' shouted Andrew.

'Shut up!' said Mike irritably.

Suddenly, as they rounded the bend a huge, wide digger came towards them.

Mike hooted ferociously but the digger refused to stop. It ploughed resolutely on. It seemed as though they were going to be thrown over the edge of the cliff. Lucy screamed and Andrew threw himself on the car floor. Mike quickly turned the wheel, crossed the lane and drove up the grassy bank on the other side. The digger ploughed on.

'Get the number!' shrieked Mike. Between them they remembered it and with shaking hands Mike wrote it down on the back of his hand. They sat in silence for some minutes.

'That was a brilliant bit of driving, Mike' acknowledged Andrew.

'You saved our lives,' said Lucy. Mike gave a grim smile then suddenly put is head between his knees. After some seconds he got out of the car and walked round it.

He then banged the bonnet of the car with his fist.

'The front wing is scratched,' he shouted, 'that bloody digger!'

Lucy and Andrew looked up, shocked at the vehemence then suddenly they burst out laughing. Mike looked annoyed then joined in the laughter. They felt better for it as they were all shocked.

'Come on' said Andrew, 'Father John is expecting us. We'd better get a move on.'

The lane wound round until it came to a main road which led into a rather dreary Council Estate. In the centre of the estate was the Church of the Sacred Heart and beside it a small modern house with the name –'The Sacred Heart Presbytery'. 'Here we are' said Lucy. Mike parked the car in the small drive and they got out of the car and went up a path between two patchy lawns. Despite the dull house and garden, there was a big rose bush by the front door in full bloom.

The door was opened by a tall, thin man probably in his fifties. He was generally untidy with a mop of greying black hair which hung over the thin face. He was dressed in clerical black but in places the black was turning to green. 'Now before you come in. What do you think of my beautiful roses? Have you ever seen such a shade of yellow – nearer to gold, I'd say?'

Lucy reached over and sniffed one,

'They have a lovely smell.'

'They have indeed – the scent of heaven – I say to myself as I go in and out. Now come in, come in. I know the good Edith sent you but you must explain yourselves what it is all about.'

They followed Father John into a comfortable sitting-room. Unlike Edith's there were very few books and the room was quite tidy.

'I keep me books upstairs' he said with a laugh, as though reading their thoughts, 'Mary Golightly – that's the lady who helps me keep the place tidy – now she's got no respect for books at all and if I stick a piece of paper in a book to mark my place, she just takes it out and throws it away, so I keep them in me bedroom. She doesn't go in there. Now you mustn't think I'm complaining about her. She's a wonderful woman and where would I be without her? Now sit down, sit down and tell me what it's about.'

'We understand you were a friend of Frank and Mary Tremayne's,' began Mike. Father John's face immediately changed. His smiling expression became one of pain.

'And proud to be so,' he mumbled.

'Well I am Mike Nichols, Mary's brother. This is Lucy Hammond who worked with

Mary and this is Andrew Tremayne, their son.'

Father John leapt up as if electrified. He rushed round to shake their hands. He was almost quivering with emotion.

'We are investigating their murder,' continued Mike, 'and we wondered if you could help us.'

Andrew felt that Mike was being rather pompous and nearly laughed at Father John's reply which rather destroyed the gravity. 'Are you indeed? God love yer.'

He remained silent for a minute and then said, 'And what makes you think they were murdered?'

Mike was rather disappointed with this especially after Edith's confidence in their suspicions. They all three explained their reasons for suspecting murder and after each reason, Father John would knock it down and suggest that it could have been an accident. In the end, Mike said in rather a belligerent tone,

'So you're not going to help us?' Father John looked very serious. He looked at

Andrew,

'How old are you Andrew?'

'Seventeen,' muttered Andrew. He was close to tears,

'And do you really think that someone murdered your Mam and Dad?'

'I do and I shall find out who did it and why. I can't walk away from it.' 'Good lad,' said Father John quietly, 'I agree with you, in fact I know that they were murdered but . . .' He looked round at the three of them, 'this is a dangerous business. I'm not being fanciful when I say that you are putting your lives at risk. I also agree with the good Edith that Emlyn was murdered. I will help you but you must take care.' He looked at his watch,
'It's half-past one and I for one need my lunch. How about if I send out for some fish and chips and we can talk while we eat? This will take some time.' The others nodded in agreement. Father John picked up the phone and to their amazement spoke in Welsh. He laughed when he saw their faces,
'Oh I'm just showing off! But you know here in Moel-y-coed, we have the best fish and chips in Wales.'

Ten minutes later found the four of them sitting round Father John's dining room table enjoying the Moel-y-coed chips. They all agreed that the quality of the fish and chips was excellent. In due course Father John put down his plastic fork, wiped his face with his handkerchief and began,
'I was introduced to the Tremaynes by Edith, the reason being that the Welsh or British book that they were working on appeared to be more of a religious book than they had hitherto thought. They had tracked down the book to a monastery in Brittany which partly explained its religious nature. The book, known as 'The

Good Book of Oxford' got its name because in the middle ages it was owned by Walter, Archdeacon of Oxford. He didn't write it but was believed to have translated it into Latin and then back into Welsh. Some people thought that it had originally been written by Tysilio, a seventh Century Welsh monk who eventually founded the monastery of St Suliac in Britany.

I won't go into all the details but the book was an amazing and a valuable discovery. Many ancient manuscripts had claimed that they had used it including Geoffrey of Monmouth's *History of The British* and Geffrei Gaimar's *Histoire des Anglais.*

The monks at the Brittany monastery were very proud of the ancient manuscript but were unaware of its value and importance. As it was written in old Welsh, they were unable to read most of it. They did however have a small section, which had been translated into Latin. This translation had probably taken place at a later stage as unlike the Welsh version, it was beautifully illuminated. This section which had a particularly Christian flavour was their greatest treasure. They trusted the Tremaynes and were anxious to help them. The monks felt that the words were so beautiful that the whole world should have the benefit of them. They were also very excited about having a translation of the rest.' 'But why' interrupted Lucy, 'did they keep it a secret? Why didn't they tell the whole world about it? I was working on the Gaimar. I would have loved to have known about it.'

Father John looked across at Lucy,

'Yes,' he said, 'that was the hardest thing for Mary. She told me about you, Lucy, all about you, how you were working on the Gaimar and what a wonderful job you were doing. She had tears in her eyes when she said,

"I can't bear not telling Lucy. I feel as though I'm cheating her, depriving her of something that would be a delight to her."' Lucy looked puzzled.

Father John continued,

'Then why didn't she tell you? Because she loved you Lucy, loved you like a daughter and could not put you in any danger,'
'But how could reading an old book be dangerous?' asked Andrew.

Father John sighed,

'The monks thought it was dangerous. They were able to cite many people over hundreds of years who had lost their lives over it.'
Mike looked puzzled,

'But surely that was just superstition?'

'I thought that at first. I thought it surprising that Christian monks should be superstitious but when I read part of it, I found it very challenging. A great chunk of it is about money, wealth and the use of it.'
'But surely,' argued Mike, 'nobody nowadays would take notice of an old book. Edith said that Jesus was crucified because of what he said in the gospels and that people have suffered because of the gospels since. I can understand that but this is the twenty-first century. Very few people in Britain take much notice of the gospels never mind an ancient, old book. Who would be threatened by it?' 'That's it Mike. You've hit on the point. The people threatened by this book are the rich and powerful. They have the most to lose.'
'But' continued Mike, 'there are lots of books being written which attack the rich and powerful. I have read them myself and encouraged others to read them but you don't feel in danger. The rich just think you're a lunatic and carry on getting richer.'
Father John laughed,

'Once again Mike, you have put your finger on the problem. You see anyone reading *The Good Book* would not feel it to be lunacy to sell up and give all his wealth to the poor. Despite the feelings of the monks, Mary and Frank couldn't think that the book could be dangerous but they respected their wishes and agreed to keep it secret during the translation process but as time went on they began to see the dangers.'
Andrew looked puzzled,

'How was that?'

'Well, you may not know this but the research that your parents were doing was sponsored by a local business man, a Mr Hayden Lewis.' 'Oh we know all about him,' said Mike aggressively. 'What do you know about him?' asked Father John.

'We know that he is the son of Sir Gareth Morgan-Lewis who wanted to give my parents money and who now wants to give me some,' said Andrew turning to
Mike,

'Did you ever look them up? You said you were going to'

'I did' said Mike, 'but I couldn't find much about them – a list of his various marriages and businesses, not much.'
'Well your parents and I found out a great deal about him but before I go any further, are you going to accept the money, Andrew?' 'Certainly not!' said Andrew fiercely.
Father John laughed,

'You're probably right but not altogether wise, but to continue, it's quite usual for wealthy businesses to sponsor research. It works to the advantage of both sides. Quite often an organisation will sponsor research into cancer or something like that and of course it's very good for their image.'
'Do they often sponsor historical research?' asked Andrew.

'Not very often' said Lucy, 'that's why we were so grateful to Hayden Lewis. At the beginning, none of us knew who his father was. He just seemed to be a very nice man who had become a friend of Mary's. He was always popping in to see how we were getting on.'

'And I suppose he liked the fact that the Tremaynes were often on the telly, gave him some kudos,' said Mike.

'No, he wasn't like that. He didn't seem to be interested in that sort of thing at all. He wasn't flashy with his money. He was just a good friend who was honest and genuine . . .' Lucy broke off rather lamely.

'Yes,' said Father John, 'that was certainly the impression I had from Mary. That's why she, foolishly I suppose, told him about the *Good Book of Oxford*. Lewis had been very interested in Geoffrey of Monmouth's book and he was very excited about the discovery of *The Good Book*. It was Lewis who put them in touch with Emlyn. He seemed to have many academic friends. Everything was going well and the translations were beautiful. That was when I got to know them both. Edith introduced them to me as they wanted to discuss the implications of the religious sections of the book. We had some wonderful afternoons talking about the book. It really was remarkable. The passages about money and the use of wealth could have been written for today. There was one more section of the book that they were to receive from the monastery and then they intended to first of all show you, Lucy and then they thought they would publish it just as it was, but translated into English.'

'Were the monks happy with that?' asked Mike.

'Yes, very happy and they were ready with the last sec... see they didn't want it published until it was complete, well as complete as it could be. That's when things started to go wrong. They hadn't told anyone about the last section, simply because at first, they didn't know of its existence themselves. One day, Hayden Lewis came to Mary and told her that as the book was nearing completion, he had told his father about it and he was willing to offer millions of pounds for the book. He would publish it and sell it all over the world. Mary was horrified. She told Lewis straight away that it was out of the question. *The Good Book* belonged to the monastery. She and Frank were doing academic research and were not a money-making concern. Apparently, Lewis looked disappointed but not too surprised. He appeared to accept the situation. Mary was shocked that he had told his father about *The Good Book*. I think she was probably quite gentle with him but made her feelings plain. He was apologetic and Mary felt that to be the end of it. She was however, very distressed about it and came straightaway to Frank and then they came to me to discuss the implications.' Father John turned to Mike, 'Like you Mike, I looked up Sir Gareth and couldn't find much but I then looked up all his connections and contacted some of my own. He emerges as quite an unsavoury character.' 'I thought he was a philanthropist, gave a great deal to various charities,' said

Lucy

'Ye-es he did, does. One doesn't want to condemn the man but motives are not always pure. I suppose for all of us, they are mixed.'

'So what's the low-down on the man? What's he done?' asked Mike eagerly.

Fr John laughed,
'Why do you dislike him, Mike?'

Mike looked slightly embarrassed,

'Well, rich man, arrogant, thinks he can do as he likes – all that sort of thing.' 'He is certainly a rich man, fabulously wealthy and it's difficult to find out exactly where it all comes from. He's covered his tracks well. In recent years he's been very lucky in his investments or perhaps very wise. He was born in Canada from quite a poor family in Toronto. Then he was known as 'Gary Morgan'. He married a local girl, an American, whose father owned a drug store. Her name was 'Stacy Loue Schmidt. When her father died, Gary took over the business but concentrated on the Pharmacy side of things. The rumour was that he was drug running but it was never proved. He invested in the pharmaceutical business and became very rich. They had a daughter, Wendy, who married a Ken Hardcastle. His father, Roger, ran a newspaper business which was largely pornography. We do know that Gary became a partner in the business and helped it to become very successful. At that time he changed his name slightly taking part of his wife's Christian name and became Gareth Morgan-Lewis. He then dumped Stacy-Loue and married an American heiress, Amy Armitage. By then Gareth was very rich, having made a fortune in pharmaceuticals and then with the newspaper. Amy owned an American newspaper. Gareth turned it from an Iowan state newspaper to a national one. Gareth then became very respectable. He decided that he had a noble Welsh heritage and has since spent a lot of his time in the UK. He bought a house in Cardiff as well as one in Chelsea. He supports Plaid Cymru financially and anything Welsh, football teams, rugby, the arts but took care to give to English charities as well hence the knighthood. He was obviously delighted with the knighthood as it has enabled him to hobnob with the rich and famous in London. His wife, Amy died a few years ago and he has since become quite a socialite.'

'Wasn't there some talk about him marrying Lady Eleanor Purbright?' said Lucy

Father John smiled,

'Quite likely but I don't follow the society news.'

'Where does Hayden Lewis fit in? He doesn't seem to be that sort of character.

He's a quiet, pleasant, academic person' asked Lucy.

Father John frowned,

'There's a bit of a mystery there. Gareth had three children, Wendy Hardcastle, who as far as I know still lives in Detroit, then he had two sons by his second wife, Bryn and Hayden. Bryn appeared to be the favourite as well as the eldest. He was lively and good-looking and seemed all set to follow in his father's footsteps but he was left behind in America and is now, never mentioned. He may have had a drug or drink problem. He certainly wasted a great deal of his father's money. Hayden has been more or less brought up in England. He did well at school and went to a Welsh University. He doesn't seem to have associated much with his father in recent years and lives a fairly quiet life. He is obviously very rich and presumably the money comes from his father as he hasn't done much himself, that is, as far as I know.'

'Father John, What did my parents think of Hayden Lewis?' asked Andrew. 'I think your mother knew him better than your father did. She was obviously quite shocked that he had told his father about *The Good Book* but I think she just put that down to filial affection. I don't think she blamed him for what happened subsequently.'

'What did happen?' asked Mike.

'Your parents were summoned to appear before Sir Gareth. He came to Ebbchester and invited them to a posh lunch at the Majestic Hotel. From what I understand he started off by being perfectly genial and congratulating them on the work they were doing. He then went on to tell them of his Welsh credentials. He believed himself to be descended from the Welsh nobility. The Wynne family were kings of Gwynedd in North Wales and can trace their ancestry back to the time of King Arthur. I think he even suggested that he might be descended from the good king. I imagine the Tremaynes listened politely and refrained from laughing. He then went on to say that he had read Geoffrey of Monmouth's History of the British People and was enthralled by it. It 'proved' the noble history of the Welsh or Britons as they were then and showed what a tragedy the Anglo-Saxon invasion was. He talked about the research of Geoffrey of Monmouth and asked them about the monk, Tysilio and whether they thought *The Good Book* had been written by him. I think Mary and Frank were quite impressed by his interest and all the research he had done. They told him that they hadn't reached any conclusions as they hadn't finished their research.

He then said that he wanted to buy *The Good Book of Oxford and* was willing to pay some inordinate sum for it. Mary told him that the book didn't belong to them and so they couldn't sell it. He then became quite vehement and said that he would find out who owned it and he was determined to own it. Mary was very anxious not to mention the monks as she didn't want Gareth going there and demanding *The Good Book* so by way of a diversion, she said that when they eventually published the translation he could buy a copy. Now that really put 'the cat among the pigeons' as the saying goes.'

Father John laughed and sipped his tea, 'Sir Gareth then said that he didn't want them to publish it "as it was". Mary was puzzled and asked him what he meant. He told them that he only wanted the historical and personal bits published, in other words he wanted all the religious bits left out. Mary asked him why. He said that they were of no interest to him and the Church had no business interfering with economic affairs. I think it was Frank who pointed out that although the Christian Church along with other religions banned usury in the middle ages, they had relaxed their views in recent years. Sir Gareth then got very huffy and said that it wasn't anybody's business how he had made his money and he didn't want 'nosey parkers' interfering in his life and he had given a great deal of money to the various churches and Christian charities.' 'He sounds a complete nut-case' said Mike.

Father John laughed again,

'I'd say he probably has a few problems. Anyway Mary said they couldn't possibly leave anything out of a translation. I think he then went purple in the face, practically accused them of eating their dinner under false pretences then completely reverted to his former, charming self, saying how he had enjoyed meeting them enormously and he hoped they would meet again soon.' 'It sounds as though he decided to use other methods,' said Andrew. 'What other methods could he use?' asked Lucy.

Andrew explained to them about his talk with his Uncle Simon and how Mary and

Frank had been given the money.'

'He was probably the sort of man who thinks everyone can be bought,' suggested Father John thoughtfully.

'Father John' asked Lucy suddenly, 'have you got any of the *Good Book*?'

Father John looked hesitant,

'I have some of the translations, the religious ones that the poor man wants thrown out.'

'Please could we read them,' Lucy persisted.

Father John smiled,

'I'll look them up and I will send you copies of what I've got. It will take me a while to sort through things.' He looked at his watch, 'I will have to go in a minute. I've got to go and see a poor old soul who has had a stroke.'

The others stood up

'Father John,' said Mike 'We are extremely grateful for all your information. If you think of anything else, please let us know. I think Lucy has given you our addresses and phone numbers and we will look forward to reading some of *The Good Book*.'

They went out to the car. Mike was just beginning to drive out of the gate when

Father John came running up. He handed Mike an envelope, 'Instructions' he said, 'You may as well have it now as later'.

Mike looked puzzled and they drove off.

They drove along the cliff top overlooking the sea. The sea was sparkling in the afternoon sun and the seagulls were chirping overhead. Lucy suddenly said,

'Oh do let's drive down to the beach. It looks so lovely, so inviting. It's ages since I've been to the sea-side.' Without a word, Mike swung the car down a little lane which led down to the shore.

To the slight consternation of the others he took the car down a stony track and parked on the beach itself.

They raced across the sand to the water's edge. Mike and Lucy were wearing sandals which they immediately removed and paddled into the sea. It took Andrew somewhat longer to remove his trainers and socks but he rolled up his jeans and joined the others splashing around in the water. He couldn't resist kicking the water over Mike and was rewarded by being thoroughly drenched. Mike then started showing off by managing to spin pebbles three times along the surface of the water. Andrew could only do it twice. They were then amazed by Lucy's prowess, managing six jumps. Try as he would Mike couldn't beat it. He then gave a shout and rushed to the little promenade. He came back with three ice-cream cornets. They strolled along the water's edge, licking the ice-creams as the sun became lower in the sky.

'This is lovely!' said Lucy, finishing off her ice-cream, 'I suppose things have been a bit heavy lately.' She put her arm through Andrew's and walked along with him. He nearly dropped the remains of his ice-cream with embarrassment and pleasure. His pleasure, however, was short-lived as Mike attached himself to Lucy on the other side and in this fashion they made their way back to the car.

Chapter Fifteen

'Will you come in for a bit of supper?' asked Lucy as Mike pulled in outside Lucy's flat.

'No thanks, Lucy. I've got to work tomorrow. We'll grab something when we get back. We'll be in touch. There's a lot to think about.'

'Yes, there is,' agreed Lucy, 'but apart from everything, it has been a lovely day.

Oh! Is that someone's phone?'

'Yes it's mine,' said Mike scrabbling around to find it, 'Hello, Mike Nicolls here. . .

. What! When! Oh no! This is terrible! Yes, I have your number on my phone.'

Mike slowly put his mobile phone in his pocket. He looked up, white-faced, 'Father John has been murdered. This time there is no pretending it was an accident. He was stabbed to death and his house has been ransacked. That was
Mary Golightly, the housekeeper.'

Lucy gasped in horror and put her hands over her face. She looked up at Mike

'The poor woman, I suppose she found him.'

'No, she didn't said Mike, 'Edith found him but she asked Mary to tell us. Mary said Edith has gone away and can't be contacted. She will write to us.' 'What do we do now?' asked Andrew hoarsely.

'I think we'll go to that pub down the road, The Red Lion, otherwise, I don't know,' said Mike.

Mike parked the car and they wandered down the road to The Red Lion. They were in a daze. Andrew felt as though he was going to be physically sick. Lucy could hardly walk. She held on to Mike's arm as they walked along. Once in the pub, Mike suggested that they sit outside as it was more private and it was a nice evening. Lucy and Andrew sat down and Mike went to the bar to order drinks.

The tears rolled down Lucy's cheeks and she clutched Andrew's shaking hand.

'Do you think it was our fault?' she whispered.

'Perhaps,' Andrew choked.

When Mike arrived they were both weeping silently. He put a brandy in front of them both and Andrew noticed to his relief that he had provided a half of bitter for himself.

'Drink that up,' he said, 'I have ordered some sandwiches and tea.' Both Lucy and Andrew protested that they couldn't eat but Mike declared that they must eat as they had things to do.

'We need to be doubly determined,' he said, 'and for that we need clear, strong minds.'

Lucy and Andrew dutifully drank their brandies.

Mike produced a pen and an envelope from his pocket.

'What do we know so far?' He answered his own question. 'We know that there have been four murders, Father John, the professor and Mary and Frank.' 'And from what we know, that we are dealing with someone who is ruthless, powerful and wicked,' said Andrew, shakily.

'We also know' said Lucy, 'that the person is so powerful that he can influence the police.'

'And possibly the government,' said Mike, 'we now need to look at our suspects.' 'We have Ken Weston,' put in Lucy.

'And Sir Gareth' suggested Andrew.

Mike sighed,

'But, we have no evidence against them.'

Their conversation was interrupted at this point as the waiter brought the tea and some very chunky 'ploughman's' sandwiches. They waited for a few minutes then Lucy began,
'It's a pity we don't have that policeman's name. It would be so useful to have the police on our side,'. Andrew looked thoughtful 'Do we know any policemen?' He looked at Mike, 'didn't we have some distant cousin who was a policeman?'

'Yes, Barry Turpin – dead.' They all remained silent for some seconds. Suddenly Mike sat up, 'Johnny Judge!' he shouted.
'Who is Johnny Judge?'

'A bloke I was at school with, nice enough, well-behaved that sort of thing, not a mate of mine but decent.'
Lucy looked disappointed,

'But if you weren't very friendly with him, he's unlikely to do you a favour.' 'Oh I don't know about that. His Mum was very friendly with mine, went to church together, ran jumble sales and his brother . . .'
'What about his brother?'

'He was older – had the – I mean liked my sister, Mary.'

'So his family were sort of family friends?' suggested Lucy.

'Yes, I suppose so. I think his mother may have been at the funeral. I don't think she came to the reception. I don't know where he is living but I think my mum said something about him hoping to be an inspector. She could probably find out.' 'That would be good,' said Andrew, 'but we need to find out more about our other suspect, Sir Gareth.'
'Yes,' agreed Lucy, 'we had a bit more information from Father John and from your Uncle Simon but we need more.'

'I was thinking about that,' said Andrew rather hesitantly, 'Uncle Simon said Hayden Lewis wanted to see me about that money. I have no intention of changing my mind about it but if he thinks I might change my mind, it might be a way to find out more about his father. I can't say I welcome the chat but it might be useful.'

'Oh I shouldn't worry about Hayden Lewis. He really is a nice man. He was very kind to your mother. I'm sure he will accept your decision,' said Lucy.

'OK, I'll get on to that. Is there anything else we need to discuss?'

'Yes there is.' Mike's voice was unusually serious, 'Father John gave me a package just as we were getting into the car. I don't know how you feel but I'd rather not look at it now. I haven't the concentration but tomorrow Andy and I can peruse it, but . . .' Mike trailed off, sighed then started again, 'If you remember Father John said he would send it to us or something to that effect and then he changed his mind. I wondered – I know this sounds a bit fanciful – whether he thought there was a chance his house was bugged.'

Lucy frowned, 'Edith might have thought that was a possibility. She said she would contact us by post, poor Edith, her two best friends murdered. She must be afraid.' Lucy was silent for a minute ' Death to those who read The Good Book', she added in a low voice.

Mike and Andrews immediately pounced on her,

'We mustn't think like that'

'That's superstition!'

Lucy looked near to tears. Mike put his arm round her,

'We're all thinking the same thing but we must try to put it out of our minds. That brings us to the next consideration' he said briskly, 'We are all in danger – all three of us. We might be bugged as well.'

'Isn't it possible to look for them?' asked Andrew.

'We could try but I think they are very sophisticated now. You might need some kind of electronic equipment to find them. I have two suggestions – if all three of us want to continue with our investigations, we could try and throw them off the scent. For instance Lucy could pretend that she is too frightened to continue and
Andy could have a nervous breakdown.'

Lucy smiled, 'and what about you?'

'Oh I could just revert to being a lazy slob.'

'Would we have to communicate by letter as well?' asked Andrew.

'We could but we could also have some kind of code that we used on the phone or in emails.'
'But surely they would be clever enough to break it?'

'Not if they didn't know it was code – for example. If we wanted to say that we needed to meet we could say something like, "I'm going to a party tomorrow" or "I'm finishing my essay on Thursday". We would need quite a few ordinary sentences as they would get suspicious if we went to too many parties' 'Yes,' agreed Andrew, 'and if they thought we had given up the chase, we could have very boring conversations.'
Lucy rummaged in her handbag and produced a notebook and some pens. She tore out some pages and gave them to each of the others.
'We had better get started on the code' she said, 'I know it's late but we have to organise our communications.'

Mike nodded his approval and they spent the next ten minutes sorting out code words. Despite their sorrow and anxiety they managed to find it quite an entertaining exercise so that when they left the Red Lion, they were all a little more composed. Mike also noticed that the 'ploughman's sandwiches' had all been consumed.

Chapter Sixteen

'Hello! Is that you Mike?

'I'm glad you got back safely. I'm feeling very jittery at the moment.'

'I know, I expect we all feel the same. I don't know how to say this Mike but I feel I can't take any more. I just need a break. I am so scared. I wake up in the night, terrified. I also need to get back to work. My research is suffering. I know it hasn't been the same for me without Mary but I have my career to think about. I really need to concentrate more on the Gaimar.'

'What's that about Andrew? I am so sorry. I suppose it was to be expected. He took the deaths of his parents very badly. Poor boy! Is he very depressed? Well at least he's trying to get on with things. I suppose he will eventually go back to his grandmother's.'

'So you are taking a break as well. Good idea – perhaps we were imagining things. It was getting a bit out of hand. I am hoping to go to the cinema with some friends on Thursday – try to go back to a normal life. Do keep in touch. I've really enjoyed our friendship.'

Mike sat down at the kitchen table thoughtfully.

'What was all that about?' asked Andrew

'Lucy is going to back out'

'But she can't. We depend on her.'

Mike shook his head and pointed quietly to their sitting room, 'Come and watch some television Andy, take your mind off things. You are getting too overwrought.'

They went into the other room and Mike switched the television on. He flicked through the programmes and stopped at a football match and turned the sound up.

He whispered to Andy,

'We should be OK with that noise. That was Lucy. She was brilliant. She made it sound so normal. I said you were on the verge of a breakdown'

'Thanks'

'Andy, you know it was what we agreed. She wants us to go to Ebbchester on

Thursday.'

Andrew brightened,

'She used the code?'

'Of course she did. You realise of course that I've switched the telly up so we can't be heard?'

'Yes but does it have to be quite so loud?'

'I don't know but better safe than sorry. We need to look at Father John's notes. Perhaps we could look at them here and then go down the road to the Pizza place and we can talk freely.'
'Good idea.'

Mike reached inside his jacket and brought out the papers. He spread them on the coffee table in front of them. There were some photocopies of what looked like old Welsh documents and with them some translations. They looked with dismay at Father John's spidery handwriting. He had typed the translations but handwritten notes in the margins – things like "this could be expressed better". Mike smoothed out one of the translations and they began to read – *We are material beings. God designed us to love material things. He created a beautiful world, mountains, lakes, trees, flowers, animals and most of all, beautiful people. He saw that it was good. Human beings are created in the image of God and so we too are creative. We love to create beautiful things, poetry, music, paintings, beautiful buildings. We create tools for our work, food, clothing, shelter. God works with us. He provides the wood, the stones, the skins and we work with him to provide for our needs and those of our families. We need to earn money for this.*

Then why did Our Blessed Lord say that 'the love of money was the root of all evil'. It is because it is what is in our hearts that is important. Jesus too must have loved material things. Did he not have a seamless garment that even his executioners did not want to destroy? Perhaps this was woven by his mother with unutterable love. Surely he must have loved it? Did he not also love the beautiful temple in Jerusalem?

Mike stopped reading,

'This is good stuff but surely nobody would be murdered because of it?'

'We need to continue,' said Andrew, 'there is more here.'

Did Jesus strive to be a rich man? When Satan offered him all the riches of the world, what was his reply?
No it is the love of wealth for its own sake and for the power it gives us that destroys us.

How do we gain wealth? It can be because we have been successful with our crops but have we worked our labourers too hard? Have we rewarded them enough for their labour? Have we then sold our crops at an extortionate price?

If we have plenty and our friend is poor, it would be good to give him money to buy seed. But if we fear for the next year's harvest and fear that we may not be able to feed our own children, then we may lend the money to our friend and he will pay us back but we must not indulge in usury. We must ask only for what we have given him. How is it just to ask for more? And if he struggles to pay it back how much more will he struggle if he has to pay interest.'

'I can see why Sir Gareth wouldn't like that but I mean nobody is going to take any notice of that in the modern world. The economy runs on borrowing and interest.'

'Yes but Mike, that doesn't make it right. I mean you have given me quite a bit of money in the last few weeks but you won't be asking me for interest.'

'You never know,' said Mike darkly, 'anyway, let's read on'

It is wonderful to give each other gifts, to share our good fortune with others. It is wonderful to receive gifts, to humbly accept the fruit of another's good will. But is it wonderful to receive a gift of money that has been stolen? By doing so we share in the theft. Is it right to accept a gift of money that is the result of oppressing others? No! By accepting it we share in that oppression.

But you may say, 'I can use this money for good purposes. I can feed the poor or build a church.'

No the food will be ashes in the mouth of the poor and such a church would be a mockery to God.'

But you may say, 'if I do not take this money, either someone else will or the rich man will continue to use it for evil purposes.'

No, the rich man and the other receiver of the gifts will have to answer to God for their actions. It is not for you to consider this.

*But you may say, 'Jesus ate with prostitutes and tax-collectors.
Was he condoning wickedness?'*
*'No, the heart of Jesus is filled with pity and mercy for these poor
children of God.*

Wasn't his constant prayer – sin no more?'

Mike put the paper down,

'This bit finishes here.' He screwed up his face, 'I can see why the
lovely Sir Gareth wouldn't want that to be published in his name.
It's a bit close to home for him with his dodgy dealings.'
'And if Mum and Dad had been reading that, they certainly
wouldn't want to accept his money.'
'I don't suppose they would have accepted it anyway but they
certainly couldn't after reading that.
'Is there any more, Mike?'

'There seems to be just scraps – a sentence here and there –
listen to this' *If I have money left to me that I have not earned,
do I deserve it? No! If I have worked very hard but have been
over-paid for my labours, do I deserve it? No, again! If I have
amassed a fortune by honest hard labour, what is to be done? I
must constantly look to my fellow men and see to their needs.
Am I being generous in doing this? Will I be rewarded in Heaven?
No, I just doing what is necessary but if I refuse to do this, if I
hoard my money, if I expect thanks and adulation for only doing
what is right , what then? I must expect the wrath of God, I must
give everything to God – my heart, and above all my purse. I
must be honest in my dealings with money even if I have to
endure Poverty, even if my house should fall down.*
'Father John has high-lighted that in his translation'

Andrew laughed,

'That's a good one. It's really challenging. It will challenge me now
I am such a rich man!'

'Speaking of your untold wealth, what about your visit to Hayden Lewis?' 'Yes, I must telephone him. Lucy scribbled down his phone number for me before we left Ebbchester. I could phone him now.'

'Good idea!'

Andrew went into the other room and Mike switched off the television. He marvelled at the change in Andrew. Rather than relapsing into nervous collapse, he had become more determined and energetic. He was, however, quite worried about his young nephew. It was clear that to continue with their investigations was dangerous and he was conscious of the fact that it was he, himself who had introduced Andrew into this danger.

Andrew returned. He was about to speak when Mike said in a loud voice, 'I'm glad you phoned Mr Hayden Lewis. He will be able to explain to you about the money. I know you want to follow your parents' wishes but it could be very useful to you. Shall we watch the end of the match?'

While the television was on, Andrew told Mike the gist of the conversation. He had had no trouble getting Hayden Lewis on the phone and he had just said that his Uncle Simon had suggested that he talked to him. Hayden Lewis had seemed very friendly and pleased that he should wish to meet him and had made an appointment for him on the following Thursday.

'That should work well as Lucy suggested we go there on Thursday. You could get a single ticket on the train and then come back with me in the car.'

'Why don't you go on the train as well? Then you can come straight from school and there is less chance of you being followed.'

Mike thought for a minute. He loved his car and was reluctant to go anywhere without it. He also felt a responsibility for the safety of Lucy and Andrew.

'OK' he said, 'I can see that makes sense.'

Chapter Seventeen

Andrew stood in front of a modern detached house in the middle of Ebbchester. It looked rather strange as most of the houses in Ebbchester were tall, Georgian or Victorian, terraces. It was at the end of the street so Andrew assumed that the land had once been somebody's garden. He walked down the path through a neat and colourful garden of Geraniums and lobelia and rung the bell. He nearly laughed out loud as the bell tune was Men of *Harlech.* A tall, thin, grey-haired man opened the door. He ushered Andrew in, saying,

'Mr Nichols, I presume. Mr Lewis is expecting you. Would you please wait here?' Andrew sat on the proffered chair which was covered in pink damask. He was bemused. Was the tall man Hayden Lewis's butler? He didn't know people had butlers these days. They were for people like Bertie Wooster or Poirot. 'Mr Lewis will see you now. Please come this way.' Andrew followed the 'butler' into a comfortable sitting-room.' The room was carpeted with a thick, beige pile.

The French windows opened on to a well-tended lawn surrounded by more

Geraniums. Hayden Lewis got up from a rose-colour, leather sofa to greet him. 'Hello, Andrew. I am so pleased you could come! I see you have already met my man, Barnes.'

Barnes nodded at Andrew and Andrew smiled back. Hayden Lewis turned to Barnes.

'I'm sure our young friend would like some lemonade on such a warm day.' Barnes went off to procure the lemonade. 'Do sit down, Andrew. I'm delighted to meet you.' They both sat down on the pink chairs.

'Before we start, Andrew, I must offer you my deepest sympathies on the deaths of your wonderful parents, such a tragic accident.' Andrew mumbled his thanks.

'I knew your parents well. We were great friends. We spent many a convivial evening together. They were doing amazing work. I tried to support them as much as I could, financially of course and procuring television and radio appearances. Your mother, especially was a great favourite with the public. I was at the funeral of course and had a great chat with your grandmother, such a lovely, brave lady.'

'Yes, she is,' murmured Andrew.

At this stage Barnes came in with the drinks, lemonade, as ordered for Andrew and something else for Hayden.

'Bottom's up' said Hayden, cheerfully, raising his glass. Andrew raised his tumbler. 'Well, to get down to business. I suppose you've come about the gift of money given by my father to your parents.'

Andrew opened his mouth to speak but Hayden waved him aside.

'Before you say anything, I want you to know that the gift was made absolutely to your parents. There were no strings attached and it was theirs to do exactly as they wished with it. My father as you probably know is a very generous man and the gift was for - two million pounds.' Hayden said the last few words slowly so that the enormity of the gift might sink in. He then said, 'And it will all come to you as the heir.'

Andrew smiled,

'Well that's a great relief – I mean, the fact that they could do what they liked with it. I know they were going to give it to an African village so I will do the same.'

Hayden frowned.

'Andrew, how old are you?'

'Seventeen,'

Hayden smiled,

'Andrew, I remember when I was seventeen. I thought I was quite grown-up but looking back. I can see that in fact I was quite irresponsible. I knew nothing of the world I –'
Andrew interrupted,

'Whether I know nothing of the world is not the point. I am quite old enough to obey the wishes of my parents.'
Hayden sighed,

'Andrew, Andrew surely you realise that that was their wish while they were alive. I can assure you that their wish for you would be quite different. If they were looking down from heaven now they would surely wish that you would take the money to secure your future.'
'Well, I don't want the money. I shall give it away.'

'Andrew, you must give it some time. It is early days yet after your parents' accident.'
'It wasn't an accident. They were murdered.'

'Now, Andrew. I am not going to listen to such silly talk. I know you have been influenced by some unscrupulous people. You must put that out of your head. It will only cause trouble for you.'
Andrew felt foolish not because he believed his parents to have been murdered but because he knew that he shouldn't have mentioned it. He was, however feeling extremely irritated.'
'In any case why should you care about whether or not I accept the money?' 'Andrew, you are the son of my dearest friends. I am concerned about your welfare, just as your father would be.'
'That is very kind of you but you have no need to worry about me. I have a house, money in the bank and relatives who care about me and who would look after me.'
Hayden turned round and stared out of the window. When he turned round, his face had taken on a look of suffering.' He put his hand on Andrew's shoulder. 'Andrew, you loved your father didn't you?'

'Of course I did.'

'Well I love my father too. He is a great and wonderful man. He wanted your parents to have that money for their own use and he wants the same for you.' 'But if I have the money for my own use, I am free to give it to whomsoever I please.'

'Yes of course but don't you think my generous father deserves something in return?'

Andrew looked puzzled,

'But what could he want from me? I have nothing to give him.'

'Andrew, if your father gave you a generous gift what would you say to him?'

Andrew laughed,

'Thanks Dad.'

'Exactly,'

'You mean he just wants me to say "Thank you". I can do that if that's what he wants.'

'But you can't if you give it away.'

'Of course I can. I can thank him on behalf of the village. I can write him a thank you letter.'

'Andrew, my father is an old man. He may not have many years to live. He would like a simple ceremony where he gave you the money.'

'You mean he wants everyone to know about it?'

'Oh Andrew, that is an unkind way to talk about a generous, loving old man.' 'But if he is so generous and loving surely he would want the money to go to

Africa? Mr Lewis, I don't think there is much point in continuing this conversation. I have decided what I shall do with, what is after all my own money. It's really no one else's business. I came to see you because my Uncle Simon asked me to. I thought I could explain to you my situation but it seems impossible to do so.' Andrew looked up at Hayden Lewis and to his horror, saw a face contorted with anger and hate. Hayden Lewis turned once again to look out of the window and when he turned round his face was once again benign and smiling.

'Well I can see you are a determined young man. I'll just ask you one thing, wait for some time before you do anything rash.'

'Well, I can't do much until Uncle Simon has sorted out the will.'

Hayden smiled,

'Of course, It's been lovely meeting you Andrew. I hope it won't be too long before we meet again.'

'Thank you for seeing me and for the lemonade.'

Chapter Eighteen

'I suppose after a while, we'll have to vary where we meet,' mused Mike, 'in case our enemies realise what we're doing?'
'It would help if we knew who they were' said Lucy.

'I think it must go back to Sir Gareth. He's the one with the money and influence.'

'Yes, he obviously pays people to do his dirty work.'

'Or threatens them. He's got some hold over the Police and the universities. Lucy,

I'm starving. Shall we order something to eat?'

'Don't you think we should wait for Andrew?'

'Well, we could order a drink – what do you want red or white?'

'Aren't you driving?'

Mike banged his fist on the table,

'I'm sick of this. You are as bad as Andy. No I'm not driving. I came by train.'

'I'm sorry, Mike. I really didn't mean to offend you.' Lucy reached over and took

Mike's hand. Mike stopped himself from pulling it away. He forced a smile, 'Oh, sorry I'm a bit touchy about that sort of thing.' It really was quite nice having Lucy holding his hand. 'Here's Andrew,' said Lucy standing up and waving.

Andrew came out into the garden where the other two were waiting. He sat down heavily into a chair and put his head into his hands.

'How did it go then?' asked Mike impatiently.

'Are you all right, Andrew?' asked Lucy. She could see that Andrew was near to tears. He looked up,
'It was terrible and I was terrible.'

'What do you mean?'

'I said all the wrong things, rubbed him up the wrong way and probably scuppered everything we're trying to do.' 'I'm sure that's not true,' said Lucy.

'Come on then tell us what happened,' sighed Mike, 'but before you start let's have a drink.' He waved to the waiter and ordered a bottle of house red.
Andrew stumbled through his conversation with Hayden Lewis.

'And this is the worst bit' he said, 'He kept on about my parents' accident and I couldn't stand it anymore. I just came out with it. I said that they were murdered.' Lucy and Mike were silent for a few seconds then Mike said,
'What was his reaction?'

'Oh, he said that it was "silly talk" and that I'd been listening to "unscrupulous people".
'That means me' laughed Mike.

'But it's important,' said Lucy thoughtfully, 'it means he knows.'

'Knows what?'

'He knows that we believe your parents were murdered and that we are investigating it'
'How would he know that?' asked Andrew

'Well somebody knows,' said Mike, 'otherwise there wouldn't have been all those murders and now it looks as though we have proof that the Lewis family are involved. You did well, Andy!'

'But' said Lucy, 'It doesn't necessarily mean that Hayden is involved in the murders. He might just have heard about it from his father.'

Andrew turned to Lucy,

'You like Hayden, don't you?'

Lucy smiled,

'I don't know. He was always so polite and interested in what we were doing and he did donate money to the department for research. It wasn't huge amounts but we were always grateful for anything.'

'Did my mother like him?'

'She was grateful for the money. The department needed it. I think she found him slightly irritating.'

'In what way?'

'Well we knew he had a very rich father and so was probably very rich himself but he made a point of being very humble and telling us about his simple life-style and his ordinary house.'

'Did you go to his house?'

'I didn't, I don't know whether Mary ever did.'

'Well, it wasn't that ordinary,' said Andrew, 'He made out he was terribly friendly with my parents. He said something like, "we spent many a convivial evening together".

'Did they go out drinking together?'

Lucy thought for a moment,

'I've no recollection of such occasions. That's not to say they didn't happen but I'm pretty sure they didn't. Your father didn't care for him and didn't have much to do with him.'

'Perhaps,' Mike interjected, 'he didn't like the way he was getting too pally with my sister.'

Lucy laughed,

'I don't think it was that – probably more to do with Frank's socialist principles.

What did you think of him Andrew?'

'Oh, I didn't like him at all. In fact I thoroughly disliked him.'

Mike seemed pleased,

'I don't think I would have liked him either. From what you have told us he sounds most obnoxious.'
'I didn't like his house, his garden, his furniture or his face.'

Lucy laughed,

'I can see you didn't like him. He was usually very polite and quite charming.' 'Possibly but what I don't understand is why he wants me to accept that money. I know he wants his father to have a big show of giving it to me but surely that's not so important.'
'You will have to be careful, Andy. Your parents refused it and look what happened to them!'
Lucy grimaced,

'Oh Mike don't say things like that but it is a bit of a mystery.'

'It's all tied up with *The Good Book of Oxford*. Sir Gareth saw the money as a bribe for *The Good Book*'
'But why should he want to bribe me?' said Andrew, 'I don't have any information about *The Good Book*'
'But he doesn't know that,' said Mike, 'and in any case you do. You have read some of it and we have in our possession stuff from Father John.'
'But,' said Lucy, 'they must have more than us. They took whatever Mary had and they ransacked the Professor's house.'

They sat in silence for a few minutes. Suddenly Andrew turned to Lucy,

'Lucy, if Sir Gareth wanted to publish whatever stuff he's got, could he do it?'

Lucy thought for a minute,

'No-o, I don't suppose he could as we would know that he had stolen it.' 'So, all his efforts to secure the means to glorify his Welsh heritage are useless, but if he bribed me, he could say that the information he had, was given to him by my parents.'

'But why go to all this trouble? I mean he may want to be a great Welsh leader but surely it's not worth committing murder for?' said Mike.

'I think,' said Lucy thoughtfully, 'that sometimes when people become very rich and powerful, a kind of megalomania kicks in. They must have their own way and keep increasing their power, also' she added, 'we must remember that he wouldn't have committed these murders personally, he would have had someone else to do it. I mean it's much easier to drop a bomb on someone than to stick a knife in them.'

'And that reminds me,' said Mike, 'thinking of our humbler suspects, I must get on to our friendly policeman. I need to find his phone number but I don't want to use the phone and mobiles can be hacked.'

'And if he is helpful we don't want to put him in danger,' said Lucy.

'I think it's time I visited my mum. What do you say, Andy to a trip to Letbury It might re-inforce the idea of you having a breakdown?'

'Good idea,' said Andrew, 'I'd like to visit Grandma but Hayden knows I'm quite sane,'

'On the contrary, he probably thinks you are completely off your trolley!'

Chapter Nineteen

'What a lovely surprise!' said Margaret Nichols as she doled out more potatoes on to Mike's plate, 'more for you too Andrew? That's good. Hasn't the weather been lovely lately? My strawberries have been wonderful this year. You must take some back with you.'

'Thanks, Mum. That would be great. The meals at Flat 13 have certainly gone up a notch or two with the arrival of young Andy.' Margaret looked surprised,

'I didn't know you were a good cook, Andrew.'

I'm not,' Andrew looked embarrassed, 'Mike's exaggerating.'

'Mum' said Mike, 'You remember Johnny Judge?'

'Of course I do, I see his mother just about every week'

'Would you have his phone number?'

'Oh I don't know about John's. I certainly have Brenda's. I didn't think you were that friendly with John.'

'I'm not really though I always got on well with him. It's just that I wanted to ask him something about the police force. A boy at school is interested in joining,'
Mike lied cheerfully.'

'Oh, yes, John would be just the person. He's an inspector now you know. I think he's a detective. Oh, I've just thought, I do have his address and telephone number. I usually send him a Christmas card. He's got a lovely wife, Virginia. They are expecting a baby in January. I'll get you the number after lunch.'

They enjoyed a splendid lunch and then went for a walk on the heath. Mike asked his mother if she would mind if he phoned John from her phone.

'Our phone's on the blink. I'm going to sue BT. It's outrageous.'

'That is bad,' said Margaret, 'I should think you need a phone with your job. Of course you can use our phone.'

Mike took the phone into the garden. He noticed that John lived in Stevenage which wasn't too far on the A1.
'Is that you John? It's Mike Nichols – yes you're right – long time no see. I'm visiting a friend in Letchworth and I thought I could pop in and see you. There is something I want to ask you. No I'm not in trouble. It's just a query and I thought as I was in the area. How about Monday evening . . . Tuesday any good? OK then, Tuesday . . . dinner, Oh that's very kind of you. I hope I'm not putting your wife to too much trouble, I've heard she's expecting. Oh you do all the cooking! Amazing! Well I won't worry too much about putting you out. No I don't think I have changed much. I expect you have, married man and all that, oh mad as ever, ha, ha – I'll look forward to seeing you.'
Mike sighed. Andrew joined him in the garden,

'Did you get through?'

'Yes, terrible, terrible.' Andrew looked concerned,

'Is everything all right?'

'No, the man's a complete idiot, a plonker of the first magnitude. No wonder he's in the police, suit him down to the ground.'
Andrew laughed,

'Mike, if you are going to make any headway with him, you will have to look kindly on him.'
'I know, I know. He's a decent chap. I've known him all my life. He was a real creep at school – well-behaved, that sort of thing. The trouble is he still sees me as the "naughty boy". I can feel it. I'll have to think of a way to make him take me seriously.'

'You could try looking smart in your best suit – well only suit and have a haircut.' 'Yes, I could do that. I've got time to get the suit cleaned before Tuesday. Can you think of anything else?'

'Well, what do we want from him? We want him to check up on Ken Weston. Do we want him to investigate the Birford Police?'

'I suppose I could play that by ear.'

'What are you going to tell him?'

Mike considered,

'I think I will have to tell him more or less everything. I will have to trust him.'

'Do you think you can?'

'I think so. I don't think he ever liked me much but our families have been quite close. I think that will count for something. I don't think he will betray us but whether he will have the will or courage to help us I don't know. He is, I should think, a very loyal, honest policeman.'

'Well that's something and it's certainly worth a try.'

'Hello Mike! Have you been for an interview or something?'

Mike looked embarrassed by his spruce appearance. He laughed foolishly,

'Oh, I went for lunch with someone.'

John giggled in a conspiratorial fashion,

'So it's a young lady in Letchworth,'

'Letchworth? Oh yes, Letchworth, no it was work related.'

'Come in, come in. Let's go into the lounge. It's more comfortable in there.

Virginia is out, meeting up with some old chums – just like us eh?'

They went into a comfortable room. It was quite small but tastefully furnished with interesting pictures on the wall. John pointed to them,
'Virginia is quite artistic, as an amateur you understand.'

'Did she paint these?'

'She did that one over there of the tree and this one of the boat. Most of the others are done by friends of hers at the art club. They're a bit modern for my taste but they are quite colourful.'
'They are,' agreed Mike, 'I particularly like the one of the tree. The shape is lovely and it almost looks like a human being.' 'Yes, I think that was the intention.'

Mike admired some of the others, quite sincerely, which obviously pleased John.

'Are you ready to eat? I did a casserole in the slow cooker so it's ready.'

'Great! I'm always ready to eat.'

John went into the kitchen and brought in a steaming casserole dish. They tucked in and Mike was effusive with his praise of the dinner, once again with obvious sincerity.
John suddenly looked very serious,

'I know you probably don't want to be reminded of it but I must offer you my condolences about the deaths of Mary and Frank. It was a terrible, terrible accident.'
Well that's what I want to talk to you about. We, that is, Andrew, Mary's son, Simon, Frank's brother, the solicitor and me. We don't believe it was an accident.' 'What!' John looked horrified.
Mike went on and told the story of their investigations. He slightly exaggerated the part played by Simon as he felt that John would be impressed by him.

John looked thoughtful,

'Mike, this is terrible, murders, theft and lies. I am shocked by the reaction of the Birfordl police. Someone powerful must have got to them. I'm sure you are right about that. It is very telling that someone of the stature of Simon Tremayne is convinced. You must have had a terrible time. I am so sorry and Andrew too. He must be about fifteen now.'
'Seventeen.'

John shook his head. Mike was pleased as he was obviously moved and shocked by the story.
'But what can I do to help?'

Mike looked at John. He was pleased by the way things had gone so far but now he had to be careful.
'I don't know, John, whether you can do anything. I have one or two requests but

I don't know whether it's possible and I don't want to put you or your job at risk.' 'Well tell me and I will be the judge of that'

'As I told you our friend, Edith had a visit from a policeman who identified the fingerprints of a Ken Weston. Would it be possible for you to find out anything about him?'
John considered,

'I could do that. I would have to think of a reason for looking him up that wouldn't cause suspicion but I could probably think of something. If I found out anything should I write to you about it?'
'That would be great!'

'You said a few things?'

'Well, this might be more difficult. We want to find out who is trying to stymie the police especially the Birford police.'

'Now that might be more difficult but wait a minute. I have a friend in the Birford police, Adrian Hollinsworth. We trained together and have kept in touch ever since – Christmas cards – that sort of thing. I think he's in the vice squad now. I could ask him to put out a few feelers. He needn't know everything.'

'Is he trustworthy? I mean could the powers above have got to him?' 'I'm pretty sure he is trustworthy. I shouldn't think he would be corrupt but it could be that the police have been told not to touch this or that because of some kind of sensitivity.'

'Thanks John. You're a pal!'

John smiled,

'I hope so Mike, I hope so.'

At that moment John's wife, Virginia made an appearance. Mike was astounded at the sight of an extremely beautiful, young woman. After kissing John, she turned to Mike with an entrancing smile, put her hand out and said,

'You must be Mike, one of John's oldest friends, I understand?' 'Er, yes,' stuttered Mike, accepting the handshake.

'Mike's been admiring your pictures,' said John. Virginia turned to Mike once again with that wonderful smile,

'That's very kind of you, Mike. We can't help but be pleased when someone admires our daubs.'

Mike muttered something indistinct, then turned to John,

'John, I must be off. Thank you very much for your hospitality. I hope we will be in touch again very soon.' Then, having gained his composure somewhat, he turned to Virginia, 'It's been lovely to meet you. I must say I am amazed that old Johnnie here has got himself such a lovely wife!' Mike said this with complete sincerity but it produced great guffaws from John with such statements as 'Mike's always been a bit of a wag.'

Mike hurried down the garden path and drove quickly away.

After a while he realised that he was driving far too fast and so slowed down. Why was it that he only had to be in the presence of a good-looking woman and he would fall apart?

Chapter Twenty

Mike turned the radio on loudly.

'Andy, I've got a letter from Edith!'

'Great what does it say?'

'She says that she is writing to me as "the leader of our little group".'

Andrew sighed,

'I'm sure she says something other than that.'

'She doesn't say much. I think the poor old thing is still in a state over Father

John's murder. She seems to be in constant communication with Mary Golightly.

Apparently the funeral is next Tuesday.'

'Does she know whether the police have any leads on the murderer?' 'No but she thinks they are taking it seriously and she volunteered to be interviewed herself.'
'That was brave of her.'

'Yes it was, but she doesn't think they took much notice of her. She told them about The *Good Book* but she thinks they saw her as a bit of a nutcase. Anyway, here it is. You read it.'
Andrew picked up the letter and tried to make sense of the spidery writing. 'Poor Edith!' he said, 'she has the two deaths of her best friends. She seems quite convinced about the bugging and is taking precautions. We have to reply to a P.O. box.'

'Yes, she looks so eccentric but she's obviously very intelligent, a pity the police took no notice of her but you can't blame them. It doesn't mean they have been corrupted,'

'But those Cardiff police who investigated the professor were. Poor Edith. I expect she's pretty scared.'

Mike nodded,

'Yes, I'm sure she is but she is also angry and determined to get at the truth. I don't think she will stop whatever the consequences for her. She says she is willing to translate any more bits of the *Good Book* we can lay our hands on. She also says she has one or two more bits. We have some small passages in the stuff from Father John that need translating.'

'I think somehow or other the key lies in *The Good Book of Oxford*. Shall we go to the funeral? Edith says she is going in disguise!'

Mike laughed,

'I shall look forward to seeing that, though she says that if we go we mustn't speak to her.'

'What about Lucy? How do we let her know?'

'I don't think there is any harm in just phoning her. I mean we are not doing anything particularly secret. We could pick her up on the way and tell her about the letter.'

The following Tuesday, Mike, Andrew and Lucy made their way once again to Cardiff. After a short discussion about whether to stop for some refreshment, they decided against it and arrived at the Church of the Sacred Heart, half an hour early. Mike was beginning to grumble about the lack of refreshment but they soon realised that their earliness was fortunate as the church was already full. They managed to find a seat in a side aisle and settled down to listen to the organ playing. It appeared to be quite a grand affair with the Archbishop concelebrating mass with about twenty priests. They could hardly fit in the sanctuary especially as there were about thirty altar servers. The grandeur and solemnity was somehow lessened by the fact that the choir was composed of the local schoolchildren. The bishop gave a moving sermon about death hardly mentioning Father John but just before the end a young priest stood up and told some funny stories about Father John and so the congregation left the church smiling. Everyone was invited for some refreshments in the church hall.
'I think we ought to go,' said Mike who was obviously hungry.

'But we are not part of his family or the congregation,' said Lucy.

'But Edith might want to communicate with us. We could just have a cup of tea,' protested Andrew. They went into the packed hall and were surprised to find that tea wasn't part of the plan. There were tables covered by bottles of wine and crates of beer on the floor as well as soft drinks. They found glasses, Mike grumbling about having to be the driver. He had orange juice, Andrew, beer and Lucy, white wine. They wandered about.
'I can't see Edith, said Andrew.

'Don't look now,' said Lucy but she's standing by the stage with a big, black hat, half covering her face. She is all in black, including her hair.'
Suddenly someone tapped Lucy on the shoulder,

'Hello, I'm Mary Golightly. I have a package for you from Edith. Have you seen her? You wouldn't recognise her.'
Lucy laughed,

'Yes I have. Isn't she wonderful?'

'She is indeed. Listen I have my instructions. Have you a handbag? Yes I can see you have. Don't point to it. I shall now go and get something to eat and you do the same. After about ten minutes, I shall go to the ladies' lavatory. It's just by the door where we came in. After a few minutes, follow me in and I shall give you the package.'
Mary drifted off and Lucy told the others her instructions.

Andrew laughed,

'This is real cloak and dagger stuff!'

Lucy did as instructed and some time later returned to Mike and Andrew.

'Shall we go now?' she said.

'I haven't eaten my food yet,' complained Mike, holding a plate laden with sausage rolls, pieces of pork pie and other delicacies.
Lucy took a piece of pork pie from his plate,
'This pie is pretty good.'

Andrew followed suit and took a couple of scotch eggs.

After some protests from Mike, the food was consumed and they returned to the car.
'Where do we go now?' asked Mike as he drove along, 'Do you think we are being followed? Don't look now but there's a white van behind us. It's been there for about ten minutes.'
After a while the van turned off at the traffic lights and the road behind them was clear.

'Let's turn into that pub, The Caernarvon Arms. The car park is behind it so nobody could see the car from the road,' suggested Lucy.

Mike did so, pulling the car well out of sight of the road. They went in and found a suitable quiet corner. Mike ordered drinks and then Lucy took the package out of her handbag. There was a copy of another page of translation, entitled *The Golden God* and a piece of paper containing an address. They looked at it, The Laurels, 84, Church Street. There was no post code.

'That could be anywhere,' said Andrew, 'There are loads of roads called Church Street'

'And,' said Mike, 'loads of houses called The Laurels, imagine giving your house such a boring name.'

'Oh, there's another piece of paper here. It's a short letter from Edith.' Lucy looked at it. 'She says she found the address with some documents she had from Mary. She meant to give it back to her but never did. She wonders if it was of some significance.'

'I suppose it must be in the centre of a town,' said Andrew.

'Why?' said Mike.

'Because only roads in towns are called "street", and it must be near a church.' 'There are plenty of country churches,' said Mike.

'I think it's probably in Ebbchester,' said Lucy, 'I mean that's where Mary lived.

How about if I check it out?'

'Good idea,' said Andrew, 'Shall we look at *The Golden God*?' 'Yes, I'll read it out,' said Lucy.

When Moses came down from the mountain with the two stone tablets containing the Ten Commandments, he must have been full of excitement and expectation. He must have been longing to tell the Israelites, what had happened to him and to show them these wonderful tablets of stone which were to be famous throughout the world, which were to be the basis for human law. But - -what did he find? They had melted down their gold to make a false god, a golden calf!

This is what is happening to us today. We scorn false gods. We would not prostrate ourselves in front of a golden calf! Would we not? Is not the world continually in obeisance to the golden god? The groats, the shekels, the guineas, the denarii, yes, the pieces of silver! Are these not our gods?

The world is continually at war. Why? Because of a patch of rich land. Families are at war. Why? Because of inheritance, because of dowries, because of good land. We are boastful if we are rich. We are jealous when we are not. We are willing to lie, cheat and fight for the Golden God.

Does God not weep for his golden rival? Is his heart not rent for the foolishness of Man.? Did our beloved Lord not point the way when he told the rich young man to sell all he had and give it to the poor?'

Lucy stopped,

'Edith says she could not make out the next bit.'

'It's good stuff,' said Mike, 'It's a pity so much is lost.'

'Don't forget we have more from the French monastery,' said Andrew.

'Yes, we need to go over there. I've still got a few weeks of school.'

'And term hasn't finished at Ebbchester.'

'I could go,' said Andrew, 'my French isn't that brilliant but I've only got to pick the stuff up.'

'I could telephone them,' said Lucy 'and pave the way. I could telephone from the porter's lodge or one of my friend's houses and we could fix a date.' Andrew looked excited.

'I'll look up trains and boats or planes.'

Chapter Twenty-one

Lucy spread the map of Ebbchester on the table in front of her. She had been tempted to look up Church Street on Google then realised that this could probably be traced so she had invested in a map.

She looked for churches. Ebbchester seemed to be full of churches. Lucy wondered vaguely how they all kept going. She found 'Church Road, Church Lane and even Church Avenue but no 'Church Street'. She felt frustrated and cross that she had wasted £7 on this useless map. She began to fold it up, then realised that there was an index on the back. She found it – 7F!

Church Street was on the very edge, to the east of Ebbchester, fortunately although she lived fairly centrally, her flat was on the east side.

She decided that her first task would be to go and find The Laurels. She wouldn't use her car but she could cycle.

Lucy looked out of the window. It was raining, not a good day for a couple of miles, cycling. She was going to put it off for a day then realised that the rain could work to her advantage. She possessed a capacious cycling cape with a large hood. Anyone seeing her cycling along would not recognise her.

About half an hour later, Lucy found herself cycling along Church Street. It was quite a long winding road but she could see a church at the end of it. The houses were mostly large terraced houses with three or four stories. She found number eighty-six, then eighty-two. Where was eighty-four? Lucy dismounted and looked around. She realised that The Laurels was set back from the road. The entrance was via a little lane. Lucy looked around. There was nobody about. She walked quickly down the lane towards the house. It was the same design as the other houses but detached. It looked quiet and there was no sign of life.

Lucy decided to investigate the road behind Church Street so she quickly retraced her steps and cycled round the corner. In the narrow street behind, she could see the back of The Laurels. She strained her eyes but there were blinds at all the windows. She felt that it was inhabited but could see no-one. As she stood there, an old man came out with a black plastic bag and threw it into a dust-bin.

Lucy cycled back home. She wondered why there were blinds at all the windows.

Perhaps the old man was just a care-taker?

She decided that she must try and watch the house and see who came and went. She reflected sadly that policemen on 'surveillance' usually had a nice warm car to sit in.

Still, it was June and despite the rain, it was quite warm.

Lucy decided that there was no time like the present so she made herself a flask of coffee and some sandwiches. She waited until 8 o'clock for the traffic to die down. By then the rain had completely stopped so she put on a 'hoodie' and with a rucksack on her back, she set off.

Lucy parked her bike a couple of streets away, then walked to The Laurels. She noticed a small children's playground quite nearby so she was able to conceal herself there behind the hedge. The Laurels appeared to be in darkness but when she looked closer, there were lights on behind the blinds. She waited for about an hour but nobody went into or came out of The Laurels. Lucy was beginning to get cold and stiff. She decided to walk round the playground. As she did so she noticed some shadowy figures going down the back street behind The Laurels.

She waited until the coast was clear then went down the quiet street. Unfortunately, there was no children's playground but there were a few parked cars. Lucy chose a big Mercedes, then crouched down behind the bonnet. She watched the back entrance to the house. She saw a man come down the street. He was covered by an umbrella, even though the rain had stopped. He pressed a belly button and then went in. Scarcely two minutes later, Lucy could see another man approaching. He looked older and had a black scarf wrapped round his neck. Lucy saw two more men enter the house and then decided it was time for her to go. She was about to stand up when she heard footsteps coming closer. She crouched down again by the Mercedes. To her horror, the engine started up and the car was driven off swiftly, leaving Lucy sprawling on the ground.

The following day Lucy debated what to do next. She assumed that *The Laurels* was a house of disrepute. But why would Mary have this address among her papers? One knew that these places existed but usually there wasn't much you could do about it. There must be something different about this house or was it because of someone who frequented it? Lucy decided that she would continue with the vigilance.

But first she had another job to do. She had already tried to get through to the monastery in Brittany but to no avail. Lucy went down to the porter's lodge to try again. Unlike Mike, she found dissimulation difficult but this time it was made easier by Jim, the porter,

'Want to use the phone again, Lucy? Come in here in the small room. Nobody will disturb you in there. Lucy, gratefully, went into the little room attached to the porter's lodge and this time managed to get through to the monastery. She spoke to a brother Luke and explained why it had taken so long for them to get back to the monastery. She didn't tell him about the death of Mary and Frank but told them that much of *The Good Book* had been stolen. She felt very embarrassed at having to impart this knowledge but Brother Luke appeared unfazed. He said it was part of the history of *The Good Book*. Lucy wondered whether he would be willing to give the rest of the document to Andrew but he seemed delighted at the prospect of meeting the son of Mary and Frank. They agreed on a few possible dates and Lucy said that Andrew would telephone them to confirm it. She explained that his French was not very good. He said that Father Bernard spoke perfect English so it would be no problem. Lucy wrote down all this information and posted it to Mike's Streatham address.

That evening, Lucy went again to *The Laurels* and watched the same procedure. The only difference was that at about nine o'clock, she heard a piercing scream. It appeared to come from the top story and immediately afterwards she heard the banging of a sash window which she assumed had inadvertently been left slightly open. She hurried away in case someone came to see if anyone had heard it. Lucy felt quite disturbed by the scream but kept telling herself that it could mean nothing; somebody could have fallen or trapped their finger. She felt weary with her surveillance but was determined to keep it up.

The following day, Lucy went to visit a bird-watching friend and asked if she could borrow his binoculars. He was excited as he thought Lucy was going to take up bird-watching. She felt she had to disillusion him and made up a story about going to visit a safari farm. Lucy felt somewhat ashamed as she realised that with practice, mendacity became easier.

That night Lucy took the binoculars to The Laurels. She found it difficult to see anything in the dark but she did discover that nearly all the windows in the house had bars on them. She really wanted to talk to Mike about it.

Her wish was granted the following day as Mike rang up. He was clearly speaking in their accepted code for most of the conversation. He said,

'Andy's gone on holiday. He was beginning to seriously crack up. I think some sea and sunshine will do him good. How are you now? How's the research going? I'm sorry we took up so much of your time with our crack-pot ideas. I think we'll give it a rest for a while but it would be good to see you. How about dinner tomorrow night?'

'That would be lovely, Mike. The research is going quite well but of course, I really miss Mary. I think I am relieved that we are discontinuing our investigations at least for a while. It was beginning to get very stressedl. Where do you want to meet?'

'How about *Le gros Chat*? I've always wanted to go there.'

'Mike, that's really expensive!'

'For you Lucy, no expense spared.'

With that, Mike rang off. Lucy was amused and also very pleased at the thoughts of seeing Mike again.

Chapter Twenty-two

'Can I help you Sir?'

'We want a table for two.'

'Over here, Sir, by the window?'

'How about that table in the corner, over there?'

'Yes that's fine.'

Lucy and Mike settled themselves at the table in the corner, Mike showing some embarrassment at the waiter's desire to take and hang up his luminous workman's jacket.
'I think we'll concentrate on the menu for five minutes before we get down to business,' said Mike.
'Do you want a starter?'

'Yes, let's have the full works.'

Lucy gave him a quizzical look. Mike looked slightly embarrassed.

'Actually, Lucy, just before he left for France, Andy had a letter from his Uncle Simon, you know, the lawyer. He was a bit worried about Andy's finances, especially as it's taking a while to sort them out so he sent Andy a couple of thousand pounds to keep him going for the time being, I mean he will eventually be quite well off and he very kindly sent me a couple of thousand pounds to cover his keep so you see I'm a rich man too.'
Lucy laughed,

'Well, I've always wanted to go out with a rich man so I will have a splendid starter!'
Some minutes later, Lucy said,

'This table is good as nobody could hear what we say and we are not too near anybody else.'

'Yes, I think the waiter was a bit surprised at us wanting a dark corner. He probably thought we were on some illicit romantic assignation. Speaking of romantic assignations, I hope you didn't mind me phoning you up and asking you to dinner. I thought it would be easier to visit you if it was thought we were romantically involved.'

'Oh that's a disappointment! So this nice meal is just a ploy to throw them off the scent.'

Mike blushed and stared hard at the menu.

'No-o, not exactly, it's a sort of mixing business with pleasure.'

Lucy laughed,

'Would it help if I looked dreamily into your eyes?'

'It's not absolutely necessary but it might be a good idea.'

They both laughed to cover their embarrassment. It occurred to them that they had never been alone like this before. Andrew had always been there.

'So what's happening with Andrew?'

'He's gone. He got the train to Stansted and he's getting a Ryanair flight to Dinard.

He should be there by now. Oh that reminds me . . .'

Mike looked swiftly round the restaurant and then passed Lucy a plastic bag. 'I bought us all cheap mobile phones with new sim cards. They will be difficult to trace. I think we will need to keep changing the sim card. I was a bit worried about young Andy going off on his own.'

'That's a good idea, Mike. We will have to memorise our new numbers and make sure the phones don't fall into the wrong hands.'

'My next bit of news is my visit to my old school chum, Johnny Judge. You know he had the most amazing wife, I couldn't believe it, an idiot like that.'

'What was amazing about her?'

'Well, she was a real looker, long, blond hair and a beautiful slim figure. She's a great painter and –'

'Mike is this really relevant? Did he agree to look up Ken Weston?'

'Yes, he did. He seemed really anxious to please me. I don't know why. I didn't get on with him at school. He was always one of the goody-goodies.'

'He probably secretly admired you, wanted to be 'cool''

Mike looked pleased,

'Perhaps that was it, anyway I got a letter from him yesterday. He said he found it quite easy to check on Ken Weston. He has got "form" as they say. He is a petty criminal who has been to prison a couple of times for robbery and G.B.H. The description John got was that he was the sort of chap who didn't have many ideas of his own but tagged along with the others and did as he was told. He is said to be quite dangerous as he is described as, "amoral". John photocopied a picture of him.'

Mike looked round furtively, then passed the picture across to Lucy.

Lucy laughed,

'He should be easy to recognise with that red hair,'

'He could dye it.'

'But he couldn't change that nose. Is he around at the moment? I mean not in prison.'

'I have an address for him. I could pay him a visit.'

'Where does he live?'

'On a big Council estate just outside Birford.'

'I should think you would need some big, hefty backup.'

Mike sighed,

'I know but most of the men I know are weeds like me.'

Lucy looked at the tall, thin gangly figure across the table and smiled.

'What do you want me to say? No you're not weedy, you're a big, strong muscle man?'
'Yes, something like that.' Mike looked rather wan. Lucy took his hand,

'But I'm sure you are as brave as a lion and anyway, you are a very nice chap'

Mike smiled,

'Thank you Lucy but I'm not sure I want to be nice. I think I would prefer to be tough and dangerous.'

Lucy burst into peals of laughter. Mike took her other hand,

'Lucy, be quiet. We don't want to draw attention to ourselves.'

They sat for a few seconds holding hands then Lucy detached herself quickly and said,
'We had better finish our food this "Canard a l'orange?" is getting cold.'   'Do you think we are being watched?' said Mike with his mouth full of steak and kidney pie.'

'Well I did wonder about that man in the long coat, but he's gone out now.'

'You're being racist, Lucy, just because he's Asian.'

'I am not,' said Lucy indignantly, 'you are the racist even thinking about it.' They argued about this point for some minutes. It was beginning to get quite heated when the waiter came over to ask if they wanted any pudding. Mike chose sticky toffee pudding and Lucy chose cheesecake. After the waiter had gone, Mike grinned sheepishly,

'Sorry about that, Lucy. I suppose I have just been trying to impress you.' 'Why would you want to do that? I mean we've been working together for a while. I know what you are like.'

While Mike was thinking of an appropriate answer, the waiter returned with the puddings. Mike poured out some more wine.

'Well, you had better tell me what you have been up to.' Lucy recounted her story of *The Laurels*.

Mike looked worried,

'Lucy, I don't think you should go there anymore.'

'Why not?'

'It could be dangerous. It's obviously a dodgy set-up.'

'Well, I'll be careful.'

'Lucy, you must not go there again on your own,' Mike said in a very stern voice.

Lucy looked cross,

'I'll go there if I please. Who are you to tell me what I must or must not do?'

Mike looked downcast,

'I was only concerned about you,' he said in a quiet voice.

Lucy relented. She took his hand again,

'I know Mike, but I'm used to doing what I please. I'm sorry.'

Mike looked up,

'I know, I'll come at the weekend and stay a couple of nights in the Travelodge down the road and we'll go together. It might be fun. Lucy smiled,

'OK, but this surveillance business isn't fun.'

'It might be if we held hands.'

Lucy pulled her hand away quickly and concentrated on the cheesecake. 'Of course you could stay with me. I do have a bed-settee in the sitting room,' Mike poured out some more wine. 'Sounds nice but I might not be able to control myself.'

'Oh that wouldn't be a problem as I certainly could.'

Lucy suddenly giggled and Mike joined in. They realised that they had had quite a lot to drink and maybe it was time for some strong coffee.

Chapter Twenty-three

Andrew was pleased with himself. He had very rarely travelled great distances on his own. He remembered once when his parents were in America going on his own from his Grandma's to Cornwall to a horse-riding holiday. He also had been on a French exchange visit to France but that had been with the school.

He left the airport in Dinard and boarded a bus which would take him to the Formula One Hotel where he intended to stay the night before getting a train to Rennes where he was to be met by one of the Benedictine monks.

Although it was summer time it was beginning to get dark when he left the bus. He looked around for the hotel. There were quite a few cheap hotels in the area and at first he couldn't see the Formula one. He went down a lane in front of him and turned a corner and there in the distance was a neon sign proclaiming 'Formule Un'. He smiled with relief but as he walked towards the sign, he was suddenly grabbed from behind, a gag tied round his mouth and then thrown into the back of a van. At first Andrew lay still, petrified with terror but after a while his anger and frustration took over and he rolled about frantically trying to undo the gag.

He was driven for some miles and then the van pulled in.

The back door of the van opened and then two men appeared. They spoke in

English. One of them laughed,

'You weren't expecting that now were you?'

Andrew looked at him. He was a big man with dark bushy eye-brows. Andrew was terrified but he wanted to recognise these men again.

'What do we do now?' asked the other man. This one was red-haired and overweight.

'We'll search him and then tie him up. We will find a quiet spot where we will persuade him to give us some information before we finish him off.'

The red-haired man sniggered,

'We'll need somewhere to dispose of the body.'

'Oh there's plenty of woods round here where we can dump him. It might be days before anyone finds him.'

They set to, emptying Andrew's pockets and his rucksack. They took his money and were anxious to find his mobile phone. To Andrew's relief they were satisfied when they had found his smart Phone and didn't notice the tiny mobile phone in the back pocket of his jeans. They found the photo-copied papers that he was to deliver to the monastery but fortunately they didn't carry the address. While they were searching him, Andrew didn't see much point in resisting but they amused themselves by smashing their fists into his face and chest, now and again and after tying him up, they kicked him a few times. Andrew said very little. He was speechless with fury. He gasped now and again with the pain but tried not to scream or cry. He was thrown into the back of the van again, this time with his hands and feet bound. They set off once again.

After he recovered somewhat from his ill-treatment, Andrew tried to loosen the ropes round his hands and feet but to no avail. After what Andrew estimated was about an hour, the van pulled in again. Andrew was afraid this was where the 'persuading' might begin but he was relieved to see bright lights and to smell petrol. He tried to bang against the wall of the van to attract attention but as the van pulled out of the Service station, the red-haired man opened the back door, climbed in and gave him a kicking.

'That's to warn you not to do that again,' he said, laughing. The man jumped down and pushed the door to and went to join his friend in the front. They pulled out into the main road. They weren't travelling very fast as the road was bumpy which was painful for Andrew. As they went over a hole in the road, Andrew noticed that the back door had not been shut properly. He tried to roll over towards the door. The van slowed down. Andrew thought it was because they had noticed that the door was open but it was because they were turning into a main road. Andrew realised that he would have to act quickly as they were picking up speed. He rolled as fast as he could to the door but it didn't open enough for him to roll out. The van was going faster but the men were playing loud music at the front so fortunately didn't hear him rolling about. He tried again and this time with the momentum of the speed he was able to roll out of the back of the van.

He lay on the ground, completely winded and almost unconscious with the pain of the fall. As he came to he could see the van in the distance with the door flapping about. The men would surely notice this. Andrew tried to move. He could hear a car coming towards him. It would surely run over him! He tried rolling again and after some effort managed to roll into a ditch just before the car reached him. He lay there for some time. He wondered if the men had noticed his disappearance. Andrew groaned. He could hardly move. He had aches and pains everywhere. He wondered if he had broken some bones as the pain in his shoulder was excruciating. To his horror he suddenly heard the voices of the two men. They were shouting and swearing and cursing each other for what had happened. They were wandering down the road aimlessly, every now and again looking in the bushes.

'There's not much point looking. We can't see a thing.'

'In any case, he's probably dead by now. He's done the job for us.'

'We'll have to come back. The boss will be furious if we don't find him. We'll go to the next service station and get some powerful torches.'

To Andrew's relief they set off again in the van but he knew he had to move. The ditch was wet and he began to shiver with cold. He managed to get himself to his knees. He had to find a way of breaking the ropes. He looked around but could see nothing that would be of any use. Then he noticed that his knee was wet with blood. He sighed. It was not surprising with all the beatings he had had, but something was sticking into him. He moved. It was a piece of glass. He moved again and could see it glistening in the darkness. He tried to bend to put his hands near the glass. It was very difficult to find a good position. This was going to take him hours! Fortunately once he got going rubbing the rope against the glass, it broke more quickly than he expected. He must now free his feet. His hands were so sore and cold that he could hardly use them. Eventually, he freed his feet but it took him some time before he could crawl out of the ditch and begin to walk. All the time, Andrew was aware that the men could return at any moment. He tried to hobble across a field away from the road. Progress was slow and it was a while before he could actually run, but run he must. At the other side of the field, he had a job finding a way out. Andrew could see a hill looming up in front of him. He heard a noise and looked round. There were horses in the meadow. 'A horse, a horse, my kingdom for a horse,' he muttered. Unfortunately, the horses were not saddled but Andrew was desperate. He chose what he thought was a small calm-looking horse. He clutched at the horse's main and dragged himself up on its back. He kicked his heels into its flanks and he was off. They arrived at the top of the hill then the horse galloped down the other side. Andrew wanted to go fast but not this fast! He couldn't stop the horse. He had no rein and clutching at the horses main didn't seem to work. He managed to steer the horse a little with his knees but after a while he just clung on for dear life. He knew the horse was bolting. The horse was now going faster and faster towards some trees. A branch caught the horse and Andrew was flung off. He lay for some time on the ground and was relieved to see that the horse was all right as it was galloping away back towards where they had come. He tried to stand up but fell down again. 'I'll just rest for a while until I feel better,' he thought.

After a while he was unconscious. He would have remained unconscious if it were not for a loud clap of thunder and some heavy drops of rain on his face. Andrew was now aware that he was feeling decidedly unwell. He realised that he must find some shelter. He struggled to his feet and tried to run through the woods. Running became impossible. He no longer had the strength and the jolting was very painful to his shoulder. He tottered onwards. He heard the sound of a
car ahead. Perhaps he could flag it down? No, it might be the enemy. He arrived at a narrow road. He could see a light somewhere in the distance. The rain was becoming torrential. If he headed towards the light there might be shelter. Andrew took a few steps to cross the road, then he tripped and collapsed by the roadside.

Chapter twenty-four

Mike arrived in Ebbchester on the Saturday morning armed with torches, binoculars and various disguises. When he showed Lucy the disguises she was convulsed with laughter. She tried on a dark wig.

'That's brilliant, Lucy,' said Mike, 'You look totally different without your long, blond hair'. He put on a Rastafarian wig.
'Stop laughing Lucy! I think it looks pretty good.'

'But Mike, you have a particularly, pale face,'

'I'm not that pale and in any case, anyone can have a Rastafarian hair style.' 'You can't wear it Mike. I wouldn't be able to stop laughing.' Eventually he agreed not to wear it or the false beard or moustaches. The weather was not good so they would not look out of place with their hoods pulled up. Lucy kept the wig on and they set off for The Laurels. They thought it would be useful to go once again in the daylight.

They took cover behind the hedge in the children's playground. As it was a Saturday there were a few children playing on the swings but there was a shed alongside the hedge and they managed to squeeze between the shed and the hedge. They took out their binoculars and surveyed the windows. They could see nothing. The blinds were drawn and there seemed to be no light coming from any of the windows.

They moved round to the lane behind the house. There was very little cover but there was an old skip on the opposite side of the road. They crouched behind it and once again took out their binoculars. The light was better on this side of the house.
'Lucy! Third window on the right, second floor.'

Lucy trained her binoculars on the window. A girl was standing at the window looking out. She was holding the bars. Lucy could see her thin face quite clearly.

She looked about sixteen years old. Her face was distraught with grief and fury.

Suddenly she began to shake the bars fiercely. Lucy and Mike could hear nothing but they could tell that she was shouting. In a few seconds, a woman appeared beside her and banged her shaking hands with a heavy stick. The girl withdrew her hands with what was obviously a cry. Then the woman slapped her viciously and dragged her away from the window.

Lucy and Mike stared in horror.

'It looks like slavery' whispered Lucy.

'It could be human trafficking,' said Mike.

They had seen enough. They walked like Zombies round to the front of the house.

A car drew up and waited for them to walk past before it drove through the gates. Lucy and Mike walked past and when the car had driven through the gates, they nipped back into the children's playground. Mike was fumbling for his binoculars but Lucy had her small ones ready. A man wearing a camel coat got out of the car. His face was half-hidden by his large fedora but he glanced round furtively, probably to make sure no-one was about.

Mike had at last got his binoculars out.

'Too late,' he sighed, 'I don't suppose you saw anything, Lucy. Lucy! What is it?

You look as though you have seen a ghost.' 'It was him!' she gasped.

'Who?' said Mike.

'Hayden Lewis.'

'Are you sure?'

'Ninety-nine per cent.'

'Come on Lucy, this is getting dangerous. We had better go.'

'Mike, the car's coming out. Let's wait until it's gone.' 'I'll get the number.' Mike scribbled it on to his hand.

Mike and Lucy took the bus back to Lucy's flat where they had some lunch. They were both in sombre mood.

'I suppose we should inform the police,' said Lucy.

'They wouldn't believe us about Hayden Lewis,' said Mike.

'No they wouldn't, not on my remote glimpse but those girls, Mike! They must be rescued.'

At that moment, Mike's phone rang.

'That will be Andy,' he said confidently.

Lucy watched anxiously as she saw Mike's face go pale and heard his gasps of horror. He put the phone down.

'Andy was captured beaten up and is very ill,' he said in a rush.

He shook as he stood by the table. Lucy fetched him a chair and made him sit down. She found some cheap brandy that she had been using for cooking and gave Mike a drop.

She too was shaking so she poured out a glass for herself.

'Now, when you're ready, tell me slowly what has happened.'

Mike gulped down the brandy,

'They didn't know the whole story as Andy wasn't capable of much communication. All he seemed to communicate was that he didn't want to go to hospital.'

'Tell me what you know,' said Lucy patiently.

Mike began to come to??

'Apparently he was found unconscious in the road by two nuns who were coming back late at night after visiting a sick patient. They initially thought he was drunk and called for help and took him into the convent. There they discovered that he was badly injured, a broken collar bone and broken ribs. He was soaking wet and delirious. The nuns at that convent are a medical order and so were able to make him as comfortable as they could. At first they didn't think he would last the night. They had to sedate him as he kept shouting and yelling.

During the next day, he began to come back to life and they discovered that he was a "lovely young man".' Here Mike laughed. 'He told them that he had been captured, beaten, escaped, rode a horse! and arrived on their doorstep, unconscious. They were anxious to inform his relatives and he gave them the phone which had my number on it. They said he mumbled "Mike" but was still calling for his Mum and Dad in his sleep. I didn't think it was the time to tell the good sister that his Mum and Dad were no longer with us but I said I would go over there. In fact I must get on to it right away.'

'Mike, would you mind if I came with you?' Mike looked at Lucy's white face.

'Lucy, I should love you to come with me, but,' here he smiled, 'I don't suppose it would make any difference if I told you that I don't want to take you into danger.'

Lucy smiled back,

'Well we had better start organising flights, but Mike,'

'What?'

'Those girls, Mike, we can't just abandon them.'

Mike thought for a minute,

'What if I make an anonymous phone call on my new mobile and tell the Police what's going on. They won't get Hayden Lewis but it might save those girls.'

'Yes, let's do that. Actually, it might be better if I make the call.'

'I think you are right. They might take more notice of a well-spoken young lady, like yourself, but we'll do it just before we set off and then I'll throw the phone away.'

'But we might need it?'

'I've got another one with another sim card.'

They spent the next hour organising their transport to Brittany. They decided to hire a car as they could then bring Andrew home. As they approached the car rental place, Lucy telephoned the Police, telling them that *The Laurels* was being used for prostitution and she believed the girls were trafficked and being used as slaves. The policeman asked for her name but she told him that she couldn't give it as she would be in danger. She then rang off. After they drove off in the hired car, Mike stopped by the river and threw the phone into the water.

They boarded an over-night ferry to Brittany and booked a cabin so they could get some sleep. They had some breakfast on the boat before it docked then were able to drive straight to their destination as described by Sister Marie-Bernadette on the telephone.

Chapter Twenty-Five

After Andrew had collapsed by the roadside, he found himself regaining consciousness every now and again for a few seconds each time. He knew he was now too weak to move. He was soaking wet and very cold. Every part of his body was aching and he was grateful to relapse into unconsciousness. At some stage he heard voices and was pleased to notice that they were women's voices. The voices stopped and then he felt himself being lifted on to what he later knew to be a stretcher. He was aware of being taken into a building that smelt of flowers and polish. People tried to speak to him but he wasn't able to answer. He knew they were speaking in French. He tried to say, 'Je suis malade' but he drifted off again.

When Andrew regained consciousness, he found himself to have been stripped naked and some women in white were washing him gently and putting ointment on his cuts and bruises. He tried to mutter, 'merci'. They looked up, obviously pleased that he spoke and then gave him something warm to drink from a cup with a spout. He drank it quickly and they gave him some more. He moved to try and pick up the cup but gasped with the pain in his shoulder. Andrew learnt later that they then gave him an injection for the pain.

It was some hours before Andrew became conscious again. When he opened his eyes, he was aware of a white room with people dressed in white moving about.

He said,

'Am I in heaven?'

A beautiful young lady with a white veil came across to him and smiled, 'Non, Monsieur, you nearly went there but I think now you will have to wait a while.'

The nurse took his temperature and then she said,

'Could you eat? Un petit repas?' Andrew nodded. He noticed that his left arm and shoulder had been strapped up but he had the use of his right arm, but when some food was brought to him, he didn't have the strength to use it. The nurse fed him with some soft food but he fell asleep while eating it.

During the course of the day as Andrew became less drugged, he realised that he was in a convent being looked after by nuns. He was able to tell the sisters something of what had happened to him but his mind was still blurred. He realised that he was ill. He was feverish and every now and again he would shout out. The sisters asked him repeatedly about his parents and how they should contact them. He appeared puzzled but eventually was able to say, 'Mike – my mobile'.

That night Andrew slept well. The fever appeared to have left him and his temperature became nearer normal. He woke up as the sun streamed into the bedroom. He opened his eyes. Someone was holding his hand and stroking his hair. As his eyes became adjusted to the light, he saw who it was, 'Lucy!' he whispered.

One of the sisters came into the room.

'Are you in heaven again this morning, Andrew?'

Andrew looked at Lucy,

'Oh, yes, this is certainly heaven!'

'I can see you're a lot better this morning, Monsieur Andrew,' Sister Thérèse laughed and went out.
Andrew looked puzzled,

'How did you get here? Where's Mike?'

'By boat and car and Mike is enjoying some breakfast.' Andrew smiled. Things seemed to be normal.

Lucy explained how Sister Thérèse had telephoned Mike and about their subsequent journey across the channel. At this point Mike came into the room and nearly caused Andrew a relapse by slapping him affectionately on the shoulder.

After Andrew recovered, he began to tell them what had happened to him. At one point the shock of his experiences became too much and he burst into tears. Lucy who was also weeping put her arm gently around him. Mike turned and walked towards the window. When he turned round, he said,

'My goodness, look at the two of you. We're going to drown in a minute with all this emotion. It's lucky I'm a hard man with no feelings. Come on now Andy!

What happened next?'

Andrew wiped his eyes and smiled,

'Sorry about that' he mumbled and continued with his tale.

After he had finished, Lucy said,

'Thank God for these good nuns. They really saved your life.'

'What I want to know' said Mike, 'is how those thugs got to know what you were doing.'

'We did say on the telephone that Andrew was going away on holiday,' suggested

Lucy, 'they could have been watching him.'

'But even if they did that they wouldn't have been able to get to Brittany in time.

Andy, how did you book your flight?'

'On line.'

'They must have hacked into his computer' said Mike, 'they will know all your contacts and conversations.'

'I don't have many contacts and I don't go on facebook or anything like that.'

'Well that's good but I suppose they will have hacked into my computer and Lucy's. I don't think I've put too much on mine and I'm not on facebook either. I was thinking about doing a blog but I never got on to it. What about you Lucy?'
Lucy looked embarrassed,

'Actually I am on facebook but I very rarely write anything on it and I have never put anything on the computer about our investigations. What about our journey,
Mike? Did we book anything on line?' Mike thought for a bit,
'No we didn't. I rented the car from that car rental place round the corner from your flat and we just drove to Portsmouth and got the first boat that went to Brittany.
Now Andy, what did these ruffians steal from you?' Mike was in dynamic mode.
'They were looking for my phone. I was pleased when they took my smart phone as they didn't bother looking for another one. I'm afraid I left my ruck-sack in the van.'
'So' continued Mike, 'they will have all the information about where you were going.'
'Not everything,' said Andrew, 'I have my passport. It was in the pocket of my jeans and I wrote the address of the monastery on my arm. It wasn't with the papers.'
'Good thinking,' said Mike, 'let's have a look at it.'

Andrew rolled up the sleeve of his hospital pyjamas and gasped in dismay,

'It's gone! The sisters cleaned me up!'

'Andy! You are the most priceless idiot!' Mike shouted.

'Mike, you mustn't shout like that. Andrew's not well and maybe one of us will remember it.'

'Do you remember it?' Mike snapped.

Lucy admitted that she didn't.

At that moment Sister Thérèse entered the room.

'Is everything all right?' she said. She looked round at the embarrassed faces and Andrew with his sleeve rolled up. She smiled as she understood the situation. 'I washed Monsieur Andrew's arm and I copied what was written on it. I have it here.'
Sister Thérèse delved into a voluminous pocket in her habit and produced a piece of paper.
'Voici!' she said and handed it to Andrew.

Lucy rushed over to her as she went out of the door.

'Merci, merci, ma soeur. C'est trés importante'

Lucy returned into the bedroom where Mike was looking rather shame-faced. 'Well, we have the address,' she said cheerfully, 'I suggest that you two stay here for a couple of days until Andrew recovers a bit and I will go to the monastery.' 'No, you won't,' said Andrew and Mike in unison. Lucy looked surprised.
'They can't know where we are!'

'But Lucy, they will be looking for Andy in this area.'

'And in any case, now we can all go together,'

Mike and Lucy looked at Andrew. Before Mike could make some tactless comment, Lucy said,

'Andrew, you have done brilliantly so far,' she smiled, 'riding the horse and everything but now you have to recover. Fortunately because of your kind Uncle Simon, we have some money. Mike has already given something to the good sisters. They were very reluctant to take it but Mike explained that you didn't want to go to a hospital and we would be grateful if you could stay a bit longer and then we can take you home.'

'These nuns are very competent, Andy. That Sister Brigitte is a qualified doctor and did operations and all sorts in the bush. Sister Bernadette is a dab hand at delivering babies!'

Andrew who looked as though he was going to protest, burst out laughing. He then shouted in pain. The others looked at him in consternation and Sister Thérèse rushed in.

'It's all right sister,' gasped Andrew, 'they are making me laugh and it's too painful,'

'I think' said Sister Thérèse, 'that it's time your guests left you for a while so you can sleep.'

Lucy and Mike agreed and backed out of the room. Andrew put his head back on the pillows and looked as though he was asleep already.

Sister Thérèse walked down the corridor with them.

'Would you like a bed for the night? We do have some accommodation here.'

Mike looked at Lucy and she shook her head. Mike spoke,

'That is very kind of you, Sister, but there is a job we must do first.'

Sister Thérèse nodded,

'I can give you directions to the Benedictine Monastery at Saint-Remy. It is about forty kilometres from here, but first you must have a meal. Sister Bernadette is preparing it now. It will be very simple.'

'Thank you sister,' said Mike, 'that will be great.'

The 'simple' meal turned out to be a wonderful mushroom omelette accompanied by home-made bread and home-grown vegetables and salad ingredients.

Lucy and Mike then set out with instructions for finding the monastery.

They arrived at the village of Neuf-Chatel. Then looked around for the monastery.

'It isn't here,' said Mike, 'Sister Thérèse must have got it wrong.'

'I don't think so,' said Lucy excitedly, 'look'

He pointed to a nearby hill and on the top, a church spire was visible. It appeared to be in the middle of a wood.

'Come on,' said Mike, 'Get back in the car.'

'Couldn't we walk?' suggested Lucy, 'It's such a lovely day.'

They set off up the hill. As they reached half-way, they both silently wished that they had come by car.

'Let's stop and look at the view,' said Lucy. They sat on a log by the side of the pathway. Everywhere was silent.

'This is very beautiful,' said Mike, 'I suppose France is such a big country compared with England, that they are able to have such quiet areas. The only thing you can hear is the birds.'

Lucy was surprised as Mike didn't usually express such sentiments.

'Yes it is beautiful,' she agreed, 'and somehow so very French.'

'Your mother was French, wasn't she? Did you spend much time in France?' 'When I was young,' answered Lucy, 'my grandparents were alive and my mother's brother lived in Marseilles. He had a jolly family of four boys. I loved visiting them. My grandfather died when I was six but my grandmother lived until I was thirteen. After she died my Uncle Maurice and his family emigrated to Quebec. We visited them a couple of times but I haven't seen them for years. My mother died when I was fifteen and so there wasn't so much reason for visiting France, apart from the cathedrals and beaches and that sort of thing.' Lucy stared ahead, tears not far from her eyes. 'Poor old thing,' said Mike, taking her hand, 'that must have been very hard.'

They were silent for a few minutes then Mike said,

'I could sit here forever, with you, Lucy looking at this view but we had better plod on.' He pulled her up and they set off again. Mike kept making silly jokes and Lucy understood that he was trying to counteract his previous sentimentality. At the top of the hill they came to a vineyard. They walked along the path in the middle to the entrance to the monastery. They saw a great bell on the end of a rope. Mike pulled it. They both nearly jumped out of the skins as the great noise rang out in the silence. A tubby little monk came to the door wreathed in smiles. He chattered away in French to Lucy and Mike understood that Père Bernard was expecting them. They were ushered into a small parlour. Mike looked around. One wall was lined with books and on one hung a huge crucifix. Mike went over to look at it. 'This looks very old, Lucy. This place must be choc-a-bloc with old masterpieces.' At that moment Père Bernard came in. He came up behind Mike.

'I see you are admiring our crucifix. We call it 'the Montpelier Crucifix' because it was found in an old church there that was destroyed during the war. It has been estimated as being fourteenth century. It is very beautiful. Is it not?'

Mike turned to face the tall, thin man in front of him. When he wasn't smiling he looked quite austere and somehow remote.'

'It is beautiful,' said Mike, 'I hope it wasn't English troops who destroyed the church.'

Père Bernard smiled wistfully,

'We love our old churches and wonderful works of art but sometimes there are more important things, matters of principle, you understand?' He turned towards Lucy. 'I understand you are relatives of Monsieur and Madame Tremayne?' 'I am just a friend and colleague,' said Lucy, 'I worked with Mary Tremayne and this is Mike. He is Mary Tremayne's brother.' Père Bernard shook hands with them both. 'I understand from the sisters of Saint Jean Baptiste at Neuf-Chatel that monsieur

Andrew was attacked. How is he now?'

'He is much better,' said Lucy but the papers he was carrying were stolen. As you know much of the documents that you gave us in the past have been stolen.'

Pere Bernard nodded,

'I understand. *The Good Book of Oxford* is a revolutionary document. It is natural that it should cause trouble.'

Lucy and Mike were slightly taken aback by the statement. Then Mike said,

'Because of this, we will only take photocopies of your Latin document.'

Pere Bernard smiled,

'You must come and see it.'

He led them down some long passages into the church. Mike was amazed at the church. It was very high and narrow. Much of it was filled with the choir stalls where the monks sang the offices. There were some monks there, saying their prayers. Mike wondered about them. What had led them to live this quiet, celibate life?

The church was obviously very old and was in need of repair. Many of the walls were covered in paintings that were very faded.

Pere Bernard led them into a transept and there was a glass case. He opened the lid. 'Here it is,' he said quietly, 'as you can see it is very, very old. I think it is the oldest thing we possess.'

They looked in awe at the pages in front of them. It was an illuminated manuscript. The colours were still bright and glowing. There were sheets of tissue between each page. Pere Bernard turned over a few of the pages. 'I think it would be difficult to photocopy,' he said, 'but I think we could photograph it. Pere François has a very good camera. I will ask him to do it.'

Pere Bernard closed the glass case and they followed him back to the parlour. 'I will go and find Pere François,' he said and then we will have some refreshment.'

He returned about ten minutes later.

'He is doing it now,' he said.

Lucy turned to him and said,

'Pere Bernard, I am puzzled.'

'Why is that, Mademoiselle?'

'When you met with Mary Tremayne, you gave her documents which were not as fragile as the book you have here.'
Pere Bernard smiled,

'Ah! That is easily explained. The papers that I gave to her were not as old as the ones in the glass case because they were later translations probably by an English monk. I think the original book was all in Latin then it was translated into the Celtic language, the language of the Britons, similar to our own language of

Brittany. It was then at a later date translated back into Latin.'

'Did you give Mary everything you had, apart from the book in the glass case?'

Pere Bernard hesitated,

'Not quite, we have a few more passages that were of a particularly religious nature that were particularly treasured by the Abbot. He was reluctant to relinquish those. It wasn't that we didn't trust Madame but well –'
Pere Bernard spread his hands in a particularly French gesture.

'As it turned out it was lucky that you held on to them as you would have lost the lot,' said Mike.
'No, we haven't lost everything as over the centuries there were various copies made and we still have some. Also, your sister was kind enough to send us some of the translations into English, made by the good professor and his assistant, Edith O'Leary. Here at Saint-Remy, we of course speak French. We have no difficulties with Latin and we also have those who know, German, Italian, Spanish and English but although some of us are familiar with the Breton language we are not experts in ancient Welsh, so of course we were delighted with the English translations. I think there will be some pages that have been destroyed.' 'My nephew, Andrew was bringing you the passages that we have. Fortunately we have photocopied the translations but a lot of the original stuff has gone,' said Mike.

'But it's wonderful that you have so much here!' said Lucy excitedly, 'between us we will be able to get a clear idea of the book.'

Père Bernard looked pleased and also quite excited.

'Yes, it will be for you now, Mademoiselle and your young friends to publish it in

English and perhaps we will subsequently publish it in French. I think it is time.'

Lucy clapped her hands with joy,

'Oh if only we could! Wouldn't it be wonderful?'

Mike laughed,

'Now don't get carried away, Lucy. We've got to get safely back to England first.'

Pere Bernard nodded,

'C'est vrai. We will pray hard for your safety. Now come! Refreshment!' He led them into a long refectory where he seated them at a well-scrubbed wooden table. He left them for some minutes, then returned with a tray with bottles of wine and glasses, olives, cheese and a couple of baguettes.'
'This is our own wine,' he said proudly, 'you may have noticed the vineyard when you came in.'
He poured out generous measures of the cold white wine and they tucked into the olives, bread and cheese.
Pere Bernard held up his glass,

'To *The Good Book of Oxford*!'

Lucy and Mike repeated the toast enthusiastically.

'This wine is wonderful, merveilleuse! Formidable!' said Mike enthusiastically. Pere Bernard moved to pour out some more but Mike caught Lucy's expression and reluctantly said,
'I'd better not, driving.'

'Mademoiselle?' said Pere Bernard holding the bottle.

'Oh yes please,' said Lucy ignoring Mike's black looks.

At that moment Pere François appeared with the photographs.

He gave them to Mike and Pere Bernard suddenly appeared with some bottles of wine.
'A present from Saint Remy,' he said.

Mike suddenly looked much more cheerful. Pere Bernard was also holding in his hands some sheets of paper,
'Photocopies' he said, 'you may find them useful.'

After thanking the monks for their help and their presents, Mike and Lucy set off to make their way back to Neuf-Chatel. As they proceeded along the quiet lanes they discussed their visit.
'I think that was very successful,' said Mike.

'Yes,' said Lucy. Mike turned to look at her.

'What's troubling you?'

'Nothing more than usual. It's just that if only we could solve these murders, I should be so pleased to take on *The Good Book of Oxford* along with the *Gaimar*.

Those monks seemed keen that it should be published and I think we owe it to

Mary and Frank to do it. I suddenly feel full of enthusiasm for the task.'

'Lucy,' said Mike, 'If you would just like to carry on with your research, that's fine.

Andy and I could do the investigating. It is dangerous.'

'That's not what I meant at all!' snapped Lucy, 'but if you want me off the case so that you, brave, strong men are not hampered by a weak, foolish female, that's
OK by me.'

Mike sighed,

'And that's not what I meant either and well you know it but if you want to play the role of the poor, slighted, unappreciated woman, go ahead.'
They drove on in silence for about half an hour. Suddenly Mike pulled into a layby.

He turned to Lucy,

'Mike,' she said and at the same time he said,

'Lucy.'

They both looked embarrassed and then began to laugh. They both apologised and Lucy said,
'Let's be friends.'

Mike gave her a quick hug, then covered his embarrassment by starting the engine.
'Best be off,' he said, 'Andy will be waiting.'

Chapter Twenty-six

Andrew was restless. His shoulder was still sore but apart from that he felt he was now back to normal. He was worried about Mike and Lucy. His own experiences had made him very nervous. He looked at his watch, four-thirty, surely they would be back soon!

Andrew slipped off the bed and walked around the room. He knew he was still shaky on his legs but as he walked things became easier. He looked for his clothes. Soeur Marie-Claire had washed them. They were ironed and folded neatly. He could see that there were one or two blood stains that were still there but the good sister had done a splendid job. He put them on. He would be ready to go when they arrived.

Andrew sat on the edge of the bed and looked out of the window. The sun was shining and he could see cornfields and sunflowers. It all looked so peaceful and wholesome. He thought about the horror of the day of his arrival. He shut his eyes. He must stop thinking about it.

The peace was suddenly disrupted by the sound of a car engine. Andrew backed into the room in panic. It could be his tormentors. He heard raised voices. Lucy and Mike were arguing about something. Andrew sighed. He wished his uncle got on better with Lucy. Mike was so loud and thoughtless and Lucy so gentle and sensitive. He loved Mike but he did have the ability to rub people up the wrong way. He was so tactless!

Within seconds, they were in Andrew's room – still arguing!

'Hi, Andy, I see you're dressed and packed and ready for off,' said Mike cheerfully. 'Mike, I don't think Andrew is well enough for a long journey. You can see how pale he is. He's too weak,' said Lucy.

'I'm fine, Lucy, really I am,' protested Andrew. He felt touched by Lucy's concern and in his tender state, it nearly brought tears to his eyes but he looked the other way quickly. He didn't want Lucy to think he wasn't ready as he wanted very much to go home, even to Mike's grubby, Streatham flat.

'I haven't got a bag to pack,' he said light-heartedly, 'they didn't even leave me a toothbrush!'

Lucy sighed. She knew she had lost the argument. She went in search of Sister Therese to thank her and to say good-bye. Sister Thérèse was concerned about

Andrew as his illness wasn't just broken bones. She explained to Lucy how Andrew had been de-hydrated and was still suffering the after-effects of pneumonia. She also said that Andrew was still in a state of shock after his frightening experiences. Lucy said they would look after Andrew and take him to see a doctor when they returned. She promised Sister Thérèse that they would keep in contact and let the sisters know how Andrew was.

Although Lucy was distressed to hear how ill Andrew had been she was amused at the affection the sisters had for Andrew after such a short time. While Andrew went to say good-bye to the sisters, she took Mike aside and told him what Sister Thérèse had said. Mike nodded and said,

'I'll make sure he's OK.'

Lucy smiled. She knew she would have to be content with that but she did trust Mike to a certain extent as she knew he was very fond of his young nephew.

The journey to St. Malo was uneventful. Andrew and Lucy slept most of the way. Lucy felt ashamed of sleeping so much but the evening was warm and she couldn't keep her eyes open. On board the ship, Mike ordered fish and chips and chocolate brownies all round and they all felt better. They sat at the table in the cafeteria and discussed their future plans.

'We don't seem to have any,' said Andrew.

'I will contact a Latin scholar, I know and he will translate the documents we've got from Saint Remy,' offered Lucy.

'He,' said Mike, 'I suppose you have a great many of these academic admirers.' 'The gentleman, I was thinking of,' said Lucy in a very cold, clipped voice, 'Doctor

Addison, is at least fifty years old.'

'Ah,' put in Mike, 'a doctor, now that's an attraction in itself.'

'Knock it off, Mike,' said Andrew as he looked at Lucy's angry face.

Mike laughed and went to get some drinks. After a couple of glasses of house red, they all relaxed.

'I've an idea,' said Mike.

Andrew looked up hopefully,

'What's that?'

'I know a chap who's a pretty good computer hacker.' 'I suppose he's a criminal,' sighed Andrew, 'and in any case what use is that to us?'

'He might be able to find out who has been hacking into our computers,' said Mike slowly and patiently, 'and he's not a criminal. He has been inside for hacking but only for a few months.'

'But Mike,' protested Lucy, 'we don't want him to get into more trouble.' 'He wouldn't because this time he's on the side of the angels – us! He's finding out who is breaking the law and in any case he enjoys it.'

'How do you know? And how do you know him?' asked Andrew suspiciously. 'Oh I used to teach him,' laughed Mike, 'he liked me. I spoke up for him at his trial. I'm sure he would do it.'

'I suppose it would help if we found out who was hacking into our computers,' said Andrew hesitantly.

'Oh, I'm pretty sure it's Sir Gareth or one of his minions,' said Mike but it would be useful to know for certain.'

'But,' said Lucy, 'if it is one of his minions, we are no further on. It's like the breakins and the other things, we can't connect them to Sir Gareth.'

'But the more evidence we have the better,' said Andrew, 'and there's more chance that one of them might give himself away.'

'OK then, is it agreed that I contact young Mervyn?' 'Agreed,' laughed the others.

They had restless nights in their cabins and were wakened by loud music at six o'clock in the morning. They had a quick cup of coffee before they set off. None of them could face the 'full English breakfast' offered by the ship.

Mike drove out of Portsmouth and Andrew promptly fell asleep again. Lucy was determined that she wouldn't sleep but didn't feel in the mood for conversation. They drove towards Ebbchester but as they neared their destination, Lucy wondered vaguely where they were going as she thought they were taking a wrong turn.

'Wake up Andy! We're here,' said Mike. Lucy looked puzzled,

'Where are we?'

'This is my Mum's,' said Mike, 'I thought it would be best for Andy for a while.'

'Good idea,' said Lucy, 'Does she know we're coming?'

'I gave her a quick ring when we stopped for petrol. She was delighted. Come on

Andy! Wakey wakey.'

Andrew got out of the car rubbing his eyes,

'What are we doing at Grandma's?' He laughed, 'I suppose you're after some breakfast.'
They went into the house and were warmly greeted by Margaret Nichols and she did indeed provide them with a hearty breakfast. When they got up to go, Mike said briskly,

'We are leaving you here for a bit, Andy.' Andrew was aghast. 'But . . ' he protested.

'I would be so pleased if you would keep me company for a while Andrew,' said Margaret. Andrew felt unable to say any more.
Mike and Lucy set of towards Ebbchester.
'Thank you for doing that, Mike. It was kind of you. Andrew can have a good rest with his grandma.'
'Oh, I didn't do it to please you,' said Mike curtly.

Lucy sighed,

'I am aware of that but it was kind.'

'Not that I wouldn't do things to please you.'

'That would be nice.'

'When's your birthday. I could buy you a present.'

'February.'

'That's no good.'

They drove on in silence for a while.

'I could buy you a present anyway.'

'You could.'

'What do you want?'

'I can't think of anything at the moment. This is a bit sudden.'

'Have you got a ball dress?' Lucy laughed,

'No, I did have a party dress but it's worn out.'

'I'll buy you one then.'

Lucy burst out laughing.

'Don't be ridiculous Mike. In any case, I don't go to balls.'

'I thought they had them at your posh universities.'

'They have May balls. They are finished now.'

'Well when they have the next one, I will take you.'

'I shall look forward to that.'

They drove on in silence for some minutes. Then Mike said,

'Andy's in love with you. You know that don't you?'

'Don't be ridiculous Mike. He's only seventeen,'

'Well that doesn't mean anything. I was younger than him when I fell in love with the Maths teacher. Boys often like older women.'

'Did she reciprocate the devotion?'

Mike considered,

'I doubt it. Most of the boys were in love with her. She was a well-built woman. She wore these tight dresses with plunging necklines. When you put your hand up to say you couldn't do a sum, she would come to your desk ..
'Mike I don't want to know!'

'No, probably not but a lot of chaps couldn't do their sums. It's natural I suppose but Andy's not like that, pure as the driven snow I should think, perhaps not, but he obviously likes a different type.' 'And what type would that be?'

'Oh the ordinary type, not too exciting, not the glamourous type, safe, I suppose.' 'Interesting,' relied Lucy drily.

At that moment they arrived at Lucy's flat in Ebbchester. Mike lifted Lucy's bag out of the boot and carried it down the pathway. Lucy unlocked the door.

'Aren't you going to invite me in?' asked Mike.

'Actually Mike, I'm a bit tired. Sorry to be unsociable.'

'Oh that's OK. I'm a bit tired myself. Anyway keep in touch. You've got the new

Mobile?'

Lucy nodded and to her surprise Mike bent down and kissed her on the cheek.

'See you,' he shouted and got quickly into his car and drove off.

Lucy looked down the road after him.

'Ordinary! Safe!' she exclaimed and turned into the flat.

Chapter Twenty-seven

Andrew lay back in a comfortable armchair and dozed. His grandmother had gone to bed and he was watching television. He was awakened by a loud noise and he realised the news had finished and a horror film was beginning. He reached lazily for the controls and switched to *Newsnight*. Someone was being interviewed about the economy. He supposed he ought to be interested.

Andrew was feeling lethargic. He had been nearly a week with his grandmother and had quite enjoyed the comfort, the good meals and the attention. Initially, though he had been quite cross with Mike for not consulting him, he had been relieved to spend some time in Sitbury to recover.

'And now,' said the TV presenter, 'I will turn to Lord Farquar. I understand Sir, that you are going to relinquish the government of Farquar Delaney Enterprises.' 'Yes, that's right,' said Lord Farquar, 'I've been at it long enough. It's time for me to go.'

'Will your son take over?'

'No, Gerald's never been interested in making money. He's a barrister. That takes up all his time. There are plenty of competent people who can take over.'

'I have heard that you intend to get rid of some of your considerable wealth.'

Lord Farquar laughed,

'Yes, it is considerable isn't it? I suppose I'm worth a billion or two. I actually intend to get rid of all of it, well most of it anyway, should have done it years ago instead of wasting my life.'

The presenter looked surprised,

'You have hardly wasted your life. You have run an extremely successful business, provided jobs for thousands and built up a considerable fortune.'

Lord Farquar gave a rueful smile,

'Ay, there's the rub. I didn't need a fortune. I was already comfortably off. I come from a privileged background – everything I could want – silver spoon and all that.

I have been reading something interesting lately, an old, very old book, chap I know showed me extracts. It made me think. I was brought up a Christian, public school, Anglican chapel and all that sort of thing. Most of us are familiar with the well-known quotations about wealth – 'eye of the needle', 'blessed are the poor' and so on but I suppose we know them so well that we don't give them a thought and go on making money as though it's a good thing to do.'

The presenter looked puzzled,

'Would you say you have had a religious experience?'

Lord Farquar chuckled,

'Oh I don't talk in terms like that, far too sensational for a dried-up old

Englishman like me but perhaps you are right.'

'Have you decided what you are going to do with your money?'

'Yes, I have but don't ask me what. I don't want any begging letters from anyone.

I have made arrangements.'

'What does your son think about losing his inheritance?'

'Oh Gerald's fine. He's got enough, a good career, beautiful, talented wife and two lovely children. What more could he want? In any case you have to do what is right even if the house falls down.'

Andrew shot up out of his chair. He had read those words, 'even if the house falls down'. Sir Alfred must have seen '*The Good Book*'. He reached for his mobile. It rang a few times, no answer. Where was Mike? Surely he was at home in the middle of the week?

The phone rang.

'Mike I've been trying to get hold of you where were you?'

'I heard the phone ring. I was on the lavatory if you must know. What's the problem?'

'Switch on '*Newsnight*'. There's an old boy who's read the *Good Book*.

'How can he have read it?'

'I don't know but switch it on.'

Andrew went back to the television.

'Thank you, Lord Farquar. That was very interesting. I do hope your good book will be available for us all in the future.'

There was a close-up of Lord Farquar, smiling, 'Indeed, indeed,' he said.

Andrew sighed in frustration. He must have missed something while phoning Mike. The phone rang again. It was Mike who asked him to go over in detail what he had heard. Then Andrew said, 'I'm so sorry I missed the last bit.'

'Oh that's OK, I can probably get it on the internet, but this is important, Andy. I suppose Sir Gareth must have shown it to him.'

'It's odd though as Sir Gareth had the opposite reaction to it.'

'That's because,' said Mike, 'Sir Gareth is a crook and Farquar is an honest man.' 'How do you know?'

'It's obvious. Farquar is one of the old school, aristocracy as far back as Moses. Played cricket and doesn't lie, public school, 'good man with the willow', hates rotters and cads, *Fifth Form at St Dominics*.'

'I've never heard of St. Dominics.'

'It's a book, you chump.'

'I thought you were a good socialist and didn't like all that kind of thing – Tory toffs and suchlike.'

'I don't but the Tory toffs are just jumped-up rich people. They are not the real aristocrats like old Farquar. I'm not keen on them either. I'm a socialist. I disapprove of the class system but it doesn't stop me recognising a decent person.'

'I'll take your word for it, but Mike, what can we do about it? Does this change anything? And Mike, I have been grateful to stay with Grandma for a while but I have now recovered completely. I need to return to HQ.'

Mike laughed. He thought for a minute,

'How about if I come over on Saturday and pick you up and . . . .'

'That's fine, but I was going to say, Lucy could come over here. It's not far for her and we could have a meeting and plan our next steps.'

'Yes,' agreed Mike, ' Lucy and I will have something to report by then.'

'Have you spoken to the hacker?' 'Not on the phone. See you Saturday.' Mike rung off.

Andrew was excited. He felt as though things were happening. It would be good to see Mike and Lucy on Saturday. He must tell his grandma that he was leaving. He knew that when she said that she was lonely, she was saying it to make it difficult for him to refuse to stay but he believed that she must be lonely and in any case she was his grandma and he was devoted to her. He would tell her tomorrow.

'Grandma, Mike phoned last night and I said that I was feeling better and would be ready to return to Streatham with him. He suggested that he came and picked me up on Saturday and that Lucy came as well. Would that be all right?'
Margaret smiled,

'Of course, Andrew as long as you do feel better. You certainly look better than you did last week. I expect you will all be wanting lunch.'
'Grandma, you're wonderful.'

'Andrew, I don't want to pry. I know you three are up to something and you told me you went to France because of the research that Mary and Lucy were doing but I know that's only part of the story and I suspect there is danger in it for all of you. I couldn't help noticing, Andrew that you were very bruised which obviously wasn't the result of pneumonia. I'm saying this because if it's possible I should like to help. I don't want to know what it's all about as I think you are shielding me from worry but I do live near Ebbchester and I do have quite a large house which you could make use of. You and Michael are both very precious to me and I know

Mary was very fond of Lucy. If there is anything I can do to help, I will do it.'

Andrew went over to Margaret and kissed her,

'Grandma, you are more than wonderful! I do appreciate everything you do' Andrew was impatient for Saturday. He wondered whether Mike had managed to get his computer hacker. He wondered whether Lucy had managed to find a translator for the documents that they had brought back from France. In the meantime he looked up Lord Farquar on his grandmother's computer. He thought that it should be safe from the hacker. He had heard of Lord Farquar as he was a well-known member of the aristocracy as well as being a successful banker. He learnt that Lord Alfred Farquar had a huge country mansion in Sussex. Markwood House had been in the Farquar family for hundreds of years. The family owned a vast estate in Scotland and some very valuable property in the City of London. In 1976, Lord Alfred married Martha Delaney, an American. Her father, Robert, was an American banker and Martha, being an only child would inherit the Delaney fortune. Robert and Alfred decided to combine their assets and the Farquar and Delaney, Known as 'F&D' enterprises became a huge name in Merchant banking.

Alfred and Martha had two children, Gerald and Rowena. Rowena, after achieving a first class honours degree in Cambridge, entered a convent where she became a medical missionary. Gerald also did well at University and after spending some years in the family business, changed direction and became a barrister. He married the beautiful, intelligent Charlotte Taylor-Smith whom he had met at

Cambridge. The wedding was a top society event, much being made of Charlotte's 'humble' background as a grammar-school girl and the daughter of a local postman.

Lord Alfred, despite his wealth was a Labour Peer and was known for his egalitarian principles and honesty.

Andrew was puzzled by this information. He couldn't see Lord Alfred as a friend of Sir Gareth and they obviously had opposing views.

Chapter Twenty-eight

'This is very kind of your Grandma, Andrew,' said Lucy, 'providing us with a secure room to meet, is just what we need and it only takes me ten minutes on the bus.' 'And lunch thrown in. Good old Mum,' agreed Mike.

'But what's your news,' said Andrew impatiently, 'have you been in contact with the hacker?'

'Young Mervyn is working on my computer as we speak,' said Mike, 'but I have no idea how long it will take him.'

And what about you,' Andrew turned to Lucy, 'have you got someone to translate the Latin?'

'Doctor Addison,' said Lucy with a sideways look at Mike, 'has the papers and he has agreed to translate them and we are indebted to you Andrew for watching

Newsnight and recognising a quotation from *The Good Book*.'

'I have looked up Lord Alfred,' said Andrew, 'but I can't see any connection with Sir Gareth. He's a different sort of person and they obviously have opposing points of view.'

'They might just go to the same club, or bump into each other at a meeting of bankers,' suggested Mike.

'It could be,' said Lucy hesitantly, 'that Sir Gareth wanted someone more prestigious to read the book to give it more credibility. He wasn't to know what

Lord Alfred would think.'

'Yes,' agreed Andrew, 'he probably assumed that a rich person would have the same point of view as him.'

Mike looked thoughtful and screwed up his face as if in pain.

'What is it Mike?' asked Lucy solicitously.

'I don't know,' said Mike, 'I feel this business with Lord Alfred might be quite important but I don't know how and also what we can do about it.'

'Well,' said Lucy, 'I am now officially working on *The Good Book of Oxford* as well as the Gaimar. I went to see my new, temporary supervisor and asked him if I could work on it and he just said, "Of course, of course, carry on". He was rather sweet actually and said, "I know it's been very difficult for you Miss Hammond but we do appreciate the fact that you are keeping going."'

'Sweet!' scoffed Mike, 'I bet he was. He probably thought Christmas had come early having to supervise someone like you. Did he really call you, "Miss Hammond"?'

'Yes,' said Lucy, demurely, pretending not to understand Mike's implications, 'he's about eighty and I don't think he's even aware of the new 'Ms' form of address. But to get back to the point, as I am now the official researcher into *The Good Book*, it would be quite appropriate for me to contact Sir Alfred and ask him tactfully how he got hold of it.'

Mike banged the table,

'Good thinking, young Lucy! That's just what we need, an entry so to speak. I suggest you write to him. An old boy like that probably doesn't know how to work a computer and probably holds the phone about a mile from his ear and bawls at it. My grandad used to do that.'

They all laughed especially as Andrew knew that Lord Alfred was only in his mid-sixties, but they all agreed that a letter with the University –headed notepaper would be the best bet.

'Mike, have you heard any more from Johnny Judge?' asked Andrew.

'No, not since he told me about Ken Weston. He was going to look into the Birford police. I might give him a ring. I don't want to pester him or make life difficult for him but I might try and think of some excuse to contact him.'

'So,' said Andrew, 'you both have things to do. What about me? What can I do?' 'you've got the most important job of all,' said Mike, leaning across the table and looking seriously at Andrew.

'What's that?'

'Making my dinner when I come home from school.'

Andrew got up quickly, went round the table and pulled the chair out from underneath Mike who was still leaning across the table. Mike collapsed on the floor.

'You stupid, lunatic oaf. I could have broken bones.

The following day Lucy composed her letter to Lord Alfred. She didn't know exactly how one should address a lord but decided that 'Lord Alfred' was the simplest. The heading was the Arts faculty of the University of Ebbchester and she addressed it to Lord Alfred's country home, Markwood Castle. She looked at her final draft:-   *Dear Lord Alfred,*

I was interested to hear you speaking on Newsnight last week.

I recognised your quotation from 'an ancient book' as being from

The Good Book of Oxford. I am researching into this book at Ebbchester   University, following the untimely death of my colleague, Mary Nichols.   As the research is not yet finished and so not published, I am curious to know   how you came by a copy of the book. I should be grateful if

you would let me know as if there are other copies in existence, this is of great   interest to me in my research.

Yours faithfully,

Lucy Hammond

Lucy was not quite satisfied with the letter but decided to send it off as she was anxious to receive a reply and realised that the letter might have to travel from Lord Alfred's country house to his London home.

She was aware of her impatient anticipation of a reply and so was astonished when three days later she received the following reply,

Dear Miss Hammond,

I was delighted to receive your letter and look forward, with great anticipation, to discussing with you, the wonderful, Good Book of Oxford. I was shown a copy of part of it by an acquaintance, who had been given that part by your late, distinguished colleague, Doctor Mary Nicholls.

I shall be in London next week for a debate in the House which I must attend. I should be delighted if you would do me the honour of taking tea with me in the House of Lords tea-rooms. I suggest 5.00 pm on Thursday. Please will you let my secretary know if that is convenient. I shall tell the man at the door to expect you.

Alfred of Markwood.

Lucy gazed at the letter. It was far beyond her expectations. So he probably did get the extract from the Good Book from Sir Gareth! Lucy smiled as she re-read the letter. She noted that Lord Alfred referred to Sir Gareth as 'an acquaintance' not 'as a friend'. Once more Lucy was impatient. She couldn't wait to tell the others. She looked at her watch. Mike would be at school. She decided to text him – phone me when you can. Andrew might be home now but she didn't want him to tell Mike first. As she pondered this, her mobile phone rang.

'Mike, I thought you'd be teaching.'

'I've got plenty of free lessons at the moment. What is it? Are you all right?'

'Yes, of course.'

'There's no of course about it. Something awful could have happened to you. You don't realise what a shock you gave me. My heart turned over!'

'Sorry Mike' said Lucy penitently, secretly rather pleased at the movement of the heart. She told him about the letter from Lord Alfred. Mike was excited,

'That's brilliant! Can I come with you?'

'You'll be at work.'

'I could get some time off. I mean – the House of Lords!'

'I didn't think you were impressed by that sort of thing.'

'I'm not but I'm sure the head would be – Mr Nichols won't be here today. He has an important meeting at the House of Lords. Yes that would go down well'

'You're not invited.'

'Well, when you phone you could say that it's important for Doctor Nichol's brother to attend.'

'I couldn't.'

'You could.'

'Maybe but I won't.'

'Why not? Don't you want me to come with you?'

'No'

'Oh, I thought you might need some moral support.'

Lucy was about to reply in a sharp tone but she could hear that Mike sounded quite crest-fallen.

'Mike, it would be great to have your company. It really would but I think I might be better able to talk to Lord Alfred on his own. He might be more forthcoming and in any case, he might think it's rather rude to bring some-one else along, even Mary's brother.'

'I expect you are right. These old boys love to chat up a beautiful young girl. He's probably hoping that all the other old codgers in the Lords tea-rooms take notice.
I expect they will say,

"Look at old Alf. He's got a very beautiful lady friend!"'

Lucy burst out laughing at the picture,

'I'll let you go back to work, Mike. You do me good!'

'That's all right then,' replied Mike pleased, 'I hope to do you good more often.' <u>Chapter Twenty- eight</u>

Lucy crossed the road from the tube station in trepidation. She looked up at Big Ben. She had been to Westminster many times and as a schoolgirl had been taken round the House of Commons and the Lords. But this was different. She was going to have tea with a Lord, a very famous, well-respected Lord. She wondered whether Mike would really be unimpressed by meeting a Lord. Lucy found the entrance to the House of Lords and saw the policeman at the door. She suddenly drew back. She looked down at her summer dress and jacket. Should she have worn something smarter, more formal? She was wearing sandals. They were her best sandals but still they were only sandals. She spoke to herself severely,
'Lucy Hammond, don't be so silly. You can't go back and change now and in any case, Lord Alfred probably won't notice what you are wearing'

She marched purposefully up to the policeman and told him her name. Before she had time to say any more, the policeman smiled at her. 'Lord Alfred told me to expect you. Come with me, love.'

Lucy smiled back. She felt quite reassured by his obvious Yorkshire accent. She followed him up some stairs which to her surprise led on to a terrace overlooking the River Thames. The policeman led her to a table, a little bit set apart from the others.

'Your guest, My Lord,'

A tall, thin, white-haired man stood up and shook hands with Lucy, then pulled out a chair for her to sit down.

'Miss Lucy Hammond, I presume. May I call you Lucy?'

Lucy smiled,

'Of course.'

'Then you must call me Alfie. That's what my friends call me.'

Lucy had to stop herself from choking with laughter as she remembered Mike's comments. To hide her embarrassment, she turned to look at the Thames,

'What a lovely view you have here!'

'Yes, I thought it would be better out here. It's a bit stuffy inside. Now, how do you like your tea?'

'With milk and no sugar please.'

Lord Alfred laughed,

'Oh I didn't quite mean that, my dear. I meant – Earl Grey, or lap sang, or just ordinary Ceylon?'

'Oh ordinary please.'

Lord Alfred waved to a waiter, who came over,

'Tom, we would like two ordinary Ceylon teas and some of your best cakes.' He turned to Lucy,

'I do like a cake in the afternoon. I hope you do and you don't have to worry about your figure, my dear, what a pretty frock! You know poppies are one of my favourite flowers.'

'Thank you,' said Lucy smiling. She refrained from mentioning that the flowers on her dress were anemones.

The tea and cakes arrived with some tiny sandwiches. Sir Alfred filled his plate with a pile of sandwiches and a large slice of chocolate cake. Lucy took three small sandwiches and a piece of carrot cake.

Lord Alfred tucked in, then turned to Lucy with a chocolate smeared face. 'Now' he said, wiping his fingers on a table napkin, 'tell me about yourself. You must be a very clever girl, working with the great Mary Nichols.' 'Well I did a History and Archaeological degree and then specialised in old manuscripts. My mother was French and so I am bi-lingual which was useful.' 'French! A wonderful people I always think, so cultured and erudite. A pity they didn't stick it out during the war but I suppose they had their reasons. Now tell me about how you came to be working on *The Good Book of Oxford*.'

Lucy told him about how she had read Geoffrey of Monmouth's *The History of the Kings of Britain* and how Mary had suggested she studied Gaimar. She said that this 'Old book' was mentioned and that Mary had finally got a copy from the monks in Brittany. She didn't mention the fact that she had been excluded from this. 'How did you get to read it?' she asked, 'we hadn't published it and it is still being translated.'

Lord Alfred looked slightly embarrassed and hesitant.

'I'm very sorry, my dear, if I wasn't supposed to have it but it was shown to me by someone and I don't know whether he should have done that or whether he should have had it in the first place.'

'Sir Gareth Lewis,' said Lucy. Lord Alfred looked up in surprise.

'Well as you know that, I don't have to protect his name, but how did he get hold of it?' Lucy hesitated. She wasn't sure how much she should tell but decided that lord Alfred was not an enemy and would be discreet. She told him about how the book had got into the hands of Sir Gareth and mentioned the fact that he was interested in it because of his Welsh ancestry. She half expected a man of Lord
Alfred's pedigree to be a bit scathing but he said,

'Yes that was very interesting. I do think we have neglected the Celts. They are a fascinating race but I was quite taken with the religious sections and the pages on the use of money. You probably know that I have had a very privileged background and during the course of my adult life I became a very successful business man. My beloved wife was an American and I teamed up with her father, Robert Delaney, Bobby they called him, you know what these Americans are like! She herself, was a rich heiress. I didn't marry her for her money, though, you mustn't think that'
Lucy nodded her assumption that she didn't think that, but he continued,

'She was beautiful, beautiful in every way, so full of fun and so good. There was no guile in her. She was always completely truthful.' He laughed, 'it could be a little awkward at times. I lost her twelve years ago, cancer.' 'I'm sorry,' said Lucy quietly.

'No, no, I was very fortunate to have her for thirty-five years, a girl in a million, a girl in a million. Now where was I? Yes money, it just seemed to fall into my lap. I suppose there was a certain achievement at being successful in what I did and money is always attractive but I never needed it. I tried to be reasonably generous and give to Charity and all that sort of thing but I didn't doubt that I had a right to it, that it should belong to me. It seems strange that an ancient book should make me think differently.' Lord Alfred looked thoughtfully at the boats passing down the Thames. He screwed up his face and sighed, 'I was brought up a Christian, you know and I am well-versed in the scriptures. My school saw to that. I know all about the difficulties of the rich getting to heaven, the eye of a needle and all that but I suppose we hear these things so regularly, church, home, school and so on and they become so familiar to us that we don't give them another thought. I say "we", my dear not because I am including you but I mean people like me, the over-privileged.' Lord Alfred sighed, looked into the distance then turned again to Lucy, ' Yes that is a remarkable book. How are you getting on with it?'

'We have had some difficulties as some of it was stolen after the death of the

Tremaynes.'

'Good Heavens! How do you know it was stolen, not just mislaid?' Lucy hesitated. She didn't know how much to tell.

'All Mary's notes were gone and all copies of the passages from *The Good Book*. I thought other members of the department must have them but nobody had any knowledge of them. The copies held by the Welsh professor who was translating it, also disappeared.' Lucy decided not to mention the murder. It all sounded too sensational.

Lord Alfred frowned. He looked worried,

'Funny you should say that but I've mislaid my copy. I looked for it again when I knew I was seeing you but couldn't find it – just put it down to poor memory – old age, Alzheimer's they call it nowadays, but it could be more sinister. Why do you think someone would want to steal it?'

'The sections on money are very radical and quite persuasive. Many people might see it as a threat. It has a history of causing upset.'

Lord Alfred sighed,

'Money, money, money – the love of it does seem to be at the root of a great deal of evil.'

Lucy agreed. Lord Alfred smiled,

'My daughter, Rowena, now she's taken a vow of poverty and is perfectly happy with that. She decided to enter a convent – Roman Catholic like her mother – did medicine at your place – Ebbchester – qualified medical doctor – joined medical missionaries. I thought I was going to lose her but she comes back regularly and is as mischievous as ever – always was – full of fun – must entertain those nuns – great girl.'

'You have a son?' said Lucy tentatively,

'Yes Gerald, good lad – joined me at the bank for a while then took up Law – suits him better – more serious than his sister don't y'know but he's got a lively wife.'

Here Lord Alfred burst out laughing,

'Keeps him on his toes all right – Charlotte – beautiful girl, full of life, don't know why she married him – good chap but not lively enough for her.'

'Aren't they happy together?'

'Oh yes, happy as Larry, she goes to all the night clubs and society dos mostly without him but doesn't ever look at another chap, thoroughly decent girl, a wonderful mother – two children, Hugo and Sebastian, very bright like their mother. I don't know where they got 'Hugo' from – sounds a bit foreign to me. You must come and meet her sometime – get on well – clever girl like you.' Lucy smiled thinking of Mike's assessment of her as being 'not glamourous or exciting' and felt that she didn't really want to meet the lovely Charlotte.

Chapter Twenty-nine

Lucy left the House of Lords thoughtfully. She had enjoyed her conversation with

Lord Alfred and found him to be a very nice man. She wandered down Abingdon Street towards Parliament Square without thinking where she was going but suddenly she was aware that she was being followed. She was determined not to look round and to keep in full view of everyone.

She went across the middle of Parliament Square and sat down on a low wall. She was aware of the person behind her moving towards the wall. He sat down beside her. Lucy looked straight ahead.

'Well it's like that is it? Now you've been hobnobbing with the aristocracy you don't even recognise me.' Lucy gasped, sighed with relief and then laughed,

'Mike! What are you doing here?'

'Oh, I got out of school early so I thought I would toddle along to see how you got on with the Lord.'

'Oh, Alf and I got on like a house on fire.'

'Alf? Did you really call him that?'

'No but he asked me to. He really is rather sweet, terribly old-worldly and says things like "don't y'know" I didn't think people said that sort of thing any more.' 'You've obviously been moving in the wrong circles but did he say anything of significance?'

'Not really,' said Lucy thoughtfully, 'It was Sir Gareth who gave him the copy of the extracts from *The Good Book* and another thing, it looks as though it has been stolen from him.'

'That's interesting,' said Mike, 'do you think he is just pretending it's been stolen so he can't return it to you?'

'No, he just thought he had mislaid it. He blamed it on old age and of course that could be true but in the circumstances . . .'
'That seems unlikely,' finished Mike, 'anyway tell me what he said.'

'He talked mostly about his family but I'll tell it all to you as closely as I remember it.'
Lucy related her conversation with Lord Alfred as nearly and exactly as she could.

When she had finished Mike said,

'He seems to have an eye for the ladies – his wife, his daughter and his daughter – in-law!'
Lucy laughed,

'Yes he does but it's a kind of gentlemanly, old-world courtesy. I think he probably does put women on a pedestal.'
'Pretty ones!'

'Probably but I expect he only meets the sort of women who have plenty of money, wear expensive clothes and are generally very well turned out, apart from his daughter of course. He's very impressed with his daughter-in-law.'
'Yes, I've heard of her, Charlotte Farquar. She's often in the news, a real looker, hob-nobs with all the aristocracy, even royals.'
'Mike, do you think all this has any relevance? Does it take us any further?

'I don't know. As you say he could easily have mislaid the Good Book extracts but '

'But what?'

'I don't know, Lucy. I think we should follow up every lead and somehow although the old boy seems decent enough, he is very rich, very aristocratic and very influential. There must be something there.'

'I think you're right,' said Lucy, 'and at the moment we seem to be at a standstill.' 'Oh I don't know about that. I heard from Johnny, an interesting development.
Ken Weston has been arrested.'

Lucy sat up in excitement,

'That is interesting. What's he been arrested for?'

'Well that's the interesting thing. Johnny said in his short letter that, "it might have some relevance for your case". I don't know more than that. He said he would come and see me but I think I ought to go over there.'
'Yes, that's only fair and anyway . . .'

'What do you mean – anyway?'

'I just thought it would give you a chance to see his gorgeous missus again,' said Lucy smiling.
'Now Lucy, I'm surprised at that comment. I fear I'm leading you into bad ways. I say that sort of thing but it's usually because I'm jealous. Surely a pure girl like you couldn't be jealous of my admiration for a friend's wife?'
'Shut up Mike!'

Mike sighed in an exaggerated way.

'Now you are sounding like my nephew. He is continually rude to me. But I suppose I will have to put up with it. Now to get to the point – how about going for some dinner?'
'Mike, I'd love to but for the past hour I have been eating cakes and sandwiches, not to mention scones with cream in them.'
'Well we could go for a drink and when the results of your greed have been dissipated we could go for the meal?'
'Sounds good.'

Chapter Thirty

Andrew was feeling decidedly disgruntled. He was bored. He knew that he had now recovered from his injuries in France but he felt that Mike was ignoring him. He knew that Lucy was going to the House of Lords and that Mike was planning another visit to John Judge but what could he do? To make matters worse he was suffering from toothache. Before Mike went off to school, Andrew had asked him for the name of a local dentist and Mike's reply had been,

'Don't know, never use one, perfect teeth.'

Andrew decided to look one up on the internet. He found a local one, a Stefan Crystowsky and rang up the reception. He said that he was in a lot of pain and it was urgent. The receptionist told him to come immediately and that the dentist would try to fit him in as soon as possible.

Andrew checked the address on the internet and set off. He only had to walk a few hundred yards. The young receptionist was friendly and gave him the forms to fill in to say he wanted to be treated on the National Health.

Andrew sat down in a comfortable armchair and looked around. There were four other patients, waiting to be seen but he could see that there were two dentists at work. He calculated that he shouldn't have to wait more than half an hour. He walked over to the magazine rack. There didn't seem to be much that would appeal to him. He picked up a magazine on cars. It took five minutes for him to realise that He didn't know a thing about cars. He went back to the table and rather shame-facedly picked up a magazine entitled *Royalty and Celebrity*. Underneath the title was the message – *Find out what they're up to – who they know – where they go!*

Despite his misgivings, Andrew thumbed through the magazine in a desultory way.

Suddenly he saw a headline,

'The lovely Charlotte Farquar – more thrills and spills!'

Underneath was a picture of a very glamourous woman stretching out a long, elegant leg as she emerged from a racing car.

Andrew read on. Apparently Charlotte had driven a racing car around a well-known racing track in the company of the famous formula one driver, Peter

Kenilworth. He commented that she was,

'Absolutely fearless and obviously very experienced in driving fast cars.'

Underneath the article were the words,

'Whatever will Charlotte do next? – turn to page 41 for more about our beautiful heroine!'

Andrew turned to page forty-one. There was a close-up photograph of Charlotte in evening dress accompanied by a handsome young man who was smiling down at his companion.

Andrew gazed at the photo. She certainly was very beautiful. She had big, blue eyes with long dark eyelashes and the most entrancing smile. Andrew then looked at her companion. He looked familiar. Underneath the picture were the words,
'Charlotte's escort for this evening was Hayden Lewis, the son of the multibillionaire, Sir Gareth Morgan-Lewis. But don't think there's a scandal here! Charlotte is never short of escorts but we know that the love of her life is her stay-at-home husband, the honourable Gerald Farquar. We also know that
Hayden's name has been linked with glamourous socialite, Annabel Penhaligon-

West, the daughter of the billionaire, Marcus Penhaligon-West.'

'Andrew Tremayne to see Mr Krystowski' boomed over the inter-com. Andrew put the magazine back on the table then hurried into the consulting room. Twenty minutes later he was back in the waiting room, making an appointment for the following week. After anaesthetising the gum the dentist had taken out the exposed nerve and put in a temporary filling. Andrew looked round for the magazine but was disappointed to see a young girl reading it. He picked up another edition of the same magazine and watched the girl out of the corner of his eye. The receptionist looked surprised that he was still there. 'Have you finished your appointment Mr Tremayne?'
'Yes, yes, I'm just waiting for my father to give me a lift home.'

Andrew gasped. What had he said? He suddenly felt as though someone had punched him in the stomach. He had had many lifts from his father in the past but now? There would be no more. The girl put the magazine down and picked up another one. While the receptionist had turned her head to answer the phone, Andrew picked up the two magazines, shoved them under his jacket and walked out.

As Andrew walked down the road, his heart seemed to be beating at an alarming rate. He wasn't sure whether this was because of his theft of the magazines, a rather painful experience at the hands of the dentist or the sudden vision of his father. He tried to control the tears as he staggered along.

As Andrew approached the flat he saw Mike just leaving. When he saw Andrew he looked horrified,

'Andy, me old mate, what's the matter? You look terrible!'

'Thanks, I've just been to the dentist. What are you doing home from school this early?'

'Oh I thought I would give Lucy some support. The dentist! It's no wonder you look grim, sadists the lot of them!'

'How do you know? You never go.'

'Oh my mum used to send me when I was a child, complete waste of time. Why go if you have nothing wrong with your teeth? They just get damaged by being poked about and hammered with steel instruments, anyway let's go and find something to brighten you up.'

Mike re-opened the door, went upstairs and made Andrew sit in the best armchair. He then presented him with a glass of whiskey. Andrew looked at it dubiously,

'It might not go well with the anaesthetic.' 'Drink it!' ordered Mike.

Andrew did as he was told and quickly felt the colour coming back into his cheeks.

He did feel better.

'Thanks Mike' he said 'but don't let me keep you from your assignation.' 'It's not an assignation. She doesn't know I'm coming. It will just be a pleasant surprise.'

Andrew looked a bit sceptical about 'the pleasant surprise' but Mike made his way through the front door, once more, calling out,

'Don't save dinner for me. I may be late. I'll eat out.'

Andrew leaned back in the chair, shut his eyes and fell asleep.

About an hour later, Andrew woke up. He was a bit shocked that he had been sleeping at four o'clock in the afternoon. He felt hungry. The numbness had gone down in his mouth and he was ready to eat. He stood up and removed his jacket. To his surprise the two stolen magazines fell out. He had forgotten all about them. He went into the kitchen and rooted around for some food. Eventually he came back into the sitting room with a cup of tea and a pile of peanut butter sandwiches. He picked the magazines off the floor and placed them on the table, sat down and began to read them. He was particularly interested in information about Hayden Lewis and the Farquar family. He discovered that Hayden Lewis was a relative newcomer to the society pages and that he was often at the same events as Charlotte Farquar. He also discovered that in recent weeks he had become involved with Annabel Penhaligon -West. Annabel was frequently described as 'lovely', 'beautiful' and 'glamourous'. This puzzled Andrew, as depicted in the various photographs, Annabel didn't look at all 'lovely'. He saw a very thin, rather scrawny, young woman who seemed to have a constant bored expression. Charlotte Farquar was quite different as apart from being obviously beautiful, she was always smiling and seemed to exude an air of energy and life. Andrew looked at her and said out loud,

'I like you Charlotte and if I was in your company I would surely fall for you, not just for your beauty but for your love of life and friendliness. I think I would be intoxicated by you.' He put the magazines down and sighed,

'It's just as well I won't ever meet you. You wouldn't even notice a star-struck seventeen year-old. I think you would be kind though.'

Andrew then decided to look up these characters on the internet. He already knew quite a bit about Hayden Lewis and the Farquar family but he discovered that Annabel Penhaligon-West was a fabulously wealthy heiress. Both her parents owned vast estates in Cornwall and the Midlands and her Father's family had made a fortune in the last century from China clay in Cornwall. Her mother was descended from a successful Birmingham manufacturer. Andrew couldn't quite find out what they did now but gathered that they had been very fortunate in their investments.

He looked again at a picture of Annabel on the arm of a smiling Hayden Lewis and wondered whether wealth made a girl 'lovely'. He was surprised at his own cynicism.

He looked up Charlotte Farquar and discovered that her father was a butcher in Leeds and that her mother was a teaching assistant. Charlotte had gained various scholarships to Oxford and had achieved a first-class degree in PPE. She met Gerald Farquar at Oxford and seven years later, after Gerald had been called to the bar, they were married in Saint Anne's Catholic Cathedral in Leeds. They had two little boys, Hugo and Sebastian, aged five and seven. The internet article made much of Charlotte's humble origins and her acceptance into 'elite society'. She didn't work believing that her little boys needed a 'full-time Mummy' but she did indulge in various escapades, riding a horse at great speed through the 'Burlington Arcade', flying a light aircraft and landing in the parkland of Weyborough Castle. Charlotte sailed 'close to the wind' with some of her escapades but her personal life seemed to be irreproachable.

Andrew tried various websites to gain more knowledge of Hayden Lewis.

He first of all found a factual biography of Hayden Lewis which gave him a little more information than one he had previously read. He had assumed, because of Hayden's association with Mary Nichols that Hayden had been to university at the prestigious Ebbchester. It turned out that Hayden had been to a private university which was financed by his father, Sir Gareth. The 'Morgan-Lewis University' was situated in South Wales and had a good reputation particularly for scientific research as Sir Gareth had obviously poured a great deal of money into it. It also had a very successful Welsh department which looked into Welsh history and promoted the Welsh language. Andrew was surprised that he had never heard of it. Apparently Hayden had gained a lower second class degree in Sociology. Andrew shut the lap-top and stared ahead. He wondered whether this information was useful. It backed up Sir Gareth's interest in everything Welsh. Did it tell him anything about Hayden? He wondered whether Hayden had applied to UCAS in the normal way or whether his father's private college was his only chance of a degree.

Andrew decided to investigate further. He pressed all the buttons in italics. He discovered more information about the 'Morgan-Lewis'. Most of the students appeared to be from North America with Welsh sounding names or were genuine Welsh speakers from Wales. Despite this oddity, the students seemed to be of a high calibre and went on to other prestigious universities to do research or to carry on with their studies.

Andrew then had another idea and looked up Doctor Thomas from Cardiff University. He discovered that Doctor Thomas had gained his first degree 'cum summa laude' at 'Morgan-Lewis', and had then done a doctorate at Cambridge before taking up his present position in Cardiff.

Andrew pressed a button marked 'biography' and found that Doctor Thomas was Canadian and had originally worked on a newspaper owned by the Morgan-Lewis group.

'Interesting', said Andrew to himself, 'now for more information on Hayden'.

About half an hour later after fruitlessly pressing many 'leads' to Hayden Lewis,

Andrew came across an article from *The Observer* which mentioned Hayden Lewis. The article was one of many which was suspicious of the increasing power of the Morgan-Lewis empire and was mostly about Sir Gareth. It talked about his background and hinted at previous shady dealings. It didn't say anything about Sir Gareth which Andrew didn't already know but spoke rather scathingly about Hayden. It mentioned the elder 'disgraced' son then described Hayden as 'the beautiful boy'. The writer accepted that Hayden was 'handsome and charming', described his intellectual achievements as 'mediocre' and then went on to describe him as 'weak', 'Daddy's boy'. The writer said that it was a mystery as to what Hayden actually did, other than attempting to 'constantly please Daddy'.

Andrew was puzzled. He thought the article was unpleasant. It was nasty about Hayden without actually saying anything. He wondered what Hayden had done to the writer to incur such malice. He looked for the name of the author, *Jane Pearson*. He looked her up and discovered that her previous job was on the *Daily National Post*, a Morgan-Lewis newspaper. Andrew assumed that the newspaper hadn't treated Jane very well or perhaps she had 'something going' with Hayden and had found out about the lovely Annabel. He noticed that there was a 'reply' to the article from *The Daily National Post* so he looked it up. It accused the Observer with getting its facts wrong, threatened to sue the newspaper and at the end said,

Far from having 'mediocre intellectual achievements,' Hayden Lewis was recognised in many academic circles as a scholarly person with a gifted, enquiring mind. He was a great friend of the late Mary Nichols and was of enormous assistance to her in her research.

Andrew looked up in disgust – How dare they say that? He quickly revised his opinion of the unfortunate Jane!

<u>Chapter Thirty-One</u>

'Mike, you're drunk!'

'I am not. I have been out for a meal and had something to go with it, and if you must know, I came home on the tube.'
Andrew sighed. It was now nearly midnight and he had been waiting for some hours to discuss his findings with Mike. He knew it wasn't reasonable to be annoyed but he was.
'Oh it's just that I wanted to discuss something with you,' he mumbled.

'That's fine. The night is young'

Andrew tried not to be irritated by Mike's obvious good humour but managed to relate to Mike, his revelations. He calmed down when Mike was obviously excited by them. After he had finished, Mike was quiet for a few minutes, then he said,
'As I see it there are four points of interest,

One – Hayden's relationship with the Farquhar's

Two – the Morgan-Lewis University,

Three – Doctor Thomas

Four – Jane'

Andrew was pleased that Mike had listened to his narrative and amazed at his lucidity.
'Do you think there is anything we can do?' he said.

'Yes, of course there is. There are lots of things. I don't know that there is much we can do about Doctor Thomas but it is interesting that that Morgan-Lewis obviously has some hold over him. Perhaps he was hypnotised.

About the Farquars – you know Lucy went to see the old boy at the House of Lords. She seems to be quite taken with him, charming, courteous, likes pretty girls, what what!'
Andrew laughed,

'I'm sure Lucy is a good judge of character.'

Mike screwed up his face,

'I don't know about that. She was quite taken in by Hayden Lewis and so was Mary. A handsome face and charming manner is particularly appealing to women.'
Andrew stopped himself from mentioning the fact that a pretty face was often the downfall of many men.
'But despite that, I think we can leave the Farquars to Lucy. Sir Alfred seems to be quite taken with her, well he would be wouldn't he, a stunner like Lucy? Anyway, he wants to introduce her to the lovely Charlotte. Lucy's not that keen. I can understand that. No-one with any sense would want to hobnob with those kinds of people.'
'What kind of people?'

'You know – hooray Henrys, chinless wonders, stick in the mud conservatives.'

'Lord Alfred is a Labour peer.'

'Champagne socialist but then aren't we all? But to get back to the point, I said to

Lucy that she should put her socialist principles to one side and . . .'

'I didn't know she had any.'

'Had any what?'

'Socialist principles.'

Mike looked shocked,

'Don't be ridiculous, Andy. You can't think a lovely, sensible girl like Lucy doesn't have principles! But she is willing to go back there if Sir Alf invites her to try and find out what is going on. He wants her to meet Charlotte but I think it's more important for her to meet the son.'

'Yes' agreed Andrew, 'I think you are right. We don't know much about him. He may be the one who knows Hayden. Is there anything that we could do to find out more about the Morgan-Lewis University?'

'I was thinking about that,' said Mike, 'It's possible that they could have taken copies of the *Good Book* there, as they have all these Welsh scholars, but we would need to find a way to find out.'

'I suppose,' said Andrew thoughtfully, 'that someone might be making translations quite innocently without being involved in the Morgan-Lewis machinations.'

'Yes, that's true and if one of us could get to know one of the students they might unwittingly give us some information. It's a pity that it's the end of term, we could have sent you on a course there.'

'But,' said Andrew, 'I could be thinking of applying there.'

'Brilliant!' said Mike, 'I wonder if there's some way we could involve Lucy. She's not old enough to be your mother but she could be your teacher, adviser or sister.'

Andrew laughed,

'She could. We could ask her what role she'd be most comfortable with.' 'Don't ask her to be your lover, that's all' said Mike darkly. Andrew spluttered,

'Even if she was, imagine introducing her to a tutor as "my lover"?'

Mike ignored the comment and went on,

'The other interesting connection is the lady with the viper's pen.'

'Jane'

'I think it would be quite easy to get an interview with Jane. All we need to do is to suggest that we have some dirt on Hayden Lewis.' Andrew looked uneasy. Mike turned to him,

'I know you have a tender conscience, Andy but fortunately I haven't. I think I could do that but at the moment my priority is a visit to young Johnny Judge.'
'Oh!' said Andrew, 'What's happened there?'

'They've arrested ken Weston. I don't know on what charge but Johnny said, "it might be of interest" to us. He wanted to call on me but I said I would go there.' 'Yes that would be more suitable.'

'Why? And don't say, so I can see his lovely wife.'

Andrew laughed,

'I wasn't going to say that. I just meant – well your flat I mean . . . .' 'What exactly do you mean?' asked Mike menacingly.
'I think I'll go to bed now, and you've got to get up early tomorrow.'

The following day, Andrew phoned Lucy. He knew he needed to be careful as it was important that the visit to the Morgan-Lewis University needed to be kept secret.
He started off by deliberately saying that since they had decided not to pursue their investigations, he hadn't seen her and wondered how she was.
'Oh, I'm fine,' she said, 'I've been working hard on the Gaimar and I hope to have a good holiday in the summer.'
'That's brilliant,' said Andrew, 'going anywhere nice?'

'Oh we haven't decided yet.'

'Going with a friend?'

'Yes, I've got a new boyfriend. What are you doing with yourself at the moment?'

'Nothing much, I'm going to see my Grandma this evening.'

'Are you? That's good. I'm sure she will be delighted to see you.'

'She will and I'm looking forward to a good meal. I might stay a few days.' 'That's great, well I won't keep you. I'd better get back to good old Gaimar. It was lovely to hear from you Andrew.' Andrew put the phone down. He was pleased as Lucy saying that his Grandmother would be 'delighted' to see him told him in their code that she would be coming to his grandma's but he did not like the reference to a 'boyfriend'. Could it be true? He shook his head. She was surely trying to make the conversation more authentic. He would put it out of his mind. He wouldn't think about it.

Chapter Thirty-two

' So,' whispered Andrew, as soon as his grandmother had left the room, 'what's this about a boyfriend?'
Lucy laughed but coloured slightly,

'Andy! Don't sound so fierce. I think you would prefer me to have robbed a bank!'

'So you have got one!'

'No, no, it was a joke, just a joke.'

'Oh, well, it doesn't matter anyway, I mean there's no reason why you shouldn't have a boyfriend.'
'Quite, now tell me, Andy, what did you want to talk about.'

Andrew told her about his findings and in particular about going to visit the Morgan-Lewis University. Lucy was quite excited.
'I think we should go soon before the research students leave for the holidays. I think I should go as I am, another research student so that it gives me a reason to talk about *The Good Book of Oxford*. I could be your aunt or cousin, someone associated with a university, who was advising you'
'Cousin, I think. Do you think we need assumed names?'

'Well, you do. You need to be a bit Welsh. I'm not sure about me.'

'How about Geraint Evans?'

'That's been done. You could be Geraint Jones. Half the people in Wales are called

Jones. Perhaps our fathers could be brothers and I could be Jones too, Myfanwy Jones. That's nice. If I had a false name, I could phone up and book an appointment. What do you want to study?'

'I originally wanted to do Physics, like my dad but I'm not sure now. Do you think I ought to say Welsh History or something?'

'No, I'll see to that and we don't want to make them suspicious. What A levels have you been studying?'

'Maths, Further Maths, Physics and . . . .' Andrew looked embarrassed.

'Well, I did an AS level in Chemistry and . . .'

'And what?'

'French, My parents thought I ought to study an Arts subject or a language, so I chose French as I got an A* in it at GCSE but as you can tell from our trip to
France, I'm useless at it. Mike's better than me and he only got a C, years ago.'

Lucy laughed,

'Yes, Mike does tend to hide his light under a bushel but you did very well in France and by the time I saw you, you weren't exactly at your best. I think that we will go along with those subjects exactly as they are, except that you will already have taken the exams.'

'They might wonder why a bright lad like me would want to go to a rubbish place like Morgan-Lewis.'

'It probably isn't rubbish if you want to do scientific research but we could say that although you are a really, bright lad you are not likely to do as well as expected because you have been ill or something. It's partly true anyway.' 'Yes, I don't want to sound like a weakling so perhaps I could have had a skiing accident. I did go skiing after Christmas.'

Andrew suddenly felt choked up as he remembered the skiing holiday he had had with his parents and his Uncle Simon's family. Lucy took his hand,

'That sounds great, Andy.'

'As long as I don't start blubbing.'

'It doesn't matter if you do. They will just think you are remembering your accident and the loss of a brilliant career. I will look up the prospectus of Morgan Lewis tomorrow. Oh here comes your Grandma with the dinner. Mrs Nichols, this looks delicious!'

The following Saturday, Mike set out to drive to Stevenage to visit John Judge. He felt very curious about the arrest of Ken Weston particularly as John had said that it had some bearing on the Tremayne's case.

John had invited him to lunch which was always a draw for Mike. He wondered too if he might once again set eyes on the lovely Virginia.

He was in luck, as this time it was Virginia who cooked the lunch.

'I hope you like curry, Mike. This is one of Johnny's favourites,' said Virginia as she came in, carrying a large steaming dish. John jumped up to take it from her.

'Thai Green Curry,' he said proudly, 'everyone likes this.'

'Of course,' beamed Mike who had never heard of it, let alone tasted it.

The curry was indeed delicious and Mike made a mental note to recommend it to Andrew. He gave it fulsome praise which he could see pleased both Virginia and John.

He was hoping for some pudding to follow but John placed a bowl of fruit on the table saying,

'We don't usually have a sweet but we do have fruit which is of course healthier.' Mike agreed with perhaps less enthusiasm. He supposed that this practice enabled Virginia to keep her sylph like figure. He picked up a banana, wondering as he did so whether he would prefer puddings and a wife with a less perfect figure. He decided that he wouldn't mind her eating fruit as long as she made puddings for him.

After demolishing a satsuma, Virginia got up from the table,

'Please excuse me. I am going to an art exhibition this afternoon. I'll leave you boys to your discussions.'

After a few desultory comments about their health and the weather, Mike decided it was time to get down to business.

'So what's this about Ken Weston?'

'Well, it's all rather strange,' John lowered his voice as if someone might be listening.

'This is all highly confidential, you understand?' 'Of course,' whispered Mike.

John continued,

'Ken was arrested about ten days ago in Walthamstow in east London for a petty burglary. He wasn't granted bail as he had bashed someone on the head and the man was still recovering in hospital. I heard about it as Ken's accomplice, Barry Lambert was from Stevenage and there had been a similar burglary here about six weeks ago. In both cases a house had been broken into and ransacked as though the perpetrators were looking for something. The two cases were also similar in that small amounts of money and jewellery were taken, the likelihood being that it was just what the burglars had seen lying around. The only difference was that in the robbery in Stevenage, there was no-one in the house and so nobody was hurt.'

'So how does that affect our investigations into the death of the Tremaynes?' 'Well in the course of the police investigations, the houses of the two men were searched. In the two houses, the police were surprised to find manuscripts in the ancient Welsh language.' Mike sat up excitedly,
'*The Good Book of Oxford*?'

'We don't know for certain. It seems strange that Ken and his friend didn't find them because the police found them relatively easily.'
'Perhaps they didn't recognise them for what they were.'

'I suspect that was the case. They were photocopies. They were just left in a pile of academic documents and nowhere was *The Good Book of Oxford* mentioned.'
'What about the people they belonged to?'

'They said that they had been sent the manuscripts by academic friends for them to look at and possible translate but neither of them spoke Welsh. I would like to question them further.
The policemen, who did the search, unsurprisingly had never heard of the book.

When the manuscripts were mentioned to me, I said I was interested and because I went to university and they think I'm some kind of intellectual, they agreed to leave that with me. I also said I had a friend who was knowledgeable about old manuscripts. Another interesting fact was a letter, found in Gary's house. It was just signed with the letter 'Z''
'What did it say?'

'I have a copy here.' John showed Mike an A4 sheet of paper with no address or date. The words on it were typed. It said,
Fix brakes and steering as arranged, ready for Tuesday.

At the bottom of the page, written in bold and large type were the words,

---

Burn This.

John laughed,

'The stupid thing is nobody would have even noticed that piece of paper if it wasn't for those two words, as Ken is a car mechanic'
'I wonder,' said Mike, 'why he didn't burn it.'

John sighed,

'I suppose there could be various reasons. I mean if Ken was to take the instruction literally, he would need to have a fire or at least a match. In the past everyone would have had access to both but if he didn't smoke and had an electric cooker, it would have required a bit of an effort and he may just not have got round to it. On the other hand he may have kept it as a safeguard to blame someone else for his actions. He could then say he was 'told' to do something or he could have used it for blackmail.'
'It only gives us 'Z' which doesn't really incriminate anyone. Was there a date on it? I mean if it was a computer printout it would have had a date on the bottom.' 'No, it was just like this copy. The 'Z' might not be as useless as you think as if we found other communications from 'Z' it would build up the evidence.'
'Have you found any other missives signed 'Z'?'

'No not as yet but then we haven't looked. There are many police authorities who don't communicate everything to each other.'
John looked at Mike with a sad, expression,
'Mike, do you remember what day of the week, Mary and her husband died?'

'No, but I can easily find out.'

'I don't want to bring it up yet,' said John, answering Mike's unspoken question, 'because as far as the police are concerned the episode was an accident. They would wonder why I was connecting the two. We need to find more evidence before we go ahead.'

Mike looked at John with gratitude. He appreciated the 'we' that John used and he knew that he could be confident that John would do what he could. 'About the Birford Police, I contacted Adrian who said he would look into it. He phoned me last week to tell me that he had found nothing. Wilkinson seems to be highly regarded. The men like him and he is a very competent police officer.

Those men who investigated the so-called 'accident' didn't have anything to add.

They seemed to accept it was an accident and. . .'

"And what?'

'Well I know it's very painful, Mike but the fire was so huge and so hot there was nothing they could find.'

'I know,' said Mike, 'but what did they think caused it? Did they really think Frank was drunk?'

'I don't think so. They seemed to assume that he had some sort of seizure or a heart attack.'

'Did anyone contact his doctor?'

'I think someone did but he said that Frank never went to the doctor's, had never been to hospital, never had any examinations and so they had very little to go on. There was one thing that Adrian said about Wilkinson. I don't know whether it is of any significance. Apparently on some social occasion, a group of police officers including Wilkinson were having a drink. They were talking about holidays. Someone had just come back from Wales. He said what a nice place the little town of

Cardigan was then he turned to Wilkinson and said,

'Of course you know the area, didn't you work in Cardigan for a while?'

Wilkinson fairly snapped at him saying,

"No, no, I was much further north."

This happened some time before I asked Adrian to investigate Wilkinson but he was curious and looked up Wilkinson's career. Wilkinson hadn't worked as a policeman in Cardigan but Adrian found out from a former secretary that Wilkinson had lived and worked in Cardigan for some time before he joined the police force.'
'Did he investigate it further?'

'No he just thought that Wilkinson had been telling the truth in so far as he wasn't a policeman in Cardigan but he was curious as to why he just didn't say so.'
Mike laughed,

'It sounds as though a bit of sleuthing in Cardigan might be profitable! But Johnny, what happens now?'
'Well I will pick up the manuscripts. I think they are probably photocopies. I don't know. I assume your friend Lucy would be the person to contact and I can quite legitimately contact her. It would be better if I contacted her directly so I should be grateful if you would give me her address. It would be useful if you could find the date of the car crash and the police will continue to question Barry and Ken and to investigate Mr Z.'
'Thanks Johnny, you're a good friend.'

As Mike drove back towards the A1, he mused to himself about Johnny Judge. He felt guilty about all the nasty things he had thought and said about him. It was true, he was very different from him but there should be room for all sorts of people. Johnny was a thoroughly decent chap. Mike looked around him at the leafy lanes between John's suburban home and the motorway. Different but very pleasant he thought, pleased at his new tolerant, philosophical outlook. The car swerved,

'Concentrate, Mike, stop this distraction' he told himself as he turned the wheel of the car. The car didn't respond, Mike swore loudly. He pressed the brake. No response. Mike swore even more loudly. He pulled at the handbrake. The handbrake of this old car had never been very effective but it did respond slightly, but caused the car to swerve even more dangerously into the middle of the road. Mike looked ahead. There was a bend in the road but he knew the car would not go round the bend. He was facing the sturdy stone wall of a country house. Mike acted quickly. He released his seat belt, opened the door, brought his knees up to his chest, and threw himself into the road. At the back of his mind, he knew this was dangerous as the car was going at about thirty miles an hour.

Mike rolled into the road banging his head in the process. He heard another car coming towards him.

'This is it.' He said as he lost consciousness.

Chapter thirty-three

At the same time that Mike was going North to Stevenage, Lucy and Andrew were going West to South Wales. They decided that they would address each other as 'Geraint' and 'Myfanwy' so they would get used to it.

'What I don't understand, Myfanwy,' said Andrew, 'is why they wanted us to go on a Saturday. Most people are not working on Saturdays.'

'The woman in Admissions said that next week was going to be pretty hectic as it was the end of exams and there would be 'vivas' and results and that sort of thing, whereas today she would be there and some young Physicist whom we could talk to. It might be better for our purposes, I don't know.'

Andrew shrugged his shoulders,

'Well, it's a nice day for a trip to the countryside. This is a great car, Lucy. How fast will it go?'

Lucy slowed down from her eighty miles an hour speed,

'Seventy miles an hour' she said, 'The people who owned it before me recommended it as it did a lot of miles to the litre.'

'I was learning to drive,' said Andrew sadly, 'Perhaps you could teach me Lucy, I mean Myfanwy.'

'Why don't you ask Mike? He's the one with a car.'

'I think I would rather learn on a newer car. The MG is fun and all that but not very reliable.'

'I think we should practice our stories. We are both Welsh but brought up in

England – hence our accents. Our fathers were brothers, Hywel and Emlyn Jones.

They came from North Wales and went to Bangor University. They moved to

England for their jobs but loved Wales and we went frequently for holidays to the North Wales Coast and Snowdonia. We can say that because it is partly true. You used to go with your parents to Llandudno and I have been walking with a student group in Snowdonia.

Lucy and Andrew rehearsed their backgrounds during the next hundred miles, then Lucy pulled into a service station.

'We set off from your grandmother's very early. I think we should have some breakfast,' she said.

While they were eating, Andrew perused the map.

'We need to turn off at junction 25A' he said, 'towards Abergavenny. It looks to be in a very remote place.'

'Yes I should imagine it is very picturesque. The original buildings were part of a stately home.'

'It doesn't look as though it would be very lively for students,' remarked Andrew. They set off again and managed to arrive at the reception entrance at ten minutes to eleven. Lucy sighed with relief,

'Ten minutes to spare! I thought we would never get here – all those winding roads!'

At the reception desk, Lucy asked for a Mrs Nerris Evans. The young receptionist pressed a few buttons and Mrs Evans appeared promptly. Mrs Evans was a large lady with an extremely wrinkled face. She had long, black, obviously dyed hair, tied back in a bun. She was, however, very smartly dressed in a navy-blue suit, mauve blouse and expensive jewellery.

'Myfanwy and Geraint?' she said as soon as she saw them, 'I hope you didn't have too much difficulty finding us.'

Lucy assured her that they didn't.

'Come into my office,' she said and they followed her into a spacious, comfortable room. The walls were lined with pictures of Wales; some were photographs, others, paintings.

Lucy immediately exclaimed at the lovely pictures and Andrew muttered in agreement.

'Well we are so lucky to live in such a beautiful country,' said Mrs Evans, 'now to business — you must be Geraint.' She turned to Andrew and put out her hand.

Andrew shook it warmly and managed a smile. Lucy smiled too as she was amused that Andrew was following her instructions so carefully.

'So what makes you think Morgan-Lewis is the place for you?'

'Well, I er . . . want to do Physics and I have heard that it is a good place.'

'Who told you? Where did you get your information?'

Andrew looked helplessly at Lucy. She leaned forward, saying,

'I am a research student in a university. Geraint was worried about his A levels. He was expected to get at least 3 A stars but following a skiing accident he was unable to keep up his studies as he would have wished. He realised his results would not really show his capabilities so he came to ask me for advice.' 'Why doesn't he repeat the year?' asked Mrs Evans sharply.

'I'm afraid I just didn't want to,' said Andrew, 'I know it's probably my best option but I don't relish the thought of going back to school in September when all my friends have gone off to university.' Andrew said this with sincerity and Mrs Evans looked sympathetic.

Lucy continued,

'Although we are both Welsh we hadn't heard of Morgan-Lewis but I discovered the prospectus and I thought it might suit Geraint. I know it is private and his father would have to pay for him but I think my uncle would be pleased to pay to ensure that Geraint gets the opportunities that he needs. In any case nowadays all students end up in debt.'

'That's true,' said Mrs Evans, 'but you can get loans you know,'

'There are a couple of other reasons why this place attracted me,' said Andrew.

Mrs Evans looked up and smiled. She looked as though she was mellowing a bit,

'And what would those be, young man?'

'I am quite passionate about Physics and I read on the internet that there are opportunities here to do post-graduate studies which I would love to do. Also because I have lived all my life in England, I would very much like to learn more about Wales and if possible learn the language.'

Mrs Evans looked pleased,

'Yes, everyone here has the opportunity to learn Welsh. It is part of the basic curriculum. Are you good at languages?'

Andrew coloured slightly,

'I did get an A star for GCSE French and I am er, did, A level French but I'm not expecting to do brilliantly.'

'Well that sounds promising. I shall give you some forms to fill in. You can fill them in now or fill them in later and send them. Then I shall introduce you to our young Physicist.

'Oh I'll send them,' said Andrew.

'Yes, that will give you time to think about it,' said Lucy.

'Right, well come on then. I will take you to the Physics department.

Mrs Evans set out at a fast pace out of the old building across a courtyard, into a modern four story block, up two flights of stairs and down some long corridors.

She flung open the door of a laboratory and called out,

'Alun, here are your visitors!' with that she departed briskly.

A tall, thin, gangly, young man appeared from behind a large desk. He went to the door and looked out, saying,

'Has the old witch gone?' Lucy looked up in surprise while Andrew giggled.

Alun took of his glasses and wiped them,

'She's not your mother or anything is she?'

Alun didn't wait for an answer, but replaced his glasses and held out his hand, first to Lucy and then to Andrew, 'Alun Morris' he said.

Andrew was about to say, 'Andrew Tremayne' when Lucy quickly broke in with,

'Myfanwy and Geraint Jones.'

Alun laughed,

'Properly Welsh then.'

Both Lucy and Andrew looked slightly embarrassed. Neither of them were good liars or deceivers. Andrew reflected that Mike would have taken it in his stride but perhaps a fake Welsh accent and a smattering of 'boyos' would have soon been detected.

Alun seemed to sense their embarrassment,

'How about a cup of coffee? I make a good brew up here in the lab. I have all the equipment.'

Lucy and Andrew agreed gratefully. While Lucy watched Alun making the coffee, Andrew wandered round the laboratory.

'Coffee up!' shouted Alun and produced a battered tin containing a variety of biscuits. As they drank their coffee, Andrew asked Alun various questions about the equipment in the lab. They seemed to be having a good discussion and Andrew was obviously impressed by the expensive instruments. Lucy was impressed by Andrew's knowledge and interest in the subject. It was a side of him she hadn't seen before. After the coffee, Alun took Andrew round the lab and talked to him about the research he was doing. Lucy looked aimlessly out of the window at the lovely view which stretched out towards the Brecon Beacons.

When they returned, Alun turned to Andrew,

'What I want to know is why the hell would a young lad like you want to come to a place like this?' Andrew looks slightly startled. It was really the same question asked by Mrs Evans, only phrased differently.

'What's wrong with it? He asked rather timidly.

'What's right with it? Is more the question. Look it's fine for me. I am very keen on the research I'm doing and old Sir Gareth pours money into this place like water. I hope to get my Ph.D. and then to move on in the academic world. I am able to run a car so I can get about. But for undergraduates it's a disaster. There's hardly any transport and the nearest clubs are about forty miles away. We do have a students' Union of sorts and there is a bar which is something as the nearest country pub is a two mile walk.

The countryside is beautiful and some of the students go mountaineering and rock-climbing but not everyone's into that and a good view isn't every young feller's idea of heaven and another thing, there are very few girls and those that are here haven't been chosen for their looks, probably by that old bat, Nerris.' Andrew looked taken aback so Lucy gave the same answer that they had given Mrs Evans without stressing the Welshness. Alun looked thoughtful. He turned to Andrew

'I can see your point about not wanting to repeat the year and if you've got a wealthy Dad so much the better but if I were you I wouldn't go back to your old school. I'd keep all the notes and perhaps nick a few from your friends of the bits you've missed as it sounds as though you have had good teachers, but you could go somewhere else or try a Sixth Form College. I think some of them are fun. If you are doing French, go over there, get a holiday job there or live with a family for a bit. Tell me, are you really that keen on all this Welsh stuff?'

Andrew looked embarrassed,

'Not really, I like Wales but we thought it would help to get in.'

'It certainly does. Don't get me wrong. I love Wales. I have lived here all my life and if it were possible I would like to go on living here but – you probably don't know much about Gareth Morgan-Lewis. He's a complete nutcase. I doubt if he's got a drop of Welsh blood in him but I think he sees it as a way to joining the aristocracy. He can't pretend that he's related to the Windsors or any of the Dukes so he tries to claim some Royal Welsh ancestry. He has been over here a couple of times. Last time he gave a speech in the Union all about being Welsh. He was quite poetic about it and very persuasive. I think he must have been swotting up some of Hitler's speeches about the Arian race and just changed it to 'Celtic'. I felt quite moved myself for a while but some of them were quite bowled over.'

'Are most of the students here Welsh?' asked Lucy.

'Yes or purport to be,' said Alun, 'you see that's another thing. Most Universities have a good mix of nationalities, races, colours, religions and so on but here they are all white and English/Welsh speaking. It's not good. Universities should be places where you broaden your outlook not make it narrower.'

'Do the people here share your opinions' asked Lucy.

'Good God, no. There are 'thought police' here. One has to be careful. For most of them it's "Welsh, good, everything else, bad."'
'Aren't you afraid of speaking like this to us?' continued Lucy.

Alun smiled,

'I am a bit but I am impressed by your young cousin, here. I think he will make a great Physicist and you – well. It's a bit of a monastery here.' He turned away in embarrassment but then turned back and continued,

'I do rather like some of the 'Welsh bit'. I mean the Celtic History has been neglected and some of the research here is great. The Welsh department were given some very interesting old documents to translate recently. I have a friend in that department and she showed me some of them. They really were wonderful.' Both Andrew and Lucy tried not to show their excitement at this statement.
Lucy said,

'Oh that is interesting. I have been working on something similar myself, *L'Estoire des Engleis* by Geffrei Gaimar
'Oh! Have you? Are yours in Welsh?'

'Some pieces but most of it is in French and Latin. Yours must be very old. Do you know what it is called?'
'No, it's strange but they seem to be very secretive about it. Lizzie, that's the girl I know, said they would have been very annoyed if they knew she had shown it to me.'
He suddenly looked mischievous, 'would you like to see it?'

Lucy sighed,

'Oh I would love to but I don't want to get anyone into trouble.'

'That's OK. There's hardly anyone here but I know Lizzie is as we are going into

Builth Wells for lunch. Just wait here.'

Alun rushed off. He was away for some time.

Lucy and Andrew looked at each other in excitement. They could hardly believe their luck!

'I expect he's having to persuade her,' said Andrew. 'Yes, poor girl. I hope we are not putting her job in danger.' 'Or her life' said Andrew ominously.

Some minutes later Alun returned with a pretty young girl. She was slightly built with curly brown hair held back by a blue ribbon. Lucy thought she looked like Alice in Wonderland.

'I'm sorry we kept you waiting,' she said in a pleasant, lilting Welsh voice, 'but Alun thought it would be better to photocopy it as only some of it has been translated and then you can take your time and do the rest yourself. I just work in the office. I'm not academic or anything but I do think some of it is rather lovely.' 'This is confidential,' put in Alun, 'I don't want Lizzie to suffer for it, so don't spread it around.'

Lizzie looked up at Alun,

'But I might be moving anyway,' she said, 'I've applied to the Central Wales

College to do A levels so I might be going to University myself soon.'

'Not for a while yet, love,' said Alun. He gave a mass of photocopied sheets to Lucy,
'I hope you enjoy it'

'Thank you so much,' said Lucy, 'this is wonderful'

Alun picked up his jacket to leave and they all moved out of the building.

He shook hands with Lucy and Andrew.

'It was great to meet you,' he said and turning to Andrew said, 'and I don't want to see you here in September.'

Lucy hurriedly put the papers under her coat as her handbag wasn't big enough and they made their way to their respective cars.

'That went off really well,' said Andrew as they drove down the country lanes. 'Yes it did. I haven't had time to look at the photocopies of the *Good Book* but it looks as though there's a lot there. Yes it did go well for us but . . . '

'But what?'

'Oh nothing much, I feel sorry for Lizzie. That's all'

'You mean because she might get into trouble for giving us the photocopies.' 'Possibly,' said Lucy thoughtfully, 'but it's just that you can see she absolutely worships Alun.'

'How do you know?'

'Didn't you see the way she looked at him?'

'I didn't notice but what's wrong with that?'

Lucy laughed,

'You are not very observant, Andrew. Oh it's just that she's about eighteen and he must be at least thirty and I'm sure he's fond of her, encouraging her to get an education and so on but . . .'

'You think he will let her down. I suppose he will but she must be aware of the difference in ages and I suppose it's just sort of hero worship and well, he seemed a really nice chap. She'll get over it. When she goes to College, she'll probably meet a dashing young fellow of her own age. It may be Alun that ends up broken hearted!'

Lucy laughed again,

'You're probably right and it has been a good day. Shall we stop in the next town for some lunch?'

'Not in Builth Wells!'

Chapter Thirty-Four

Mike tossed from side to side. He was in pain. His head hurt. He opened his eyes.

He heard a voice say,

'He's coming round.' He shut his eyes again. He didn't want to 'come round'. He wanted to go back to sleep and shut out the pain. He couldn't. He groaned. He wanted to swear violently but he couldn't. He opened his eyes again and grabbed his head. All he could utter was,
'Oh no, oh no, oh God!'

He felt someone injecting him in the arm. Someone said,

'That should ease the pain a bit.' It did.
Mike opened his eyes again. He could see a man and a woman both in white overalls. The man was leaning over him, 'Are you all right? Can you speak?' he said.
Mike muttered a 'yes'.

'I hope the pain has eased a little. We gave you some morphine. Has it helped?'

'Yes, thank you, yes, yes. Where am I?'

Mike felt the inanity of the question as soon as he asked it. He also felt very stupid. He should know where he was but he didn't.
'Good,' said the man, 'You are in Welwyn General Hospital. You have had serious concussion. Can you remember what happened?'
Mike looked up at the ceiling. This was a hospital. He was here for concussion.

Why? He didn't know.

'I don't know anything,' he said. The woman then spoke, 'What's your name?' she said.
'Mike looked at her blankly.

'Don't worry. You have lost your memory. It will probably only be temporary. Just shut your eyes and go back to sleep. You will be right as rain by tomorrow.'

Mike felt a surge of panic. He didn't know his own name! He didn't want to be here tomorrow. They might put him in a straight-jacket and throw him into a lunatic asylum! Fortunately for his peace of mind, he fell asleep almost immediately.
He felt someone gently tapping on his shoulder,

'Mr Nichols, you have a visitor,'

Mike opened his eyes and looked up. A tall thin man stood in front of him. He had dark hair cut very short and a small, trim moustache. He was casually, well-dressed, wearing a polo-necked sweater, a tweed jacket and brown corduroy trousers.
Mike looked at him,

'A policeman?' he said.

'Quite right,' laughed the man, 'poor old Mike. You don't look too good. I hope it's not too painful'
'Ah,' thought Mike, 'my name's Mike. I'll tell that nurse. She will have to let me go.'
He looked again at the man, 'Johnny,' he said slowly.
John Judge looked relieved,

'They told me you had lost your memory. I suppose it often happens but you seem to be getting it back.'
Mike tried to sit up,

'Johnny,' he said, 'You shouldn't be here! They tried to kill me. Go quickly! Go

Johnny, you've got a wife and a child to think of.'

Mike lay back and clutched his head. He felt agitated, distraught. Everything began flooding back. John walked across the room to a nurse who came over to Mike. She gave him a couple of tablets in a little cup and gave him some water.
'Drink this, Mr Nichols. It will help you feel better.' Mike looked suspiciously at the tablets.

'They are just painkillers,' whispered John.

Mike took them, then shut his eyes for a few minutes. He felt better.

'It's true though, Johnny. You shouldn't be here.'

'Can you remember what happened?' asked Johnny, gently.

'Yes, I think so,' said Mike, 'I left your house and was driving down a country lane. I was admiring the scenery, wondering if I would like to live in the country and then we were going down a hill with a bend at the bottom.'
'We?'

'Me and the car,' said Mike irritably, 'I thought it was just the distraction but the brake didn't work and neither did the steering wheel. I was going full pelt into a big brick wall. I thought I'd had it.' Mike thought for a bit.
'I don't remember anything else,' he said, 'until I woke up here. How do you come to be here?'
'I had a message that there had been an accident on Heathbury Hill and that someone was injured. I immediately thought of you even though I thought it unlikely so I drove over there. You had already been taken off in an ambulance but I recognised the car.'

'Was it recognisable then? I thought it would have been burnt up like Mary and Frank's'

'It didn't catch fire. I don't know why. There was a young sergeant there who was just about to get a local garage to tow it away. I thought there was a possibility of foul play so I just got him to put some blue tape round it. I have sent some of the fingerprint lads over there to see if they can find anything and then I will get a mechanic to go over it to see if there is any evidence of foul play.'

'There definitely was foul play. I can tell you that,' said Mike belligerently. 'I know Mike,' said John patiently, 'but if we don't find any evidence they could just say you were asleep at the wheel just like poor Frank.'

Mike sighed,

'Mary and Frank! I suppose I got off lightly, but we know it wasn't Ken. He's safely locked up. Isn't he?'

'Yes he's been in custody for over a week so he doesn't seem a likely candidate.'

Just then a nurse came in and said,

'Mr Nichols, there are two more visitors here, your nephew and a young lady, a

Miss Lucy Hammond. Do you feel well enough to receive them?'

'Of course,' said Mike impatiently, 'send them in.'

The nurse went off and they could hear her telling Andrew and Lucy that they must not tire the patient.

Andrew came in first. He looked pale and strained,

'Hello Mike, are you all right. Have you got your memory back?'

'Of course,' Mike laughed, 'nothing wrong with me. I am ready to come home.'

Lucy then came in,

'Oh Mike! What a terrible thing to happen! Can you speak?'

Mike laughed again and John found a chair for Lucy and put it by the bedside.

Mike reached over and took her hand.

'Lucy did you come by car? You could take me home.' Lucy looked doubtfully at Mike's bandaged head.
Mike continued,

'Andy, this is Johnny Judge. Do you remember him?'

Andrew looked at John

'Yes, I remember seeing him at Grandma's. It's good to see you Johnny.'

John laughed and shook Andrew's hand,

'I remember you but you've grown a lot. How old are you now? Fifteen, sixteen?' 'Seventeen,' said Andrew coldly – grown a lot! 'And this is our good friend Lucy.'

'I've heard a lot about you Lucy,' said John.

Mike then proceeded to tell them everything that had happened. Andrew looked on with irritation as Mike continued to hold Lucy's hand.
'You can tell by her face that it's annoying her' he thought, 'why is Mike so insensitive?'
As they were speaking the nurse returned and told the visitors that Mike needed to have something to eat and to rest.
Mike sat up,

'After I've eaten, my friends could take me home. They've got a car.'

The nurse smiled,

'I think you will need to spend at least one more night here. I'll check with the doctor.'

A trolley was wheeled round to Mike's bed and he was given his evening meal. It didn't appear to be very appetising but Mike fell on it with relish and demolished it within minutes.

'That was good,' he said, 'now where are my clothes?'

'Not so fast, young man,' said the man in the white coat who has suddenly appeared, 'You have had very serious concussion and we need to do a few more tests before you can leave. I was just coming along to advise that you had a brain scan. I think that if that's OK, your friends might be able to pick you up tomorrow.

He turned to Andrew, Lucy and John,

'I suggest that you wait in the waiting room down the corridor and someone will bring you the results of the scan'

Mike sighed but lay down and accepted the decision.

'See you in a few minutes,' he called out as the others were led down the corridor.

While they were waiting, John explained the situation with regard to Gary Weston. Lucy and Andrew told him about their trip to Wales.

'That sounds as though it could be very useful,' said John. He turned to Lucy,

'If I were you, I should put copies of everything you've got from The Good Book of

Oxford, into a safe.'

Lucy and Andrew agreed.

'I don't think Mike is really ready to go home,' said Johnny, 'Who will look after him?'

'Well if he goes to Streatham, I will,' said Andrew rather huffily, 'but we could take him to his mother's in Letbury'

'Good idea,' said John, 'it would be useful as I could visit him there when I get the results of the car investigation. I often pop down to see my mum so it would be easy enough to call in.'

'That sounds like a good plan,' said Lucy, 'and here comes the nurse with the results.'

The nurse opened her folder,

'You will be pleased to know there is nothing wrong with Mr Nicholl's brain,' she said.

'Are you sure?' said Andrew, 'Perhaps you need to do another one?'

John gave a great guffaw but Lucy looked shocked. The nurse ignored Andrew's comments.

'Who is offering to take him home?'

'I am' said Lucy. The nurse turned to Lucy,

'Telephone in the morning after half past eight and ask for Azalea ward and whoever is on duty will let you know. I will tell Mr Nicholls as I think it would be better if he didn't have any more excitement.'

They all left the hospital together then John Judge said 'Goodbye' to Lucy and Andrew.

'He seems a very nice man,' said Lucy, 'I don't know what Mike had against him.' 'Oh Mike only likes weirdos like himself. He despises anyone who is just ordinary and decent.'

Lucy laughed but she was rather surprised by the oddly bitter tone of Andrew's reply.

Chapter Thirty-five

'Andy, will you do me a favour?'

'What's that?' Andrew answered sleepily.

He and Mike were sprawled out on Margaret's sofa watching back episodes of *Top Gear,* Margaret having gone to bed.
'Well there are two jobs that I said I would do, one, going to Cardigan and see if I could suss out something about the lovely Inspector Wilkinson and the other was going to visit the sharp-tongued Jane. As you know I am practically back to my old, healthy self but I am not quite as quick off the mark as usual and I wondered if you would go to Cardigan, while I visit Jane. I think I would be better doing that as I am harder than you and more suspicious, also she's a woman and . . .'
'You are an experienced ladies' man'

'Well, you have to admit it, I do know a bit about women, what makes them tick and that sort of thing.'
'Mmm,' said Andrew, 'and it's not as far to go as Cardigan. I'll go tomorrow, might as well get on with it. Let's think of some ways of finding out about him. The following morning, found Andrew on the train to Cardigan. The journey took some time as he had to change at Birford. Andrew recalled his trip to Birford to visit the Chief Inspector. It seemed years ago and yet it was only a few weeks. He had felt so nervous and had been still very shaky after his parents' deaths. Now he felt much more confident. He had reluctantly to admit that he was grateful to Mike for helping him recover.
The night before, they had agreed that the best thing to do was to go to the Police Station first. After getting off the train, Andrew looked for a taxi. He found one, got in and said rather grandly,

'Cardigan Police station please.' The taxi driver looked surprised but Andrew took no notice and stared out of the window but to his embarrassment, the taxi went a few yards round the corner and stopped.

'Cardigan Police Station,' called out the taxi driver.

Red-faced, Andrew handed him a five-pound note and hurried into the Police Station.

'And what can I do for you, young man,' asked a young sergeant behind the desk. 'I wonder if you can help me,' Andrew began, 'I'm trying to track down a relative of mine, a Peter Wilkinson, I believe he was a policeman here some years ago.' 'I could look in the register,' said the obliging sergeant.

Andrew thought he was going to get a large file but he just switched on the computer.

The sergeant looked through the files on the computer then looked up,

'I can't find a Peter Wilkinson' he said, 'there was a Nigel Wilkinson in 1992. Could that be the one?'

'No' said Andrew disconsolately, 'but thanks anyway.' He turned to walk away. He was just walking through the door when a constable, an older man approached him.

'I overheard you asking about a Peter Wilkinson.' 'Yes' said Andrew hopefully.

'Well a Peter Wilkinson used to live next door to my sister about ten years ago.

But he was nothing to do with the police.'

'That could be him,' said Andrew, 'Do you know what happened to him?' 'No,' said the constable, 'but I remember the name as he was quite friendly with my sister's family for a while and then left in a bit of a hurry.'

'Does your sister still live there,'

'No, she moved to Birmingham but some of the neighbours still live there. She keeps in touch with one of them. They might be able to help you.'

'That's great,' said Andrew, 'Could you give me the address?'

The policeman wrote it down and handed it to Andrew who then asked for directions. He decided to walk. It was a nice day and Acacia Avenue was quite a long, winding road so it shouldn't be too difficult to find.

The constable had said that his sister had lived in number seventy-two so Andrew tried number seventy. A young woman with a baby in her arms answered the door.

'I'm sorry we've only lived here for two years,' she said.

Andrew tried seventy-four. An old man answered the door.

'Yes, I remember Peter Wilkinson,' he said, 'come in. Cup of tea? I was just about to brew up. Do you want one?'

Andrew thanked him and stepped into the house. He was surprised to find it meticulously clean and tidy. He noticed pictures of ships on the walls and a model ship on a table.

'Were you in the navy?' asked Andrew.

'Forty years,' said the man, 'I joined up as a young lad in the war. I've seen some action; I can tell you. I was at the battle of Cape Manahan you know.

Andrew expressed interest.

'Terrible it was. My ship was torpedoed but some of us managed to get away.' He then proceeded to describe the gory details at great length.

'You certainly did see some action,' said Andrew.

The man put a tray down on a highly polished table.

'I did. I was at the battle of Anzio. You must have heard of that.'

Andrew wondered how he was going to re-introduce the subject of Peter Wilkinson. He felt he must show some interest in the exploits of the old man who was obviously lonely and was enjoying the occasion.

After going into all the details of the battle of Anzio the old man said,

'But you wanted to know about Peter Wilkinson?'

'Yes,' said Andrew, 'I need to get in touch with him on behalf of a relative.' 'Well I don't know where he is now, so I can't help you there but I did know the lad, lived next door for a while, was always pleasant and obliging. I used to have a dog and he would take it for a run and look after it when I went to my sister's, nice lad but I think he got into a bit of trouble.'

Andrew tried not to sound too interested,

'What happened?'

'I'm not really sure, I think it was probably drugs. All the young people seemed to be into that sort of thing at the time.' Andrew nodded.

'And then he had this girlfriend, pretty girl, long, blond hair, Stacy, yes, that was her name and of course he was a good-looking lad. Well she used to come regular-like, stayed the night as often as not. Well it was none of my business and the young people nowadays have different ways of carrying on. In my day, it wouldn't have been allowed.'

'How did you know he was on drugs?'

'I'm coming to that. This girl committed suicide, terrible thing, strung herself up. Poor lad, he was in a bad way. They had an inquest and it seemed she was an addict, heroin, I think, and he was blamed, he'd been supplying her. I suppose they were both at it. Well everyone thought he was going to be arrested but he wasn't, at least I don't think so. He worked for a local newspaper, reporting, that sort of thing, called himself Dai Evans on the newspaper, thought he'd be a bit Welsh I suppose being in Wales and writers do have their pen-names don't they? Anyway, the owner of the newspaper was very kind to him and gave him another chance. Someone said it was that famous man, Sir Gareth Morgan Lewis. He's a good man gives a lot to charity. Well Peter left then and someone said Sir Gareth had paid for him to go to University, treated him like a son, he did, a good man.'

'That is interesting,' said Andrew, 'You have been very helpful,'

'Sorry, I can't tell you what happened to him.'

'Oh I'm sure your information will help me to find him,' said Andrew, 'Do you know of anyone else around here that might have kept in touch with him?' 'Oh I don't know. The young couple the other side moved to Birmingham. Wait a minute! He and Kevin Morris were very pally, used to play football together. He might know.'

'Where does he live?'

'Other side of the road – odd numbers, eighty-three I think. Try there.' Andrew stood up.

'Thank you very much for your help. It has been very interesting talking to you especially about your wartime experiences.'

'Yes, they are interesting aren't they? It's been a pleasure talking to you. I hope you find what you want.'

Andrew waved goodbye, walked down the path and crossed the road. He felt quite excited. He had had a bit of unexpected good luck with the garrulous old man but he was puzzled. Why should Sir Gareth take all that trouble to protect him?

He knocked at the door of number eighty-three. A woman came to the door whom Andrew estimated to be in her sixties.

'Can I help you?'

'Does Kevin Morris live here?'

'No, dear, he did. I'm his mother, Kathleen Morris, but he's working in Cardiff now. He's doing well there. He works on the docks. Do you want his address?' 'A phone number would be good or an email address but perhaps you could help me. I'm trying to track down a long lost relative, Peter Wilkinson. Did you know him.'

Mrs Morris pursed her lips in disapproval.

'I did know him, though he was known as Dai Evans round here, and I regretted it, sorry him being your relative and that but he was a bad un. I was glad when he left, not a good influence on our Kevin.'

'Do you know what happened to him?'

'He should have been locked up, that's what, dealing in drugs and sending a young girl to her death but he got away with it. I always say it's who you know what matters.'

'And who did he know?'

'Oh some rich toff, that Morgan-Lewis, Dai was friendly with his son. I think they worked together. I suspect that he was mixed up with the drug- dealing as well. I wouldn't be surprised; I mean why else would he have used his money and influence to keep Dai out of Gaol? That's the trouble with this country, one law for the rich and another one for the rest of us. Well I mustn't keep you talking on the doorstep. Come in and I'll give you Kevin's number'

Chapter Thirty-six

'Thanks Mum, Sticky Toffee pudding is one of my favourites,' said Mike, helping himself to another bowlful.
'And mine,' agreed Andrew.

Margaret Nichols laughed,

'You both have a great many 'favourites' when it comes to puddings. Will you clear the table when you've finished? I'm just going to watch the next episode of
Downton Abbey.'

'Well, Andy, you seem to have done really well in Cardigan. I'm glad you went instead of me. You were able to gain their confidence.'
'I did with the old man. We were good mates by the end of it but I didn't with the woman. She was very suspicious of me. It was strange the way they both had such different views of Wilkinson.'
'Oh, I don't think it was strange at all,' said Mike, 'The old man was able to look at him from a distance whereas the woman was protective of her son. Imagine if you had a kid, you wouldn't want him associating with drug addicts would you?' 'I don't know that he was an addict. The girl was but they said that he was a drug dealer.'
'That's worse, isn't it? And it looks as though the lovely Hayden was at it too. He's a strange character, handsome, charming, well-spoken, attractive to women, rich and yet he seems a real deviant. You can't help wondering why. I mean he has everything he could want. He doesn't even need to work.'

'Perhaps he's bored,' said Andrew thoughtfully, 'and I suppose his father didn't set him a good example. He is very respectable now but he made his fortune by very questionable ways. He probably didn't have much of a conscience when it came to drugs or pornography.'

'Do you know what I think,' said Mike, 'I think he's a bit dim. Old Gareth didn't have much of an education but he was certainly very sharp. I always feel rather sorry for these chaps that have celebrity parents. They can never match up.' 'I suppose my parents were sort of celebrities,' said Andrew sadly.
Mike snorted,

'They were clever and nice people. They didn't want to be celebrities and in any case you will do just as well academically and be quite a decent person.'
'Thanks Mike.'

'I suppose I'm the problem there, my sister and brother-in-law being so successful and me sort of letting the side down.'
'But you don't value 'success' in that way so it's not as though you've failed.'

'No that's true but I don't know what I want.'

'That's probably true for most of us.'

Mike laughed,

'You are turning into quite the philosopher. Now to get down to business – tomorrow I am going to see Jane. I emailed her and she emailed straight back. She's very keen to meet me. It will be useful having that extra tit-bit of information, you found out today.'
As Mike finished speaking, there was a ring at the door. They heard Margaret going to answer it.
'I wonder who Mum's late visitor is,' whispered Mike, 'she seems very pleased to see him.'

The door opened,

'Michael! It's your old school friend, John Judge. He is visiting his mother and just called in on the off-chance you might be here.'
'Johnny,' said Mike warmly, 'good to see you. You've met my nephew before haven't you? Come and sit down. Have a glass of wine or beer if you prefer.' 'Just a small one then,' said John.
'I'll leave you to it' said Margaret and returned to her programme.

John seated himself at the table beside Andrew while Mike poured glasses of beer for the three of them.
'I've got some interesting news,' said John, looking rather pleased with himself.

'Come on then, Johnny, let's hear it. Don't keep us in suspense,' laughed Mike. 'Well the police mechanics went over your car with a toothcomb and guess what?'
'Johnny, I'll throw this beer right over you if you don't get on with it,' said Mike'

'Ken Weston's prints are all over it.'

'But,' said Andrew, 'hasn't he been locked up for two weeks?'

'Yes,' said John 'but if for instance there was just a small leak in the brake fluid, the car could be driven for a few hundred miles before the brakes failed and there would be something similar with the steering. When did you last use your car?
Mike, before you came to Stevenage?'

Mike thought,

'I would have to check with my diary but I think it was about three weeks ago. I don't use it for school and not much round London or when I'm going to have a drink.'
'Where do you leave it?'

'Just on the road outside the flat, we don't have parking restrictions here. It's just a matter of driving round 'til you find a space. My last parking spot was in Oak Hill
Road. It's round the corner from here.'

'But surely,' said Andrew, 'he would have worn gloves.'

'I thought that,' said John, 'but the mechanic said that it was difficult to work on tiny nuts and bolts with gloves on and in any case, he had spilt a great deal of petrol around and would have expected the car to blow up.'
'With me inside it,' muttered Mike, while Andrew muttered,

'Like Mum and Dad.'

'Why didn't it blow up?' asked Mike.

'They didn't really know. They think it was because it was an old model and was possibly tougher.'
'I always said it was a good car,' said Mike, 'So what happens now?'

'Because this happened on my patch, I will be able to go over to Walthamstow and question Ken myself which will be useful as I can ask him the right questions, if you know what I mean.'
'Things are beginning to move,' said Mike, 'Andy, tell Johnny about your revelations about Wilkinson.'
John Judge was interested to hear what Andrew had to say. He sighed, 'It's an odd situation. Wilkinson is thought to be a good policeman and these revelations could destroy his career but I couldn't use them in any case as they are only hearsay and the most dangerous part is him being the tool of Sir Gareth and we have no concrete evidence for that.'
'I don't think we want to destroy his career,' said Andrew.

'I do' muttered Mike.

'But' continued Andrew, 'If we were able in some way to destroy Sir Gareth's evil influence, that would be the ideal solution.'

'I agree,' said John, 'In that way he could continue to be a good policeman. I think it would be a great relief to him.'

'I don't understand you two,' grumbled Mike, 'That man is a bent cop. He has covered up crimes, wicked crimes like the murder of my sister and brother-in-law.

He should be sent to prison, never mind losing his job.'

'I agree,' said John calmly, 'but we can only do so much and ninety per cent of the time he is a good policeman. He fell into a trap when he accepted that man's protection. I doubt if he had any idea where it would lead and he was only a young boy at the time.'

'Well, we are working on the Morgan-Lewis family,' said Mike, 'I am visiting an arch enemy of young Hayden's tomorrow.'

They then told John about 'Jane' and the newspaper.

'Yes,' he said, 'it's good to gather evidence from lots of different areas.' John stood up.

'I'd better go' he said, 'Virginia will be wondering what's happened to me. I will be in touch. I won't phone. Are you likely to be here much longer, Mike?'

'I shall be here all week. I phoned school and as there's not much going on, they said to take the week off so I shall stay here.'

'That's great. I shall call again later in the week. It may take a few days to get any information out of Ken but we'll keep at it so, toodlepip.' 'Thanks John,' said Andrew and John left.

Mike snorted,

'Toodlepip! Just when you think he's being comparatively normal!'

'Mike!' said Andrew, 'he's doing his best to help us and he practically saved your life.'

'No he didn't. It was that driver that decided to call an ambulance instead of running over me, but you're right. He is being very helpful so we will have to put up with him.'

Chapter Thirty-Seven

The following morning, Mike took the train into London and then took the Piccadilly line to Kings Cross. He wasn't feeling quite up to his usual confident self as he had taken the bandage of his head to discover that half his head had been shaved. His mother had put a large plaster over his wound and Andrew had helped him cut the rest of his hair to make it match. It was a difficult job as he wanted some hair to cover the plaster. He was very scathing about Andrew's efforts and in his own words felt that he looked like a 'freak'. Andrew found him an old baseball cap. He tried it backwards and forwards and declared he looked like 'an American backwoods idiot' either way. He had tried to make up for his head by wearing a suit but that didn't go well with the cap so decided 'smart casual' was the thing. Andrew had proclaimed his efforts as 'scruffy casual' but it had to do.

Mike approached the reception desk and asked for Jane Pearson. The receptionist hardly looked at him, just at the computer to confirm that Jane was expecting him. She asked him to 'take a seat'.

After about five minutes a woman of about his own age appeared. She was dressed all in black. She had black hair, black nails and black eye-liner. She even wore black lipstick. Her black dress was very short and revealed long, slim legs clothed in black leggings. Mike was immediately attracted by her and wished his own appearance wasn't so unfortunate. He thought that he might adopt a posh voice to ameliorate the impression. This immediately proved inappropriate as she addressed him in a strong Liverpool accent,

'Are you Mike Nichols? Come on up then.'

They went up in a lift, went down a corridor and entered a small room. 'I don't work here,' she said, 'everything is open plan, but I use this room for private interviews. Do you want a beer?' She opened a small frig' and tossed him a can of lager. She then opened a small cupboard and took out several bags of crisps.
Mike began to feel more relaxed as he sipped his beer and crunched the crisps.

'So what can you tell me about horrid Hayden?' she said.

Mike smiled,

'You first,' he said, 'I read something you had written in *The Observer* and then I looked you up and realised you had worked on *The Daily Post*. Was that with
Hayden?'

'Not exactly,' she said, 'He popped in and out, the boss's son, you know. Occasionally he wrote an article about something that interested him. At first, I really liked him. He was polite, good-looking and friendly and obviously fancied me. I hung around with him for a while. After a bit I began to get bored with him and actually found him rather strange. We had nothing in common at all. I am quite a strong Socialist and he, well I don't think he had a thought in his head apart from going on about 'immigrants' or 'scroungers'. It really started getting on my nerves but I have to confess, I did enjoy the lavish dinners, hotels and presents. I was planning how to tell him that our relationship was at an end when he suddenly disappeared and I never saw him again apart from in magazines on the arm of a super-rich girl.
He emailed me, *nice knowing you, now moving on.* I was livid. It was my own fault of course. I had been prepared to spend nights with him in exchange for a few bracelets and chocolates. I suppose I was acting like a whore.'

'What do you mean when you said you found him, "rather strange"?'

Jane sighed,

'Various things really, he seemed obsessed with his father. He would say things like, "My father was really pleased when I did that" – I mean the man was nearly forty for God's sake! And he was a bit kinky, I won't go into details. I had always prided myself on being a bit – live and let live- if you know what I mean' Mike nodded in his most worldly-wise fashion.

Jane continued,

'He would then say things like, "Don't you think it would be amazing to commit a spectacular crime, something that was never solved." I went along with that for a while. I've always liked films about bank robbers and suchlike. I assumed it was just a joke but then he would say things like, "but the greatest crime is murder, don't you think?" I mean robbing banks is one thing but Murder! I still assumed it was just a joke but he seemed to be obsessed with it. I think he thought because I wasn't exactly straight-laced that I would approve of anything. He didn't seem to understand that although I might not be too strict about paying my fares on the bus and was willing to have a relationship with him, that didn't mean that I was completely amoral and do you know in the end I thought that was exactly what he was – amoral. He was charming, kind to old ladies and children but underneath a bit of a monster. I know that sounds extreme and is partly coloured by his rejecting me but looking back, I think he was amoral'
Mike agreed,

'I think you are probably right. I do have various incidents that I believe he was involved in but unfortunately at the moment no proof or concrete evidence.'

'What sort of things?'

'I believe he was mixed up with a people-trafficking business and had a house in Ebbchester for that purpose. I also believe he has bribed or blackmailed various policemen because when we reported this house to the police, it was quickly closed down and nothing was done.'

'When you say "we" who do you mean? Are you a private detective? Or a government spy?'

Mike laughed,

'Maybe a bit of both,' he said mysteriously.

'I see you have a head injury. Did you get that in the course of your investigations?'

'I did,' said Mike this time quite truthfully, 'we are investigating him in regard to a couple of murders but there's nothing I could tell you at the moment and we wouldn't want him to know we were on his track.'

Jane looked at Mike critically,

'Are you sure you're not having me on?'

'No,' replied Mike, 'I do honestly believe he has been involved in at least two murders. I'll tell you what I'll do. If we get any clear evidence and think there is going to be a prosecution, I'll let you know. OK.'

'Be quick about it,' said Jane, 'These stories spread like wild fire. Anyway, how about taking me for lunch?'

Chapter Thirty-eight

As Mike sat dozing in the train, he reflected that he had had a good morning. Although Jane couldn't provide any more evidence against Hayden, she had reinforced their conviction that he and his father had something to do with the death of the Tremaynes and subsequent deaths. He had also enjoyed his lunch with Jane. She was the kind of confident, original person that he had always admired and she actually saw his head wound as something to be respected. He had ordered a stupidly expensive bottle of wine, knowing that he couldn't compete with Hayden in that line, but he felt it was necessary and he had loved it. He smiled as he remembered Jane's 'I've enjoyed this, Mike, are we going to meet again?' – Quite a compliment! He wondered why he hadn't taken her up on it. He had just muttered, 'I'll let you know if there is any news.' What a fool he was, a woman like that, ready and willing! He let his head drop and nodded off. Mike was woken some time later by the ringing of his phone. He fumbled about in his pocket and just got to it in time.
'That you, Mr Nichols?'

'Yes, who's that?'

'Ah, the blurred voice, been having a midday tipple, Mr Nichols?'

'What the? Oh it's you.'

'Yes, Montague Carruthers.'

Mike laughed, this was the name his old hacking friend, Mervyn Carter, had devised for himself,
'Hi Monty, how's things?'

'I was wondering if you fancied a night out in a friendly hostelry. How about *The*

Horse and Hounds?'

Mike considered. He didn't really want to say on the phone that he was staying with his mother and he didn't really feel like 'a night out' but if Mervyn had something to tell him . . . .'

'OK Monty, *Horse and Hounds* – eight o'clock?'

Mike sighed. The train drew into a small station. He got out, walked down the platform, climbed the steps to the overhead bridge, descended and waited for the next train to London.

'I can't believe it?'

Mike sat with a pint of beer in his hand opposite Mervyn Carter who was similarly supplied. He put the beer down on the table. 'I can't believe it.' He repeated.

Mervyn laughed,

'Well, you've got no choice. The hacked phones are heard in an address in Watford and then they are sent to a computer in Mayfair and your computer emails are sent to the same computer.'
'Do you know who picks them up?'

'No, the computer is registered just as 'Farquar'. The house belongs to Lord Alfred but is officially the home of his son, Gerald and his family. I believe Lord Alfred spends a great deal of time there with his son and his family. His official home is Markwood Castle.'

'Mervyn, do you know how long this has been going on?' Mervyn looked at his scribbled notes.
'The phones, that is yours and Lucy Hammond's from ??? and your computer from ??? and Lucy's from ??'

Mike thought for a minute. Of course the hacking wouldn't have started until well after the Tremaynes' death.

'Is it still happening?'

'Yes and I think efforts are being made to track all your mobiles. They haven't really succeeded as yet.'

'Do you know who's doing it. I mean the Farquars are the recipients but they must have paid someone to do it.'

Mervyn screwed up his face,

'I have a pretty good idea but I'm not going to say. I don't know for certain and I don't want to get anyone into trouble and I don't want to get into any more trouble myself, besides you don't need to know. You have the Farquars.'

'Fair enough,' said Mike, 'but I've got one more question.'

'Fire away.'

'Does the hacker or the address in Watford have anything to do with the Morgan-

Lewis family?'

'What! Sir Gareth and that lot, no of course not, as far as I know, nothing whatsoever.'

'Thanks Mervyn, worth every penny.' Mike handed over a plastic bag containing a plastic box filled with twenty-pound notes'

Mike stood up,

'I'd like to sit chatting, Mervyn but I've had a long day.'

'Yes, you're looking a bit green. I suppose the head is taking its toll.'

Chapter Thirty-nine

Inspector John Judge arrived at an East London Police Station at eleven O'clock on Monday morning. He was shown into the Inspector's office, given a cup of coffee, heard about the Inspector's daughter's acceptance at Oxford, discussed the lovely, sunny weather, then he finally asked,

'Have you had any revelations from young Ken Weston?'

'Not much, we'll see what you can find out. Are you ready to get started? Ken has his solicitor with him'

'Yes, of course.'

Inspector Judge was led down to the cells. He went in and was surprised at the appearance of Ken Weston. He was older than he imagined. He estimated him to be in his mid- sixties. He had bright, red hair and a very large nose. 'Come in to my drawing-room, Inspector,' he said, 'I heard you were coming, pleased to meet you.' He stood up and held his hand out. Inspector Judge ignored it.

'So, I hear you have admitted the burglaries in Walthamstow and Stevenage.' 'Inspector, Inspector, don't think I'm going to be caught like that with my brief here an'all. You know I had nothing to do with any break in, in Stevenage.'

'I see you are a car mechanic, by trade?'

'That's right, having trouble with one of your Rolls Royces? Don't worry I'll fix it in a jiffy.'

'Yes you are good at fixing cars, Ken, aren't you?'

Ken looked slightly uneasy but laughed,

'Course I am.'

Inspector Judge picked up a file and thumbed through the pages. In reality there was nothing much in it but the length of time he spent looking for the right page was making Ken Weston agitated. 'Ah here it is,' The Inspector picked out a closely written page, 'We have an old

MG registered in London which has your prints all over it.'

Ken was obviously restraining himself from showing his shock,

'I do work on lots of cars. I can't remember every single one.'

'Ah! But the work on this car was not to mend it but quite the reverse – to make it crash.'
'How can you know that?'

The Inspector smiled,

'Oh but I think we do.'

At this stage, the solicitor interrupted,

'Mr Weston is answering no more questions.'

'That's right' said Ken looking relieved and smug. He folded his arms and sat back.

The Inspector nodded at the young policeman who was sitting by the door.

'Interview terminated at twelve fifteen' he said.

John returned to the Inspector's office. He found him in front of a pile of papers.

'Paperwork, paperwork, paperwork,' he said and they both laughed.'

'Did you get anything out of him, cocky devil isn't he?'

'Not much but I managed to put the wind up him. The solicitor wouldn't let him say any more. I think it's important that he doesn't know whether the driver of the car was killed or haw damaged the car was. If he thinks he might be tried for murder, he might come clean on the robberies.'

'I'll let him stew then.'

The following day Mike got up late. Andrew was aware that Mike had arrived very late at night and that he was still recovering from his head wound but he was impatient. Mrs Nichols went out shopping and Andrew slouched in front of the television watching programmes about antiques. At about midday, Mike put his head round the door, 'Any breakfast left?' he said.

They went into the kitchen and Andrew put on some toast.

'I'm starving,' said Mike, 'how about a fry-up?'

'Grandma's gone shopping,' said Andrew, 'and she'll be making lunch when she gets back. Come on Mike, tell me your news.'

'Well the main news is that my mate, Mervyn reckons that our phones and computers are being tapped by one of the Farquars!'

'I don't believe it. That can't be true!'

'Well, it is and he reckons that the Morgan-Lewis family have nothing to do with it.'

'Well we know that can't be true.'

'It could mean that the two families are in cahoots,' said Mike thoughtfully as he put another piece of bread into the toaster.'

'Well we know they know each other. We've seen the pictures,' said Andrew, 'but

I would have put the Morgan-Lewis family as the prime movers.'

'Me too,' said Mike, 'and I got a little bit more insight into Hayden from the lovely Jane.'

'Oh I'd forgotten about her. What was she like?'

'A stunner!'

'I don't mean what was she like to look at. I meant as a person.'

'She was dressed all in black, clothes, hair, lipstick, everything.'

'She sounds weird'

'She was great, really alternative, original – you know what I mean. She had her own set of morals, worked things out for herself.'
'Probably immoral,'

'Andy you are so bourgeois, such a little prig! She was wonderful, hung loose about everything. She fancied me. That was obvious. We had lunch together.'
'But what did she say about Hayden?'

'Dim, kinky (sexually), talked about committing crimes, especially murders, threw his money around.'

'So I suppose he dumped her and stopped throwing his money at her.'

'More or less but I think she is truthful. She's intelligent and perceptive.'

'Must be if she fancied you. Are you going to see her again?'

'I don't know. She wanted to. I mean I could have had her.'

'You are so crude! You have a very low opinion of women.'

'No I don't. I'm a feminist.'

'Like hell. You look at women as sexual objects and then use them for your own ego.'

'When you are a few years older, young Andy, you will be capable of expressing an opinion but talking of women, we need to get in touch with Lucy.'

'You are not fit to be in the same room as Lucy, not even on the same planet.' Andrew stormed out of the room but later, he did agree to telephone Lucy and leave her a code message to come and visit them on Thursday evening.

Chapter forty

'Thank you Mrs Nichols. That was a wonderful dinner,'

'Do call me Margaret, Lucy. I hope we are friends.'

Lucy stood up and put her arm round Margaret,

'Of course we are, Margaret. I will call you Margaret, Andrew calls you Grandma and Mike calls you Mum.'
'Yes, aren't I lucky to have all these young people around me.'

'Don't worry about the washing up Grandma, we'll do it won't we Mike?'

'Yes, it's easy with a dish-washer, particularly when Mum has already rinsed the plates.'
Margaret laughed,

'I'll let you get on with it then. I'm off to my bridge evening.'

'Make sure you win tonight, Mum, those prize chocolates were lovely!' Margaret went out.
'Coffee?' said Andrew and went into the kitchen to prepare it.

'OK,' said Mike as they sat round the dining-room table with their coffee cups, 'we have a few things to discuss tonight. Lucy, did Johnny Judge get in touch with you about the pages from *The Good Book*?'
'He did. I photocopied them all and put them in the safe, sent the Welsh ones to Edith and gave the Latin ones to my friendly Professor, you know my eighty year old lover,' Lucy said, smiling at Mike.
'And have you heard any more from the Farquars?'

'As a matter of fact I have. I received a very posh invitation to a 'supper party' from Lord Alfred. He wants to introduce me to his glamourous daughter-in-law.

He was very pressing that I should come but I'm not going.' 'Why not?' said Mike and Andrew together.

'I don't see the point. I've no wish to meet the beautiful, exciting Charlotte. I have written a refusal. I meant to bring it with me to post but I forgot it.'

'Good,' said Mike. Lucy looked surprised, 'I don't care what you say. I'm not going. As you know Mike, I am a very boring, ordinary person and I know it's pride, sour grapes, call it what you like but I don't like being out-dazzled by this beautiful, daring, adventurous woman.'

Andrew felt quite choked up. He wished Mike would say how beautiful Lucy was.

He didn't have the courage to say it himself. Instead, Mike said,

'We'd better tell you our next piece of news.'

Mike then told Lucy about Mervyn's discoveries about the hacking. Lucy's reaction was the same as the others,

'I can't believe it!' and then, 'What about the Morgan-Lewises?'

'Well, we do know they have connections,' continued Mike, 'Hayden found out about *The Good Book from* Mary. He then told Sir Gareth and showed him a copy. Sir Gareth showed it to Lord Alfred. We have also seen pictures of Hayden hobnobbing with Charlotte Farquar. Although the two families appear to have little in common, they do move in the same circles.'

'So you would like me to go to this social gathering to see what I can find out?' 'We would be very grateful if you would Lucy,' said Andrew, 'I know you don't want to and it might be painful for you but . . .'

'Never mind painful, it might be bloody dangerous,' put in Mike. Andrew looked shocked but Lucy laughed,

Of course I will do it. I can't see myself being in any danger from Lord Alfred.'

Mike put his hand on Lucy's arm,

'Lucy, Lucy, you are continually taken in by these charming old men. You must be more discriminating.'

'And when precisely have I been taken in by a charming old man?'

'Well, this Lord Alfred. You sounded practically in love with the man, the way you talked about him.'

'Mike, don't be so ridiculous and in any case, I haven't been taken in by him. I believe him to be a kind, honest man and I will continue to think so unless you prove otherwise.'

'But Lucy,' began Andrew, 'the phone-hacking!'

'There are two other adults who live in that house. It could be either of them.' 'That's true enough,' said Mike, 'when you go, try and talk to the son, Gerald. We know nothing about him.'

'He's a barrister,' said Andrew.

'I know that but we don't know what kind of person he is.'

'I got the impression from Lord Alfred that he was a quiet, hard-working, rather staid sort of man,' said Lucy.

'That's just the sort who would like you, Lucy,' said Mike kindly, 'You could do well there.'

'Thank you, Mike,' said Lucy, glaring at him.

'That's all right' said Mike cheerfully, 'it's quite a gift chatting to these quiet types. He seems the most likely to have hired the hacker – still waters run deep - as they say.'

'When is the party, Lucy?' asked Andrew.

'Next Wednesday, eight o'clock.'

'I'll come with you,' said Mike

'You can't' said Andrew, 'you're not invited.'

'I didn't mean, going to the party, you idiot, I will just hang about outside, just in case.'

Just then there was a ring at the doorbell. Andrew went to answer it. He returned to the dining room with Inspector Judge.

'Johnny,' said Mike, 'good to see you. I don't think you've met Lucy.'

'I met her at the hospital and I've corresponded with her about the manuscripts.'

John reached over to shake hands with Lucy. 'All here,' he said, 'the three

Musketeers!'

Lucy and Andrew laughed politely and Mike sighed heavily. After a few seconds he said,

'Any news for us, Johnny?' John sat down at the table.

'It's coming on. I think we're getting there. On Monday, I told him we had his fingerprints on an MG. He was clearly shocked. He covered it up quite well, saying that he had worked on hundreds of cars. I then said we knew that he wasn't intending to mend this car but to damage it. His solicitor then interrupted and said he would answer no more questions.'

John took a sip of water from the glass, Lucy had offered him.

'Does he know it was my car? Does he know that it didn't blow up?' asked Mike. 'He probably knows who the car belongs to but he has no more information. He doesn't know whether you are alive or dead.'

'So he doesn't know whether it is a murder charge,' said Andrew.

'No he doesn't. He must guess that the car didn't blow up as intended but I have dropped hints which might lead him to believe that Mike might be on a life-support machine and likely to pop off at any minute. I saw him again this morning and the solicitor obviously wanted to find out whether or not it was a murder charge. Ken was much quieter and less confident than the other day. I produced the letter from 'Z'. He said he didn't know who 'Z' is and I am inclined to believe him but he did incriminate himself to a certain extent by almost acknowledging the letter.'

'Well he would have to wouldn't he? It was found in his house,' said Andrew 'Well criminals are very quick to say something was a 'plant'. I said that I wanted to discuss another incident where a car had been tampered with. I said that on this occasion both passengers had been killed instantly so whoever fixed the car would be guilty of murder.'

'How did he respond to that?' asked Lucy.

He was in a panic and despite the solicitor's restraining arm, shouted,

"That was nothing to do with me." I left him then as I knew the solicitor wouldn't let him say any more but I think it would be good for him to stew for a few days.'

'Well done, Johnny,' said Mike and the sentiments were echoed by the other two. John then asked Mike how long he would be staying with his mother. Mike explained that he intended to return to London on Sunday night to be in time for school on Monday. He suggested that Andrew remain but Andrew was reluctant. 'I can easily visit you in London. I am often there for meetings and so on.' He pulled out a note pad, 'I haven't got your London address, Mike.'

'There's no need to come trekking over to Streatham. We could meet in town and if I'm working, Andy could come.'

Lucy and Andrew smiled, knowingly at each other as they understood Mike's unwillingness for the finicky John to visit his flat.

Andrew, however agreed enthusiastically about going into town to see John. They arranged a code whereby John could name a time and place.

John then got up to go, 'Toodlepip' said Mike.

John laughed sheepishly and reddened slightly.

'What was all that about – toodlepip -?' asked Andrew.

'Oh it was just what he said to me last time we met, silly chump, toodlepip! I ask you?'

'Mike, you embarrassed him. Couldn't you see that?'

Mike laughed,

'Serve him right, oh here's mum. Did you have a good evening? Did you win?' Margaret put a box of chocolates down on the table. 'Yes we did,' she said, 'but I'm in two minds about those chocolates. What happened to the clearing up?'

Chapter Forty - one

'Good-morning Mr Weston, I hope you have spent a pleasant weekend.' 'Very funny, very funny,' replied Ken Weston.
'Inspector,' interrupted the solicitor, 'I have been discussing the situation with my client and we should like to make a statement' 'And what would that be?'

'My client, Mr Weston admits the break-in. He says the assault on Mr Bradshaw was unfortunate and unintended. He is sorry about that. He admits that he was requested to tamper with a car and offered money by a person known as 'Z' but he had no intentions of harming the driver. He thought 'Z' intended it as a joke.'
Inspector Judge turned to Ken,

'Well, Ken, I'm glad you are beginning to see sense. You know that your situation is serious. At the moment the person who was driving the car is still alive unlike the two people in the previous case. Now don't start getting agitated and turning to your solicitor. I know that on both these occasions you were pushed into it by someone else. It wasn't your wish to kill anybody. It is 'Z' who is the murderer.' 'Oh it wasn't 'Z' for the first one,' said Ken.
The solicitor sighed, shut his eyes and leaned back in his chair.

'I think I need some time alone with my client,' said the solicitor.

Inspector Judge looked at his watch.

'Interview suspended at ten minutes past eleven', he said.

The following day, Andrew was delighted to receive a telephone call from Inspector John. Although the phone call was on a new mobile, they continued with the code. Andrew replied,

'I shall relax with a good book' which translated meant, 'I will meet you in the restaurant in Oxford Street.'

Andrew got there in plenty of time and ordered a coffee for himself while he was waiting. He soon spotted John entering the restaurant. He waved to him and John came over and sat down opposite him. He picked up the menu,

'We'd better have some lunch. What will you have? I've been here before and I can recommend the steak and kidney pie, a bit heavy for lunch time but very nice all the same.'

Andrew said he would have the same. They waited until they had been served then John said,

'I have two things to report. I visited the two houses where we found the manuscripts and they are both owned by teachers. They are not university men. One teaches Classics in a private school and the other one teaches History in a college of further education. He studied Classics at University but can't get a job with Classics so he has been teaching History for some years. They were both approached by a man called Edmond Croft who asked them if they could translate some documents from the Latin. They agreed to do so and were grateful for the money offered as neither of them are rich. When the manuscripts arrived, they both found very little in Latin but most of it in ancient Welsh which they couldn't translate.

In the meantime, David McCarthy, the one from Stevenage, had contacted a friend in Bangor who speaks Welsh and was about to send it off when Croft contacted him and said to hang on for a bit. The other chap was thinking of something similar but hadn't got a Welsh contact. It was after that, that their homes were broken into.'

'Edmond Croft doesn't appear to be a very efficient character,' said Andrew.

'No he doesn't, positively bungling in fact.'

'I wonder why he didn't send the manuscripts to the Morgan-Lewis University?'

John was thoughtful,

'Two things I think, one, the manuscripts have arrived in their hands in dribs and drabs, some from Lucy, some from the professor, some from Edith. The other thing is I believe there are two forces at work here, probably loosely connected but operating separately.'
'What makes you think that?'

'My interview with Ken Weston,'

John then went on to tell Andrew about his interview with Ken, the previous day.

Andrew was excited,

'So he's practically admitted that he was involved in the murder of my parents!' Andrew sat back in his chair and closed his eyes. He suddenly felt full of strange emotions. John waited for a minute, then said in a matter of fact tone of voice, 'He has, but his lawyer will probably get him to backtrack. I could have gone back to him after a short while but I think it is better to let him sweat a bit. If he has a couple of bad nights dreaming of a lifetime in prison, he will be more ready to ignore his brief and plead for his life.'
'But has he anything to gain by admitting it?'

'Not a lot, but I put it to him that the real murderer was the one who asked him to do it, which is true in a way and it's not just admitting it that's important but all the information that comes with it. That's what we call, "helping the police with their inquiries". Come on Andy, your pie is getting cold.'
Andrew noted that the tall, lean Inspector had already wolfed down his steak and kidney pie, so he set to, to finish his. John was already looking hungrily at the sweet trolley.
'I think I'll have cheesecake. What about you?'

'Black Forest Gateau,' muttered Andrew through a mouthful of pie.'

Chapter Forty-Two

'What do you mean, you haven't got the dinner on because you're not hungry?' 'Well I had steak and kidney pie with chips and mixed vegetables for lunch followed by Black Forest Gateau, coffee and mints and I had half of a nice bottle of Burgundy.'
'OK, Andy, who bought you this feast?'

'Johnny Judge.'

'How come? By the way, Inspector Judge to you.'

'He telephoned me and I went,'

'Huh! Without me. Any news?'

'Quite a lot actually,'

'Come on then, tell Uncle Mike.'

When Andrew had recounted his morning's adventures, Mike was excited, 'Things are certainly moving. Johnny takes things slowly but he probably knows what he's doing.'
'We must tell Lucy,' said Andrew.

'I shall be seeing her on Thursday. She's going to that party.'

'Are you really going to go with her?'

'Yes, I am a bit anxious about those Farquars. There's something going on there and at the moment Lucy is on her own with them. I shall hire a car to take her and then skulk around outside.'
'But what use is that if she is in danger in the house? She may not have time or the opportunity to email you.'

'Ah, you have to trust your Uncle Mike. I have a device whereby you just press it and it buzzes somewhere else. Look at this.'
Mike produced a small object about half the size of a mobile phone and gave it to Andrew.
'Put it in your pocket. I will go outside. You wait for a little while then press the big red button. You can easily press it in the pocket and I will receive the signal outside. I will then come in.'
'OK'

Mike went outside, Andrew looked out of the window. It was raining. He could see Mike standing by the roadside. After a while, Mike put his jacket over his head. Andrew waited a bit longer. Mike moved down the road to wait under a bus shelter. Andrew pressed the button. Mike rushed out of the shelter and back to the flat.
'What was that about, keeping me standing in the rain?'

'Well we need to check that it works properly. We can't have poor Lucy being kept waiting when she has called for the cavalry.' I want my dinner,' snapped Mike.

'You shouldn't have done this Mike but it's really kind of you' said Lucy as she stepped into Mike's hired car.
'Lucy, you're all dressed up!' said Mike.

'Well it's not often that I go to a supper party in ?Mayfair.'

'You certainly scrub up well!'

'Thank you Mike. I assume that's a compliment.' Mike set off towards London.
'It's true though, Lucy'

'What's true?'

'That you will outdazzle any woman at that party.'

Lucy smiled,

'Thank you Mike.'

'As we're going along, I'll tell you our latest news.'

Mike proceeded to tell Lucy about the Inspector's interrogation of Ken Weston.

Lucy was pleased,
'So we've done it, Mike.'

'We haven't got there yet. Ken hasn't admitted it formally.'

'But that doesn't really matter does it? We know, which is what matters.' 'That's true. When we stop I'll show you this little gadget which you can put in your pocket.'
'I haven't got a pocket.'

'What! Where do you keep your money and everything else?'

'I've got a small handbag.'

'Oh I suppose that will have to do but a pocket would be better.'

Mike stopped the car a few yards from the Farquar's house. He showed Lucy the gadget that he had devised for her safety.
'And when you are ready to leave, text me.'

'You don't want me to press the red button?'

'Oh no! don't do that. If I heard that I would come crashing into the Farquar's house at great speed with a baseball bat in my hand.'
'Have you brought one with you?'

'Brought what?'

'A baseball bat.'

'Of course I haven't I'm speaking figuratively, well, good luck and Lucy,'

'What?'

'You really do look lovely,' he added rather shyly.

'Thank you Michael and . . . thanks for everything.'

Lucy disappeared past the iron railings and up the steps of the tall, Georgian house. Mike sighed, what did she mean by 'Michael'? Perhaps she felt like his mother? He drove the car into a nearby cul-de-sac and shut his eyes. He had brought some books from school to mark. Perhaps he would do that later. Lucy looked up at the tall house. It was well lit, lights on in every room. She wondered how big the party was going to be. She merged into the crowd in the hallway.
'I don't know that gentleman in the tall hat, do you?'

'Yes, he's the earl of somewhere or other. Toby and I met him at Ascot last year, very charming but a bit absent-minded.'
Lucy felt ill at ease. She wondered if someone would say,

'Who's that gal in the green frock? Never seen her before.'

The group moved up the wide staircase. At the top, an imposing retainer in livery announced the new arrivals. When it came to her turn, she could hardly say the words, 'Lucy Hammond'. The announcer smiled at her and whispered,
'Am I right to say "Miss"?'

Lucy nodded and smiled back. She felt a little better and didn't feel too put out when, after she heard her name being boomed out, various people turned to stare at her. Within seconds, Lord Alfred appeared and greeted her as an old friend.

'Lucy! How kind of you to come. I thought you might be put off by such a crowd of tedious, old people. Charlotte's in the drawing room at the moment. I'll introduce you to her as soon as I can. In the meantime, let me introduce you to Roger and Lyndsey. He called them over.

'Roger, here is a wonderful, clever girl you must meet.' Lord Alfred turned to Lucy, laughing at Roger,

'Lucy, these two are not quite as boring as some of the others.' Roger and Lyndsey shook hands with Lucy as Lord Alfred disappeared.

'Finding it all a bit dry, Lucy?' said Lyndsey.

'No not at all. I've only just arrived.'

'So have we, Roger, do you think you could push through the crowd and get us something to drink?'

'I'll try,' said Roger, manfully.

'Let's find a seat,' suggested Lyndsey. She looked through the door of one of the rooms leading off the landing and said, 'It looks quieter in there, come on.'

Lyndsey took hold of Lucy's arm and propelled her into the half-empty room.

'Will your husband be able to find us?'

'I hope so I'm gasping for a drink. Do you know many people here?'

'Virtually nobody,' said Lucy then explained very briefly her connection with Lord Alfred.

'He's a pet isn't he?' said Lyndsey, 'we know him because he's a Labour Peer and my husband's an MP.'

It suddenly dawned on Lucy that Roger was 'the Right Honourable Roger Maitland' who had been Home Secretary in the previous government.

'Is your husband a London MP or do you live somewhere else?' asked Lucy. 'We are from the North East, just North of Newcastle,' said Lyndsey, 'so it's not convenient at all, especially for our children but we managed. She then began to describe for Lucy, the life of an MP which Lucy found fascinating.

'So there you are!'

Roger came into the room, expertly balancing three drinks and a tray of canapés.

'I do apologise, Lucy, I forgot to ask you what you wanted to drink. Lyndsey likes

??? so I got you one too and if you don't like it Lyndsey will happily drink two and

I could get you something else.'

'Oh that's fine,' said Lucy who had never tasted ??? but after a few sips found it quite acceptable.'

'The dinner looks pretty good,' said Roger, 'they are setting it up in the dining room. I went in and had a quick look.'

'I hope you didn't pick at anything,' said Lyndsey.

'I didn't,' said Roger, 'well I did sample a quick beef olive. It was on a hot plate covered with a lovely sauce.'

Lyndsey raised her eyes to heaven,

'Roger, you are a disgrace! You are so greedy.'

Just then Charlotte Farquar came into the room. Everyone stopped speaking just to look at her. She was wearing a long dress of dark red, shot silk. When she moved it shone red and black and even green. Lucy thought that she was even more beautiful than her pictures, but it wasn't just her physical beauty, she exuded life and energy and her whole presence was radiant.

She looked at Lucy, 'Are you Lucy Hammond?' Lucy smiled and nodded.

'I have been absolutely dying to meet you. Pops told me all about you and about that wonderful book you have discovered.'
'Well, I am working on it but I didn't discover it.'

Charlotte came and sat beside Lucy. She turned to Roger and Lyndsey,

'Please forgive me but I'm going to monopolise your friend.'

'So, tell me all about your famous book. How did they discover it and where did they find it?'
Lucy felt that she had to be careful. She had no intention of telling anyone about the monastery, so instead she talked about Geoffrey of Monmouth and Geffrei Gaimar and *L'Estoire des Engleis.* She was relieved that Charlotte didn't pester her with questions about the discovery of the book but asked intelligent questions about the content.
'I studied Science, myself,' she said, 'but I have always been interested in History.

I have to admit, though, that I am very ignorant about early medieval History. What I found fascinating about the small section of your book that I have read, was how modern it seemed. In lots of ways it could have been written for our own times. I'm afraid I don't do too much studying these days. I am too much of a gadabout. But my main interest in life is my beautiful boys, Sebastian and Hugo. They are seven and five. Hugo has just started school. I thought he wouldn't like it as he is very shy but he loves it. He is very studious unlike his naughty big brother.'
Charlotte went on to talk at length about her boys. Then a gong sounded. 'Supper-time!' she said, 'come on Lucy, let's get there first. All the polite people will be hanging back. You must sample the delights of our chef, Pierre de Jean.

Actually his name is Peter Johnson but chefs should be French don't you think?' Lucy followed Charlotte to the dining-room. She was amazed at the size of the room. From outside one couldn't have imagined that the house would contain such a room. It had recognisable pictures on the wall. Lucy wondered whether they were originals. Charlotte saw her looking at the pictures.

'They are not all originals,' she said, 'some are just very old prints. That Kandinsky is original, so is the Lowry. They are lovely aren't they?'

'They are,' said Lucy, taking a closer look. She reluctantly turned away to concentrate on the food as the room was filling up. She noticed that Charlotte was talking to an old lady.

'You sit over there, Ida, I'll get you a selection of food and then you can eat what you want. You can't carry a plate of food, a glass of wine and your walking stick.' Charlotte took Ida's glass from her hand and let her to a seat by a small table.

Lucy heard Ida laughing as Charlotte said,

'And I'll try and find a handsome young man to entertain you.'

Lucy gazed at the food. The presentation was such that it was difficult to know what was in each dish. Lucy tried to take a variety, without looking too greedy.

Charlotte came up behind her and whispered,

'If you like avocados, that mousse is delicious. That dish surrounded by red leaves is mostly snails.'

As Lucy was helping herself to the mousse, a tall, dark-haired man spoke to her,

'Excuse me,' he said, rather shyly, 'are you Lucy Hammond?'

Lucy turned round,'

'Yes, I am,'

'I should like to talk to you. Would you mind, joining me at my table?'

Lucy smiled at the diffident, rather serious man and followed him into an adjoining room where small tables were set with cutlery, glasses, flowers and candles. They sat down.
'This is kind of you. My name is Gerald Farquar.'

'So this is your house?'

'Well it really belongs to my father but I live here with my wife and family.'

'Your wife was telling me about your boys.'

Gerald smiled,

'I'm sure she was. They are the light of her life and of mine too. I really wanted to ask you about *The Good Book of Oxford* I understand you are working on it?' 'Yes, I took over from Dr. Mary Nichols after she was killed in a car crash.'
'I heard about that. Her husband was killed too wasn't he? Tragic, really tragic,' 'Yes, it was.'
They sat for a minute, reflecting on the tragedy.

'Yes, I saw her on the television a few times, her husband too, Frank Tremayne, such a nice man!'
'He was.'

'I expect it was very hard for you, Miss Hammond, working so closely with them but so brave of you to continue the work.'
'It was a great privilege, but do call me Lucy!'

Gerald smiled. Lucy was surprised at how it altered his serious face. She realised how like his father he was.
'Thank you Lucy, that's very kind of you. My friends call me 'Gerry' so please do.' Lucy smiled, she couldn't visualise anyone less like a 'Gerry'.

'I should imagine anyone would feel privileged to work on such a book. I have only read one short extract but I was very moved by it, so was my father and
Charlotte.'

Lucy agreed,
'Yes, I think it is wonderful too but I don't think everyone would agree with the sentiments about money.'
Gerald sighed,

Yes, I'm going to be with those camels, trying to get through the eye of a needle unless I do something about it. I realise how privileged I have been but riches do present problems. I know many people would welcome some of those problems. I think it was Marilyn Monroe who said,
"I've been rich and I've been poor and I like rich better."

One wonders what is the right state to be. Should one give everything away? Are occasions like this with all this luxury, wrong?'
'Well, Jesus himself went to parties and when he turned the water into wine it was gallons and gallons.'
'That's true. And He is hugely magnanimous in his gifts to us and infinite in his mercy.'
Gerald stared ahead. He appeared to be almost talking to himself.

'What I should really like would be for politicians, people with power, so-called captains of industry to operate with kindness. Surely that should be possible? Why should we always trying to grab what's best for us personally. Can't we sometimes say,
"How can I help someone else? How can I help the poor, the unfortunate, the immigrant? We should try and appeal to what is noble, what is good in people's nature.'
Gerald turned to Lucy,

'Lucy, do you think that if everybody read *The Good Book of Oxford*, it would make a difference.'

Lucy thought for a minute,

'I think there are people who would be affected by it. It is very powerful and I felt inspired by it. It is only really the message of the gospel but it spells out ways of living that message but I suppose there will always be those like the rich young man who find it too hard.'

'Yes, G.K. Chesterton once said something like, "Christianity would be great only it's never been tried." But Lucy don't you think that everyone, Christians,

Muslims, Buddhists, Jews, atheists have a noble, selfless heart?'

Lucy considered this,

'No, I think that many people's hearts have been damaged by unhappy or even cruel childhoods and many people who do have good hearts are weighed down with poverty, hard work and anxiety. It is too difficult for them to think of other people's troubles. I think too that the modern world encourages envy. People watch the television and see enormous houses and yachts, fast cars and think – why haven't I got that?'

Gerald sighed again,

'Yes it's people like me who cause the envy.'

Lucy felt bad,

'I'd say it was more the so-called celebrities and footballers.'

'So you think there's not much hope?'

Lucy laughed,

'Of course there is hope, just think of all the wonderful people there are, doing thankless jobs, risking their lives to save somebody from danger, going to foreign countries to fight illness. I was considering too, those noble hearts you spoke of. I read a book once about someone who survived a concentration camp. She said that those prisoners who were the most generous, were not always the ones you would expect, the educated, religious or healthy but perhaps those who shared the little they had, were very often the poor, those who had been in prison, those we would think of as "rough".'
Gerald laughed,

'That is interesting, isn't it? I suppose many of us think that God approves of those of us who wear clean clothes, speak nicely, eat five portions of fruit a day, aren't covered with tattoos and don't spit in the street.'

Lucy giggled. She was enjoying talking to Gerald. She had thought him very staid which in one sense he was but there was more to him than that.
'You see, my sister, Rowena, and Charlotte, particularly Charlotte don't behave like me. They think differently – I think the modern expression is – out of the box.
They wouldn't shrink back from someone who smelt and swore like a trooper.

They would probably smile and offer him a cup of tea.'

'Yes but Gerald, we are all different. Some of us are just a bit shy. We all have different things to offer. Some people are brilliant on a human level. They can communicate with anybody, high and low, educated or not, any nationality. I imagine your wife is like that. Others communicate with the pen or they paint or play an instrument. You are a barrister aren't you? What sort of law do you specialise in?'

'Human Rights, but it's getting more and more difficult as legal aid is continually being cut. I do my best but I'm not a brilliant barrister and I'm not likely to take silk.'

Lucy looked at Gerald and felt for him. She thought that he was probably a very good barrister but he was surrounded by brilliance, his father, his wife and probably his sister and late mother.

Gerald looked at his watch,

'Forgive me Lucy, I have been monopolising you for too long and there is somebody over there who is signalling to me. He probably wants to introduce me to someone who will further my career. I have enjoyed talking to you and I hope we can continue our conversation another time. Before I go will you promise me that you will let me know when and if *The Good Book of Oxford* will be published. I should love to help to make it widely read and I do know a lot of influential people.'

'It probably won't be published for some time but I will let you know. I have really enjoyed meeting you.'

Gerald went off and Lucy thought the time had come to do some snooping round. She asked someone where the lavatories were and took the opportunity to go to the next floor. Everywhere was quiet, Lucy looked around and opened a door, a bedroom, an attractive, comfortable bedroom but there was no computer in sight. She went further along the corridor. She was about to open a door then noticed that it had a picture of a dinosaur on it. She gasped in relief, it must be a child's room. She made her way back the way she had come and do her dismay encountered someone she thought must be a waiter coming the other way. 'Can I help you?' he asked politely.

'I was looking for the Lady's toilet,' she stuttered.

'The lavatory is just behind you. We don't have a "Ladies" and a " Gentlemen".

This is just a family home.'

Lucy thanked him and dived into the room behind her. She felt very foolish and didn't feel she had acquitted herself well. She waited for a few minutes to retrieve her courage, then descended the stairs again. She went back into the dining room which was now not quite so crowded. She went to get a drink. A young waitress was clearing the table.

Lucy smiled at her and she smiled back.

'Do you work here all the time,' Lucy asked.

'Yes, I work for Mrs Charlotte. I help her with jobs in the house and with the two little boys.'
'Do you like working here?'

'Yes, I am Lucia from Romania and I came here two years ago. At first I get a job, cleaning an office. It was all right but the pay was very low and I had a terrible place to live. Then I get a job here and I am paid well, I have a place to live and everyone is kind to me. Mrs Charlotte, she talks to me like I am her sister or good friend. When my mother is ill, she pays my fare to Romania and gives me money to help my mother get well. She is a wonderful woman!'
'That is kind,' said Lucy, 'are their many people working here?'

'I am not sure the number but there is James who is a chauffeur and looks after the cars and Lily, the nanny and Isabel and Irma who do cleaning and . . .'
'Who would use the computer?'

Lucia looked puzzled,

'I suppose those who work in the office. I don't know them. They don't live here.'

Lucy smiled at Lucia,

'I hope you don't think me terribly nosey, but I have never been in such a house before and it's interesting to find out all about it. Do you know you have the same name as me? My name is Lucy.'
Lucia looked amazed,

'I think Saint Lucia is a popular saint in many nations,' she said and then carried away the dishes.
Lucy looked at her watch and saw that it was ten thirty. She knew that the party would go on into the small hours but Mike was outside and had to take her to
Ebbchester then come back to London. She went to look for one of the Farquars.

She found Lord Alfred,

'Lord Alfred, I have had a lovely time. Thank you very much for asking me to the party but I must go. Someone is giving me a lift home.'
'Of course, my dear,' he pulled her down so he could whisper in her ear, 'Alfie' he said.
Lucy laughed and nodded,

'Of course, Alfie,' she said.

Lucy pressed Mike's mobile number, then hurried down the stairs. As she did so,

Charlotte hurried after her. She caught Lucy on the steps outside,

'I know you have to go, Lucy but it's been great meeting you. I shall insist that you come again when nobody else is here.' With that she kissed Lucy on both cheeks. Mike's car was already waiting for her, so Lucy turned and waved to Charlotte and got into the car. Mike drove off,

'Well, I'm glad you're safe. Was that the lovely Charlotte who was kissing you goodbye?'
'Yes, she's really nice, Mike. They all are.'

Lucy proceeded to tell Mike about her evening.

'So you see Mike, it can't be one of the Farquars. It must be someone who works in the office downstairs. Everyone says how nice the Farquars are.'
Mike drove along in silence for a while,

'A bit too nice, don't you think?'

'What do you mean?'

'Well, when my sister was alive, she once had a party at my parents' house. It was when she was first married and I can't remember the reason for the party. I was still at school and was only allowed in at the beginning. Now you have met Mary and Frank and my mother. Wouldn't you say that they were all nice people?'
'Of course,'

'And my dad was pretty good too. Now those people leaving the party wouldn't have been talking about how nice my family were.'
'They might have,'

Mike shook his head,

'No they would have been saying what a good time they had, repeating someone's joke, saying so and so had too much to drink, whether they liked the food.'
'But that would be because they all knew each other. A stranger like me, would probably say how welcoming your sister was or something like that.'
'I don't know, Lucy. There's something not right.'

Lucy was silent for a while,

'I do know what you mean but it would be hard to visualise any of those as a criminal or a computer hacker.'
'Still, I'm glad you enjoyed it.'

'I did and I wouldn't mind going back again if they asked me.'

'That's what I'm afraid of. You have been lulled into a sense of security by all that niceness.'
'Don't be ridiculous, Mike!'

Chapter Forty-Three

'Well here we are again,' said Inspector Judge cheerfully as he entered the prison cell. He noticed that Ken Weston was looking pale and thinner. His solicitor looked decidedly frosty.

'Last time I spoke to you, you said that the first car's so-called accident wasn't commissioned by 'Z'.' 'Yeah' muttered Ken.

'That's interesting,' said Inspector Judge, 'Who was it?'

'Oh I don't think I can tell you that.'

'Well, it would make things a great deal better for you if you could, because, don't you see, then we would have the real murderer.' Ken looked appealingly at his solicitor who nodded.

Ken hesitated,

'I did some work on a car for this posh gent. He paid me well and we got chatting like and he asked me if I would do a job for him. He said it was for a joke on some friends of his. Well it was difficult to refuse. It seemed harmless enough and he was a real toff. I mean I didn't think he would do anything illegal.'

'So it came as a shock to you when the two people were killed?'

'Yes, it did. I was terrified but he said that the police knew about it and said it would be OK. They just thought it was an accident. They thought the driver was probably drunk, I mean he might have been?' Ken looked up hopefully at the Inspector.

'Did this 'toff' give you his name?'

Ken wriggled,

'Not really.'

Inspector Judge leaned forward so that his face was close to Ken's. He said in a gentle voice,

'Now listen to me Ken. We know that you didn't willingly commit murder but unless we find who was the real murderer, it will look bad for you.'

Ken shuffled about,

'Well I might not have got it right and it's a few months ago but it was quite an ordinary name. I think it was Aidan, Aidan Lewis.'

'Thank you Ken. That will be very helpful. Now if I showed you some photographs of men's faces, do you think you could pick him out?'

'Oh I think so.'

'Now Ken, my next question, did Mr Lewis have any further contact with you? Did he ask you to do anything else?'

Ken looked hesitant. He looked at his solicitor who then asked if he could have a few words in private with his client. Inspector Judge then closed the interview and they agreed to meet again in half an hour.

'So you see Mike, we have quite a lot of information but still have quite a few loose ends to tie up.'

Inspector Judge and Mike were sitting in a Streatham pub. They both had pints of beer in front of them.

'That's brilliant, Johnnie, so we know that Hayden asked him to set up the car for

Mary and Frank, Hayden asked them to keep looking in the Tremayne's house and

'Z' asked him to ransack the professor's house and to set up my car.' 'Yes, that's the gist of it. He doesn't know who 'Z' is. I'm pretty sure of that. I asked him how 'Z' got in touch with him. He just said by a letter pushed through the door which he threw away.'

'I suppose we could assume that 'Z' is known to Hayden?'

'That seems likely.'

'The other thing that puzzles me,' said Mike is Sir Gareth's part in all this. We felt

from the beginning that everything led back to him.'

'Yes and Ken didn't know anything about Sir Gareth. He didn't connect him with Hayden. When I casually brought him into the conversation, he was obviously puzzled. He had heard of Sir Gareth as a rich, powerful man who gave a lot to charity, nothing more.'

'He must be connected though, surely?'

John sighed,

'He must, and I'm sure he must be behind the corruption of the police. I feel as though Hayden was his tool. It is Sir Gareth who wanted the Welsh History parts of the good book and who didn't want the other parts published and it was Sir Gareth who tried to bribe Mary.'

'Won't we find that out when Hayden is arrested?'

'I'm not sure,' said John, 'He might easily slip through our fingers. Sir Gareth is a very powerful man. He dines regularly with members of the cabinet. He has a great deal of influence in the city. He has powerful friends in every walk of life. He controls much of the press and commercial television. Although I think the police were ultimately corrupted at his bidding, instructions may have come from government sources. It is easy for them to say, "don't pursue this line of enquiry, it is about sensitive issues". It happens frequently and we don't always know why, but MI6 takes precedence over us so we can do nothing.'
Mike pondered what John had said,

'That is a terrible situation. It makes it all the more important that we get him, for the sake of the whole country.'

'You're right,' said John, 'I think we will wait and see what Hayden comes up with and then there is Andy's discovery about Inspector Wilkinson. The trouble is that could easily be by-passed. It could be denied and we wouldn't be able to prove it or Wilkinson could be quietly sacked. The best way forward would be the press or the BBC or Chanel 4 - something like that, someone who will worry away at it until everything is disclosed.' 'I do have a journalist contact,' said Mike.

'It might be necessary. Our other problem is 'Z'. We might get some information from Hayden but he's going to have a better lawyer than poor old Ken.' 'And then there's the very nice Farquars,' said Mike.

'Yes there's a bit of a mystery there. Did you say Lucy will be going back there?' 'I think she will if she's invited. I don't want her to but she likes them all and fears no danger.'

'Do you really think there is a danger?'

'Well someone, most likely killed the Professor and certainly murdered Father

John. We've got 'Z' and the Farquars. They must be connected.'

'I could find out who works for the Farquars, who would have access to their computer.'

'Good idea, John. It will give us something to work on.'

Chapter Forty-four

It was the weekend and Mike, Lucy and Andrew once again sat at Margaret Nichols' dining room table. Margaret remained a little nervous about 'what they were getting up to' but she loved having them to stay and was getting very fond of Lucy.

Mike had recounted to Lucy and Andrew, his conversation with Inspector Judge. They were both quite excited and felt that at last things were falling into place. 'And since I saw Johnnie, I have had a letter from him. He lists those people who work for the Farquars. Apart from the ones, Lucy mentioned that is James the chauffeur, Lily, the nanny, and Lucia, Isabel and Irma, there is the cook, Peter Johnson and an odd job man, Stefan. Peter and Stefan don't live in the house. The people who work in the office are Albert (Bertie) Fisher and Monika Crystowska. They live out as well. Bertie has been a private secretary to Lord Alfred for years and is probably as old as him. Monika has been with them for two years. She is there for filing and photocopying but I think she does most of the typing too. Johnnie doesn't know much about her. She is Polish, a very good worker, very competent and efficient. Bertie is supposed to be a secretary for Gerald as well but Gerald has a secretary at work and he and Charlotte would both ask Monika if they wanted something done.'

'What does he know about James, Stefan and Peter?' asked Lucy..

'James is the same vintage as Bertie and Alfred. Peter is new. He's only been there about a month. Stefan works part time, has worked for the Farquars for about two years. His English is still very poor. Charlotte gives him English lessons. Lily is quite old and has worked for the Farqhars for years. Isabel is Spanish and Irma, Bulgarian. They haven't been there for very long and are unlikely wiz kids on the computer.'

'So Monika is the most likely candidate,' said Andrew.

'But why would a Polish girl want to track our emails and phone messages?' said Lucy.

'She could be paid by Hayden or Sir Gareth' suggested Andrew.

'Bit if that's the case, why at the Farquars' home? She runs the risk of being found out, of not having the use of the computer part of the time and of general inconvenience. It doesn't make sense!' said Mike.

They sat in silence for some minutes, all three trying to puzzle out Monika's situation.

'I suppose,' said Andrew, 'Hayden might have something on Monika, she may not be Polish. She could be Albanian or something and an illegal immigrant. She may not own a computer and the only one she could use is at work.'

'I think it's unlikely that she's an illegal immigrant as the Farquars would have to pay National Insurance and that sort of thing for her but you are right, Hayden could have found out something about her and is using her, said Lucy.

'She could have murdered her Mother,' suggested Mike.

'Or be a drug smuggler or a prostitute,' said Andrew.

'She could have hacked into the Pentagon or GCHQ,' said Lucy.

'Or,' said Mike, 'she could have had an illicit relationship with a member of the royal family.'

'That' said Andrew, 'would be more dangerous for the royal family than for

Monika,'

'No, it wouldn't' said Lucy, 'because . . . .'

At that moment they were interrupted by Margaret coming in with Inspector Judge.

'The Inspector has come to visit you again,' she said rather grandly.

John turned to her,

'Margaret' he said, 'I have known you all my life. You used to baby-sit for little

Johnnie. I have no intentions of arresting you!'

They all laughed but Mike's laugh was more of a sneer. He didn't appreciate John's attempts at humour.
'John, can I get you a drink?' said Margaret.

'A glass of beer would be lovely, thank you Margaret.'

A few minutes later when John was settled with his beer, the others looked at him expectantly.
'The news is,' said John, 'that Hayden has been arrested.' The others cheered.
'Has he admitted what he's done?' asked Mike.

'Sort of, he's been acting very strangely. I think he's either very dim or he's going off his head. He seems to think asking Ken to tamper with the Tremayne's car was nothing as he was trying to please his father, "a great man". He keeps repeating that. He couldn't believe that he, Hayden Lewis, the son of "a great man" would be put in a police cell. He said things like, "but cells are for criminals, for common people, don't you know who I am, who my father is?"'
'Has the great man turned up to rescue him, to get bail?' asked Andrew.

'Not so far. He has sent him a top criminal lawyer, Sir Amos Timpson but he seems more interested in protecting Sir Gareth.'
'What exactly has Hayden admitted to?' asked Lucy.

'I think we can say amidst all the muddle that he has admitted to the car, and the searching of the Tremayne's house. I don't know that he has done much else. I think 'Z' is unknown to him. He seemed to think the actions of 'Z' were more or less acts of God in supporting his cause.'
'Did he say anything about the Farquars?' asked Mike.

'Oh yes, plenty, I casually asked him if he knew them. He then went on at great length about what good friends they all were, how Charlotte had introduced him to Annabel. How they had all gone to Ascot together and met up at Henley.' 'But nothing to implicate them? What about his father? Has he implicated him at all?'

'Only indirectly, at one point when his father was mentioned, he burst into tears.

He said he was trying to please his father but "Daddy was cross".'
'He actually said that?' said Lucy.
'Yes and then he said that Daddy forgave him and made it all right. He then went into great lengths about the goodness and greatness of his father in the middle of which he said that his father knew the police and the Home secretary and nobody would ever know what Hayden had done.'
'Well that gives us something about the great Sir Gareth,' said Mike.

'Yes,' said John hesitantly, 'but I think Sir Amos will prevent any more revelations and quite likely will get Hayden certified as being "under mental stress" or even insane which I think he probably is. The idea of being kept in a police cell probably drove him over the top.'
'It looks as though Sir Gareth didn't instigate the tampering of the car and was probably horrified at what Hayden had done?' suggested Lucy.

'I think that's right,' said John, 'but he probably came round to thinking that it was no bad thing, particularly when he had sewn up the police.'

'So,' said Mike slowly, 'we have achieved what we set out to do, that is to prove that the Tremaynes were murdered.'

'We have,' said Andrew, 'but we can't leave it there. Just think of Edith, the professor and Father John?'

'No we can't,' said Lucy, 'we also have *The Good Book of Oxford* to think about.

That is part of Mary's legacy and I want to work on it safely.'

'We all want you to be safe Lucy and we want to rid the country of the influence of Sir Gareth Morgan-Lewis,' said Mike.

'Nailing down Sir Gareth will be the difficult part,' said John, 'I think we will eventually get 'Z'. He will probably make a mistake somewhere. The trouble is he may strike again.'

Lucy, Mike and Andrew suddenly felt quite cold at the prospect.

'He has already attacked Mike,' said Andrew, 'so now, we are all in danger.'

'Don't forget, Andy, you also were attacked in France' said Lucy.

Mike and Andy looked at Lucy. They seemed to feel, 'your turn next'.

'We'll look after you, Lucy,' said Mike, 'putting his arm round her.

Lucy smiled rather thinly,

'Oh I'll be fine. That reminds me, I've had another invitation from Charlotte

Farquar.'

'I don't think you should go,' said Mike firmly.

'Mike,' said Lucy gently, 'we agreed that we need to find 'Z' and the hacker has led us to the home of the Farquars.'

'Lucy, what does the invitation say?' asked John.

'It's for tea, it's a posh invitation card with the time and place on, but Charlotte has scribbled, 'there will be just the two of us, so we can have a lovely chat and get to know each other. Pierre will make some really scrumptious cakes.'

John screwed his face up,

'It doesn't sound too dangerous and if you get close to Charlotte you may be able to find out a bit more about the household. I think any information about Monika would be useful.'

'We thought Monika was the one to watch,' said Andrew.

'I don't think it's worth the risk,' said Mike.

Lucy turned to Mike,

'Mike, I know you are concerned about me. It's very sweet of you but I must do this.'

'Sweet, sweet!' Mike snapped, standing up and walking towards the window, 'I'm never sweet. You want to get well in with all those toffs. You like them. You want to go!'

Lucy, tears streaming down her face, rushed out of the room.

'Mike!' said Andrew, 'that's not fair.'

Mike scowled at Andrew then rushed out after Lucy.

John and Andrew looked at each other in embarrassment. A few minutes later Mike and Lucy returned together.

'Sorry, over-reacted,' muttered Mike.

'So did I,' said Lucy with a watery smile.

'Well I suggest we make use of Margaret's kind hospitality and have another drink,' said John. He went out and quickly returned with a couple of bottles of wine, crisps peanuts and cheese and biscuits.

'Ah! A feast' said Mike brightening up. Margaret then came in to join them and they were soon laughing as Margaret described Mike's first day at school when he had refused to wear the uniform.

Chapter Forty-five

Lucy wandered along the Thames embankment. It was a lovely day and she watched the tourist boats going up and down the Thames. She was a little early for her appointment with Charlotte which was for four o'clock and also a little apprehensive. She had told Mike there was nothing whatsoever to worry about but she had to admit to herself that if not exactly worried, she was puzzled. It seemed strange to her that Charlotte should want her friendship so much that she had asked her to come to tea so soon after the evening party. Lucy was not afraid for her physical safety but that Charlotte might quiz her about *The Good Book* and try to persuade her to answer questions that she had rather not answer.

The whole Farquar family seemed to be enchanted by *The Book* and whereas Lord Alfred or Gerald would be sensitive and hold back, she thought that Charlotte would not. In a way it was part of her attractive, open, lively nature.

Lucy fingered Mike's gadget in the pocket of her jacket. Mike was doubly anxious as he couldn't come with her. He had a meeting at school that he had to go to. He had promised her that he would get away as quickly as possible and meet her on the embankment but if there was any danger and she pressed the buzzer, he would drop everything and come. Lucy couldn't imagine there would be an occasion when she would press the buzzer but she was touched by Mike's concern.

Lucy wandered up to the house which was facing the river. She noticed a boat moored outside the house. She wondered vaguely if it belonged to the Farquars. She mounted the steps and rang the bell. Almost immediately Charlotte appeared at the door. 'Lucy! How wonderful to see you! Come in, Come in.'

They went up to the first floor and entered a small room. Lucy was slightly puzzled by the room as it didn't look as comfortably furnished as other rooms she had seen and the carpet was quite worn. The room had two doors, the one they had entered and another one which was partially covered by a screen. There was a small old-fashioned fire-place in the room with arm chairs at either side.

Charlotte sat in one and indicated to Lucy to sit in the other.

'This is nice,' said Charlotte, 'we are all on our own, the servants all have the day off, Gerald is at work, Pops is in the House and the children will be in school until six o'clock as they have swimming after school.' Lucy smiled weakly.

'I am telling you this,' went on Charlotte, 'so you know that you can't escape and nobody, absolutely nobody, would hear your shouts. The reason I asked you to come is that I intend to kill you.' Lucy started and looked at her in amazement,

'Charlotte! You can't mean that?'

'Oh but I do. It's not that I don't like you. I think in other circumstances we could have got on well together. I still want you to think well of me. I'm like that. I want everyone to love me and on the whole I think I succeed very well. I am a very nice person. That's why I am going to explain to you why I intend to kill you.

You made a big mistake when you began to work on that book, *The Good Book of Oxford.* You probably realise that my father-in-law, Lord Alfred intends to give away all his money. He also decided the other day that he would resign his titles. Now I can't have that. I am not a greedy person. I could live quite happily on Gerald's earnings and I am not particularly interested in being 'Lady Charlotte', though it would be rather fun, but, and here is my concern, I want everything for my boys. You haven't met Hugo and Sebastian, have you? If you had perhaps you would understand.'

Lucy thought quickly. Her mind was surprisingly clear. She must keep Charlotte talking. That's what they did in books and in sieges. 'But why didn't you tell Lord Alfred how you felt?'

'I couldn't, you see he and Gerald were so excited about it. I did mention to

Gerald in passing that it affected not only him but the boys as well but he just dismissed it. He said that by the time the boys were old enough to have an opinion it would all be done and in any case he trusted that his boys – his- you notice, would be able to appreciate what had been done.'

'But surely he wouldn't want to go against your wishes?'

'You don't understand. I love my husband. I love him completely and passionately mainly because that is the way he loves me. Gerald is a quiet man, sensible, some people might say boring, but he is capable of great love, great passion. He would do anything for me.'

'Well then . . . .' began Lucy

'Hear me out,' said Charlotte, 'Gerald has two great loves in his life, me and God and I'm sorry to say that God comes first. He could not go against something which he believes to be morally right. Lord Alfred is different. He wants to do something that is morally right. He cares deeply about the poor and the deprived but he hasn't got that passionate love of God that possesses Gerald.'

'But surely you could have worked out some compromise?'

'No, I don't want Gerald or his father to think of me as a greedy, ambitious woman.'

'But how would it help to kill me. I could understand it if you killed Lord Alfred.'

'Oh No! I couldn't do that. I love old Pops. He's a great character and he loves me. No I intend to kill you because I intend to discredit the book. I have many pages from the book that Gerald and Pops haven't seen. I intend to insert scurrilous things in them, not too obvious but enough to make them think again. I am quite clever and I think I can do that.'

'Where did you get the passages from?'

'I got some from that fool, Hayden Lewis and his ridiculous father. I got some from the universities of Ebbchester and Cardiff and some from ransacking various houses. I also intend to find out where in France you got the book. I could get it form you now but I'm not into torture. No I might be able to get it from your collaborators after you are dead. They will be worried about you and might be willing to exchange information for knowledge of your whereabouts.' Suddenly there was a faint sound. It seemed to come from the next room.

'What's that?' said Charlotte.

'I didn't hear anything,' said Lucy, praying that someone had come into the house,

'You say you are "not into torture" but surely you are not into murder either?' Lucy said this slightly louder in case somebody might hear.

Charlotte laughed and produced a gun from under a cushion on her chair. 'That's where you are wrong. You may have heard that I like doing dangerous things, driving racing cars, bungee jumping, even walking on a tight-rope. Well, I hadn't committed murder before so that was a new experience. Yes, I murdered that poor old professor and that Welsh priest.'

Lucy looked at her in disbelief,

'I suppose you got someone to do it?' she said.

'No I wanted to do it myself, to have the experience. The Professor was easy. I poisoned him. I found a good poison that wasn't too obvious. I just slipped it into his tea, very easy. Father John was more challenging. I got the gun. I wanted to experience a point blank murder, to feel what it was really like. It was quite shocking but also quite thrilling. I was dressed in a jogging suit with the hood up. I knocked at the door, asked him to hear my confession, went inside the house and shot him. I didn't find much of the book which was disappointing but it was worth it – good experience.'

'And will you enjoy killing me?'

'I hope so. You see I haven't killed anyone I know before so it's a new experience. That's why I am telling you all this, so you will understand and that I can prolong the experience.'

'Doesn't it trouble your conscience to kill someone?'

Charlotte considered,

'Well I am doing it for my boys. It is a good cause. Mothers in Roman times often committed murder to further their sons' careers, Agrippina, now she was a one!'

Charlotte laughed,

'And then there was the mother of the sons of Zebedee. She asked Jesus to give them the highest place in Heaven. You see I am in good company.'
'But she didn't commit murder.'

'Well we don't know. She might have been one of the crowd that shouted,

"crucify him!"'

Charlotte picked up the gun and pointed it at Lucy.

'Now you have no need to worry. I won't miss or anything like that. I have been practising and so it should be a good clean shot.'
'But,' said Lucy, 'What will you do with the body?'

'Oh, I've thought of that. You may have noticed that there is a boat outside. It's mine and I have employed two men to work for me. After I have killed you, I shall roll you up in this old carpet, just like Cleopatra, do you remember the story?
I shall tie it up carefully. I have plenty of rope and signal to the chaps in the boat. They will come and collect the carpet – not a bit suspicious – and dispose of the body at sea. The carpet they will burn separately so there is no connection with here. I'm rather pleased with the whole plan. It's rather good don't you think?'
'Well actually, I'm not happy with it at all.'

'I can understand that but I am going to give you a full five minutes to repent of your sins and make your peace with God. I'm not going to send you into eternity, like Hamlet's Father, "unhouseled, disappointed, unnanealed." I suggest that you remove your hands from your chest. That way it will be cleaner. There is nowhere you could run to. If you ran to the door, I could quickly shoot you in the back as you fumbled with the key, so OK five minutes starting now.'

Lucy had been trying to think of a strategy all through the conversation. She planned to dive behind the screen and throw it over Charlotte. She knew the chances weren't good as it was a few steps to the screen and Charlotte could surely catch her somewhere on her body. She did try to say a prayer, conscious that she was probably going to meet her maker.

Suddenly, the screen was thrown down and Lord Alfred strode into the room. He placed himself in front of Lucy.

'What's all this about Charlotte m'dear? Come on, give me that gun! You might hurt someone with it.'

He bent down and picked the gun from the trembling Charlotte. Lucy realised that she wasn't trembling with fear but with rage. A terrible expression had contorted her beautiful face.

Charlotte jumped up and raced for the door. Alfred made a feeble attempt to stop her. Lucy sat still, unable to move. Lord Alfred looked out of the window.

'What is she doing?' he said.

Lucy joined him at the window. She saw Charlotte, below, getting into the boat. Two men left the boat, obviously at her instruction and she drove off at great speed. She raced towards Albert Bridge and made no attempt to go under the bridge but drove straight into one of the pillars. There was a huge crash and the boat went up in flames.

Lord Alfred and Lucy watched in horror.

Alfred said over and over again,

'God help us, that beautiful girl!'

Lucy took him by the arm and he sat in the chair vacated by Charlotte. Lucy brought the other chair closer and sat holding his hand. They sat in silence for some time and then Lord Alfred began to talk. He had heard a great deal of the conversation between Lucy and Charlotte. He had caught the word, 'murder' then had put on his hearing aid. He understood what Charlotte had done but wasn't quite sure why she had done it. Lucy explained about the boys. Lord Alfred was mystified.
'Why didn't she say how she felt?'

Lucy tried to explain in Charlotte's words.

'She could have killed me instead. I am an old man,' he said wearily.

Lucy explained that Charlotte had really loved him.

Lord Alfred stared ahead,

'Had he not resembled my father as he slept, I had don't', he muttered quoting Lady Macbeth.
They sat for some time, listening to the sound of fire engines and Police cars, Lucy holding the old man's hand. The tears ran down his face.
'What am I to say to Gerald? What can I say to the boys?' he wept.

Suddenly there was a loud knocking at the door,

'Knock, knock, knock', Lord Alfred seemed to be immersed in the world of Macbeth.
Charlotte had left the door wide open and so the Policemen came up the stairs.

Lucy went to the door,

'We are in here,' she said. Two Policemen came into the room, 'Lord Alfred?' said one.

'I am he and this is a friend, Lucy Hammond,' he replied courteously.

'I am sorry to inform you that whoever was driving that boat was killed outright. I understand it was your daughter-in-law, Mrs Gerald Farquar.
Lord Alfred nodded.

'I am sorry to disturb you at this sad time but I just want to clear things up. Do you think this terrible crash was an accident or do you think there was any reason for suicide?'
'It was an accident,' said Lucy quickly, 'Charlotte was with us here and went out to drive the boat up the river. There was no reason whatsoever for her to commit suicide.' The policeman looked at Lord Alfred who looked bemused but nodded. 'There may have been a mechanical failure,' said the policeman, 'Your son will be arriving here shortly, so I will leave you.'
The policeman left. Lord Alfred looked questioningly at Lucy.
Lucy, who was now also crying, clutched both his hands,

'There's no reason for them to know. Is there? What good would it do?'

'Oh Lucy, I don't know. We're not supposed to lie to the police.'

'Well we don't know for certain that it wasn't an accident. Do we?'

'But what shall I say to Gerald?'

'Nothing, just comfort him in his sorrow. He doesn't need to know.'

'Is that possible? Do you think she was insane Lucy?'

'Possibly, I didn't know her very well but I immediately liked her. She seemed to have so many good qualities. I think we should concentrate on them.' They heard some people coming upstairs. Lucy looked down and saw the gun lying on the floor, almost under the chair. She quickly picked it up and put it in her handbag. Gerald came in with a tall, young woman.

'Gerald, Rowena,' cried Lord Alfred and appeared to crumple up.

'What are you doing in here?' asked Rowena and took her father by the hand and led him into the comfortable drawing room. Lucy and Gerald followed.
'What happened ?' said Gerald weakly. He was ashen white.

'Charlotte had invited me over for a chat, Lord Alfred arrived and then she decided to go on the boat. It was such a lovely afternoon,' Lucy finished lamely. 'She was a very good driver,' said Gerald, 'but I suppose it was inevitable. She would do these dangerous things. Oh Charlotte, my beautiful Charlotte.' He suddenly broke down. His sister put her arms round him, then she went to the side board and poured out four glasses of brandy. They sipped them quietly, glad of something to do. After a while, Lucy stood up,
'Do you mind if I go,' she said, 'I don't think I can do anything else.' Rowena walked down the stairs with her.
At the doorway, she put her arms round Lucy and whispered,

'Thank you Lucy, I won't ask you any questions but I know this family are indebted to you. Goodbye and thank you again.'

Lucy said nothing and walked quickly away. When she was some distance and out of sight of the house, she sat on a seat facing the river in the sunshine. Things looked normal. She saw some rowers practising; another cruise boat went cheerfully down the Thames. Could all this have happened? Was she imagining things?

She leaned her head back and shut her eyes.

'Lucy, Lucy, I'm so sorry. I got your buzz and came straight out but I went as far as Waterloo and then the line was down. I came out and I couldn't get a taxi for ages. Are you all right? I'm so glad to see you. What happened?'

Lucy looked at Mike's agitated, anxious face. Suddenly she started to shake. She threw herself on Mike's shoulder and began to weep uncontrollably.

Mike put his arms around her,

'Lucy, Lucy what is it? Oh my poor Lucy, what happened? My precious Lucy, has someone hurt you? I'll kill him if he has.'

Lucy smiled through her tears,

'No more killing,' she sobbed. Gradually she told Mike what had happened. He constantly blamed himself for not being there.

'Mike if you had turned up, she would have shot you.'

'Well I would have risked that,'

'But it wouldn't have helped me and anyway I don't want you dead.'

'Don't you Lucy?'

'Of course I don't. You're one of my best friends.'

'friends, I suppose you have lots of friends, but Lucy what are we going to do about Charlotte?'

'What can we do?'

'Don't you think we should tell the police what really happened?'

'Mike, No! I gave my word.'

'What about Johnnie?'

'I'd forgotten about Johnnie but we can't tell him Mike. We can't.'

'Ok, we'll leave it for the moment and we'll think of something.'

Lucy put her head back on Mike's shoulder,

'Thanks Mike, you're a good friend.' 'Mmm, friend,' said Mike.

Chapter Forty-six

Lucy had a bad night. She was staying with Margaret Nichols. Mike has insisted that she was 'in no fit state' to stay on her own and Margaret on seeing her had recognised immediately that she had 'had a bad shock'. Margaret knew about the death of Charlotte Farquar. It was in all the news bulletins with pictures of the wrecked boat. Someone had even taken a film of the boat in flames on his phone camera. A policeman had been interviewed and had said that Mrs Farquar had been having tea with a 'family friend' before the accident. In a later bulletin, the 'family friend' had been named as 'Miss Lucy Hammond'.

Lucy was shocked that the accident had so much coverage but relieved that she didn't need to explain to Margaret what had happened.

After delivering Lucy to his mother, Mike had something to eat and then went straight back to Streatham. Lucy made him promise that he would only tell

Andrew what had happened and would not say anything to anyone else, even to

John. He had promised but had said,

'We will talk about it later'

As Lucy tried to sleep she kept wondering what Mike had meant by those words. When she did finally drop off, she dreamt that she was surrounded by policemen with Mike in the middle, pointing their fingers and truncheons at her, and shouting,

'Liar, liar.'

She woke up in a sweat but was grateful that it was only a dream. Lucy turned the light on and picked up a novel by her bedside. In no time she was asleep again but this time she dreamt that Charlotte was pointing the gun at her but it wasn't the beautiful Charlotte but a Charlotte who looked like a monster. She pulled the trigger and it was as though Lucy felt the bullet going through her. She felt herself shouting, 'No! no!' Lucy opened her eyes. She wasn't dead. She wasn't in Heaven. She was here in Margaret Nichols' comfortable house. She heard a soft knock at the door. The door was pushed gently open, 'Can I come in Lucy?'

'Oh Margaret, I'm so sorry, I've wakened you up. I'm afraid I had a nightmare.' Of course you did. You have been through a great trauma. I've brought you some hot milk. I find that helps me if I have a restless night. Take these paracetamol.
They might help.'

Margaret put the tray on a side table. She had brought two drinks, one for herself and one for Lucy. She had also brought in a plate of biscuits. Lucy remembered such an occasion with her mother when she was a small child and felt comforted.
Margaret sat on the side of the bed.

'Was Mrs Farquar a great friend of yours, dear?'

'No, I hardly knew her. Her father, Lord Alfred was interested in my research and invited me to tea at the House of Lords. It was fun and he is such a nice man. Then he invited me to a party. He wanted me to meet Charlotte. She was very welcoming and kind and I really enjoyed meeting her husband, Gerald. I was a bit surprised at being asked to tea again by Charlotte but they were all so nice, I decided to go.'
Lucy stopped talking. She was reluctant to say much more.

'So sad,' said Margaret, 'such a pretty girl!'

'She was,' agreed Lucy, 'such a shock for her father-in-law and for Gerald. I don't know how he will get over it and of course those two little boys.' They both sat in silence for a minute.

'Still, I'm sure you were a great help to them, Lucy and you mustn't regret anything.'

Lucy sat munching the biscuits and wondered what Margaret meant. She hadn't said anything to Margaret and she knew that Mike hadn't but it was as though Margaret Knew. Lucy wished with all her heart that she could tell Margaret everything but she knew she could not, nevertheless Margaret was a comfort to her. Eventually Margaret stood up and said,

'Now shut your eyes and go to sleep and remember none of it was your fault.' She bent and kissed Lucy goodnight and finally Lucy went to sleep. The following day, Lucy spent a pleasant morning with Margaret, shopping, baking bread and talking about everything except the tragedy of the day before. After lunch Lucy decided to go for a walk. She walked up a nearby hill and gazed down at the lovely view. Everything looked so peaceful, so tranquil. She picked some daisies then sat down on a log. She looked down at the beauty of the daisy, the colours, white, yellow, pink and green, the beautiful symmetry of the flower, a 'lily of the field'.

She then thought of the beauty of the human being, worth so much more than the tender little flower in her hand. She thought of Charlotte, the most beautiful woman she had ever seen, beautiful, not only in face, and figure but with a lovely smile, an enchanting personality. She was intelligent, thoughtful, considerate, loving and a charming companion and hostess. How could it be that such a woman was a murderer? Lucy could hardly say the word, even silently. Was she right to keep quiet about what Charlotte had done? Was the spirit of Father John crying out for Justice? She wanted to protect Gerald, Sebastian and Hugo but was truth more important? Could they base their happiness on a lie?

Lucy walked slowly down the hill. She walked past a small, ancient parish church. She stopped to admire it, then noticed that the door was open. She went in. She went up to the front of the church and sat down. She admired the beautiful, old rood screen and looked round at the lovely church.

'Oh God, what am I to do?' she thought, 'tell me what's the right thing to do.' 'The end doesn't justify the means but I haven't exactly lied have I? Charlotte didn't say she was going to kill herself and maybe that wasn't her intention. It seems likely but we don't know. She wasn't depressed either. When I went in she was very cheerful and in the end she was angry but not depressed. Would Father John want revenge on his killer? That's not likely and even if he did it's not possible as she's dead but what about his friends and relations? People often talked about 'Justice' and 'closure''. Lucy tried to think whether if someone close to her was murdered whether it would matter to her to find the killer. She supposed it would be important if a serial rapist or child molester was on the loose but this didn't apply here but then again the relatives didn't know that the murderer was dead.

She sighed and clutched her head. She didn't notice the old clergyman shuffling down the aisle. He stopped when he saw Lucy and heard her heartfelt sigh.

'Are you in trouble my dear?' he asked.

Lucy looked up,

'Not really,' she smiled, 'I've just got a problem and I don't know what to do.'

The old gentleman sat down beside her,

'Do you want to talk about it?'

'I'd love to but I can't. I've got to decide between two evils or perhaps between two good things. It's really between honesty and charity.'
'I see,' said the old man, 'Usually Charity wins as it is of course the greatest virtue but I suppose it depends on the extent of the dishonesty.'
'It's not so much dishonesty as a lack of honesty, if you see what I mean. It's a matter of not saying something, keeping something back.'
The old priest was silent for a while. Then he said,

'A long time ago, when I was a young priest in my first parish, one of the choir boys stole a large sum of money from the church. It was obvious who did it and the boy more or less admitted it but he wasn't at all repentant and in fact was quite insolent. I didn't like the boy and I called the police. I thought it was the right thing to do. It would teach him a lesson and it was a terrible thing to steal from the church. I learned later that the boy's father had left the family and that the mother was very poor. She was a good woman and tried to come to church when she could but I didn't know her. When her son came to trial, she had a nervous breakdown and the children were taken into care. I don't think the boy was sent to Borstal or anything. The state was more merciful than me but I never saw him again. He never came to church again.'
Lucy sat quietly for a while,

'It still troubles you?' she said.

'Yes I suppose it does. I know God has forgiven me but sometimes it's hard to forgive oneself. I suppose I was the one who learnt the lesson. I'm sure your situation isn't like mine but if there is a choice I should go for charity.'
Lucy smiled at the priest,

'Thank you, I think that has helped.' He stood up and shuffled off. Lucy sat in silence for a few minutes then left the church.

As Lucy approached Margaret's house, to her horror she saw John Judge walking towards her. He was the last person she wanted to see at the moment. She couldn't escape him. He had obviously been to Margaret's to see her and now he was waving to her.
'Hello Lucy, just the person I wanted to see. Have you got a few minutes? I'd like to have a chat.'
Lucy's heart sank but she couldn't avoid it.

'Yes of course,' she said.

'Have you been to the "Copper Kettle"?' he said, 'they do some very nice muffins there. Do join me for some tea.'
They walked along into the town chatting about the lovely weather.

When they arrived at 'The Copper Kettle' John took a tray of tea pots and muffins into the garden at the back of the café.
'This is lovely!' said Lucy, 'You can see the river in the valley.' 'Yes it is pretty,' said John.
Lucy poured out the tea and they tucked into the muffins.
Eventually John said, 'Mike would be very annoyed if he knew I had come to see you.' 'Would he?' said Lucy.
'Yes, I spoke to him on the phone and he said that you had had a terrible experience and nobody was to trouble you. He wouldn't even tell me where you were but that wasn't difficult to guess.'
He looked at Lucy and put his hand on her arm,

'Lucy, I am really sorry about what happened to you and I promise you that I won't trouble you for long.'

Lucy stared down at the flowered tablecloth, 'Here it comes' she thought.

John began again.

'I just want you to know that my brief is what happened in Hertfordshire. I am not supposed to know anything about what goes on in London or in Cardiff for that matter. I knew about the phone-hacking and the Farquars because Mike told me about it. I couldn't use the information that Mike had about phone-hacking as that wasn't authorised by the police.' John looked at Lucy and smiled, 'I only know about the tragedy on the river because I watch the news. I saw the report on the news of your statement. I have no reason to question it. As far as I am concerned this has nothing to do with my enquiries with Ken Weston.' Lucy looked up at John. She realised she was trembling.

'But Lucy,' said John gently, 'that doesn't mean I can't make some guesses. You needn't worry, I shan't make use of these guesses but I don't think we have to worry any more about 'Z' or phone-hacking?' Lucy nodded.

'I don't know why she did it or what she intended to do next but I imagine it was something to do with inheritance. You needn't acknowledge these guesses. I know you would tell me if you thought someone's life was at risk so we'll leave it at that.'

Lucy suddenly realised that tears were running down her face. She tried to speak but couldn't.

John put his hand on Lucy's arm,

'I know from what Mike said that you have had a frightening experience. Mike didn't want me to see you. I think he thought I would bully you into telling all you knew. That isn't necessary. I thought I would come despite Mike's reservations because I felt you would be worried. I just wanted to put your mind at rest.'

Lucy smiled through her tears,

'And you have, John, thank you. I have been anxious about what to do. I suppose the only thing that worries me now is Father John. Won't his family want answers?'

'I investigated his family. There are not many of his close family left. His mother died about two years ago and his father has been dead for a long time. He has two brothers, one of whom is in America and an older brother who is a farmer in Ireland. I can't see them making a fuss. It will probably go down as 'an unsolved case'. Maybe years in the future some new evidence might turn up and they could re-open the case but it would seem unlikely. Are you all right, Lucy? You look a little pale.'

When John had mentioned evidence, Lucy remembered the gun that was still in her handbag. She must get rid of it!

'No I'm fine John, very relieved. Thank you very much for coming to see me. It was so kind of you.'

'No problem. I'll be off now. I'll be in touch. I don't think we need to worry any more about phones.'

John Judge went off and Lucy wandered back to Margaret's thinking how she could get rid of the gun. She had thought that she would throw it in the Thames but she realised her throwing skills weren't that good and in any case there were too many people around.

'You have another visitor,' said Margaret as Lucy went through the kitchen door, 'I'm just going to see Mrs Kennedy. I'll probably be a couple of hours. She does like a chat. Sister Magdalene is in the sitting room.'

Lucy was puzzled and slightly apprehensive. She wondered if Sister Magdalene had anything to do with Father John.

As Lucy entered the sitting room, a tall, attractive young woman stood up to greet her. Lucy suddenly realised who she was.

'Rowena!' she exclaimed.

Rowena laughed,

'I'm afraid I gave Mrs Nichols my religious name. I thought it was better than saying, "Rowena Farquar" I hope you don't mind me coming?' 'Of course not' said Lucy. They both sat down.
'Before we say anything, I want to tell you that I know more or less what happened. My dad was very distressed and I knew something had happened which Gerald and I didn't know about. I admit I was curious, nosy if you like but I thought it would help Dad to talk about it. He did eventually. It was a bit garbled but I understood. Dad was also very concerned about you and I said I would go and see you.'
'I haven't told anyone apart from the two people I have been working with and they won't tell anyone.'
'Lucy,' said Rowena gently, 'I didn't come here to check up on you. I came to make sure you were all right.'
Lucy looked up at Rowena. She was simply dressed in a white blouse and navy skirt with a crucifix round her neck. Her dark brown hair was tied back. Despite the simplicity of her attire, Lucy saw before her a very striking woman. She not only had a lovely face but exuded strength and personality. Lucy knew she could trust her.
'I think perhaps I had better tell you the whole story,' she said.

Lucy began by telling Rowena about Mary and Frank and their subsequent deaths then proceeded to tell her about Mike and Andrew and all their investigations. When it came to her conversation with Charlotte, she found that it was so imprinted on her mind that she could remember it word for word.
When she had finished Rowena just stared in front of her.

'It's worse than I thought,' she said, 'I didn't really know about the professor and Father John. Dad knew something and kept saying, "she was a murderer" but he obviously didn't catch everything. Poor Charlotte, poor Charlotte, God rest her soul.'

Lucy waited for Rowena to recover, then she said,

'Rowena, you knew Charlotte. Did she ever give you a clue as to what she was really like?'

'No, she didn't. You met her. She was incredibly beautiful. She must have been aware of that but somehow it didn't seem to matter to her. She was always charming, always kind and considerate. She was a good and faithful wife. We knew that in the kind of life she lived she must have had many temptations. She was pursued by Hollywood stars, so-called celebrities, even by politicians but we never had reason to believe that she was ever unfaithful to Gerald and she was a wonderful mother, she had a nanny but she tried to do as much as she could for those boys. She was always playing with them and would sit up all night if one of them had so much as a temperature, and yet . . . .'

'Yet what?'

'Well I said, "You met her" which was obvious but I suppose I meant that you knew her as well as I did. She has been married to Gerald for nearly ten years and I have seen a lot of her over the years but I didn't feel as though I got to know her any better than the day I met her. In some ways the conversation that she had with you tells us more about her than the hundreds I had with her, her passionate love for Gerald and the boys, her love for Dad and perhaps her vulnerability.' 'Yes,' said Lucy, 'it was as though even when she was preparing to kill me, she didn't want me to think badly of her.'

'I met her parents yesterday,' said Rowena, 'they seemed very nice, ordinary people. They put her death down to the fact that she was a "bit of a dare-devil". It was almost as though they expected it. They were desperately upset, of course. I think she was a good daughter and went to see them regularly with Gerald and the children. She was very generous to them.'

'Did she look like them?'

'Well you could see certain likenesses but I don't think either of them would ever have been beautiful.'
'Do the boys look like her?'

Rowena laughed,

'Not at all, Sebastian is the image of Gerald and perhaps Hugo looks a bit like her dad. It's as though she rose from the sea like Venus and she was a one-off. I know that sounds very fanciful.'
'Perhaps it's just as well,' said Lucy.

'I also wanted to say,' said Rowena hesitantly, 'that if you feel you have to tell the police, please don't hesitate to do so.'
'I have to admit that I was worried about that but I saw our policeman friend, John Judge this morning and although he had an inkling of what had happened, he said that it wasn't on his patch and he wouldn't make any enquiries about what happened in Chelsea. That's not to say that I won't be questioned again by the Metropolitan Police but I'm not bothered about them. I wouldn't have liked to deliberately deceive John because he has been such a good friend.'
Rowena laughed,

'But you don't mind deceiving the Met?'

'I won't tell them any lies. I was in the room with your father when Charlotte left. She didn't say she was going to commit suicide and we didn't expect her to do what she did. Also we don't know for certain that it was suicide.'

Rowena smiled at Lucy,

'Lucy, what you are doing is very brave. If everything came to light, you could be charged with obstructing the course of Justice and if something like that happens you must tell all but . . . .'
Here Rowena trailed off. Her eyes filled with tears.

'Rowena,' said Lucy, 'I spoke to Gerald at the party. I liked him very much. He is a good man who passionately loved his wife. I should like him always to think well of her. I haven't met Charlotte's parents but I should wish the same for them but most of all if possible I should like to protect those little boys. They must grow up with fond memories of their beautiful mother. As time goes by the memories will fade and maybe Gerald will provide them with a new mother but that's in the future.'

'Lucy, I will always be grateful for what you are doing. Would it be possible for us to be friends?'

Lucy sighed and shook her head,

'I don't think so Rowena. I should always be a reminder of a tragedy. I don't think we will forget each other and please remember me in your prayers.'

'Oh I will, I will and I will continue to thank God for you, and Lucy . . . .' 'Yes?'

'Will you pray for me too?'

Lucy smiled,

'Of course I will. I will pray for all your family but I think you are probably better at praying than me. I expect I will see news of the Farquars in the media from time to time and I hope the news will be happy.'

'And we will see news about *The Good Book of Oxford*. I shall look forward to its publication.'

'That will need your prayers,' said Lucy, 'It seems to have caused many tragedies over the centuries.'

'It will do nothing but good,' said Rowena firmly and stood up, 'thank you, thank you Lucy.'

The two women hugged each other and then Rowena left.

Lucy sat for some time, quietly crying. She thanked God that she now knew what to do. She had had three answers to her prayers.

Chapter Forty-seven

'Margaret, you have been wonderful! I'd love to stay longer, particularly for your cooking! But I had better go back tomorrow.'
'Well, it's been lovely having you here, Lucy,' said Margaret as she divided the steak and kidney pie into two, 'but I can understand why you want to get back to your work'.
Lucy looked round the comfortable dining room with the photographs of Mary and Mike as children on the mantelpiece.
'Margaret, is that your mobile phone flashing?'

Margaret picked it up,

'I suppose someone has sent me a text. I'm not very good at picking these things up. I hope it's not urgent. Oh! It's Michael. He says he's coming this evening to make sure you are all right. Oh dear! He says to save dinner for him. I only made enough for two.'
'Margaret, there's plenty here. We'll just take a piece off these two portions and I can see you have loads of vegetables. We'll eat ours before he gets here and then he won't notice that our dinners are smaller than his – we're not as greedy as he is!'
Margaret laughed,

'Yes he does like his food. I don't know how he keeps so thin. He always looks as though he is starving.'
As Lucy and Margaret ate the pie, Lucy felt strangely excited. She was slightly anxious in case Mike wanted her to reveal all to the police but would be pleased to see him. She needed to talk to someone who was as informed as she was about the whole investigation and she hoped that Mike might have some ideas about disposing of the gun.
'Steak and Kidney pie! Great! I hope you have saved some for me.'
Mike came bursting into the dining-room.

'We have, Michael. I'll just go and warm it up.' Margaret went into the kitchen.

'Mike, we need to talk,' whispered Lucy.

'We'll go for a walk after we've eaten. It's a lovely summer evening and still quite early.'

'Will your mother mind us abandoning her?'

'Of course not, she knows I've just come to see you.'

Margaret came in and put a generous dinner in front of Mike.

'Thanks Mum. You've done a good job on Lucy. She looks a lot more healthy than when I last saw her. She's getting quite fat!'

'Michael! You mustn't say such things. Lucy may not know you're only joking. But

Lucy has had visitors to cheer her up, Johnnie Judge came and a very nice lady,

Sister Magdalene.'

'Johnnie Judge! What did he want?' Mike looked furious. He stabbed viciously at his potatoes, 'Mum, I thought Lucy and I might go for a walk after dinner if that's all right. I might take her back to Ebbchester as she hasn't got her car.' 'Of course, it's a beautiful evening. Perhaps you could show Lucy the lake?' After they had cleared the table Lucy went upstairs to get her handbag. 'I don't know why you need that,' said Mike, 'we're not going shopping.'

They walked for some yards away from the house then Mike almost shouted,

'What the hell did Johnnie Judge want? I told him to keep away from you.' 'It's all right Mike.' Lucy told him what had happened. 'I was actually very relieved to see him.'

'I can see that,' grumbled Mike, 'but he should have told me.'

'Why?'

'Well you are my responsibility, not his.'

'Mike, it's very kind of you to be concerned about me but I am not your responsibility.'
'Yes you are. You are my . . . .'

'You're what?'

'Friend, I suppose,' said Mike lamely, 'and who is sister Magdalene?' Lucy told him.
Mike groaned,

'This is certainly a complicated business you have got yourself into. Well don't look so cross. I know it's not your fault.'
'There's another complication,' said Lucy.

'Oh no! What's that?'

Lucy looked round furtively then opened her handbag and showed Mike the gun.

He gasped in horror,

'Where on earth did you get that?'

Lucy told him, then she said,

'I was hoping you might help me get rid of it.' Mike thought for a while.
'Your mother mentioned a lake.'

Mike brightened,

'Yes, good old Mum. Lucy, they hire out boats that you can row into the middle of the lake. I think they go on quite late in the summer time. If we run we might get there in time.'
'OK, let's run,' said Lucy.

Mike grabbed her hand and they raced down a pathway through the woods, then on to a bridleway. Lucy was out of breath and gasping but Mike took no notice and dragged her along. Eventually, after about a mile, they arrived at a huge lake which looked beautiful in the setting sun.

'Hiya George,' shouted Mike to a man who was sorting out the boats.

'Well if it isn't young Michael Nichols. It must be years since I've seen you.'

'We wondered if you had a rowing boat we could hire?'

'Michael! It's nearly nine o'clock. I'm just putting them away.'

'Please George. I told my girlfriend about Letbury Lake and she would love to have a trip on the lake – just a short one?'
George gave Mike a knowing look,

'Well it does look very romantic at the moment, everything pink in the setting sun. I'll tell you what. You take that little boat over there and you can put it in the shed yourself. I'll give you the keys and you can leave them under that green pot and I'll be off home.'
'Thanks George, you're a pal.'

George guffawed and proceeded to clear up singing 'Roaming in the Gloaming with a lassie by my side,'
Mike pulled the boat into the water and helped Lucy in. He pushed off. Lucy waited to get her breath back,
'Your girlfriend! Setting sun! Roamin in the Gloamin!'

Mike laughed,

'Well it worked and in any case you are a friend and a girl so what's the problem?'

He looked around,

'You must admit, this red sky reflected in the water. It is beautiful.'

Lucy leaned back in a comfortable cushioned seat while Mike took the oars and rowed out into the middle of the lake. The water was calm with hardly a ripple and there wasn't a soul in sight. The only sound was an occasional bird calling to its mate as it flew over the lake. Lucy shut her eyes. It was lovely, so peaceful and she would soon get rid of that hateful gun.
'This would be a good spot,' called Mike as he stopped rowing, 'it is very deep in the middle and I think we are just about there. Give me the gun and I'll chuck it in,'
'Willingly,' said Lucy and took the gun out of her handbag and handed it to Mike.

He looked at it as it lay in his hand.
'I've never held a real gun before,' he said, 'I've had a go at those rifles in the fairground. I'm a pretty good shot, though I say it myself. I used to have cowboy outfits with guns. I used to practice the quick draw.'
Mike stood up in the gently rocking boat and twirled the gun in his fingers. Then he put it in the belt of his trousers and pulled it out quickly. He nearly fell on top of Lucy.
Lucy laughed,

'Mike you are a fool. Somebody might see you and they would know where we have dropped the gun. Please Mike, get rid of it.'
Mike leaned over the side of the boat and pointed it towards the water. He pulled the trigger. The noise was deafening and gave them both a shock. Mike dropped the gun and it sank into the water. He turned and went to the back of the boat and sat by the trembling Lucy.
'Lucy, I'm sorry. I think part of me thought it wouldn't be loaded.'

Mike suddenly stopped. He turned pale,

'Lucy, that bullet was meant for you!'

Lucy nodded and sobbed on Mike's shoulder. He put his arms round her. He was trembling too.

'Lucy, Lucy, thank God for that old man.'

They clutched each other as the boat drifted into the sunset.

Chapter Forty-eight

Andrew was feeling pleased with himself. He had enjoyed a good day. He went to the Science Museum and watched a scientific model being set up. He was particularly interested in it as it concerned the topic that his father had been working on. The museum was fairly quiet as the school holidays hadn't started yet and the man and woman who were setting up the model were very helpful in answering Andrew's questions. They were impressed by his knowledge of the subject.

'My dad used to work on it,' he explained.

'What's your father's name?' asked the girl whose name he gathered was Tracey.

'Frank Tremayne, but he's dead now,'

'Oh, we knew Frank. He was at Ebbchester. He was great!' said the young man.

'Yes, he was,' mumbled Andrew.

Tracey put her hand on Andrew's shoulder.

'We heard what happened to both your parents. It was a terrible tragedy. I'm so sorry.'
Andrew nodded, ashamed at the tears he couldn't prevent.

'I'm hoping to study Physics like my dad,' he said.

The young man looked at his watch,

'Time for a coffee,' he said. He turned to Andrew, 'won't you join us? I'm Marek by the way.'
'Thank you, I will. I'm Andy.'

Andrew had enjoyed chatting to Tracey and Marek. They were research students at Imperial College and after the coffee, Marek showed him round the College, particularly the laboratories where they worked. Andrew decided on the spot that he wanted to go to Imperial College to study Physics. He felt almost light-headed with the joy of his decision. It somehow put him in contact with his father and he knew that this was what he wanted to do. As he travelled back to Streatham, he was alone in the railway carriage and he said out loud,

'Dad, I'm going to study Physics like you. I will do my A levels next summer and I will get A stars for all of them and then I will go to Imperial College, get a first and then do research. I hope you can hear me.'

It was strange. It was as though he heard his father's laughing voice coming back to him,

'Steady on, Andy. There are a lot of decisions there and a lot of work to be done. A stars and a first eh! But I'm delighted you want to study Science. I can't help thinking it's the best thing ever! Go for it, Andy. Go for it!'

'I will, I will,' shouted Andrew and was somewhat embarrassed as an old lady got into the carriage at the tube stop.

After Andrew left the tube train and was leaving the station, he noticed a headline in one of the free papers that were stacked up in a container. It read,

'Sir Gareth Morgan-Lewis taken in for questioning by the Police.'

Andrew picked up a newspaper and read that following the arrest of Sir Gareth's son, Hayden, certain facts had emerged that made it necessary to interview

Hayden's father. The newspaper stressed that,

'There is no question that this distinguished man is accused of any wrong-doing.

He is merely, helping the Police with their inquiries.'

Andrew had been looking forward to telling Mike about his day and was now also wanting to talk about the arrest. He wondered if Mike had had any information from Inspector Judge.

As Andrew entered the flat, he saw a note, pinned to the wall,

'Back late, gone to visit Lucy.'

Andrew was cross, he was disappointed as he wanted to talk but he was cross that Mike had gone on his own to see Lucy.

'Why didn't he wait for me?' he said out loud, 'I could have gone with him to visit

Lucy.'

Muttering to himself, Andrew prepared some beans on toast and then sat down to watch the news to see if there was any more about Sir Gareth.

On the six o'clock news it was purely that Sir Gareth was 'helping the police with their inquiries'. A solicitor was interviewed who said quite categorically that nobody suspected this 'kind and generous pillar of the community' of anything but that he was concerned about his son who was undergoing 'distressing mental health problems'.

Andrew then turned over to watch a tennis match. He wasn't normally very interested in tennis but he became quite engrossed with a hard-fought match between an American and a Spaniard. He was quite cross when the end of the programme was interrupted by 'breaking news' but sat up in amazement to hear that 'Sir Gareth Morgan-Lewis had now been arrested'. The BBC promised more information on *The News at Ten*.

Andrew waited patiently for the news but the only thing that he heard was that someone had come forward with more evidence. The solicitor came on briefly to say that he was sure that the matter 'would soon be cleared up satisfactorily'. Andrew was about to switch off the television when he saw a man entering the police station. He couldn't see clearly because the man was surrounded by reporters and flashing lights but he recognised the man as Stuart Martin, a good friend of his parents.

Andrew was puzzled. He couldn't think what Stuart could have to do with Gareth

Morgan-Lewis. He switched the channel to BBC 2 and was pleased to see that *Newsnight* was very interested in the arrest of Sir Gareth. They had found out that the charge was 'perverting the course of Justice'.

A friend of Sir Gareth was saying that it was obvious that Sir Gareth had been trying to protect his son, 'something that any father would do and I think all those of us who are fathers would sympathise with that.'

Another person being interviewed had looked into Sir Gareth's murky past and purported that Gareth was 'no stranger to dodgy dealings and criminality.'

The interviewer was shocked by this statement and said,

'But surely, Sir Gareth is renowned throughout the world for his generosity to good causes?'

The interview went on but nothing else was revealed and eventually Andrew fell asleep. He was awakened some time later, by a push from Mike.

'Wakey, wakey! You need to get yourself to bed.'

Andrew yawned, then looked at his watch,

'It's half past three! Have you just come in? What have you been doing?' 'Andy! You are not my mum. If you must know, Lucy was in a bit of a state. She had picked up Charlotte's gun at the Farquars and put it in her handbag. She wanted me to help her get rid of it.

'Good old Lucy! She was very fast thinking. Did you get rid of it?'

'Yes, we rowed out into Letbury Lake and dropped it into the water. We came back on the bus as Lucy was pretty shaken up.' 'Hmm! I can't see you being much good as a calming influence.'

Mike smiled happily,

'I think I did pretty well actually.'

Andrew didn't look convinced,

'I've got a bit of news myself,' he said. He told Mike about the news and the arrest of Sir Gareth. Mike was delighted. Andrew was always surprised at Mike's vindictiveness.
'Andy! He's an evil man. He may not have been directly responsible for the death of your parents but he certainly tried to cover it up. And probably even more important than that, he has this stifling influence over every government that's in power. He needs locking up for the rest of his life.'
'Oh, there's another thing,' Andrew told Mike about Stuart Martin. Mike didn't know him but seemed to recollect the name. 'Will Inspector Judge be able to enlighten us?'

'I expect he could,' said Mike, 'whether or not he will is another matter. He went to see Lucy so he knows our situation.'
'Why did he go and see Lucy?'

'Why? That is the question. Damned cheek! without even mentioning it to me.'

'Why should he?'

'Because it's our case. He told Lucy not to worry about the Farquars. He wouldn't let on about Charlotte.'

'Did Lucy tell him?'

'No of course not. We are not to tell anyone but I think he pretty much guessed the gist of it but he said it wasn't on his patch so it was nothing to do with him.'

'That was very decent of him. He has been helpful to us Mike.'

'I suppose so,' sighed Mike, 'it's a pity he's so . . . .'

'so what?'

'Oh I don't know, I mean toodlepip! I ask you. Oh well I'd better get to bed, school tomorrow and then a busy weekend.'

'Why? What are you doing at the weekend?'

'Aha! Wouldn't you like to know, Mr Nosy.' Mike turned to go upstairs,

'Still, I shall have wonderful dreams!'

Chapter Forty-nine

Lucy turned over in bed and switched the alarm off. She shut her eyes and went back to sleep. Suddenly, there it was again. She reached out to attack the clock, then realised it was the telephone. Who could possibly be phoning her at this unearthly hour? She sat up and picked up the phone, noticing as she did so that it was ten o'clock!
'Hello' she stammered.

'Is that Lucy Hammond?'

'Yes,' she said, trying to make her voice a little brighter.

'This is Stuart Martin. Do you remember me?'

'Of course,' said Lucy, 'lovely to speak to you again.'

'Did you see the television news last night?'

'No, I was out late,' said Lucy cautiously.'

'Well, I'm telephoning in case you or your friends might be wondering what I was doing visiting a police station to testify against Sir Gareth Morgan-Lewis.'
'Oh! I didn't know.'

'Lucy, I don't want to talk on the phone. Could I come and see you? I thought you were the best person to talk to as I know you and you live nearby.'
'Of course,' said Lucy, 'I should be pleased to see you. Do you know my address?

Now, would be fine.'

Lucy replaced the phone. She must liven up. She had such a headache. Of course it was the champagne or was it Prosecco? She smiled at the recollection. Mike had decided that after her ordeal and subsequent events, champagne was needed. He had rifled his mother's cupboard before driving her back to Ebbchester. She smiled again as she drank some water with a couple of paracetamol. She was still smiling half an hour later when the doorbell rang.

'Hello Stuart, do come in. Would you like a cup of tea, coffee?'

Stuart accepted a cup of coffee and Lucy joined him in her tiny sitting room with a black coffee for herself.

'Lucy, this is very embarrassing for me and I hope this conversation will go no further.'

'Stuart, I don't know what you are going to say so I can't promise that but I will promise to be as discreet as I possibly can be.'

Stuart smiled at Lucy,

'I know you will Lucy and I didn't need to say that but this is difficult for me.' Lucy waited for a minute as Stuart hesitated.

'It started really after the death of Katy, our lovely little girl. I think I told you that she died of meningitis, aged two. As you can imagine, Heather and I were distraught. We were beside ourselves. If it hadn't been for looking after the other two children we would have gone mad. We were also grateful to Mary and Frank to whom we became very close. I was very worried about Heather. She just wandered about in her dressing-gown, looking into the distance and saying nothing. Frank suggested that she went back to work. He thought it would distract her. This was difficult as Mark had just started school and Sophie was only three. In those days we had no money. I had just started my own accountancy business and it hadn't really taken off. Mary and Frank and some students helped us with the child care and Heather returned to the University to work with Frank. She was reluctant as she claimed that "her brain was gone." I also felt embarrassed as I knew that Frank was struggling to raise the funding for another research worker. But despite that they were pleased to have Heather back on the team. She was and is a very, very intelligent woman and her memory and knowledge of Physics was enormous. Before she left the department to have the children, she was working with the very prestigious Professor Sanderson. At first, after going back, she didn't seem capable of doing any serious work. She would come home and weep, telling me that if she didn't come up with something soon, she would be sacked. Well she did come up with something. It made her name and she was internationally recognised as an important Physicist.

She published a small pamphlet which completely altered her career. The trouble was that the pamphlet was not her work. It was that of Professor Sanderson who had died four years earlier. I didn't realise this until Frank came to see me one evening. He told me the truth and said that he was the only one who knew. We didn't know what to do. I said that I would speak to Heather. She looked at me with a sort of glazed look on her face and said,

"But it is my work. We did it together and the professor is dead."

I couldn't speak to her. I tried again about a month later. By then she was working hard with her previous energy and aptitude. When I broached the subject she was furious. She said that I didn't rust her, that I was accusing her of lying and deceit.
I can still see her, standing with her back to the window in our little dining room.

She yelled at me,

"Do you really think that I, a dedicated scientist would put my name to a lie? Do you think I have no integrity whatsoever?"
Her lovely hair is tinged with grey now but then it was a flaming red. The sun shone in behind her and her hair seemed to glow. She was very beautiful. She still is.'
Stuart stopped and wiped his eyes. He seemed to have almost forgotten Lucy's presence. He gulped down his coffee and continued,
'What could I do but apologise profusely? I didn't mention Frank as I didn't want to cause a rift between them but I went to see Frank. I asked him if there could have been some mistake. He was puzzled. We both agreed that Heather certainly believed that this was her own work. I asked Frank why he believed that it was Sanderson's work. He said that one morning, he was in the laboratory and was talking to Professor Sanderson who was bemoaning the fact that Heather was about to go on maternity leave. Sanderson told him about the work they were doing. He had said,
"Don't mention this to anyone, Tremayne. This is going to be big, a real breakthrough. Heather has been a great help to me. She has done wonderful work. Why she wants to go off and have babies, I don't know." Frank laughed about it as Sanderson was a single man who had no other interest in life but

Physics. He couldn't imagine that anyone could put marriage or babies before Physics. After that Heather did go and do a few hours work with the professor now and again and then of course he died suddenly of a heart attack.'

Stuart stopped again and almost sobbed,

'I'm sorry Lucy, I'm being very long-winded but it's important to give you all the details.'

'Of course,' said Lucy gently, 'don't worry about that. I have plenty of time.' Stuart continued.

'As I said, neither of us doubted for a moment that Heather was completely honest and wouldn't knowingly pass someone else's work off as her own. Frank and I then decided that perhaps he was mistaken and that Heather had put just as much into the project as Sanderson. We left it at that and I never referred to it again either to Frank or Heather.

Now I come to the present. Earlier this year on April 4th was Heather's fiftieth birthday. We planned to celebrate the occasion with a weekend in Paris. The flight left from Heathrow at about seven in the evening. We had our bags packed and planned to leave about three. We had an early lunch as Heather had an appointment at the hairdressers at one. I was clearing away after lunch when there was a knock on the door. It was Mary and Frank with a present for Heather. They were sorry to have missed her but joined me in a cup of tea. It had been raining but by then it was a lovely day and we were all so light-hearted. I went into the kitchen to get some more milk. The kitchen looks out over a lane by the side of the house where Frank had parked the car. I noticed a man opening the door of the Tremayne's car. I thought he was about to steal it so I raced out of the back door. I saw the man quite clearly but when he saw me he turned and ran. I told Mary and Frank what had happened. Frank looked at the car and everything seemed in order so we assumed that I had prevented a car theft. The Tremaynes were duly grateful and set off home. Heather arrived back within minutes and we set off for Heathrow.

We had a lovely time in Paris, going to the theatre and to posh restaurants. We had no time to look at an English newspaper or English television. We stayed three nights. On the way back, Heather had a message on her mobile from her sister that their mother wasn't very well. Heather lived comparatively near her Mum so she texted back that she would go straight over there. We picked up the car at Heathrow. Heather dropped me off at the house and went straight on to her mother's. I wandered into the house, picked up some letters and newspapers we had forgotten to cancel and went to turn the heating on. I then noticed a headline in *The Guardian* – "Well-known academic couple killed in car crash" It still didn't register until I turned the paper over and saw Frank and Mary smiling up at me.

I read the short article over and over again. I was so shocked it didn't seem to register with me. Then I absent-mindedly picked up my letters. There were one or two I put aside to read later, bank statements, that sort of thing, then I picked up one I thought looked more interesting. I can remember exactly what it said,
"Dear Mr Martin,

You will have heard by now of the accidental death of your friends, the Tremaynes. We know that before they set out on their last, fateful journey, you saw a man interfering with their car. This is to let you know that this incident had nothing whatsoever to do with the car accident of your friends, and to warn you that if you thought the right thing to do was to report it to the police, it would definitely be the wrong thing to do. We have conclusive proof that your wife took the credit for the String Theory article in 1995 And that she and you have profited by that deception. I have many avenues to the media and to the government, at my disposal and it is quite likely that I could make sure that your wife went to prison for such a serious deception of scientific knowledge.
I am also very, very rich and powerful and without the help of the police I could ruin your business, discredit you and your wife and inflict great harm on your children.
I hope I will not find it necessary to do any of those things.

A well-wisher."'

Stuart sat for a moment with his head in his hands. He looked up at Lucy, 'What could I do? I knew that if I showed the letter to Heather, she would pooh pooh it. She would say it was a lie and that I must go to the police immediately, but I couldn't risk it. I suppose in the end it was the threat to our children that filled me with fear and then of course I thought that whatever I did, it would not bring back the Tremaynes.' Stuart looked up again, 'It's no use, whatever excuse I make, I was a coward.'

Lucy looked at Stuart and covered his shaking hand with hers,

'Stuart, I don't know that any of us would have acted differently, but did you have any idea who might have sent the letter?'
'Yes, from the start, I believed it to be Sir Gareth Morgan-Lewis. I knew Hayden

Lewis had been funding some of their research and I knew something about Sir Gareth offering them money which they had refused. I didn't know what the research was about but I knew that Mary was furious.'
'Do you know how he got hold of information about Heather's research?' 'I don't know and that's what baffles me. You see by that time I was convinced that Heather had deceived no-one. Frank was the only person who had suspected it but before he died, Heather was her normal self. Of course we will always have the wound of the death of our child but if Heather had thought that while she was suffering and obviously unwell she had done such a thing she would have owned up to it immediately. No I didn't believe that but I did fear the might of the Lewis empire.'
'But now you have gone to the police?'

'Yes, when I heard about Sir Gareth – helping the police with their inquiries – I thought the time had come. I have to confess that I was motivated mostly by hatred. These last few months, I have been eaten away with hatred, for the killing of my friends and for the damage done to my wife and family.'
'Does Heather know now?'

Stuart pulled his hands through his hair,

'Yes, she knows. It has done our relationship no good whatsoever'. Stuart smiled ruefully, 'She is incandescent. She thinks that I think she was guilty. She is furious that I didn't show her the letter. She thinks I am the most cowardly man that ever lived but it was Heather that suggested that I tell you.'

Lucy had to smile at Stuart's description of Heather's anger. She could smile because she knew that Heather's anger would not last.

'What did you tell the Police?'

'I told them about the man in the car, about our trip to Paris and subsequent letter. I said I believed the accusation about my wife was utter rubbish. I admitted to being afraid, a miserable coward and I told them why I suspected Sir Gareth and why it was only when he was he was in the custody of the police that I had the courage to come forward.'

'How did the police react?'

'They were very practical, showed no emotion or scorn. I was shown various "mug shots" to see if I could pick out the man in the car. It was easy to pick him out as I had quite a good look at him and he had one or two noticeable features. The man had only been shown in the press with his head covered. My instant recognition of the man helped. They took the letter and gave me a copy. They said the accusation of blackmail and threatening behaviour were very serious and on that account arrested Sir Gareth. I have to confess I am still afraid of his power, wealth and influence but it is a huge weight that has been lifted from me and I feel with

Heather alongside me I can put up with anything.'

'Did Heather say any more about the accusation against her?'

'She says she can dispel any doubts that I had about her in two sentences but at the moment she doesn't feel inclined to do so. I could tell she was curious about where the story came from.'

'Yes' said Lucy thoughtfully, 'we need to look into that. It matters for Heather's sake and also it might clinch Gareth's guilt and that's to everyone's advantage.'

Stuart was despondent,

'I wouldn't know where to start.'

Lucy hesitated,

'Stuart, I have the germ of an idea. I promise I won't compromise Heather or reveal anything unnecessarily but would you mind if I made one or two inquiries?'
Stuart brightened,

'I'd be very grateful, Lucy and you know, now I've told the story twice it doesn't seem quite so bad. I don't honestly think Heather would mind. She is completely confident in her own innocence but I don't want her to be subjected to the "no smoke without fire" thing.'
'Of course not' replied Lucy.

Stuart stood up,

'Thank you Lucy for listening to me. I am extremely grateful. I won't take up any more of your time. I'd better go and have another shot at making my peace with
Heather.'

'Good idea,' laughed Lucy.

Chapter Fifty

Andrew decided that he would return to his grandmother's for a while. He needed to sort out a school for September. He didn't want to return to his old school in Ebbchester because although the house was still there, he had no intentions of living there on his own. Now that he had decided where his real interests lay he felt quite enthusiastic about going back to school.

Andrew also felt that he needed a break from Mike who had been acting very strangely lately and didn't seem willing to include Andrew in any of his activities. Margaret was of course delighted to see her grandson and set about organising his favourite foods. They had just had lunch together when there was a phone call.

'It's Lucy for you, Andrew,' said Margaret.

Andrew felt his chest contract in a leap of Joy.

'Hi, Lucy,' he said as nonchalantly as he could.

'Andy, will you be in this evening? I've a favour to ask you and I can't explain it on the phone. Tell Margaret I will eat before I come as I'm a bit tied up with work.' 'Of course! Anything for you Lucy,' replied Andrew in his most debonair tone. Andrew was curious as to Lucy's request and was pleased that she had asked him for the favour and not Mike.

Lucy didn't arrive until nine o'clock that evening and Andrew was wondering if she had changed her mind. Margaret as usual left them alone and Andrew was pleased that Lucy looked grateful.

Lucy recounted to Andrew her conversation with Stuart. Andrew told her that he had seen Stuart on the television.

When she had finished, Lucy said,

'We are all wondering where Gareth got his information. I think it is important that we find out for Heather's sake and also to confirm that Stuart's anonymous letter was from Gareth. I was wondering whether Professor Sanderson had any connection with Gareth's Welsh University. After thinking about this I telephoned Stuart. Heather answered the phone. I was a bit embarrassed at first but she soon put me at my ease as she knew Stuart had been to see me. I told her about The Morgan-Lewis University. She said that she had heard of it as some useful research had been done there in Physics but she didn't think Professor Sanderson had any connections there. I was disappointed as that was the only idea I had but about an hour later, Heather phoned me and said that she remembered that 'Dickie' had a very good friend who was at Aberystwyth. He talked about 'Hughie' quite a lot, mostly about Physics. They obviously discussed their research together and often met socially. Heather had met him a couple of times. She thought 'Hughie' might very well have ended up at the Morgan-Lewis place but she was having difficulty in tracing him so we don't even know his full name or whether he is still alive.'

'If only we could trace him,' said Andrew, 'but what do you want me to do?' 'I was wondering if you could get in touch with that Alun chap. He is in the Physics department and might have heard mention of 'Hughie'. I am going to be away tomorrow so I can't do it but you seemed to get on well with him and you have an appreciation of Physics so I think you would be the best one to do it. I spoke to

Mike and he agrees with me.'

Andrew looked at his watch,

'It's a bit late now but I'll get on to it first thing tomorrow.'

'Thanks Andy. You're a gem.'

Lucy stood up, then bent over and kissed Andrew lightly on the cheek. Andrew went to the door and waved to Lucy, then went up to bed where he had his favourite daydream. Lucy was being threatened with a gun when Andrew strode into the room and snatched the gun from Charlotte. As he did so Charlotte fired the gun giving Andrew a small flesh wound. Lucy was obviously very grateful and devastated at Andrew's wound which bled copiously. It was a pity it hadn't happened that way but it made a very comforting daydream!

The following morning, Andrew set about tracking down Alun Morris. He phoned the University and was disappointed to find that Alun had taken two weeks holiday. Andrew must have sounded disappointed as the Welsh voice then said,

'If it's urgent, I can give you his mobile number.'

Andrew said that it was and wrote down the number which he then phoned. He got Alun straight away and asked if it was possible to see him.

'Sorry, mate I'm on holiday for a couple of weeks. I'm staying with the girlfriend at the moment and we are off to Gran Canaria tomorrow. You're not thinking of
Joining Lewis Uni are you?'

'No,' said Andrew, 'It's about something else, a rather delicate matter actually.'

'Oh' Andrew could sense that Alun was curious, 'where are you now?'

'I'm staying with my grandmother at Letbury'

'I'll tell you what I could do. I could meet you half way. Could you get a train to Tewksbury? I could meet you there in the *Red Lion*. It's very near the station. Shall we say eleven o'clock? That gives us both time to get there.'
'Great,' said Andrew, 'see you there.'

An hour later, Andrew stood outside the *Red Lion* Pub in Tewkesbury. He realised he was far too early so decided to wait outside. Fortunately Alun was also early and spotted Andrew as he drove past. Alun had some difficulty parking his car but by ten forty-five they were both inside the pub. They decided on coffee as Alun was driving and Alun also ordered a plate of cakes.

'So, what's this about?' asked Alun.

Andrew had carefully rehearsed his questions so that he could leave Heather's name out of the discussion. Alun had heard about Sir Gareth's arrest and was intrigued by it so that made things easier. Andrew explained that it was thought that Sir Gareth was blackmailing a Physics research student who worked at Ebbchester and they were anxious to find out where he had got his information.

Andrew explained that the student was a good friend of his and of Lucy.

'The only possible connection we could think of was the Physics department of the Lewis University. We asked our friend if her professor had any connections with Lewis but the only thing she could think of was that Professor Sanderson had a close friend called 'Hughie' who was at that time at Aberystwyth.

'When did this happen?' asked Alun.

'The blackmail was a few months ago but the research was done about twenty years ago'

So how old is this 'student'?'

'She's now in her fifties and still doing research.' Alun thought for some minutes.

'I know Hughie,' he said.

Andrew gasped in amazement,

'That's brilliant,' he said, 'Is he still alive? Do you know where he is now?'

'I came to the physics department as a research student about eight years ago.

We had two professors then, the Professor of Atomic Physics was Cedd Trueman

— always called 'Professor Trueman', who is still here, the other Prof was Hywel Jones who was always known as 'Hughie'. We all liked Hughie. He was good fun and could do wonderful impressions of famous people and also people in the University.'
'Where is he now?' asked Andrew.

'That's the problem. He's in an old people's home and I'm not sure if he's compos mentis.'
'Have you seen him recently?'

'Well as it happens, I saw him about a year ago. They had a celebration at the home for his ninetieth birthday. I went along as I was fond of the old boy but I'm not sure that he knew who I was. He seemed to fluctuate between being very cheerful and lucid and muttering on about things that happened years ago.'
'Do you think he could have told Sir Gareth what he knew?'

Alun screwed up his face,
'It's possible but not very likely. He was a kind old man. I'm sure he wouldn't have stirred up trouble for your researcher friend.'
'Maybe he felt strongly on behalf of his friend, Professor Sanderson. He may have felt that he had been cheated of his rightful recognition.'
'Possibly,' said Alun, 'But my money's on Cedd. He's a nasty piece of work and sucks up to Sir Gareth. The trouble is you wouldn't get any help from him. He would protect Gareth.'
Alun looked at Andrew who looked downcast.

'I think your only chance is Hughie. When I saw him, there was a crowd of people around him drinking champagne. I think if Heather would go with you . . . .'

'Heather? Who told you it was Heather?'

Alun laughed,

'Heather Martin is a well-known Physicist. She works at Ebbchester as does your friend, Lucy. Also this time you gave me your real name, Andrew Tremayne. Your father, Frank Tremayne worked with Heather and Professor Sanderson at Ebbchester.'

Andrew looked at Alun in amazement.

'How did you work all that out?'

'I can play the detective too. This is all about the death of your parents, isn't it? I don't know how it all fits in but I want you to know I'm on your side. Your parents' death was a tragedy for all of us and for you it must have been terrible. I'm no fan of Gareth. I take his money but if it comes to an end I won't be heart-broken.' 'Thanks,' mumbled Andrew, 'you think I should get Heather to go with me to see the old man?'
'Yes, it might jog his memory and it could be that his short-term memory's not too good but he might remember everything about Physics, after all it was his whole life. If I were you, I'd video the whole conversation just in case something useful comes up. Hearsay evidence is no good.' 'Good idea,' said Andrew.

'Have you a pen? The home where he is or was, is called "The sunset Experience". Awful isn't it. It's somewhere in Gloucestershire and it isn't too far away. I don't know the precise address but you can get it online. I remembered the name as it was so dreadful.'
'Thanks Alun,' said Andrew standing up, 'I'm really grateful. It was very good of you to come over here. I hope your holiday goes well.'

'If the truth were known I was a bit curious about it. I shall watch the news to see what happens to Gareth and one of these days I shall meet up with you and find out the whole story. Where do you want to go to University, by the way?'
'Imperial College.'

'Great, that will suit you. Good luck! You can wish me luck too as I intend to propose to Lizzie. She will probably think she's too young but I'm knocking on a bit.'
Andrew grinned broadly,

'That's great. Good luck then.'

They shook hands and Andrew left for the station.

Chapter Fifty -one

'Grandma, do you know Stuart and Heather Martin?'

'Yes, not well but they were great friends of your Mum and Dad. I just send them

Christmas cards, that sort of thing.'

Andrew brightened,

'So you have their address. Do you have a telephone number?

'I may have. I'll go and look.'

Margaret went off and some minutes later came back with a card.

'This is good. They moved house a few years ago and sent me a card which I just shoved into my address book. It's got everything on it Home number, mobiles and even email addresses. Here you are.'

'Brilliant, I need to get in touch with Heather,' Andrew added by way of explanation. Margaret was curious but knew better than to ask questions. Andrew spent the next couple of hours trying the various phone numbers and leaving messages. He was just about to give up when the phone rang. It was

Heather. Andrew explained about the Morgan-Lewis University and his trip to Tewksbury to see Alun. He could tell Heather was quite excited and was delighted to learn that 'Hughie' was still alive. She said that she would willingly come with Andrew to see him and would contact the care home herself and arrange a visit at the earliest possible opportunity. Andrew was pleased that Heather was going to arrange it. He sank into an armchair and switched the television on. He soon dropped off to sleep.

'Andrew, Andrew, wake up, wonderful news!'

'What is it Grandma?'

'Lucy and Michael! They've just been visiting Lucy's father and guess what!' Andrew rubbed his eyes.
'Grandma, I can't guess. What are you talking about?'

'They are going to get married! They're engaged!'

'Who are?'

'Michael and Lucy! Isn't it wonderful?'

'What!' Andrew sat up with a jerk, 'I can't believe it?'

'Neither could I, but Michael's always been one for sudden decisions. Here they are. I said I would tell you first'
Lucy and Mike came into the room, holding hands and looking slightly embarrassed. Andrew looked horrified.
'Well Andy, aren't you going to congratulate us?' said Lucy planting a kiss on his cheek.
Andrew rushed out of the room upstairs to his bedroom.

He sat on his bed with his head in his hands. He was quivering with anger.

'I can't believe it,' he kept saying, 'poor Lucy, oh how could she?'

After about half an hour, there was a knock at his door and Mike came in. 'Hello Andy. I knew you wouldn't like it but I thought I'd just let you know I did include you.'
'Include me! What are you talking about?' said Andrew angrily.

'Well I did, and Mum too actually.' Andrew looked mystified. Mike continued,

'After we got rid of the gun, Lucy was a bit tired and shaky so we got the bus back. It is a bit of a roundabout journey but we didn't mind. We went upstairs to the front. I usually do that. Well we were going along and Lucy was saying how she would miss us all after all this business was cleared up so I had a brainwave. I suggested that we got married and then she would be related to us all, so I did include you. Well Lucy laughed.'
'Of course she would,' muttered Andrew.

'She said that it wasn't a very romantic proposal so I went down on my knees. All the people on the top of the bus were laughing, including Lucy. She was laughing so much we went past our stop. Anyway we got off the bus and I said, "what about it Lucy?" She said that she didn't even know whether I liked her that much. I was amazed. Of course I told her I was crazy about her. I thought it would be obvious. I said that I didn't expect her to fall for me all at once but she might get to like me better. I mentioned you and Mum again.' 'I can't believe this,' said Andrew.
'And do you know what she said?' Andrew shook his head.

'She just said, "I Love you, Michael" just like that. Well then we started kissing and once we started we couldn't stop.'
'I don't want to hear this, Mike.'

'It took us ages to get home and then I said I would come in for a cup of tea but we never got on to the tea, I thought I would . . . .'
'This is grotesque,' shouted Andrew and pushed past Mike to lock himself in the bathroom.'
'Oh well, suit yourself' shrugged Mike and returned to his mother and Lucy who had opened a bottle of champagne.
'Is Andrew all right?' asked Margaret.

'Oh, he's seething with jealousy. Can't blame him really. He had Lucy lined up for himself, quite natural I suppose.'
'But Andy's only seventeen!' Margaret was amazed.

'What's that got to do with anything? Poor chap's got his feelings. I mean, a girl like Lucy? I put it to him that Lucy would be part of the family – didn't seem to help. Well it's not quite the same is it? – having her for an auntie?'

Margaret and Lucy couldn't help laughing. Andrew in the bathroom put his hands over his ears as he heard the peals of laughter drifting up the stairs. He wondered if he would ever again be able to leave the vicinity of his grandmother's bathroom.

He sat there for some minutes wondering what to do. He knew he ought to be able to go downstairs and act normally but he really couldn't join in the festivities.

He heard the telephone ringing.

'Andrew, Andrew, dear, it's for you,' Margaret called upstairs.

Andrew met his grandmother on the stairs and gave him the phone. He took it into the garden.

'Hello, Andrew, this is Heather. I've contacted the Sunset Home and we could go and see Hughie tomorrow. Apparently sometimes he is quite lucid and other times very confused. The person I spoke to, I think she was a Matron, said that he was very fond of 'Werther's Originals' so I'll get him some. Have you a Mobile phone that takes videos?'

'Yes, mine's quite good and easy to use.'

'Good, I'll do most of the talking and you could be doing the filming.'

'What time shall we go?'

'About two o'clock. They will have had their lunch by then. I will come and pick you up about one o'clock. Is that OK?'

'That's great. Thank you Heather that's really kind of you.'

Andrew took the phone back into the house. He met Lucy and Mike going out. He told them about the phone call. They were both genuinely delighted and congratulated him on doing such a good job. Andrew knew they were both being rather 'over the top' in their enthusiasm but he did feel rather pleased with himself. He said modestly,

'Of course we don't know if anything will come of it.' 'Still, there's a chance,' said Lucy.

'We're just going out for a drink. Do you want to come? asked Mike. 'No thanks, I want to look over some of these schools' prospectuses that I've picked up.'

Andrew went back into the house where his grandmother was watching an old episode of *Only fools and Horses*. He sat down and together they enjoyed three episodes before Andrew went to his room to look at the one prospectus he had.

'Andy! It's Heather for you,' called Mike the following afternoon.

Andrew picked up his phone and rushed out.

As they drove along, he told Heather a little of how he, Lucy and Mike had been trying to find out what really happened with regard to the death of his parents. She was very interested and impressed with what they had achieved. She said very little about her past research achievements but she did say that she 'greatly admired' Andrew's father.

As they approached the care home, there was a big sign with a colourful picture of the setting sun and the name 'The setting sun experience' in big letters.

'Poor old Hughie ending up in a place like this,' sighed Heather.

The people they met at the reception desk were, however, very friendly and helpful.

Andrew and Heather were led into a small sitting room where two people were playing cards, another was reading and Hughie was sitting in an armchair, looking out of the window. He had a newspaper on his lap but he was obviously enjoying himself watching the birds. As they approached him, he said,

'Watch that little blue tit, that great magpie is trying to get at the bird seed but the little tit keeps jumping in and beating him to it.'

'Hughie,' said the nurse, 'you have visitors, Mrs Heather Martin and Mr Andrew

Tremayne.'

'Tremayne, I know that name. Weren't you working with Bob Sanderson?'

'No, that was my dad, Frank Tremayne.' 'Of course.' Hughie looked at Andrew.

'Far too young,' he said, 'far too young. I'm getting old you know, forgetful.' 'Heather worked with Professor Sanderson,' said Andrew, surreptitiously taking out his mobile phone. Hughie turned to look at Heather,

'Of course, Bobbie's girl, there was a song. I don't suppose you would approve of that feminism and all that.'

Heather laughed,

'I don't mind. We've brought you some sweets.' She put them on a ledge beside his chair.

'Oh, I love those, my favourites. You get childish you know when you get old. I live for a sweetie.'

'Hughie, do you remember Professor Sanderson working on String Theory?'

'I do indeed, the old devil, Morrison-Scott wasn't it? Morrison-Scott. Good girl Heather, good girl. Shouldn't have done it, the old devil.' Hughie stared out of the window. He began chewing one of the sweets. His eyes seemed to glaze over. 'I told Cedd, silly, very silly. Bob, I'd like to see him again, perhaps I will, good friend, used to cheat at cards, good old Bob, liked a glass of Guinness.'

Suddenly Hughie's eyes closed and he was asleep. Andrew and Lucy tried to wake him but it was no good. The nurse came over.

'I'm afraid he will sleep now for some hours and when he wakes up, he won't be very lucid for some time.'

Heather stood up,

'Thank you, that's fine. We knew we wouldn't be able to have a long conversation.'

Heather and Andrew walked back to the car.

'I'm sorry, Heather, that was a waste of time,' said Andrew.

'Did you manage to video what he said?'

'Yes, I think I got most of what he said when he was talking to you.'

'Good, when we get back to the car, let's play it.'

Andrew was mystified. He couldn't think that anything on the recording would be of any use but once in the car, he dutifully played back what he had recorded for Heather.

'Brilliant!' she said, giving Andrew a brief hug.

'I'll explain,' she said, laughing at Andrew's baffled expression, 'the mention of *Morrison-Scott* is the key to the whole thing. You see when I was young and working with Professor Sanderson, I discovered something. It was really almost by accident as I think a lot of discoveries are. Anyway it was quite important and Dr. Sanderson was thrilled. He wanted us to keep quiet about it until it was all written up and tested properly. At the same time the department was very hard-up. We had very little money to carry on with our experiments. Also at that time there was an interesting case taking place in the courts. It was nothing to do with Physics. Two people, John Morrison and Angela Scott had worked on a translation of an ancient Aramaic manuscript. It was nearly all the work of the young man, John Morrison but Angela Scott was older and a very well-known scholar at the time. As I understand it, Morrison suggested that the work should be published as being completely hers.'

'But why?' asked Andrew.

'Money, simply money,' said Heather, 'Anything produced by Angela would get far more publicity and general credence than something written by the unknown Morrison. They agreed to split the money. Unfortunately, young Morrison was killed in a motor-cycle accident and after his death, Angela Scott was sued by Morrison's mother and young wife. While he was alive he had foolishly told them about the situation.'

'What happened?'

'They lost – that is Angela won the case. She was able to prove that the publication under her name was with John's approval and that he did indeed receive half the profits. They ruled that anybody had the right to give away the fame and fortune accruing from their own work.'

'I'm beginning to see,' said Andrew, 'you mean, you did most of the work for this Physics breakthrough and agreed that Professor Sanderson should take the credit as it would have more kudos coming from him.'

'Yes, that's exactly what happened. At the time the research team in the physics department had very little money and we needed whatever fame and fortune we could get to continue, so it was in my interests as well as the Professor's to capitalise on our project. We made sure that everyone thought the project was Sanderson's work, that must have included your father. I thought it included Hughie as he acted as if the project was wholly Sanderson's. He must have mentioned that to Cedd. There was still quite a lot to do on the project when I became pregnant and I would pop into the department now and again to do some work but unfortunately Professor Sanderson died of a heart attack very suddenly and unexpectedly. I didn't go back to work for some time after that as I had the children very quickly. When I did finally go back to work after Katy died, I drifted about for a bit and then decided to go back to the project. There was no longer any point in putting it in Professor Sanderson's name as he had been dead for some years.'

'Yes, I understand,' said Andrew 'but why didn't you tell Dad and Stuart?' 'It never occurred to me. I don't remember what I thought at the time. I suppose I thought that Frank knew and Stuart wasn't a Physicist and wouldn't have any opinions about it. I suppose all this misunderstanding was my fault. I wasn't really all that *compos mentis* at the time. As time went on I became more and more absorbed with the Physics and I probably wasn't much of a wife to poor Stuart who was just as distressed as me about little Katy. Recently, I have been furious with him for not trusting me. I know I have generally behaved badly.' Heather put her head on the steering wheel and sobbed. Andrew just felt embarrassed and couldn't think of anything to say. Heather looked up,

'I'm so sorry, Andrew. I shouldn't be subjecting you to this. Your parents were my greatest friends but you have suffered more than any of us. You have been brilliant and your little video should clear things up.'
Andrew smiled,

'Thanks Heather. I hope it helps.'

Heather wiped her eyes and smiled back at Andrew. To his further embarrassment, she gave him a quick hug.
'You're a great lad, Andrew. Your parents would be proud of you. Could you send the video to Stuart and we will take our evidence to the Police as soon as possible?'
'Yes I can do that if you give me his email address. Do you think this is enough to convict Sir Gareth?'
'Yes I do. We have the man and the car and the blackmail note. I know his lawyer is the best you can get but he will find it hard to get round this.' Heather started the car and they set off back to Letbury.

Chapter Fifty-two

Lucy turned over in her small bed in her small flat and looked at the clock – seventhirty. She didn't need to get up yet.

Lucy was very happy. She was aware that she had fallen for Mike right at the beginning of their relationship. She found the tall, lanky, young man, with his floppy, untidy, dark hair, very attractive. Lucy found his odd behaviour and 'alternative' points of view, exciting and interesting. She was over the moon that this original, 'cool' character should be attracted by her, normal, ordinary, boring old Lucy!

Lucy was also delighted by her father's obvious approval on meeting Mike. She was afraid that he might not appreciate all of Mike's good qualities.

'Good old Dad!' she thought and then, 'good old Nancy!'

Nancy had laughed uproariously at all Mike's jokes. This had encouraged him and by the end of the afternoon had achieved the reputation of a born comic and entertainer. When Lucy joined Nancy in the kitchen, Nancy had whispered, 'Lucy! He's such a dish!' This wasn't the way Lucy generally expressed herself but she was pleased nevertheless.

Lucy hugged herself and turned over again in bed. She would relive that night on the double-decker bus. She soon drifted happily off to sleep.

Lucy awoke with a start. What had she been dreaming about?

Edith, that was it! She must contact Edith. She had been so wrapped up in her own affairs that she hadn't considered Edith at all.

She had sent Edith some documents for translation but she must tell Edith that she had no need to worry about bugs any more. She could return to her home. But what could she tell Edith? How could she keep from her the name of the murderer of her friends? Lucy wished that she could talk about this to Mike. She dialled his telephone number- no answer. Lucy sat at her little kitchen table and stared out of the window. She felt the need to contact Edith immediately, after all, Edith had left her home!

The phone rang.

'Hello! Hello! This is David Beckham.'

'Oh it's you.'

'Well, that's nice. How about "hello my dearest, darling, how wonderful to hear your dulcet tones?"'

'If I started calling you "darling", you'd curl up. Anyway why "David Beckham"?' 'I thought he was the maiden's answer to prayer. I was wondering how you would react – you know – Oh how wonderful to hear from you . . .'

'Shut up Mike.'

'Well this has come very soon in our relationship. I was hoping that you might be different from my other so-called friends and treat me with respect. I thought . .'

'Shut up Mike, I want to talk to you. I need to contact Edith. What can I tell her?' There was silence for a minute or two.

'Lucy, I think you will have to use your own discretion. You are better than me at these things. I know we have all sworn to secrecy on the matter but I can't see

Edith broadcasting it to the world, can you?'

'No-o, but what if she thinks the police should be told? I mean the Professor and

Father John were her very good friends.'

'I can't see that and I'm sure she would be guided by your good sense.'

'Thanks, Michael, you're a great comfort to me.'

'I'm glad about that and how about if I came round this evening to comfort you a bit more?'

Twenty minutes later Lucy wrote to Edith. She told her that there was no longer any need to worry about bugs and that the danger had passed. She asked Edith to telephone her so they could arrange a meeting and then she could tell her the details. After posting the letter, Lucy felt better but found it difficult to concentrate on her work as she looked forward to Mike's visit that evening. She must remember to tell him that her father and Nancy wanted to come to Letbury to meet Margaret.

'Come in Edith, Come in. It is kind of you to come here. I would have come to you.'

'I know, dear,' said Edith, kissing Lucy heartily on both cheeks, 'but I've been staying with my cousin and although she's been exceptionally hospitable, I don't want to stretch her hospitality too far. Yes dear, I would love some coffee. Those cakes? Did you make them yourself? Sainsbury's? Well they do make good cakes. I've bought them myself.

Lucy and Edith sat opposite each other in Lucy's two comfortable chairs. They sipped their coffee and Lucy looked across at Edith. The last few weeks had taken its toll on the old lady. The once-green hair was now white and Edith wore a long, brown skirt, a prim, blue blouse and a comfortable if shabby, navy-blue cardigan. Lucy suspected that these articles of clothing had been given to her by the hospitable cousin. Edith looked even thinner if that was possible. 'So, my dear,' said Edith at last, 'you have something to tell me.'

'Yes, I have,' said Lucy, rather apprehensively, 'It's rather a sad story.'

Lucy then told Edith the story of the Farquars. She told her everything as she felt that if Edith was to understand the situation, nothing must be kept from her. Lucy's final conversation with Charlotte was imprinted so well on her memory that she was able to tell it word for word. Lucy looked at Edith and realised that tears were flowing down the old, wrinkled face. Lucy continued until the throwing of the gun in the lake.

They were both silent for a while, then Edith with tears still flowing said,

'That poor, unfortunate woman, how very, very sad!' Lucy remained silent, slightly puzzled.

'We must pray for her and for that unfortunate family. Shall we do it now, Lucy?' Lucy nodded, close to tears herself.

Edith took out her rosary beads and began. Lucy, who was familiar with the responses, accompanied her. They recited *The sorrowful Mysteries* together.

After they had finished, Lucy said, rather shakily,

'Do you think I was right to promise to tell nobody?'

'Of course,' said Edith fiercely, 'and you didn't have to tell me you know.' 'Edith you are so good. I just thought that well, you know, Father John and the professor – you might have wanted to see justice done.'

'I suppose it has been done,' said Edith thoughtfully, 'and in any case, revenge is not for us. If we had to protect people against a killer, we would have to do it but 'Vengeance is mine,' says the Lord. No it's not for us and that poor family! Those little boys!'

'I suppose the Morgan-Lewis family are suffering too.'

'That's true. We must pray for them as well. It's a mystery isn't it? Such evil! But I suppose, "there but for the grace of God go I" They sat silently for some moments. 'But I have got some good news, Edith.' Edith looked up.

'I'm going to get married!'

'Wonderful! To that lovely tall young man with the dark hair? I thought there was something there. Oh this is good news!'
Lucy laughed,

'Yes, you're right. To Mike, Edith you are very perceptive.'

Edith looked pleased,

'And I am going back to my little cottage with all my own things around me. That's good news too. But Lucy, I have a favour to ask you.'
'Edith, you know I would do anything for you.'

'Not so fast, what I want to ask is, May I help you with The Good Book? I don't need paying or anything but it would be such a privilege. I could help with the translating, the sorting out and being a general dogsbody. I could come over to

Ebbchester a few days a week and find somewhere to stay.'

'Edith! That would be wonderful. At the moment Michael and I are not sure where we are going to live. Whatever happens we will not be using our two flats so you could take over one of them. Michael did offer to apply for a job in
Ebbchester but I think he would like to stay on at his school so I may work in

London too.'

Edith beamed,

'Whatever it is, it would be wonderful. There is nothing I would rather do. Thank you Lucy, Thank you so much.'

Lucy laughed,

'Edith it is I who should thank you. I have been lonely working on my own. I don't work well on my own and I was used to working with Mary. You have come to me like a gift from God.'
'Well, that is a compliment indeed. I am going to take the train to Cardiff now and go back to my cottage. I shall skip all the way!'

Chapter Fifty-three

'Hello, is that you Michael?'

'It is, Mum. Are you all right?'

'Yes, I'm fine. I am a bit worried about Andrew. He seems on edge. He has been looking at schools for next year and is quite pleased about that. I am surprised at his choice. He wants to go to Linsbury Park Comprehensive. There's nothing wrong with that but he could have gone to your old school, King Edward's Grammar.' 'Oh he doesn't want to go there, load of snobs, think they are better than everyone else.'

'Well they probably are, or he could have gone to St Peter's but that's not what I'm phoning about. I wondered if you could come over on Saturday and cheer him up?'

'Oh he won't want me to cheer him up. I'm his number one enemy.'

'Well that's what I meant. I think he's upset because he's cross with you and poor Lucy.'

'Why poor Lucy? You mean she's belittling herself in marrying me?'

'Now Michael, don't start being silly. Will you come?'

'What about Lucy? I want to spend the weekend with her.'

'Of course you do but it might be better if you saw Andrew on his own. Now will you come?'

'I suppose so.'

'Thank you, Good boy.'

Mike slammed the phone down – Good boy! Andy was being a real pain. What could he do to cheer him up? Give up Lucy?   .

'I thought you would be over at Ebbchester with my future aunt?'

'Cool it Andy, Lucy has work to do. She wants to finish something off. Any way I wanted to see my mum. This is a great pie, Mum.'

'Thank you Michael. I thought perhaps you and Andrew might like to go for a row on the lake.'

Andrew glared at Mike and when Margaret turned round, he shook his head vigorously.

'That sounds like a good idea Mum. It's a lovely afternoon.'

'It's not,' growled Andrew, 'the forecast said rain,'

'We could do a bit of fishing,' said Mike cheerfully.

Margaret smiled at Mike who thought to himself,

'Good boy!'

'I've found a couple of your old rods,' said Margaret.

A couple of hours later Mike and Andrew were successfully fishing on the lake. They had done rather well and had caught some perch. Andrew was thawing a little as he had caught three and Mike only two.

'Well I suppose we had better get back,' said Mike, 'Mum could cook these for tea'. Mike put the fish in his rucksack and they rowed towards the shore. Mike stood up ready to hitch the rope on to the hook. Andrew went over to him and pushed him into the shallow water. Mike yelled at him and swore violently. Andrew picked up the rucksack and stepped out of the boat. He strode purposefully across the meadow, smiling.

He felt better!

Chapter Fifty-four

My Dear Lucy,

Although my daughter tells me, you wish to step aside from the Farquar family for the good of us all, I feel I owe it to you to communicate a little about what is happening to us and to show some concern about you.

My dear, dear, Lucy, you suffered a great deal and like Horatio in suffering all you acted as though you suffered little. I feel the need to acknowledge the trauma you underwent at the hands of my family and to thank you from the bottom of my heart for your subsequent actions or lack of them. I hope and pray that you are recovering from your terrible ordeal.

I have heard that you are to be married and so I offer you my warmest wishes for your future happiness. I offer your future husband my congratulations on his impeccable choice of a lovely wife. I hope and pray that your present happiness will push aside your hurt.

I saw you at the back of the Cathedral at the funeral. I was pleased to see you and forgive me for not acknowledging you but Rowena said I mustn't. It was a beautiful event and brought me great peace. We didn't want a eulogy but the Cardinal spoke so warmly and beautifully that I found it hard to keep the tears at bay. If you remember, he spoke of the need we all have for the mercy of God and then said how the Father would 'gather to his loving, merciful heart, this precious child'. These words and also the words of the commendation have stayed with me. I have been feeling my age recently and sometimes I just sit and ponder and these words are of great comfort.

*Gerald is managing very well. He occupies himself with his work
and has recently taken on the case of a Romanian family who
have undeservedly found themselves at the wrong side of the
law. He has spent a great deal of time with the boys and tried
hard to interest himself in such things as football and 'Star wars'.
He and*

*Rowena took them on a steam railway trip that they all enjoyed.
That was one thing that did appeal to Gerald! The poor fellow is
suffering greatly. Before I knew of your forthcoming marriage, I
had hoped that you might be the means of some consolation to
him but Rowena told me off very soundly saying, 'that wouldn't
do at all'. She can be very bossy but I suppose she is right. Gerald
did ask after you.*

*He was obviously very impressed by you. I thought it was because
of The Good Book but do you know what he said?*

*'Lovely girl, great figure, beautiful hair'. I nearly fell off my chair!
He said it so seriously as though he was talking about one of his
cases. It gave me hope. He will turn up one day with a real cracker
of a girl. I think he is a great connoisseur of beauty.*

*Rowena is still with us and although she bosses me around
terribly she is a great comfort to us all. She is on leave of absence
from her convent until September. We all went down to
Markwood recently and I was surprised to learn that Gerald and
Rowena had enjoyed their holidays there as children so I have
reconsidered getting rid of it. I have formerly passed it on to
Gerald who has ideas of using it for refugees. I reconsidered
getting rid of the title but Gerald said he would get rid of it
anyway so the boys will have to make do with 'Mr' in the future. I
have gradually been getting rid of the money, shares etc. I have
put something aside for the boys and I would like to do
something for you and 'The Good Book of Oxford'.*

*In the past the poets and artists all had their patrons. What we
would have lost if Horace and Virgil didn't have Maecenas?*

Well, my dear, I hope everything is going well for you. Let me know about 'The Good Book'. Gerald and Rowena send their love,

Your good friend,

Alfie

'Don't you think that's a lovely letter, Michael?'

'I suppose so. That Gerald sounds a real dark horse.'

Lucy laughed,

'I thought you would pick up on that. I do find it amazing, quite out of character.'

'It's not out of character at all.'

'What do you mean?'

'Well you would have thought he would have chosen for his first wife, some bookish, holy, plain girl but no! He chose just about the most beautiful woman in the world (barring one} who was also a lively dare-devil socialite and he obviously takes after his father.'
'His father?'

'Yes do you remember when you had your first conversation with him? He talked about his good-looking wife, good-looking daughter and exceptionally good looking daughter-in-law, also about the fact that they were all lively, sparkling, vivacious characters, and then his penchant for you.'
'I'm not sparkling and vivacious.'

'I wouldn't say that. Have you replied yet?'

'I have started my reply but haven't posted it. I wanted to refuse the offer of money as quickly as possible.'

'Could you use the money with regard to *The Good Book*?'

'Well the department always complains about being hard-up but we can manage.' 'What about Edith? I mean she should be paid, at least a little bit and she's got transport and living costs.'

'You're right but I don't think she would accept it.'

'She might if it came from the University.'

'Yes she might but Mike, how could we work that?'

'Sometimes, Lucy you are quite dim. You could go to the department, tell them that someone wants to donate money to enable you to have an assistant. Discuss with them what amount would be necessary, then put Alfie in touch with the department. In that way you will have nothing to do with it.'

'My lovely Michael! You are a genius!'

'I'm glad you've spotted it and I shall expect to be rewarded in the usual way.'

Chapter Fifty-five

'I see you have engaged the services of D'Artagnan.'

'Johnny, what are you talking about? Are you going completely crazy?' Inspector John Judge laughed, rather unnecessarily raucously in Mike's opinion, considering that the good Inspector had only had one glass of white wine.

'Well, I called you the three musketeers before. You would be Porthos, Athos and Aramis and now you have another member – D'Artagnan.'

'Michael,' said Lucy, 'he means Edith'

'Oh,' said Mike, 'jolly funny, but I must say, Edith you look absolutely magnificent!'
Edith giggled,

'Well it's not often I get asked out for dinner in such a posh restaurant. You are so kind!'
'It's all Andy's doing,' said Mike, 'he arranged it and is paying for it.'

'Edith,' said Lucy, 'where did you get that wonderful dress?'

'Well my father, although he was an Irishman, served with the British army in the first World war. His name was Major Michael O'Leary. After the war, he was sent to India and my mother although a confirmed pacifist went out to join him. They were newly married in 1923 and despite her misgivings about the army, my mother didn't want to be separated from him. Eventually she fell in love with India and all things Indian. She was given this dress by a Maharajah. It is pure silk and I don't often have the occasion to wear it.'
'Did your mother wear it?'

'I suppose she must have done in India but I don't remember. When we returned to Wales, she just wore overalls. She was a poet you know and she used to paint as well.'

'Have you all chosen you first course?' asked Andrew in a very self-important voice.

They all agreed that they had and after giving orders to the waiter, Andrew ordered three bottles of Champagne which were quickly brought in the appropriate ice buckets.

Andrew lifted his glass,

'I want to thank you all for everything you have done to clear the name of my parents.' They all raised their glasses. Then Lucy said, 'To Mary and Frank!'

They echoed the toast. They all suddenly fell silent. A great deal had happened in a few weeks but the death of the Tremaynes was still very recent. Then John said, 'I expect you want to know what is happening to our suspects.' The others nodded.

'Ken and Barry are still in custody and will remain so until their trial. Hayden will also remain in custody. I think he will probably end up in Broadmoor. He might not even be able to stand trial. Sir Gareth is out on bail but will surely go to prison for perverting the course of Justice and for blackmail.'

Mike was just about to ask, 'How long will he get?' when Edith came in with, 'The poor, foolish man, what a way to end up in your old age! and such a tragedy for his son. And those two other young men. Perhaps they will have time to see the sadness of what they have done.' 'We hope so, Edith,' said Lucy.

'Look who's here,' exclaimed Mike as Margaret came rushing towards them, 'you made it after all Mum.'

'Well I wasn't going to miss a party,' said Margaret, 'and I'm so sorry to be late but I couldn't miss the opportunity of visiting Eileen as she was so near in the Chelsea and Westminster hospital.' Margaret looked across at Edith,

'You must be Edith. I have heard so much about you. What a wonderful dress!' Margaret pulled a chair in next to Edith who was then able to recite her story once again for Margaret's benefit.

As the evening wore on, the conversations became more animated and the laughter more boisterous. Margaret sat and admired the young people around her. She knew that she had had more to drink than usual and was feeling rather sentimental. Despite her happiness she still had a dull, deep ache for the loss of her beloved daughter. Mary had telephoned her most days and they had laughed together over their mutual experiences. Margaret had also been very fond of Frank. She recalled how, after the death of her husband, Frank had spent a great deal of time with Michael. Michael had been just thirteen at the time and Mary and Frank were newly-married. Michael had walked around with an ashen face and hadn't cried a tear. He didn't eat. He didn't do any homework or even watch the television. Frank had taken him to football matches, played cricket with him, taken him fishing and gradually, Michael had come round. Margaret looked across at Lucy and wept a tear of gratitude. 'God works in mysterious ways,' she thought. Margaret had been given some information about what the children had been up to but she knew she hadn't got it all and she wouldn't ask. She would look to the future. Margaret suddenly realised that Edith was talking to her,

'Did you know, Margaret, I am going to be working with Lucy on *The Good Book of Oxford*? I am so thrilled and Ebbchester University is actually going to pay me!'
'Well of course they should,' said Margaret. 'I have been given little snippets to read but I am looking forward to being able to read it all. It does seem to be what it's called – a Good Book.'
'Yes, it is and despite all the tragedies, I believe it will do some good.'

'I'm sure it will, Edith. I'm sure it will'

Andrew who was sitting nearby and who, in Margaret's opinion had had far too much wine for a seventeen-year-old, suddenly said,
'You're right Edith. You're right Grandma.'

He stood up, banged his spoon on his glass then raised it high,

 '*The Good Book of Oxford*, Everyone.'

'*The Good Book of Oxford!*'